ABIDING MERCY

Center Point
Large Print

Also by Ruth Reid and available from
Center Point Large Print:

A Woodland Miracle
A Dream of Miracles
An Angel by Her Side

**This Large Print Book carries the
Seal of Approval of N.A.V.H.**

ABIDING MERCY

An Amish Mercies Novel

Ruth Reid

CENTER POINT LARGE PRINT
THORNDIKE, MAINE

This Center Point Large Print edition
is published in the year 2017 by arrangement with
Thomas Nelson.

The text of this Large Print edition is unabridged.
In other aspects, this book may vary
from the original edition.
Printed in the United States of America
on permanent paper.
Set in 16-point Times New Roman type.

ISBN: 978-1-68324-512-4

Library of Congress Cataloging-in-Publication Data

Names: Reid, Ruth, 1963– author.
Title: Abiding mercy / Ruth Reid.
Description: Center Point Large Print edition. | Thorndike, Maine :
    Center Point Large Print, 2017. | Series: An Amish mercies novel
Identifiers: LCCN 2017024002 | ISBN 9781683245124
    (hardcover : alk. paper)
Subjects: LCSH: Amish—Fiction. | Large type books. |
    GSAFD: Christian fiction. | Love stories.
Classification: LCC PS3618.E5475 A64 2017b | DDC 813/.6—dc23
LC record available at https://lccn.loc.gov/2017024002

Glossary

ach: oh
aenti: aunt
boppli: baby
bruder: brother
bu: boy
daadi: grandfather
daed: dad or father
danki: thank you
doktah: doctor
"Das Loblied": an Amish hymn
Englischer: anyone who is not Amish
fraa: wife
geh: go
guder mariye: good morning
gut: good
haus: house
hiya: a greeting like hello
jah: yes
kaffi: coffee
kalt: cold
kapp: a prayer covering worn by Amish women
kinner: children
kumm: come
lecherich: ridiculous
maedel/maed: unmarried woman/women
mamm/mamma: mother or mom

mei: my

nacht: night

narrish: crazy

nau: now

nay: no

nett: not

Ordnung: the written and unwritten rules of the Amish; the understood behavior by which the Amish are expected to live, passed down from generation to generation. Most Amish know the rules by heart.

Pennsylvania Deitsch: the language most commonly used by the Amish

reddy-up: clean up

rumspringa: running-around period when a teenager turns sixteen years old

schweschaler: sister

yummasetti: a traditional Amish dish made with noodles, hamburger, and cheese

washhaus: an outdoor laundry shed

welkum: welcome

wunderbaar: wonderful

Chapter 1

Bloomfield Hills, Michigan
Fifteen years ago

Roslyn Colepepper shuttled her eighteen-month-old daughter, Adriana, through the produce section of the Best Choice Market, the cart wheels clacking. Her daughter didn't seem to mind the thumping, unbalanced ride, but the noise was a nuisance to Roslyn and, judging by the snippy glances from nearby patrons, to others as well. She contemplated exchanging carts at the front of the store, but if she walked near the exit, she would be tempted just to leave. Doing so would put a crimp in her schedule. Her dinner guests would arrive at six only to find her unprepared, which wouldn't bode well in her vie for the president position in the Bloomfield Hills Women's Republican Club.

Her husband had been right. Instead of stressing over meal preparations, she should have arranged a catering service. After all, her housekeeper had always handled the details. Roslyn would simply choose the menu and leave the rest to Georgette, who kept the butler's pantry stocked with organic fruit, vegetables, and every soy product imaginable. Georgette's culinary skills went beyond the typical housekeeper's talent, which made it impossible to replace her when she requested a leave of absence to care for her sick grandmother.

The last girl the temp agency sent fell short. The maid purchased substandard food and ended up pocketing the allotted funds. Of course the girl denied the charges, leaving Roslyn no choice but to dismiss her immediately. Now here she was pushing a malfunctioning shopping cart down the produce aisle when she should be at home preparing for her guests.

Roslyn stopped the buggy in front of the green beans and inspected them for freshness. As she placed a handful in a clear baggy, Adriana leaned sideways in the cart, stretching her little fingers toward the bin of Brussels sprouts.

"You're too young for those, darling. Mommy doesn't want you to choke." She pushed the cart forward.

Adriana's round face puckered. "Mine."

"No, sweetie."

Tears welled in the child's light-blue eyes, then Adriana let out a curdling cry that caused several nearby patrons to look their way.

"Hush now," Roslyn whispered. "You're causing a scene." She smiled at the red-haired man stocking heads of cabbage in the case. This was why she dreaded taking Adriana anywhere without her nanny. Unfortunately, Brittany had come down with something and Roslyn had no choice but to dismiss her for the day. After all, she couldn't have Adriana exposed to those germs. Roslyn's leniency with the staff had forced her to cancel her nail appointment and reschedule the masseuse. What good was having a live-in nanny if she always had the sniffles?

While she was thinking about it, Roslyn stopped the cart and riffled through her handbag. Locating her PalmPilot, she tapped a note. *Call agency for a replacement nanny. Arrange interviews for a permanent housekeeper starting next week.* Her thoughts ricocheted a dozen directions. It'd be easier to use her cell phone to call the house and leave a detailed message on the answering machine. She needed a personal assistant. And one of those new BlackBerrys she'd heard so much about. Something sticky touched her forearm. "No—no, Adriana. Put the berries down."

Adriana jammed a pudgy fistful of raspberries into her mouth, dribbling juice down her chin and staining her pink flowered dress. A half second later, her mouth dropped open and she began pawing berries off her tongue. Managing to rid her mouth of the undesired fruit, she lifted her arms. "Up."

Oh no. Not until you're cleaned up. Roslyn had spent a small fortune in New York on her silk blouse, and she wasn't about to let dirty hands stain it. The same held true for the Jaguar.

Sticky fingers would destroy the '63 vintage cream leather interior. Granddaddy would turn in his grave if she didn't keep the car in its original state of glory.

Roslyn rummaged through her purse for the package of antiseptic wipes she'd used earlier to clean the shopping cart. Adriana squirmed, not liking her face wiped. Even after removing the raspberry residue, her daughter's mouth and lips remained red. The same bright-red shade she'd turned after eating strawberries earlier in the year—an allergic reaction that had terrified Roslyn. *Mental note: no raspberries.*

Roslyn wiped Adriana's neck and hands, then worked on the front of the dress, although it was already ruined. To ease the child's distress, she removed a box of animal crackers from the shelf, opened the package, and offered her one. Her daughter's crocodile tears evaporated quickly and, at least for the moment, she seemed content. Roslyn used the opportunity to finish shopping while still monitoring Adriana's face for any sign of hives. Within a short time, she conquered the store one aisle at a time, filling the cart with the items on her list plus a few extras.

Adriana's eyes closed and her head nodded only to startle herself awake. Roslyn glanced at her watch. Noon. No wonder everything looked good. She'd fed Adriana breakfast this morning but neglected to eat anything herself.

"I know you're tired, darling. We're going home now." Roslyn headed to the checkout.

The store wasn't that busy for a Thursday, but with only one register open, the time crawled standing in line. Another reason not to shop here when her schedule was already full. She tapped her fingers on the cart handle as the person ahead of her insisted the almond milk had wrung up at the wrong price. Roslyn called the house and dialed the code to retrieve the messages on the answering machine while the price was verified and the correction made. A twenty-cent difference cost them almost five minutes. As the clerk rang up Roslyn's items, she didn't bother watching the prices. A handful of pocket change wasn't worth arguing over. Her focus was divided between getting Adriana down for a nap, getting dinner started, and jotting down some key ideas for the upcoming fund-raising gala.

The strong autumn breeze made her wish she hadn't been concerned with someone dinging her car door, which prompted her to park in the farthest open space from the store. Roslyn hurried across the parking lot, steadied the cart next to the car without it touching the paint, then opened the trunk. As she went to grab a grocery bag, she noticed Adriana holding her hand over her ear. The poor child was prone to ear infections and had been to the pediatrician only last week. High wind exposure would most likely result in another clinic visit and more anti-biotics. Roslyn unfastened the safety strap around Adriana's waist and took her out of the cart. Her daughter's eyes closed the moment Roslyn fastened her into the car seat. Not wanting to run the risk of Adriana catching a cold, Roslyn slipped behind the wheel, started the engine, and adjusted the heat to its highest level. With her daughter situated, she went back outside to load the groceries.

Refrigerated and freezer items on the right side, nonperishables on the left. She leaned over the shopping cart to retrieve the case of bottled water and something struck the back of her head. Her mind not fully registering what had just happened, she took a step back, but another blow darkened her surroundings and she hit the pavement.

Chapter 2

Faith Pinkham peeked through the round window separating the kitchen from the eating area of The Amish Table and cringed at the large lunch crowd. Many of the tables hadn't been cleared since the breakfast surge and her older sister, Olivia, had her hands full taking new orders. Faith glanced over her shoulder at the pot of broccoli-and-cheese soup simmering on the stove. If she hurried, she could clean off a few tables before Olivia turned in the next order. Wiping her hands on her apron, she pushed the swinging double doors open with her hip.

Mrs. Meyer, one of their regular customers, shot up a quick wave from a back table. The retiree from downstate had bought a house on a nearby acre lot two years ago and had been busy planting gardens ever since. When it came to growing tea roses, Faith had never known anyone to have a green thumb like Mrs. Meyer. Tea roses are tender and prone to disease, but her bushes were lively and massive and fragrant.

Faith strode to the back of the dining area and stopped at the garden lady's table to say a quick hello before cleaning off the empty table next to Mrs. Meyer. "How are you today?"

"Doing just peachy, sweetie. Do they have you working in the kitchen?"

"*Jah*, I'm cooking." And cleaning tables.

"You poor thing. It must be blazing hot over the stove." She added a splash of cream to her coffee.

Faith smiled. The large fans in the kitchen helped exhaust the heat, but on days like today, she looked forward to soaking her feet in the creek after work. She stepped to the recently vacated table next to the window and began stacking dirty plates. Olivia had grabbed the tip off the table without taking any of the dishes away.

Mrs. Meyer stirred her coffee. "Are you doing anything special for the Fourth of July?"

"You mean other than work?" Faith chuckled. "Probably *nett*." The Amish only celebrated Thanksgiving, Christmas, Second Christmas, and Easter, but not many *Englischers* knew that.

Mrs. Meyer had an inquisitive soul. Since moving to northern Michigan, she'd shown more interest in the Amish lifestyle than most people who lived in Posen all their lives. Although Faith didn't mind answering the friendly woman's questions, she didn't volunteer anything more. If Mrs. Meyer knew about Faith starting baptism classes, she would have a slew of questions. Questions Faith wouldn't feel comfortable answering.

Faith repositioned the chairs. She would come back to wash the table, restock the condiments, and replace the paper place mats and napkin-wrapped utensils. She glanced at Mrs. Meyer sipping her coffee. "Can I get you anything? More coffee?"

"I have everything I need, sweetie."

"New order," Olivia announced, waving the carbon-copied slip on her way into the kitchen as if it were a flag.

Faith groaned under her breath. Several more tables needed to be cleaned off. Too bad it was her cousin Catherine's day off. Admittedly, Catherine was a better cook than all of them, except for *Mamm*. But then, her older cousin had worked over fifteen years at the restaurant, and over time *Mamm* had taught her everything. Olivia often voiced to Faith how it wasn't fair that *Mamm* gave their cousin the prime shifts, but Olivia was annoyed about everything lately—everything Amish, that is.

Faith positioned the dirty mugs and silverware on top of the plates. "I'll see you next week, Mrs. Meyer." She picked up the stack. "I want to hear about your roses when there's more time to talk."

"Don't work too hard in the kitchen," the woman said.

Faith wished that was an option, but people came from all over to eat an authentic Amish meal. As she headed to the kitchen, the tiny bell over the door jingled, announcing yet another customer. She liked staying busy, but at this rate, her feet would be too swollen to get her shoes off for wading through the creek. "Take a seat wherever you like," she called out, keeping her eye on the teetering mug atop her pile.

A man cleared his throat behind her. "I'm here to deliver the cherries your *Mamm* ordered, *nett* eat."

Faith glanced up and smiled. "*Hiya*, Gideon." He'd been so busy lately that today was the first she'd seen of him since Sunday service.

He lifted the gallon-sized ice-cream pails now heaped with bright-red cherries. "I knocked on the kitchen door, but no one answered. Is your *Mamm* here?"

"She's running errands." Faith moved cautiously toward the kitchen, focusing again on the wobbling mugs, then paused long enough at the double door to bob her head for Gideon to follow. Faith bumped the door with her hip and proceeded to the sink area where mounds of dirty dishes littered the counter. Their restaurant didn't have a fancy electric dishwasher. Her hands had remained chapped since she finished school after eighth grade and started working full-time almost four years ago with her mother, older sister, and cousin.

"Looks like you've been busy today," Gideon said, his gaze taking in the disarray.

Faith's face heated. When her mother or

Catherine ran the kitchen, it never looked this unorganized. "It's just been Olivia and me all morning, so we haven't had time to catch up."

Olivia stood at the drink dispenser, filling glasses with ice. "Did you hear me say you have an order?"

"*Jah.*" Faith maintained a cheerful tone. First she had to find a bare surface for these dishes. Her arms grew weaker under the weight and a mug toppled over, spilling cold coffee down her arm.

Gideon swiped a pillar of unwashed plates off the counter, clearing an empty space.

Olivia balanced a large tray of water glasses and steaming mugs on her shoulder. "I told them you'd put a rush on the order. They're in a hurry." She came around the corner and smiled when her gaze landed on Gideon. "I didn't see you *kumm* in, Gideon. How are you?"

"Fine."

Olivia backed into the door, butting it open with her hip. "*Gut* to hear." She sprang out the door, leaving it to flap in her wake.

A baffled expression overtook Gideon's face.

Faith imagined he was taken aback by Olivia's aloofness but was too polite to mention it. She strode to the counter and unclipped the order slip suspended on the wire above her. Six omelets. All different. *And* a half dozen sides of potato pancakes. How was she supposed to rush this?

She had used the last of the diced vegetables on the last order and was running low on grated potatoes.

"Does everyone have to be in a hurry today?" Faith grumbled.

"I guess I'm *nett*—in a hurry." Gideon lifted the dirty dishes he'd picked up to make room a little higher.

"*Ach*, Gideon. Why didn't you say something?" She tossed the slip on the counter and dashed over to the dishwashing area. After carefully piling one stack on top of another, she cleared a spot. "You can leave them here."

He set down the plates, then immediately rolled up his sleeves.

Faith watched in disbelief. "What are you doing?"

"Well, I'm *nett* much of a cook." He worked on rolling up the other sleeve. "But I do know how to wash dishes."

"You don't have to do that."

"I know." He plugged the stainless-steel basin with a stopper, turned the hot-water tap on, then squirted in some dish soap.

"I don't want to keep you from your cherry deliveries."

"You're *nett*." He smiled.

Faith's insides fluttered. She'd never shared kitchen duty with a man. "*Danki*, but you can leave them soaking. Once *mei mamm* returns

18

from the market, she'll relieve me from cooking, and I'll have time to catch up on the dishes."

Gideon motioned to the stove. "You should probably get started on that order." He dipped his hands into the soapy water, glanced sideways at her, and winked. "Aren't they in a hurry?"

"*Ah, jah,* that's right." Faith spun around and scurried over to the prep sink where she lathered her hands with soap. The oddity of a man with his sleeves rolled up past his elbows while not delivering a calf, but washing dishes, was a bit disturbing. In a good way.

She stole a glance over her shoulder at Gideon and sighed. Strong, kind, handsome, hardworking, he had all the traits of a good husband—for her sister, Olivia, if only she would show him a little interest. The man used every excuse possible to conjure up ways to be around her sister. Last month, when it came time for her family to host the Sunday meeting, Gideon volunteered to help her father muck the barn and set up the benches for the service. He even washed dishes today to see Olivia. Faith sighed. Her sister was blessed with creamy skin, blond silky hair, and enough smarts to teach school, yet she was dim-witted when it came to Gideon. Faith had known him her whole life, not that he ever paid much attention to her. She was Olivia's kid sister—lanky, grease-clogged pores from working over the fryer, and dark, coarse hair that tended to frizz in the summer—nothing more.

Faith turned off the tap water and dried her hands. Too much daydreaming had slowed her pace. She slid the refrigerator door open and removed the onions, mushrooms, green peppers, spinach, and tomatoes for one omelet; sausage, goat cheese, and jalapeños for another. Some naturally took longer to make because she had to fry the bacon and brown the ham. Not to mention one person wanted egg whites only, and that took more time.

A few feet away, Gideon hummed "*Das Loblied*" as he worked, an added treat to Faith's ears. Recognizing the tune as one of their Amish hymns, she hummed along while dicing vegetables. Once this order was filled, she would make him something special to eat for all his hard work. Since it was almost noon, maybe a cheeseburger. She stole another peek at him working, his head bobbing to the tune. She could get used to his help in the kitchen.

Stop it! Gideon was her sister's *bu*—even if Olivia hadn't shown interest in settling down and joining the church yet. Eventually her sister would come to see Gideon for the man he was. A good man. A patient man. A man . . . who would wait for Olivia to finish her *rumspringa* and join the church fold.

A flash of jealousy bubbled up within Faith.

Chapter 3

Gideon Rohrer managed to wash most of the towering plates and cups before Olivia zinged through the double doors with another tray heaped with dirty dishes in her arms. The job was unending. He lifted his hands out of the sink and flung the excess soap residue off with a hard shake, then reached for the tray. "I'll take them."

Olivia nodded and flashed what he'd come to discover the hard way as an insincere smile. Before he could speak, she strutted back into the dining room.

He'd spent the better part of a year chasing that smile—trying to get her back. All the while knowing Olivia was sitting on the fence, mustering the courage to jump.

Standing at the stove, Faith leaned back and pointed her spatula at him. "You don't have to do those."

"The way I see it, you're *nett* in any position to turn down help." The shelf of clean plates near her workstation was dwindling fast. Gideon scraped the uneaten food from the plates into the scrap bucket on the floor. Such a waste of good food. His parents raised him to finish everything on his plate. Lowering the dishes into the basin, he glanced at the wall clock. When he decided to stay and help, he didn't plan on still being here at noon. Even though his fruit deliveries were finished, he had promised one of his *Englisch* customers he would apply another coat of redwood stain on her deck.

Within minutes, the scent of bacon drifted across the room, teasing his senses. Faith tapped the silver bell, a satisfied smile blooming on her face as she positioned the plates of food under the heat lamps.

Olivia strode into the kitchen with yet another tray of dirty dishes. Surely that was the last of the dirty tables. She set the items to the left of the sink, on the same counter that only minutes ago he had cleared off. Without acknowledging him, she exchanged the tray for a clean one from the shelf under the island and placed it on the counter. She picked up one of the plates from under the heat lamp. "Is this the one with mushrooms?"

Faith consulted the slip. "*Jah*." She handed the next plate to Olivia. "This one is the sausage, goat cheese, and jalapeños." The sisters worked together arranging the plates counterclockwise according to how Olivia had written down the orders.

Gideon had to remind himself to get back to work. The dishes wouldn't wash themselves. He quickly scraped the food leftovers into the bucket and lowered the dishes into the soapy water. The pads of his fingers were wrinkled from having them submerged so long.

"Hey, Gideon. What do you like on your cheeseburger? American or Swiss?" Faith dropped a raw beef patty on the grill.

He shouldn't tie up her time cooking for him. Then again, the meat was already on the grill. Sizzling. Sending tantalizing aromas over to his side of the kitchen. The peanut butter–banana sandwich he'd packed for lunch was still in the buggy. Warm. Mushy. He licked his lips. "Swiss, please."

Hoping Olivia wouldn't clean off another table and bring him more dishes to wash, he scrubbed faster. He'd just finished rinsing and stacking the last plate on the drying rack when Faith pulled the basket of fries out of the hot grease. Gideon pulled the plug on the drain, then dried his hands. "I probably have the cleanest hands of all the men in the district," he said, inspecting his nails.

"Does that bother you?" She set the plate of food on the counter and motioned to a stool.

"*Nay*, but I'm sure *mei bruders* will tease me for having dishpan hands, but that's nothing new. They've always given me a hard time over something." Mercilessly. It didn't help being the youngest of six boys or that his mother often came to his defense. She wouldn't have her baby boy picked on—even though her "help" usually meant more heckling from his brothers in the end.

Faith set the ketchup and mustard containers in front of him.

His mouth watered looking at the big juicy burger with melted cheese oozing down the sides. He bowed his head, prayed briefly in silence, then opened his eyes. He squirted condiments on the meat, then reassembled the toasted onion bun over the patty and picked it up. Opening his mouth wide to take a bite, he pulled back. Faith was staring, giving him the same perturbed look his mother gave him whenever he rushed through saying grace. "What? I prayed."

"Bless this food, amen?" A smile tugged at the corners of her lips.

"And all who are at the table," he added, readying the burger to take a bite.

"Well"—her brows quirked—"I was actually looking at your hands. They do look soft."

The spunky laugh that followed provoked him to put the burger down. He stood, leaned over the counter, and snatched the dish towel.

Faith planted her hands on her hips. "You're *nett* going to waste the food I made, are you?"

"Oh, it won't go to waste." He twirled the towel at both ends and took a step toward her.

"Oh, don't you dare."

He snapped it in her direction, intentionally missing her by an inch. "You still want to talk about *mei* soft hands?"

"You don't seem to be as *gut* of an aim as you are at washing dishes," she teased.

He wound the towel again.

"Okay—okay, I give up. You have very manly hands." Giggles laced her words.

Ignoring her plea of surrender, Gideon stepped closer. His menacing chuckle made her deep blue eyes grow large. "Nervous, are you?" The clean fragrance of her lavender soap floated to him, overtaking the smell of fried food.

"*Nay.*" But her gaze darted from the towel, to his eyes, back to the towel while stepping backward. She backed into the ice chest and worked the latch.

"Order up," Olivia announced as she whizzed into the kitchen. She stopped abruptly when an ice chip, flying over Gideon's shoulder, landed at her feet. "It must be nice to have time for games." She slapped the order ticket on the counter, then, frowning, eyed her sister. "Faith, you better clean this up before someone falls." She marched back into the dining room.

Gideon stared at the swinging door, momentarily taken aback by Olivia's sharpness. "She's got a chigger under her skin," he muttered under his breath.

"Olivia is always upset with me." Faith bent down and picked up the pieces of scattered ice chips. "It doesn't matter what I do."

He squatted and collected the cubes at his feet. "That's how *mei* older *bruders* are with me."

"She despises me most days. I don't even know what I do to get her upset."

"Other than throwing ice chips?"

Faith smiled. "I'd say you have a point if Olivia were the one responsible for mopping the floors, but she breezes in, slaps an order slip on the counter, and breezes out like a princess while I'm the one stuck in the kitchen cleaning, cooking, or washing dishes. *Nett* that I mind, it's just . . ." She sighed. "Never mind."

"It's just that you'd like to be appreciated," he said.

She bowed her head. "I shouldn't have complained."

Gideon playfully took her hand as she reached for another ice chip. "Maybe we should compare our dishpan hands." He turned her hand over, pretending to inspect it. Brushing his thumb against her soft skin, an irregular *pit-pat* of his heart increased his awareness of their closeness, and he dropped her hand. "You have nothing to whine about. Your hands are way softer than mine."

"*Hmm.* I'm *nett* sure if I should be flattered you think *mei* skin is soft or insulted that you called me a whiner." She swiped the order ticket off the counter and looked it over.

If she'd felt uncomfortable about their close proximity, she wasn't showing it now. He, on the other hand, was still battling a stuttering pulse. He plopped onto the stool, picked up the cooled burger, and took a bite. He should have thought to slide his plate under the heat lamp

26

before he started chasing Faith with the towel.

Faith tossed a couple of hamburger patties on the grill, moved over to the fountain machine, filled a glass with ice, then pressed the cola button on the soda dispenser. She set the fizzing drink next to his plate. "Do you want me to warm up your food?"

"*Nay, danki*. I have to leave in a few minutes. I promised Beverly Dembrowski I would put a second coat of stain on her porch today." He took another bite and washed it down with a gulp of cola. The carbonated bubbles tickled his throat and made it hard to swallow. "I wanted to talk to you about Olivia. She's planning—" The whoosh of the swinging door behind him caught his attention. He glanced over his shoulder to see Olivia. "Back again," he choked out.

Olivia's mouth crooked, her expression unreadable. Had she overheard her name?

"The lunch crowd is growing." Olivia waved yellow slips at Faith, then slapped them down on the counter.

Faith fussed with the hamburger already cooking. She waited for her sister to leave, then faced Gideon. "I know I've helped you before, but I'd rather stay out of your and *mei schweschaler's* . . . affairs. I already told you, she hates me."

"*Hate* is a strong word," he said, wishing he could take back the lecturing tone when Faith turned her back to him. She was a close friend, the person he trusted most. This had nothing to do with his—affairs. Olivia was in trouble. "Faith," he said, pleadingly enough that she glanced over her shoulder at him, "I wouldn't bring it up if it wasn't important."

The back door swung open, and Faith and Olivia's mother, Irma, entered carrying a brown paper sack and moving slowly, as if drained of energy. "Sorry I'm late."

Noticing how winded Irma sounded, Gideon jumped off his stool and reached for the bag, which, surprisingly, wasn't heavy.

"*Danki.*" She brushed her hand against her forehead.

"Where would you like me to put this?"

She patted the counter opposite of where he'd been sitting. "Over here will be fine." Her dark-brown eyes looked dull and her ivory complexion resembled more a wintery white than the sun-tanned tones of summer. He was about to pull the stool around for her to sit when Faith rounded the corner, her face etched with worry.

Faith's five-ten height towered over her mother's five feet two inches. "*Mamm*, is everything okay?"

"I'm fine, dear." She pursed her lips in a long exhale, then smiled at her daughter, who was eying every inch of her. "Really, I am." As if ending the discussion, Irma looked at Gideon. "I see you brought the cherries I ordered."

"Eight pounds. I picked them this morning."

"*Gut.*" Irma reached into the paper bag and removed the vegetables.

Faith gathered the cucumbers, celery stalks, and broccoli and took them to the wall-sized refrigerator.

Irma inspected a head of lettuce, peeling off a few outer leaves. "Do you think you'll have more cherries?"

"Oh, *jah*. The trees are full this year." His orchard tended to be plentiful one year and scarce the next. This season he had enough fruit to supply his regular customers and stock the roadside fruit stand. Even his mother was able to put up extra jars of cherry preserves and pie fillings for the winter. He hoped the blueberries would be as plentiful, but he wasn't holding his breath. They hadn't had much rain lately. Some years the berries shriveled before completely ripening.

"I should have blueberries next week. Hopefully raspberries at the end of the month," he volunteered.

"I'll take ten pounds of each to start." Irma wiped her hands on a rag after handling the vegetables. Her gaze swept the counter. "Did you bring the invoice for the cherries?"

"The slip is in *mei* buggy. I'll go get it." He strode to the back door. Irma was usually more talkative. She always made a point to ask about his mother and his *mammi*. Sometimes she kept him there to talk about the swarms of bugs

29

destroying the crops or to offer him food. Irma wasn't making the shooing motion with her hands, but she wasn't trying to coax him into having a bowl of ice cream either.

He stepped outside, and the midday heat enveloped him. At least his horse, Bay, was in the shade of the maple and within proximity of the watering trough. The skittish three-year-old gelding lifted his head and neighed as Gideon approached. "Easy, boy." He stroked Bay's neck until he calmed down, then grabbed the slip of paper with the price of the cherries and plodded across the gravel parking lot. Irma was one of his best customers, buying whatever fruit was in season throughout the summer and multiple bushels of apples in the fall.

The screen door creaked and Faith stepped outside. "I wrapped your burger and fries in wax paper for you to take with you." She held out a brown paper bag.

"*Danki*." He'd planned to scarf down the last few bites before he left, but taking it to go was even better. "Will you give your *mamm* this?" He handed her the slip of paper.

She leaned closer and lowered her voice. "What were you going to say about Olivia?"

Nothing he could blurt out in a parking lot. "What time do you get off work?"

Chapter 4

The potato peel curled around Faith's hand as she worked the knife, her mind filled with thoughts of Gideon. Had he not mentioned that he wanted to talk about Olivia, she might have jumped to the wrong conclusion after he asked what time her shift ended. But Faith handled her disappointment by maintaining her practiced, neutral expression.

She pushed the thoughts of Gideon to the back of her mind and concentrated on a new cherry recipe. "*Mamm*, what if we put cherries and rhubarb together instead of making the usual strawberry-rhubarb combination?"

Mamm said nothing as she pressed the hamburger patty with the spatula on the grill. Obviously, her thoughts were elsewhere too.

Faith wrinkled her nose. "I guess it would be too tart, *jah*, probably *nett* a *gut* combination." She would stick to making a cherry cobbler. "Should I make a pie for the Sunday-afternoon meal?" It wasn't until Faith cleared her throat that *Mamm* responded.

"I'm sorry," *Mamm* said without looking up. "Did you say something?"

"I wanted to try to make a cherry-rhubarb cobbler. Have you ever tried that combination?"

"Sounds interesting, dear."

Her mother wasn't a lackadaisical listener, especially when it came to Faith's ideas about the menu. *Mamm* loved to create new recipes and the two of them worked together a lot, developing new desserts for the restaurant, but *Mamm* hadn't been herself since she'd come back from running errands. Come to think of it, her only errand had been for vegetables they hadn't even needed.

"*Mamm*," Faith said, eyeing her mother's slumped shoulders. Last week she'd overheard her parents discussing the struggle to make the restaurant's steep monthly payments and how they'd overestimated June's revenue. "Is something wrong? Something you're *nett* telling me?"

"*Nay*, honey." *Mamm* pressed the blood out of the beef patty, juices sizzling around the edge, then flipped it over.

Faith set the knife down, gathered the potato shavings, and tossed them into a pail. The pigs would love them mixed in with their usual slop. Faith rounded the island and glanced up at the pending orders hanging on the wire. A single cheeseburger and fries on one ticket. Two dinners of open roast-beef sandwiches and mashed potatoes on another and a sauerkraut and pork chops. "I could finish these if you'd like to take a break."

Mamm shook her head. "I have everything under control." But the weariness in her voice suggested otherwise. So did her red-rimmed eyes. "Why don't you see if Olivia needs help in the dining room?"

Faith glanced at the peeled potatoes waiting to be grated into hash browns, then over to the bucket of cherries that still needed pitting. She'd rather prepare pies and cobbler than wait tables. But something told her that her mother needed a few minutes alone, so she went into the dining room. Olivia was chatting with the locals seated at the coffee-drinkers table as she refilled their cups. Her sister's friendliness with the *Englischers* stretched beyond the expected meekness of the Amish ways. Faith scanned the other patrons in the room, her gaze stopping on a man tapping his fingers on the menu while the woman gazed about the restaurant. She'd seen the impatient gesture a time or two. Debating whether to stay or leave. Faith grabbed a pad and pen from the counter and headed for the table. "Good afternoon, my name is Faith. Have you heard about our special today?" The chalkboard displaying the daily specials was well within view, but most new customers didn't know that *yummasetti* was a traditional Amish dish.

The man squinted in the board's direction, reminding Faith that she needed to suggest to *Mamm* that they have something printed for each table since the Monday-through-Friday specials never changed.

"*Yummasetti*, green beans, roll, and a slice of shoofly pie." Faith quoted the board from memory.

The man angled the menu toward Faith and pointed to the barbecued pulled pork sandwich. "I'll take this on sourdough bread. Is the bread fresh?"

"We bake it every morning." At 5:30 a.m. to be exact.

The woman seated across from him leaned forward. "What exactly is *yummasetti*?"

"It's an egg noodle dish with hamburger, tomato paste, and cheese. It's very filling," Faith added, knowing the woman's interest had faded the moment Faith mentioned noodles. But she asked anyway with a friendly smile, "Would you like to try the special?"

"No, I don't believe so. I'll have the Cobb salad, no croutons, and low-fat ranch dressing on the side." The woman handed Faith her menu. "Also, could we get more iced tea, please?"

"Yes, I'll bring you more to drink right away." Faith turned away from the table and caught Olivia glowering at her from behind the waitress station.

"Why did you steal *mei* table?" Olivia snipped the moment Faith stepped behind the half wall.

Faith placed the menus in the wooden holder. "Just trying to help."

"I didn't ask for your help."

"*Jah*, I know. *Mamm* sent me out here." Faith

34

reached for the pitcher of iced tea, only to have her sister snatch it off the counter.

Olivia's eyes widened and she looked down at the front of her apron, now tea stained. She set the pitcher down hard on the counter, sloshing tea over the rim. "Don't laugh," she snapped, dabbing her dress with a paper napkin. "You have grease splatters on your dress."

"I'm *nett* laughing." If anything, her sister's outburst and her possessiveness made Faith sad. She tore the ticket off the pad and handed it to Olivia. "Your table requested a tea refill." Faith would stay out of her sister's way. She removed the cleaning rag from the bucket of bleach water and wiped the counter next to the coffeepots. Her eyes moistened with tears. She and her sister had never been close. *Mamm* tried to explain that the reason was the four-year age gap between them, but the truth was, Olivia was kinder to her friends than to her own sister. Faith had prayed for years that things would change, but now she wondered if she and her sister might never become friends.

Faith dropped the rag into the bleach water, then wiped her tears with the back of her hands, not thinking to wash off the residue first. Her eyes instantly began to burn and water more. Blinking didn't relieve the sting. Faith covered her eyes with her hand and went into the kitchen, blindly feeling her way over to the sink where she turned on the cold-water tap. She cupped handfuls of water and tossed them at her face repeatedly.

"Faith?" *Mamm* placed her hand on Faith's shoulder, leaned closer. "Did you get something in your eyes?"

"Bleach," she said, continuing to rinse her eyes.

"Is there anything I can do, honey?"

"*Nay*, they're feeling better." Faith blinked a few times, but the irritation persisted. She should have been more careful.

Olivia breezed into the kitchen. "What's wrong with her?"

"She got bleach in her eyes," *Mamm* said. "Grab that dish towel on the counter so Faith can dry her face on it, please."

"Sure. Do you want this?" She waved the order ticket.

Mamm took the paper and looked it over. "I'll get this started and be right back," she told Faith.

Olivia approached Faith with the towel and whispered, "You sure know how to get attention, don't you?"

Lord, I'm casting all mei *cares on You, for You care for me.* Faith had recited scriptures more and more lately to combat Olivia's sharp tongue. She wouldn't let her sister get under her skin today. She buried her face in the towel and fought the urge to set Olivia straight. *Let it go. Mamm* had been upset about something not long ago, and Faith wasn't about to get her upset all over again by seeing them bicker like toddlers. She held the towel against her face until she heard the door swing, then waited a few more seconds before peeking to see if Olivia had indeed left the kitchen.

Mamm tipped Faith's chin and inspected her closely. "How do your eyes feel?"

"Better." Or they would once they stopped watering.

"You should go home." *Mamm* washed her hands, then went to the refrigerator and removed the items to make the Cobb salad.

"I don't want to leave you shorthanded. Who's going to keep up with the dishes?"

"We can handle things. Besides, you were here early to bake bread. It won't hurt your *schweschaler* to wash dishes after we close."

Doing extra kitchen labor would certainly irritate Olivia if it meant not spending time after work with her friends. "I better stay," Faith said.

Mamm smiled. "You're so conscientious and mature for your age that sometimes I forget which of *mei* girls is older." She made a shooing motion with her hand. "*Nau*, off you *geh*."

"What about the cherries?" Their restaurant was known for homemade pies and muffins, and the display case out front had a limited selection.

"They can be pitted tomorrow. *Nau*, please take the rest of the day off. I may need you to cook again on Monday."

Faith hesitated a moment, then removed her apron. She could guess what Olivia would say tonight once they were alone in their shared bedroom. First she would grumble about having to do Faith's work, then accuse her of being *Mamm's* favorite. According to her sister, Faith always received special treatment, which wasn't true. The last time Olivia made those accusations, Faith offered to change jobs. But Olivia didn't want to get up early and make the bread. She also didn't want to give up her waitressing tips.

Faith took her mother's advice and started for home on foot in the scorching July heat. She strolled along the sidewalk at an easy pace, gazing in the store windows as she went. Their farm wasn't too far out of town. On days like today, when she was on foot, she liked to take the North Eastern State Trail, the old Detroit and Mackinac Railway line, which meant no traffic and plenty of wildlife sightings. She could watch the animals for hours, especially when she spotted a herd of deer grazing in the grassy meadow at the edge of the forest or an elk cow and calf nibbling on tree bark in the old apple orchard. Many of the townsfolk believed that during the late 1800s when timber camps were being established in this area, logging men inadvertently started the orchard by discarding apple cores. But today, she chose the crushed limestone path because the creek was one of her favorite places to sit and think. And since Gideon had left the restaurant, she had a lot to think about.

Faith removed her shoes and dipped her feet in the spring-fed creek. *The joys of summer.* She breathed in the dank scent of moss as she tipped her face upward, soaking in the warmth of the afternoon sun, a sharp contrast to the cold water. For a moment, she forgot about work and Olivia. She felt the breeze against her face, listened to the babbling sound of water and the birds chirping nearby. She loved spending time alone.

"You sure know how to get attention."

Olivia's comment earlier invaded Faith's solitude. Her sister had held a grudge for more years than Faith could remember, longer than she could recall what had even caused Olivia to be upset in the first place. Olivia had no reason to be jealous. Then again, her sister had walked into the kitchen when she and Gideon were teasing each other. No wonder Olivia accused Faith of knowing how to get attention. Now it made sense. And tonight she would be sure to set things right with her sister and ease her mind.

Faith ventured upstream, keeping her eyes on the rocky bottom so she didn't slip. The midcalf water level was low after an unseasonably dry season. Iron ore and sulfur deposits had tinted the water an amber shade and given it a metallic scent. A few yards upstream, Faith reached the clearing where last spring she had spotted a doe with its speckled fawn. On hot days like today, the deer were probably lying in the tall grassy meadow or roaming the woods scrounging acorns.

As she moved into deeper water, a smallmouth bass nibbled her toes. The tickling sensation made her jump and the splash she produced scattered the fish. A hearty laugh echoed behind her and she spun around, scanning the tree-lined bank. She spotted Gideon, perched on a tree limb that hung low over the water, and called, "What are you doing here?"

"Checking out *mei* fishing hole."

She sloshed over to him, the water rising to her knees. "I don't see a pole."

He smiled. "This isn't the best time of day to drop a line."

"*Nett* the best spot either." Unless he wanted to spend most of his time untangling lines from the cattails. She swatted away a dragonfly.

"True." He removed his boot and tossed it on the ground. "How *kalt* is the water?"

"Not bad once you're used to it." She kicked the surface of the water and splashed him with a few drops.

He tossed his other boot on dry land and jumped off the branch, not bothering to roll up his pant legs. His eyes fostered a determined glint as he moved toward her. "I didn't think you'd be off work yet."

"*Mamm* sent me home early." She backed up,

40

but not before he cupped his hand and skimmed the surface of the stream, creating a large spray of icy water. She froze. "Hey!"

"You shouldn't start what you can't finish." He sprayed her again, this time soaking her good.

Backing away from him, she tripped over a rock and plunged into the water.

Gideon laughed. "Practicing for your baptism?"

Faith cupped her hands and collected water, then tossed it at him as he tromped closer.

Blocking the shower, he leaned over her and extended his hand. "Let me help you up."

His playful chuckle gave her cause to hesitate. She squinted up at him, but wasn't able to see his face under the shadow of his straw hat and with the sun at his back.

Gideon cocked his head. "You're *nett kalt*?"

"I'm freezing." And mostly embarrassed. Swimming with a man, even though they technically weren't, was strictly forbidden. She should be more mindful of her activities. After all, she'd started taking classes to join the church. If one of the elders saw them together . . .

"Don't be a fool." He extended his arm farther. "Take *mei* hand."

Faith accepted his help and he lifted her up from the bottom of the creek. The summer breeze sent a chill through her body. Her lips trembled uncontrollably. "I should go." She turned and traipsed downstream to where she'd left her shoes.

"Why are you getting baptized?"

Puzzled by his question, Faith stopped, crossed her arms, and faced him. "Are you questioning *mei* character?" Prior to the baptism, the bishop asked the church members if they would accept the applicant as brother, or in her case, sister in Christ. She wasn't sure what happened to those who a member spoke out against. More classes? Faith had already attended three of the nine sessions on the teachings of the *Dordrecht* Confession of Faith.

"*Nay.*" He walked closer. "Most people join the church just prior to getting married. Is that . . ."

"What?—*Nay!*" On the rare occasions that she attended the youth singings, it was to socialize with people her own age, not look for someone to marry. She wouldn't turn seventeen for another three months. Besides, working six days a week at the restaurant—and long hours at that—put a crimp in courting anyone seriously. That and she happened to be taller than most of the unmarried men and was often overlooked when it came time for the girl to be asked home from a singing.

Gideon's brows creased.

"Can't someone get baptized and join the church because they feel led by God? Not everyone needs to get married—why are you asking such personal questions?" She wasn't sure she liked him being so intrusive. Perhaps Bishop Zook sent him on this inquiring mission.

As an applicant for baptism, she was under more scrutiny than others her age who were still on *rumspringa*. "Are you gathering information?"

"*Nay—jah*, kinda."

"You can tell the bishop and elders and whoever else is interested that I'm ready to join the church." He opened his mouth, but she continued. "I'm young, I know. Others *mei* age don't always know what they want. They think they'll figure it out sowing their wild oats during *rumspringa* but—" Faith clamped her lips, unable to stop shivering . . . and not because his face formed perfect dimples. "Why are you grinning like that?"

"Was I?" He sobered for an instant, but his dimpled grin reappeared. "The only one asking about you is me. *Nett* the bishop, *nett* the elders, *nett* even your parents. Just me."

"Oh." Dare she ask what piqued his curiosity? No, some things were better left unspoken. She fell silent, but that didn't stop her mind from turning over his words. *"Most people join the church just prior to getting married."*

A few minutes passed when neither of them spoke. Then Gideon veered a few steps over to a deeper section of the creek where the water was a dark copper hue. "I should've brought *mei* pole." He studied the water, his gaze darting in all directions.

She located the school of bluegill he was

watching. Even if he had his pole, the fish were too small to be considered a legal catch.

"Where there are bluegill, there's usually bass, walleye, and pike. Smallmouth bass like a hard rocky bottom and a little faster current than pike."

Standing in the shaded area of the creek for any length of time made her shiver. "I'll leave you to your fishing expedition." She plodded forward, suppressing her desire to stay and hang out longer. It wasn't right that her sister's *bu* had become such a close friend. Lately, she had spent more time with him than any of her chummy girlfriends, but that had more to do with her girlfriends being on their *rumspringa* and Faith working so many hours at The Amish Table.

"Hey, wait up." Gideon sloshed up to her. "I'll give you a ride home."

She glanced at her sopping dress. She hated the thought of someone from their district seeing her on the way home, walking with her wet dress clinging to her legs. But she'd already spent too much time alone with Gideon. Talk had a way of spreading like honey and was just as sticky too. "*Danki*, but I should probably—"

"I wanted to talk with you about Olivia."

Of course he did. Faith focused on the sandy river bottom.

"I think you should know . . ."

His pause, whether intentionally or not, drew her attention.

Concern flooded his expression. "She's getting ready to jump the fence," he said.

"With who?"

Gideon stared without blinking, pain hooding his eyes.

Faith swallowed hard. "With you?" She waited for him to deny it, but he just stared.

Chapter 5

Bloomfield Hills, Michigan
Fifteen years ago

In a matter of minutes, the FBI had converted Roslyn's eight-thousand-square-foot home into a field headquarters. Special Agent Sanderson introduced himself as post commander, then briefly introduced his team, including the only woman in the group, Special Agent Dunford, a family and media liaison specialist. Roslyn attempted to keep track of the agents' names, but with her head still throbbing from the throttling she took in the parking lot, they jumbled together. Once introductions were made, the team began setting up equipment in her husband Brandon's office.

Agents Sanderson and Dunford approached Roslyn. "While we wait for the surveillance footage from the market, we would like to ask you a few questions."

"There's a video?" Her attention flitted from Agent Sanderson's stoic face to Agent Dunford, whose expression was no more revealing.

"It's being obtained," Sanderson finally said. "We should know something soon."

Roslyn glanced at her Rolex. "Five hours later," she muttered.

Dunford tilted her head slightly, offering a sympathetic smile. "All things considered—"

"I know. Had I not been knocked unconscious, admitted into the ER as Jane Doe, you would have been involved sooner." Roslyn pushed her hair behind her ear and winced at what felt like hot irons searing her head from all angles.

"Are you okay, Mrs. Colepepper?"

No, she wasn't okay. Her daughter was missing. She glimpsed Brandon across the room, riffling through his file cabinet. Surely he wasn't looking for something for work. Their daughter was in the hands of strangers, who might—on a whim— hurt, torture, even . . . *Stop! Take control.* A burst of white dots clouded her vision.

"Mrs. Colepepper?" Agent Sanderson repeated. "Any information you can give us . . ."

"Yes—yes of course."

Agent Sanderson removed a pen and pad from his shirt pocket. "This may have been a carjacker unaware of your daughter in the vehicle. Then again, Adriana may have been the target."

"And if it was my Jag they were after, what do you think will happen to Adriana?" Snippets of information from an article she'd once read jogged her memory. A high percentage of carjackers were often ex-cons who dealt hand in hand with drug lords. Within hours, the stolen cars were stripped down, repainted, and posted on the black market. Unless the car was stolen by juveniles on a dare or joyride. But even those cars were often abandoned in some alley in downtown Detroit.

"There's a good possibility the carjacker will drop your daughter off at a hospital or fire station. We've issued an Amber Alert. Both local and state police are involved. We'll do everything we can to get your daughter back safe and sound."

"My daughter's name is Adriana," Roslyn said. "You called her Amber."

Agent Sanderson offered a weak smile. "I'm sorry, I should have explained how the Amber system works. It's an alert notification sent out automatically to the surrounding counties. We have issued notice of your daughter's abduction to law enforcement agencies as well as newspapers, radio, and TV stations."

"And they know what she looks like?"

"Yes, ma'am." He consulted his notebook. "Brown hair, blue eyes, weight approximately twenty-two pounds, height approximately thirty inches. Abducted from the Best Choice Market on Telegraph Road, last seen in a green 1963 Jaguar four-door Saloon. License plate SPOIL-1."

"She was wearing a pink flowered dress," Roslyn added.

"Yes, ma'am."

"Stained with raspberries . . . her dress." A dull, throbbing ache cinched Roslyn's throat. She should have left the store earlier instead of pacifying Adriana with animal crackers. If only she had parked closer to the building . . .

"In the meantime," Sanderson said with a slight clear of his throat. "I'd like to concentrate on people who would have had access to your schedule. I'll need the names of your household staff, a list of their duties, length of employment, and anyone who might have a grievance against you or your husband."

Roslyn drew her head back in confusion. "Where do I begin? We've had multiple people work for us over the years." Several terminated for one reason or another.

Sanderson's pen remained poised over the tablet. "Start with your current staff."

"We have two housekeepers. Milly, who works Tuesdays and Thursdays, and Georgette, who is—was—Monday through Friday."

Sanderson looked up from his notepad. "Was?"

"Georgette took a leave of absence to care for her sick grandmother."

"How long ago?"

"A month. Why?" A chill settled over Roslyn. "You don't think she had anything to do with this, do you?"

"We're not ruling anyone out at this time." Sanderson continued, "Did she leave any contact information? An e-mail or physical address?"

"No, she said she'd be in touch."

Agent Dunford broke her stiff stance and leaned forward. "And has she?"

"No, but it wasn't like we were friends on a social level. I had given her a letter of reference, so other than possibly requesting her personal recipe book be mailed to her new address at some later date, I don't expect her to contact me."

"Do you still have the recipe book?"

"Yes, it's on the shelf in the kitchen with the other cookbooks. Georgette's has a black binder."

Agent Sanderson nodded at his partner, and without saying anything, Agent Dunford left the office.

Her housekeeper forgetting to take her cherished recipe book had struck Roslyn as strange at the time. The recipes had been handed down through Georgette's family, some stretching back to her great-grandmother. She wouldn't have left such a treasure behind on purpose. An image of Adriana eating macaroni and cheese with her fingers came to mind. Her daughter loved the meals Georgette created. Who was feeding her child now?

"Is there something else you want to say, Mrs. Colepepper?"

"Georgette was very fond of Adriana," Roslyn volunteered. "On her last day, Georgette told Adriana she'd see her again soon." Roslyn placed her hand on her forehead and closed her eyes, fighting back the tears. She had to stay strong. Help with the investigation.

"Agent Dunford is dusting the recipe book for

prints, and she'll run them through the database, but we need to move on." He cleared his throat. "Mrs. Colepepper, time is of the essence. Does your daughter attend day care?"

Roslyn shook her head. "We have a nanny, but she's been sick lately. I'm in the process of having her replaced."

"What's her name?"

"Brittany Cox. She's been with us a few months and came with an impeccable background." Roslyn's gaze drifted to the wall of windows overlooking Turtle Lake and the infinity pool. Only a few weeks ago, Brittany was giving Adriana swimming lessons. The two of them got along wonderfully and Adriana loved the pool. The musky scent of Brandon's cologne wafted in the air, and she turned as his hand settled on the small of her back.

"How's your head, honey? Do you need a break?"

"I'm fine, and no, I don't need a break." She forced a smile. He wasn't often this tender.

"Mr. Colepepper." Agent Sanderson nodded at Brandon. "We were discussing your nanny."

"Brittany." Brandon's hand dropped from Roslyn's back. He folded his arms across his chest. "You don't think she has anything to do with this, do you?"

"As I told your wife, we're not ruling anyone out at this early stage." He paused a half second, his dark eyes difficult to read. "Do either of you know where Brittany is now?"

"She had a cold," Roslyn said. "I didn't want her infecting Adriana, so I dismissed her for the day." Roslyn wrapped herself in a hug. She wasn't chilly. Just lost. Empty. "I think she has a night class tonight. She attends Oakland University. Design . . . Fashion design, I believe."

"Architecture," Brandon corrected.

Roslyn eyed her husband.

"She's in architecture design," Brandon repeated.

Roslyn's headache worsened. This wasn't the time to probe her husband for answers, yet she needed to know if the past was repeating itself. "Do you know her schedule too?"

"She asked me for a job once she graduates." He faced the agent. "I'm sure you know already that I'm the president and CEO of Colepepper Hotels. She was interested in working with the design team on future projects." He glanced over his shoulder at Roslyn. "I didn't promise her anything."

Sure. Roslyn glanced at her watch. "What other information do you need from me?" Without giving the agent time to answer, she continued. "The grounds are cared for through Updike Garden and Lawn. I can provide their business number, it's in my book. I have no idea the names of all the men. I recognize some

52

every week and others come when extra work is required, like removing leaves in the fall or planting flower beds in the spring. Anderson Pool and Spa maintains the pool and patio. It isn't always the same person each week, so again, they will have to provide you with the names of their employees." She drew a breath. "I fired a housekeeper the temp agency sent last week. I think her name was K.C."

"I'll need the name of the staffing agency."

"Yes, of course. I have it in my—" Her PalmPilot was in her purse, which she'd left in the Jag. "I'll have to look it up in the phone book. My purse was in the car."

Sanderson lifted his brows. "And credit cards?"

"In my purse."

"Good. Let's hope they use the cards." The agent jotted a few notes, then looked up. "Anyone else?"

"I'm sure there are others, but I'm drawing a blank." Roslyn faced her husband, arms crossed. "What about you, Brandon? I'm sure you have an assortment of disgruntled secretaries, designers, and guest-services hosts to add to the list?"

"This isn't the time, *honey*." Brandon turned away from the agent. He narrowed his eyes at Roslyn, then stormed away, retreating behind his large hand-carved mahogany desk.

Agent Dunford reentered the room, her gaze on Sanderson. Was that a nod she gave him? Roslyn studied Sanderson, but his body language said nothing. They were probably trained to not show emotion, remain calm, but right now, she didn't think she could stand not knowing what they were thinking. "Did the agent find something? A note? A clue?"

"Let's take a break, Mrs. Colepepper," Sanderson suggested. "I know this is all overwhelming." He removed a sheet of paper from his pad and handed her a pen. "If you think of more people we should investigate, please write them down."

Roslyn nodded.

Sanderson crossed the room, spoke with Dunford in a whisper, then the two of them promptly left their temporary headquarters.

Roslyn wandered out of her husband's office, finding it impossible to walk more than a few steps in any direction without having to dodge another agent. She couldn't possibly come up with names if she couldn't think. Not only was her husband's wall-to-wall glass office packed with people, the hallway, grand foyer, and parts of the kitchen were crowded as well.

The doorbell chimed and Roslyn rushed to the front door, glad of the distraction. Only one of Sanderson's men intercepted, his body blocking the view. Relief flooded at the sound of her sister's voice. She wedged between the agent and doorframe. "Chrisla, please come in."

Roslyn narrowed her eyes at the man when he didn't immediately step aside. "This is my sister, Chrisla Hollingsworth."

"Brandon's secretary called me," Chrisla said, throwing her arms around Roslyn's neck. "How are you holding up, sis?"

"Not very well." Roslyn clung to her younger sister. "I want my daughter to come home."

"You'll get her back." Chrisla gave her a squeeze, then pushed her out to arm's length. "Your driveway looks like the time you hosted that dinner party for Congressman Morrison. I've never counted so many black SUVs in one place before."

Roslyn didn't attempt to conceal her eyes as she began to tear up. "I wish that was the occasion."

"What can I do to help?" Always the organizer, her sister jumped into action. Shedding her jacket as she walked into the kitchen, she tossed it over the back of a chair and rubbed her hands together. "I'll make coffee. You go back to doing whatever you were doing."

Roslyn wiped her face. "I'm glad you're here, Chrisla."

"I'm not going to let you go through this alone. I called Dad's office. Apparently he's campaigning out of town all this week, but I was able to obtain a copy of his updated itinerary, so I left a message at his hotel in Traverse City."

Roslyn sniffled. Their father's state senate run

had him on the road for weeks at a time with speaking engagements, and it wasn't even an election year. Her sister held much too liberal views to help with their father's campaign, but Roslyn was interested in politics and, until the nanny came down with her latest flu-like symptoms, Roslyn was scheduled to join him at a fund-raiser dinner tomorrow night. But none of that mattered now. Political views, plate dinners, respiratory infections. It all seemed so trivial.

"You should be with Brandon. I'm sure he needs your support." Chrisla shooed her away. "Go."

Roslyn fought control over her quivering lips. Brandon never needed her. But this wasn't the time to rehash the past. She went to the built-in desk at the far end of the kitchen, opened the bottom drawer, and removed the phone book. With something to keep her mind occupied, she headed down the hall toward the office. As she reached the doorway, the phone rang. The roomful of FBI agents donned headphones, and Roslyn rushed to her husband, who was seated at the desk, hand poised to answer upon Agent Sanderson's nod.

Second ring.

Roslyn gripped the back of Brandon's chair, her nails biting into the soft leather. By the third peal, she narrowed her eyes on Sanderson. With her child's life in jeopardy, she couldn't stomach the FBI dragging this out any longer.

Fourth ring.

"They're going to think we're not home." She couldn't lose Adriana forever. Roslyn lurched over Brandon's shoulder for the phone—her only link to her daughter.

Brandon snatched the receiver first. "Hello." His deep voice held a faint quiver that probably no one else in the room detected. Her husband's shoulders slumped. "Roslyn, it's for you."

She grabbed the phone and pressed it to her ear. "Yes?"

"Mrs. Colepepper, I ah . . ." Brittany coughed.

Roslyn released a pent-up breath, exhaling any patience she'd managed to retain. "Brittany, Adriana is missing. We have to keep this line open."

A brief pause preceded another coughing fit.

Roslyn hung up the phone. She had to keep the line clear for the kidnapper.

"Less than a minute," one agent announced, removing his earphones.

"Checking voice recognition," another agent said.

"That was our nanny, Brittany Cox." Roslyn faced Sanderson. "I know her voice. You don't have to waste your time with voice recognition."

"It's routine, Mrs. Colepepper." Sanderson picked up the headphones, covered his ears, then hand signaled the agent operating the computer.

Brandon pushed his chair back and stood. He reached for Roslyn's hand and led her away from the group of agents camped in his office. "Let's give them a few minutes," he said, directing her to the bay window. "They need to investigate every call."

"Oh, please. Brittany's a college kid, not a carjacker slash kidnapper. They need to put their time and effort to better use and find Adriana."

Brandon's brows narrowed a half second. "It's more than that," he said softly, as if talking to a child. "They analyze the caller's tone, speech patterns, and they listen for background noises as well." Brandon motioned to the leather couch. "Are you sure you're feeling okay? You're acting a little strange."

"Strange?"

"Head trauma. Concussion." He pointed to his head as though trying to jog her memory. "You practically pounced on the phone when Agent Sanderson had instructed us to wait for his signal."

"They were taking too long." Roslyn's insides quivered with anger or fear or both. She plopped down on the couch only to jump back up. "I can't stand this waiting around—doing nothing." She scanned the room, skimming over the group of men seated at the makeshift table, each glued to a computer screen. She counted another half dozen agents and police officers also doing nothing. Nothing except whispering to one another and sipping their lattes. Roslyn turned to Brandon. "They should be searching."

"This is going to be a long night." Brandon rubbed his forehead hard enough that his tanned skin whitened under the pressure of his fingers. "I had my secretary call Chrisla. She should be here anytime."

Roslyn eyed her husband. Lines of worry etched his forehead. "Chrisla's making coffee."

"I contacted Leon too. He's calling in a prescription. I'll send—"

"No! I won't let him pump me with drugs. I'm numb as it is." Only a few hours ago, she was unconscious on the pavement. Then waking up in the emergency room, dazed and reeling with a crushing headache, she recalled a redheaded man wearing white scrubs sitting in the corner of the room. The orderly said he'd been assigned to look after her. At first she couldn't even remember her name let alone how she ended up in the ER, but as the man made small talk about God, family, and children, details began to unfold in her mind. Along with the panic that her daughter had been stolen.

If only she could remember more. Like who had knocked her out. Was the person after the car or her daughter? For all she knew the kidnapper's face was buried somewhere in her memory.

Chrisla entered holding a tray of cups and a carafe of coffee. She placed the tray on the corner lamp table, then joined Brandon and Roslyn, who were standing near the built-in bookshelves. "Did I hear the phone ring a few minutes ago?"

"The nanny called," Brandon said.

"To talk to you, I'll bet." Chrisla eyed Brandon sharply. As a philosophy major and free-thinker, an artsy person by trade, Roslyn's sister wasn't one to hold back on her opinion, especially if she thought she could put Brandon on the spot.

Brandon's jaw twitched.

Roslyn lifted her brows at her sister and mouthed, "Not now."

Chrisla leaned closer and whispered, "Did he tell Brittany that Adriana was missing?"

"I told her, but she was coughing so hard, I doubt she was listening." Roslyn gritted her teeth. "We're not going to talk about Brittany Cox. Not today. Not ever."

Brandon cleared his throat. "Would either of you like a cup of coffee?"

"No, thanks," the sisters said in unison.

Brandon walked away, only he didn't go for coffee. He strode to the other side of the room and stopped at the workstation where Agent Sanderson was studying something on a computer screen.

As the men exchanged words, Roslyn inched forward. She didn't want to be left out of any conversation. If the agent had news to share, he needed to include her in the discussion. Her sister was busy formulating an agenda—a news conference where they would announce a reward for information—but Roslyn was focused on Brandon's concerned expression. Her husband wasn't one to show weakness. Even under pressure as CEO and president of a large conglomerate of hotel chains, he always managed to convince the board members to see things his way. She'd never seen him where he didn't have command of the room.

"Excuse me, Mrs. Colepepper." Agent Dunford rounded the desk.

Roslyn grasped her sister's arm before asking the agent, "What have you heard?"

"Nothing yet. I'm sorry." Agent Dunford stood, feet shoulder-width apart and her hands shoved into the front pockets of her navy trousers. "Agent Sanderson suggested we step into another room and continue going over the events leading up to the incident."

Roslyn froze. "Incident? This wasn't a fender bender in the parking lot. My daughter is missing."

"I'm sorry if I sounded insensitive."

Roslyn acknowledged the woman's apology with a nod, then peered over her shoulder at the agents huddling close to the computer, one man pointing at what looked like a map on the screen. *They found her.* She tapped her sister's arm. "I think they located Adriana." Her voice croaked as balled-up emotions unraveled.

"Mrs. Colepepper?"

Agent Dunford's sympathetic tone caught Roslyn's attention, and she automatically braced herself before facing the woman.

"Area mapping is a tool we use based on time and distance calculations in order to find a focal point in which to concentrate search efforts," Dunford explained.

"But my daughter's been located, right?"

"It's only one tool," Agent Dunford said. "It doesn't take into consideration all the variables."

"Then what good is it? Adriana could be anywhere by now. Out of state—out of country if her kidnappers took the Detroit Tunnel or the bridge to Canada." Pent-up emotions broke free and Roslyn sobbed uncontrollably. Her sister pulled her into a smothering hug, and when she pushed back, Brandon was standing next to them, a box of tissues in his hand.

"What did you hear?" Roslyn pulled a tissue from the box.

"Nothing concrete." The lines on his forehead deepened with worry. "Maybe you should lie down for a while, Roz."

"How can I lie down when my daughter is missing? No. I won't." Shaking her head sent shards of pain to the back of her head. She didn't dare take something for the pain.

Medication would only dull her senses, block her recollections. Bright lights spotted her vision. *Stay calm.* The spurts of blindness would pass.

"Roz." Her husband's hand capped her shoulder, turning her to the left.

"Stop. Please." She shook loose of his arm, staggering a few steps. People in the room came in and out of focus. The walls closed in. "He knew my name."

"Who are you talking about?" Her husband's arm came around her waist. This time she didn't pull away, but leaned on him for support. "Did you see the man who hit you?"

"He kept rattling on as though he knew me. Saying things . . ." Strobe lights flashed as if a hundred cameras all fired seconds apart. Roslyn covered her eyes.

"Mrs. Colepepper, do you remember what the man looked like?" Agent Dunford asked.

"Red hair."

The agent's words blended together. "What about his height? Can you tell me how tall he was?"

Tall? *Think.*

"Did you have to look up at him?" the agent prompted.

"No. No, I don't know how tall he was. He was sitting down, reading my chart when I woke up."

Brandon exhausted a heavy sigh. "She must be talking about the ER doctor."

Roslyn opened her eyes gingerly, squinting

until her focus adjusted. "He was wearing white scrubs and said he was assigned to look after me." *Think. What did he say?* Roslyn shuddered. "He knew my name."

"You're a recognized figure in the community, Roz. Your father is running for state senate," Brandon said.

"When I first woke up, *I* didn't even know my name. I didn't know where I was or what had happened." Her gaze darted from Brandon to Agent Dunford. "Didn't the emergency room have me listed as Jane Doe?"

Agent Dunford flipped through the notes she had taken earlier, then signaled one of the officers standing a few feet away. Roslyn recognized him as the first detective who interviewed her at the hospital.

The fiftysomething man stood with his feet shoulder-width apart and hands clasped behind his back. "Detective Henderson, ma'am. Do you wish to speak with me?"

"I understand your initial call to the hospital was for a Jane Doe who came in with head trauma."

"Yes, ma'am. At the time the paramedics arrived on the scene, Mrs. Colepepper was unresponsive. Without any identification or witnesses, the emergency room physician suspected foul play and reported it to the police department. I gave a copy of my full report to Agent Sanderson."

"Do you recall seeing or talking to a man in

Mrs. Colepepper's room? Perhaps the ER doctor? White scrubs, red hair?"

Detective Henderson shook his head. "Doctor Wyn is female, five four, dark hair, and glasses. She wore street clothes under a long white doctor's coat. I don't recall anyone wearing white scrubs, male or female."

Agent Dunford made a notation but looked up from the pad when the office door opened.

A tall man carrying a padded envelope in his hand glanced around the room.

"That must be the store surveillance video," Brandon said.

≈ﬔ

"May I watch the video tape again? I might have missed something." Tears streamed down Roslyn's face faster than she could wipe them away. The video recording the store provided the FBI was distorted. Even worse, the manager discovered that the outdoor camera aimed in the area where she had parked was not working.

Agent Dunford rewound the VHS tape, then handed her the remote.

Roslyn sat in the leather wingback chair and studied her black-and-white image pushing Adriana in the shopping cart. She should have left the store when the cart's wheel started clacking. She dabbed the tissue against the corners of her eyes.

"Do you recognize that man?" Her sister pointed to a man on the video standing at the end of the produce area where Adriana picked up the raspberries.

"I don't remember seeing him. But that was when I would have been busy cleaning up Adriana. She'd eaten raspberries and made a sticky mess." Roslyn looked down at her unblemished blouse. How foolish it'd been of her to worry about Adriana staining her clothes. Roslyn swallowed hard. "Her face broke out in a rash . . . like earlier this summer when she ate strawberries."

"I remember her lips turning bright red." Chrisla reached for Roslyn's hand and gave it a compassionate squeeze.

"Why did I leave Adriana in the car? If only I hadn't started the engine." Roslyn's voice strained. It all seemed unreal. A blur. She gingerly touched the lump on her head and winced.

"Adriana was cold," her sister reminded her. "You didn't know, Roslyn. It isn't your fault."

A few feet away, Brandon poured scotch into a glass—his way of taking the edge off. But this wasn't a business meeting. He wasn't trying to convince shareholders that he would increase the hotel chain's overseas revenue by 60 percent like he had at the grand opening gala in Aruba last spring.

At the chime of the doorbell, Roslyn stiffened.

The constant influx of people had frayed her nerves. Yet every time the doorbell rang, Roslyn's hope rose that maybe, just maybe, her daughter would be left on the doorstep.

Her sister stood. "I'm sure that's another one of your club members." Chrisla had told the dinner guests as they arrived that the evening had been postponed. Roslyn was grateful not to have to leave Brandon's office. She wasn't ready to face the truth. She'd placed her child alone in the car and practically handed the carjacker the keys. No one would understand, including her friends from the Republican club.

Roslyn pressed the Rewind button on the remote, then hit Play.

Brandon came up beside her chair, swirling the amber liquid in the glass. "Watching that tape over and over isn't going to change the fact that the camera angles are wrong or improve the film quality. You're only torturing yourself." He took a drink.

"I have to do something."

He raised his glass. "Would you like me to make you a drink?"

She narrowed her eyes at him. "This isn't a cocktail party."

"Just asking." He drained his glass and walked away.

Roslyn tapped her foot as she gazed around the room. At least the FBI agents didn't seem interested in Brandon pouring himself another drink. The buzz of conversations in the room ranged from the Tigers' baseball stats to the new body style on the heavy-duty Dodge Ram. She wanted to scream at them all, Brandon included. Her baby was missing and they were talking about baseball and engine torque. How dare they converse about such trivial things that didn't pertain to bringing her daughter home. She had half a mind to send all nonessential people outside to sit in the news vans with the press.

Roslyn drummed her fingernails on the arm of the chair. Idle talk would drive her crazy. She closed her eyes a moment, trying to push the useless chatter to the back of her mind. Her headache was back with a vengeance. The ibuprofen she had taken earlier had lost its effectiveness. Opening her eyes, she noticed her brother, Leon, standing in the threshold, his medical bag in hand. Roslyn stood, then sat back down when Brandon spotted his brother-in-law's arrival and went to greet Leon first. As they talked, Chrisla slipped past them.

"Brandon wants Leon to give you a sedative," her sister whispered.

Roslyn wiped her face. That wasn't going to happen.

Brandon and Leon moved toward her as though on a mission to wrap her in a chemical straitjacket.

She sucked in a breath and stood. "Leon, it's good to see you."

He greeted her with a hug. "How are you holding up?"

"I'm scared," she admitted. "We haven't heard from the kidnapper. I want . . . my baby home." The strength she had intended to demonstrate crumbled. She glimpsed Brandon staring at the mahogany crown molding. When her husband's downcast eyes fell on her, she sensed his judgment. Brandon thought this was her fault. Roslyn buried her face against her brother's neck and cried.

"Leon is going to give you something to relax," her husband said.

Roslyn backed out of Leon's embrace and stormed out of the room. Lining the hallway, several of Brandon's business associates awaited news. She shielded her face with her hand, pretending not to hear them when they asked how she was doing, and climbed the winding staircase in the front foyer. Seeking solace in Adriana's nursery was impossible. The fingerprinting crew had quarantined the room with yellow crime tape. Roslyn rasped a shallow breath, then another, and another in rapid succession. *Calm down. Focus. Breathe.* No amount of self-talk would allow her to gain control over her breathing. *Don't fall apart. You're panicking. Stop it.*

"Ma'am, is there something you need?" a white-gloved detective asked, holding a bag marked Evidence.

She needed her daughter home. Needed this day to start over.

"Ma'am," the detective said empathetically. "We won't be much longer."

Coldness spread through Roslyn's veins. She moved away from the doorway, a numbness settling into her bones. Wandering over to the staircase, she plopped down on the top step and buried her face in her hands. "God, if You're there—if You really exist—please bring my daughter home."

Footsteps tapped up the wooden stairs. Brandon sat, leaving a step between them, and tied his black leather shoe. "This waiting can cause someone to go insane."

"Or cause someone to drink. Oh, that's right, you don't need a reason to drink."

"Really? I was trying to be nice." He moved up a step, closing the distance between them, and placed his hand on her knee. "I know I haven't always been there for you—"

"Just get our daughter back. Please, Brandon. Talk to those reporters, post a reward, do something to bring Adriana home."

A stir of voices filtered up the stairway and Roslyn bolted up as an agent approached the steps. The man glanced at her, then directed his attention to Brandon. "Special Agent Sanderson would like a word with you."

Brandon's prominent Adam's apple bobbed.

"Have they found Adriana?" Roslyn blurted.

The agent lowered his head. "I'm not sure, ma'am."

"What do you mean, you're not sure?" Roslyn hurried down the stairs.

"Roz." Brandon caught her arm outside the office door. "Stay here. Let me—"

"No!" She jerked her arm free. "We do this together." She wasn't fragile. Any news of Adriana, even . . .

The throng of agents stepped aside as they approached Brandon's desk where Sanderson and his men had set up command. Sanderson motioned them over while he continued to dispatch orders over the phone.

Brandon's arm encircled her waist with a rigid hold.

Sanderson released the phone. He drew the other agent's attention to the computer screen and called out numerical codes without altering the inflection in his tone. Roslyn tried retaining the digits. Two zero seven. Same numbers she had heard him spout earlier, only this time Sanderson had dropped *alpha.* She wouldn't interrupt to ask what it all meant now. Perhaps Special Agent Dunford would explain it since she was the liaison. If she had issues with divulging coded information, then maybe one of the reporters would know.

"Do you have news?" Brandon's patience was notably thin.

"We have a lead on the nanny," Sanderson said, eyeing Brandon as if analyzing his reaction.

Chapter 6

"Of course I'm *nett* going to jump the fence. I'm talking about Olivia." Gideon tossed a stone into the river. He wasn't sure if he should be hurt, shocked, or offended that Faith would think he might be tempted to walk away from his beliefs.

"Then what makes you think she's planning to leave?"

"Olivia's been going to the library every day. Sometimes she's alone, sometimes she's with a group of *Englischers* . . . chummy." He spotted a rainbow trout making its way against the current and couldn't help but compare its struggle against the flow to his relationship with Olivia. Granted, their plans to marry had been unofficial since Olivia hadn't wanted anyone to know until after they had both joined the church. Perhaps she'd gotten cold feet about marrying him before she backed out of baptism, but because the *Ordnung* forbids marriages of the unequally yoked, their wedding plans were indefinitely put on hold— and for good reason.

Faith plopped down on the rocky embankment where she'd left her shoes.

Gideon sat beside her. "I'm worried about Olivia." His words spilled out of his mouth. Faith was a good listener and so easy to talk to that she made it easy for him not to have to censor his words.

"I don't know how Olivia spends her free time, we've never been close. But she still covers her shifts at work. She hasn't left *Mamm* in a lurch." Faith sighed. "Some people need longer to sort out their decision of baptism and joining the church. Besides, hanging out at the library doesn't seem that bad."

"We were supposed to get married."

Her smile faded. Faith shifted her attention downstream to where a blue heron fished for food. "Like I said," she said, breaking the silence, "some people need more time. And it isn't like she's drinking or experimenting with drugs like others have done on *rumspringa*."

"I'm *nett* so sure." He inhaled the scent of dank river water and let the breath out slowly. "I saw her giving money to an *Englischer*."

"And?"

"The library might be a location for drug exchange."

"I don't believe that." She grabbed her shoes and climbed the embankment.

He hadn't meant to upset her. He'd better tell her another time about the rumors he'd heard. His foot slipped on a rocky section and he came down hard on his knee. "Ouch!"

She glanced over her shoulder. "You okay?"

"*Jah.*" He limped up to the top of the embankment. A strong breeze threatened to steal his straw hat, but he pressed it firmly on his head.

Faith smiled.

"You think *mei* big ears curling under this brim are amusing, don't you *nau*?"

"Your ears aren't overly big."

"Overly," he repeated. Growing up the youngest, he'd taken the brunt of many jokes for his big ears, but seeing Faith struggle to smother her smile, he would wear his hat like this every day.

The tall grassy meadow bent in the wind, and a large flock of iridescent blue grackles took flight as dark clouds moved toward them. "*Kumm* on, it's getting ready to rain," he said. "I'll take you home."

"*Danki*, but I can walk." In no hurry to leave, she swept sand off her wet dress.

"Why are you being stubborn, Faith?"

She looked up. "Olivia's already mad at me. Things will get worse if she gets the wrong idea about us spending time together."

"That's nonsense. You're like . . . a little sister—Olivia's little *schweschaler*." He needed to make the relationship clear for his benefit as well. He'd already had his heart broken by one Pinkham woman; the likelihood of developing

75

a relationship with her sister was as slim as the sliver of sunlight peeking through the gloomy afternoon clouds. At least that's what he needed to keep telling himself. Especially after spending any amount of time with her. The woman's laugh was contagious. *Stop, Faith is a friend—nothing more.*

"You don't understand. When it comes to Olivia . . . Well, let's just say I've turned my cheek so many times, I'm dizzy."

"I'm sorry she's curt with you."

"Olivia has always thought *Mamm* and *Daed* treat me differently. Even as *kinner*, she used to say I didn't belong and that our parents should send me back."

Gideon chuckled. "That would be rather difficult."

The wind picked up and Faith turned, shielding her face. She balanced on one leg and shoved her foot into her black leather loafer, then readjusted her balance and put on the other shoe, her teeth chattering the entire time. "I have to go before someone sees me like this."

"You're wet and *kalt*. I'm taking you home." Gideon placed his hand on her back.

She stood a little straighter, building a wall of resistance in her stare, then crossed her arms over her chest and narrowed her eyes.

"*Kumm* on," he persisted. "I can get you home a lot faster."

Faith glared at him a half second longer. "Fine, I'll ride with you, but if something gets back to Olivia, or the bishop, or—"

"Don't worry. Nothing will keep you from being baptized and joining the church." He hobbled barefooted down the pine-needle path, Faith walking more than an arm's length away off to his side. Her enthusiasm to join the church was something he'd only seen in someone pledged to wed—unfortunately, he'd never seen the same glint in Olivia's eyes.

Gideon swallowed the bitter memory and fed his mind with uplifting thoughts. *It's a new day. The steadfast love of the Lord never ceases; His mercies never come to an end; they are new every morning; great is Your faithfulness.* He viewed the canopy of velvety green maple leaves above them, shaking in the breeze, and smiled, declaring to himself that no matter what trial came, his faith wouldn't be shaken. Not by Olivia, not by anyone.

"So are you still going to marry my sister when she returns from *rumspringa*?"

"She won't return."

"But if she does," Faith prodded.

"*Nay*," he said sharply, more to tamp his wishy-washy thoughts than to stifle their conversation. But Faith kept silent during the last stretch of the wooded path.

At the buggy, he opened the back end and

removed a quilt he kept stashed for winter weather. He came up behind her and draped the cover over her shoulders. "This should help warm you up. I hope it doesn't smell too much like Bay." The horse blanket was all he had. Hopefully she wouldn't recognize it as the quilt Olivia had made for him. After she ditched him, he'd found a more fitting use as a cover for his horse than on his bed.

"This is perfect." Faith snuggled into its cottony softness, pulling it tighter around her neck. "It's strange how it can feel *kalt* in the middle of summer."

Northern Michigan was unpredictable. Lake effects even in July could send a damp chill to your bones. He scanned the sky. It wouldn't be too much longer before the sun fell behind the trees, claiming even more daylight. He opened the buggy passenger door and helped gather the bulk of the blanket so Faith could climb onto the bench. "I need to run down to the river and grab *mei* boots," he said once she was situated. "I'll be back in a minute."

Gideon sprinted the few yards to the edge of the river, retrieved his boots, and hurried back to the buggy as the clouds burst with rain. "It's going to get bad fast," he said, disengaging the buggy brake.

He didn't mind getting wet. The rain would be good for his blueberry plants and apple orchard, but Bay didn't like the rolling thunder. The young, spirited horse and strengthening storm wasn't an ideal combination. Bay tossed his head. Lightning flashed and seconds later a large oak split down the middle. The cracking timber sound spooked Bay and the reins slipped between Gideon's wet hands.

Chapter 7

The sudden downpour sent streams of water fingering out over the dirt road and dumping into the ditches. Sections of the passageway started to flood as the heavy amount of runoff overwhelmed the culverts. Fortunately for Faith, Gideon had insisted on driving her home. Otherwise she'd be stranded somewhere trying to wait out the storm. As it was, Mud Lake Highway was disappearing underwater.

Gideon's face tensed as the buggy jerked in a chugging motion. No longer trotting, the Standardbred went from a clumsy gallop to a spirited run within seconds of a flash of lightning and a crack of nearby timber splitting.

"Easy, Bay. Easy." Gideon worked the reins, but the gelding kept thrusting his head forward, pulling for more length. "Hold on, Faith."

The buggy wheel dipped into a washed-out area of the road, and Faith clutched the edge of the bench with a white-knuckle grip. Jostled again, she sucked in a sharp breath and held it. As if she and Gideon were kernels of corn on a hot stove top, they popped up and back down as Bay stumbled.

It wasn't until they reached the intersection and pulled onto the pavement on Leer Road that they noticed Bay favoring his front right leg. Gideon guided him to the shoulder of the road to stay out of the way of car traffic. Accidents happened on days like today when visibility was less than a few feet.

Faith tapped his arm. "You think Bay's badly hurt?"

"Hard to say." He spoke over the pelting rain drumming the top of the buggy. "I won't know until I can get him somewhere safe and can check if his leg is swelling."

An oncoming car flashed its headlights, blinding Faith for a half second. She squeezed her eyes closed as the car sped past, a whoosh of rain spraying the side of the buggy. Opening her eyes, she peered at Gideon, who, staring straight ahead, appeared unfazed. Another vehicle passed them from behind. She focused on the yellow line dividing the road. They'd be home soon. Out of this horrific weather. Sipping a cup of herbal tea. Her mouth watered for a slice of cinnamon-raisin bread and a sip of lemon-ginger tea.

They passed Bishop Zook's farm on the left, but she didn't notice the Zooks' fence dividing the property lines until they were right up on it. On a clear day she would be able to see her farm from this distance. Her father's barn was nestled on a hillside and one of the tallest in the areas.

"This rain isn't letting up," she said, not thinking the obvious remark would cause Gideon to take his eyes off the road.

Gideon studied her. "Are you still *kalt*?"

"*Nett* wrapped in this quilt. Are you?" She lifted the corner. "I'll share."

"*Nay.*" Gideon snapped his attention back on the road.

Nay. *He said that fast. Oh, what was she thinking offering to share the blanket?* At least he was watching the road and not her cheeks blaze. Faith pulled the quilt up higher, burying her face up to her eyes. Bay's scent on the blanket wasn't too strong, but some of the loose horsehairs tickled her nose. Olivia must not know he used the quilt as a horse blanket. Otherwise she'd have something to say.

Faith breathed a sigh of relief once Gideon pulled into her drive. Home safe. Now to find *Daed.* He had a special way of treating injured animals. He would know how to care for Gideon's horse. She craned to look for light coming from the sitting room window. On rainy days like today, *Daed* was often spotted sitting in his favorite chair reading the Bible by lamplight. But that wasn't the case today. The sitting room was dark. She glanced at the barn. Although it was too early for him to be doing the evening milking, her father often found things to tinker on in the equipment room. But the barn was closed up tight with no sign of activity through the milking parlor window.

Gideon stopped the buggy next to the house. "Doesn't look like anyone's home."

"*Nay*, it doesn't."

Lightning flashed. Faith spotted her mother's clothesline down. The dresses she'd washed earlier that morning were now scattered on the ground.

"Are you going to be all right alone?"

"You need to stay," she said. Then, seeing his brows lift, her heart nearly burst with embarrassment. "Bay might not make it another three miles." Gideon's family farm was closer to Metz Township than Posen and down a pitted dirt road that was treacherous to travel even on good days. Driving home now was foolish. "What if your road is washed out? You can't risk him going lame."

"True."

"So put him in one of our stalls and wait the storm out here. It'll give Bay time to rest, and you can have supper with us."

Detecting Gideon's reluctance, she added with less emotion, "*Mei daed* knows what to do for a sprained leg. Our plow horse had problems last spring."

He twisted his body to look upward. "The entire sky is gray. I'm sure the rain won't let up any time soon, and you're probably right about *mei* road being underwater."

She motioned to the barn. "Park next to the gate, and while you unharness Bay, I'll open the stall."

"Okay." Gideon gave the reins a light tug, and Bay limped to the barn.

Faith eased the quilt off her shoulders, leaving the warmth on the bench. With it raining so hard, there wasn't a good time to jump out. Her feet landed in a pool of water and soaked through her shoes. She ran to the barn and tugged the sliding door open. Rain drenched, she adjusted her prayer *kapp* over the mound of limp wet hair. No telling how disheveled she looked. Normally she liked a hard summer rain and the fresh scent it left behind, but at the moment, she wasn't feeling fresh at all. It seemed the rain had mingled the scents of fried food embedded into her clothing from the restaurant and the stench of river water, which was hardly a pleasant aroma.

Finding the box of wooden matches on the shelf next to the lantern, Faith set the wick ablaze. She passed the first two stalls, both empty, and opened the third. It wasn't surprising for her father to be stuck somewhere waiting out the storm just as Gideon was waiting it out here.

Clumsy-sounding horse hooves clomped across the barn's concrete pad. Faith poked her head outside the stall door and frowned at Bay limping. "He's really favoring it, isn't he?"

"*Jah*," Gideon said, sadness in his tone.

Faith grabbed the feed bucket. "I'll fetch some oats while you get him settled." She eased over to the door, giving Bay a pat on the shoulder as she passed. From the feed barrel, she could hear Gideon talking softly to the horse. Faith recalled how her father had doctored the plow horse with liniment last spring. She searched the equipment room and found a jar with the milky-looking paste. One whiff of the strong medicine caused her eyes to water. She lowered the feed bucket, then handed Gideon the liniment.

"What's this?" He unscrewed the lid, lifted it to his nose, then pulled it away and coughed.

"*Daed* used it on Calliope when her leg started bothering her after plowing season."

"It worked?"

She shrugged. "I think so."

Gideon scooped a glob and squatted next to Bay. The gelding's leg must have been sensitive to Gideon's touch because he tossed his head and neighed. "Easy, boy." Gideon applied the liniment, rubbing it from the horse's forearm, to his knee, and down to the area around his hoof. Once he finished applying the medicine, he stepped back and frowned as he studied Bay.

"The liniment needs time to work," Faith said.

Gideon slipped out of the stall and stood next to Faith in front of the half door. After several seconds of staring at the gelding, he said, "I'm going to get something to dry him off. I'll be right back."

Faith leaned against the doorframe of the stall and sighed. Bay was the first horse she'd known to hang his head low without nibbling on hay or oats. The poor animal was pitiful to watch. She leaned down and snatched the oat bucket and gave it a shake to get the horse's attention. Bay lifted his head and perked his ears, but he didn't move. She shook the oats more. "Aren't you hungry, boy?"

Bay dropped his head and sniffed at the hay-covered floor.

The barn door popped open and Gideon came inside, rain running off his hat and soaking into his shirt.

Noticing the quilt from the buggy in his arms, Faith hardened her expression. "You're *nett* thinking about using that to dry him, are you?"

"I was." He used the corner of the quilt to wipe rain water off his face. "Why?"

"Gideon Rohrer. You know why." Olivia wouldn't think kindly of him using the quilt she'd made to dry his horse, injured leg or not.

His lips played into a mischievous smile. He planned to put it on the horse anyway, she could see it in his eyes as he unfolded the quilt. Faith moved away from the stall door, but instead of him going inside with Bay, he wrapped the blanket around her shoulders, his hand gently brushing against her chin as he brought the quilt around. "Better?"

His gaze soaked deep into her eyes, Faith was sure he could see her soul. She couldn't get her voice to work with him standing so close, and he seemed intent on waiting for her answer before he moved. "So"—her heartbeat galloped wildly, causing a quiver in her voice that made her words come out as wisps—"you think I'm a horse *nau*? I need toweling off?"

A soft chuckle erupted. Gideon moistened his lips with the tip of his tongue, pinning her with a gaze that turned his eyes from cobalt to a piercing indigo blue. Then as he leaned even closer to the point that his features blurred, his words about not marrying her sister echoed in Faith's mind, and she closed her eyes.

The barn door creaked open, and Faith glanced over Gideon's shoulder as her sister's shadowy figure moved into the glow of the lantern light. A whoosh of dread washed over Faith as she sank a little deeper under the cover.

Gideon turned and followed Faith's line of vision to the barn door. He jumped back, breathing noticeably huskier. Redness spread from his neck to his ears and over his face in a matter of seconds.

Olivia planted her hands on her hips. "What's going on?"

Chapter 8

"It's *nett* what you think, Olivia," Gideon said. He distanced himself a little more from Faith.

"He's right," Faith said, thrusting the balled-up quilt she'd been huddled in at his chest. "It's definitely *nett* what you think." She shot an icy look at him over her shoulder, then stormed away. A few seconds later, the wooden door closed hard, rattling its hinges.

Gideon groaned under his breath. *It's* nett *what you think.* Who was he trying to fool, other than himself? He'd almost kissed Faith. Now she was upset, embarrassed . . . He glimpsed Olivia moving into his peripheral vision and spun to face the stall. It'd been months since they engaged in a lengthy conversation. They had nothing in common—nothing to talk about.

He peered over the half wall at Bay nibbling on oats, but Gideon's mind refused to register if the horse was putting weight on his leg or not. An image of Faith's hardened expression, disappointment hooding her dark eyes, pitted his stomach.

"What's going on with you?" Olivia sidled up beside him.

"Bay injured his leg."

"I mean what's going on with you and Faith?"

"Why do you care? You're leaving Posen"—*me*—"the plain way."

She shrugged. "You look at her the way you once looked at me."

Olivia's reminiscence sounded as if she held a morsel of regret. He wasn't falling for that even if it was the truth. Up until the day they were to be baptized, she was absolute about their future. About getting married. Now he was absolute about one thing—never falling in love again with someone making plans to jump the fence.

Olivia leaned against the wooden stud framing the stall wall, a wry grin on her face. "She's everything you want. Marriage material."

"Stop it," he said.

"I suppose you've been counting the weeks until her baptism. You two secretly making plans to wed?"

"Olivia." His tone sharpened. "That's enough." He stared at her a moment, then slowly shook his head. Blinded. That was the only way to describe why he'd been drawn to her for so long.

"I liked it when you looked at me that way. When we kissed, you made *mei* toes tingle."

Don't fall for it. Look away. Guard your heart. If the rumors were true, and she'd stolen money from the restaurant till, he could never trust her again.

"These past few weeks I've been very confused."

"Months," he corrected. "You walked out of the baptism service almost a year ago."

"I've been meaning to—"

"Explain why you've avoided me?"

"I'm *nett* avoiding you *nau*," she said softly.

Gideon's muscles tensed. After months of silence she wanted to talk now? He waited a moment for her to speak her piece, then turned his attention back to Bay.

The three-year-old was standing on his foot, moving gingerly around the stall. Did Gideon dare chance taking him home? It hadn't stopped raining. Even from where they were under the hayloft, he could still hear the rain tapping steady on the tin roof.

Olivia pushed off the wall and walked away.

A part of him wanted to stop her. She owed him an explanation. Instead, he flipped the latch on the stall gate and went inside. Crouching on one knee next to the horse, he ran his hand down the length of Bay's leg. The horse jerked when Gideon touched a tender spot midway. "Easy, boy." That settled it. He couldn't risk moving Bay tonight.

The wooden floor of the hayloft creaked above him. An animal? No, it sounded more like shuffling footsteps. Olivia was in the loft. A faint jingle of what sounded like coins in a glass jar drove his curiosity to investigate. He left the stall, then eased up the wooden ladder leading to the loft. Once he reached the landing, he inched toward the small beam of light glowing in the far section.

Olivia was seated on the floor next to a flashlight, money piled in her lap, and holding a wad of cash she was too busy counting to know he was peering at her from around a beam. Flashlights were not allowed in their district and, as a general rule, anyone under twenty-one years of age and living under their parents' roof contributed the majority of their earnings to the household fund. The youth didn't accumulate large sums of cash other than to save for a horse and buggy or when a man started saving to build a house as Gideon had been. Judging by the wad of money Olivia was counting, the rumors had been right.

"Olivia!" Faith's voice rang with a sense of urgency.

Gideon sailed down the loft ladder, landing on the concrete pad inches from Faith. He eyed the blue dress, different from the wet one she'd worn at the river. "Is something wrong?"

"It's *mei* parents. Have you seen Olivia?"

He pointed to the loft. "Up there."

Faith's mouth dropped open, then she tightened her lips into a straight line. A flicker of light from the lantern she was holding illuminated her strained expression before she lowered the light and shadows filled her features.

He reached for the handle of the lantern and she

released it to him. He held it up, casting enough light to see her grimacing face. "What's wrong with your parents?"

She peered up the loft opening. "There's been an accident."

❧❦❧

Faith stepped out of the glow of the lantern and into the shadow, avoiding the spotlight Gideon had cast on her. She appreciated his concern over her parents and his attentiveness, but she needed to keep a safe distance.

"Tell Olivia that Beverly Dembrowski is taking me to Alpena." She wasn't going to leave her *Englisch* driver waiting any longer. Not in this stormy weather.

"Wait," he said, following her to the door. "I'll go with you."

"Gideon, I don't think it's wise for—"

Olivia walked out from the shadows. "Were you calling me?"

You know I was. Faith steeled her emotions. "*Mamm* and *Daed* were in an accident."

Olivia's mouth dropped open, her expression blank.

Faith spoke over her shoulder as she opened the door. "Beverly Dembrowski offered to drive us into town."

"Wait!" Olivia bolted out of the barn, lunged for Faith's arm, and stopped her. Pouring rain

92

soaked her prayer *kapp*, her hair. Olivia's face puckered. "Tell me what happened."

Faith pushed loose strands of wet hair away from her face. "All I know is that they were in a buggy accident." Color had drained from her sister's face, turning Olivia's usual peachy complexion the same shade as the whitewashed chicken coop. Faith gave Olivia's arm a tug. "*Kumm* on, let's get out of the rain. We'll find out more as soon as we get to the hospital."

Gideon followed them to the *Englischer's* parked car. "I think I should *kumm* along," he said, water running off the brim of his straw hat and landing on his shoulder. He opened the back door of the car and motioned for Faith to enter.

Faith didn't object. Her sister was upset and needed Gideon's support. But rather than climb into the backseat where Gideon was trying to direct her, Faith opened the front passenger door and slid into the car. "Thank you for taking us," she said to Beverly, buckling her seat belt.

"Not a problem." Beverly put the car in reverse. She peered at the rearview mirror, then the side mirror, and frowned. "I can't see a thing outside with these windows fogged." She rolled her window down and craned her short chubby neck outside.

"Did you hear how bad the accident was?" Faith asked once they were heading south on

93

US-23 toward Alpena. The elderly woman was a sweet grandmotherly type with gray hair, who waddled when she walked. She often poked fun at herself by referring to her figure as a perfect square, as wide as she was tall. But that wasn't true. The *Englischer* had a few more inches in height, even though, standing straight, her head only came up to Faith's shoulder.

Beverly gripped the steering wheel as a passing car splashed road water. "Hospitals have some sort of healthcare protection law that prevents them from discussing patient care information without written consent. At least that's what I was told. But I'm sure once we get there, someone will be able to give you more information."

"*Jah*, I hope so."

Faith stared at the headlights' reflection off the wet pavement and listened to the rhythmic whooshing sounds of the windshield wipers. A wheel could have dropped into an unseen pothole and thrown the horse off-balance. Traffic was unpredictable. Oftentimes vehicles whizzed past them without leaving much room on the road for a horse and buggy.

"Our gardens will sure benefit from this rain," Beverly said. "For a while I wasn't so sure my corn would reach knee-high by the Fourth of July, but it's already reached that plus." She glanced in the rearview mirror. "Gideon, do you still have cherries for sale or is the season over?"

"I still have more to pick."

"I've heard tart cherries are loaded with antioxidants that reduce inflammation and they're even good for insomnia." Beverly turned her blinker on and sped past another vehicle.

"I wouldn't know anything about that, but I do know cherries sure taste *gut* in pies," Gideon said.

Faith smiled. She often baked cherry pies for the afternoon meal after church service, and Gideon always made a point of eating dessert first so he didn't miss out on having a slice. Olivia probably didn't know that about Gideon. If she did, she didn't go out of her way to bake him anything special. In fact, Olivia avoided baking whenever possible, claiming no one needed extra sugar. Her sister was right, of course, and as a result, she didn't carry the added weight on her hips that Faith did.

Beverly continued to make small talk, asking questions about the restaurant's busyness and what size garden they had planted this year. Faith didn't mind the distraction; talking helped to make the twenty-mile trip to Alpena go by faster. Besides, Beverly appeared a little shaken too. She and *Mamm* had been friends for years.

When they reached the hospital, Faith held her hand to her chest and took a few calming breaths, which didn't work. Until she learned the extent of her parents' condition, she'd be on edge. Closing her eyes, she whispered a prayer. "Have mercy, Father."

"I'll park the car and be in shortly."

"Okay." Faith's voice quivered.

Olivia and Gideon crawled out of the backseat and waited on the sidewalk under the canopy.

The rain wasn't more than a drizzle. Faith almost wished they would walk in ahead of her, save her from the awkwardness swimming in her head. She glanced up at the red illuminated Emergency Room Entrance sign hanging above the glass doors and took a deep breath. Surely the hospital worker who had called to inform them of the accident would have said if her parents had died in the accident. *Don't panic. God is with me.*

Gideon stopped before her. "Are you okay, Faith?"

The tenderness in his tone made her want to cry. She nodded, unable to answer with words. *The Lord is my rock, my fortress, and my deliverer.*

Olivia sniffled. "I know I'm the oldest, but I don't want to be the one to ask if they're . . . alive."

Faith clasped her sister's hand. "We can do this together, Livie."

When Olivia squeezed Faith's hand tighter, hope swelled Faith's heart. Perhaps this could be a fresh start as sisters . . . or friends at least. Faith had always looked up to her big sister, wanting to do everything she did when it came to learning to cook and sew.

Gideon led the way through the automatic sliding doors and to the information desk where a long-haired blonde was seated. "We're here to see Mordecai and Irma Pinkham. I believe they were brought in by ambulance."

"Are you family?" the woman asked.

"*Jah*," Gideon replied for all of them.

Faith held her breath as the woman tapped the keyboard and eyed the computer screen in front of her.

"I'll let the doctor know you're here." She stood.

"Are they alive?" Olivia blurted.

The receptionist smiled. "Yes, ma'am."

Faith released a lungful of air.

"I'm not able to update you on their condition, however." She pointed to an area off to their right where chairs were lined up in a row and a television played in the corner. "If you'll have a seat in the waiting room, the doctor should be with you shortly to answer your questions."

The three of them entered the crowded waiting area and took the only group of chairs together, which happened to be in front of the television. Staying true to her beliefs, Faith looked at the floor and studied the worn pieces of linoleum tile in order to avoid the broadcast. Though she couldn't avoid listening to the program without covering her ears, and doing so would only make a scene.

"If you're just joining us, with me today is founder and president of the Adriana Hope Foundation, Roslyn Colepepper, who is here to talk about a mother's worst nightmare—child abduction. Welcome, Roslyn."

"It's always a pleasure to be here, DiAnna."

"The Adriana Hope Foundation is near and dear to your heart. Will you share with our viewers how the foundation came about?"

"Adriana was—*is*—my daughter. My daughter was only eighteen months old when she was abducted from a grocery store parking lot."

The airway went silent, and Faith looked up at the television screen to see the woman being interviewed dabbing her eyes with a tissue. Faith's heart tugged for the woman on the screen, a woman she didn't even know.

The camera zoomed in on the mother's glazed blue eyes as she struggled to compose herself. "This Labor Day weekend will mark the fifteenth year since my daughter was abducted."

Faith's throat tightened.

The brokenhearted mother's lips quivered into a smile. "The Adriana Hope Foundation was something good and meaningful that came out of my daughter's kidnapping. No mother should have to go through the same nightmare."

"And what an impact the Adriana Hope Foundation has made in helping to recover missing children." The host looked straight at the camera. "After the break, Roslyn will share more about how her foundation is establishing a national database for infant DNA registration."

Beverly stepped into Faith's line of vision as the talk show broke for a commercial. "Have you heard anything?"

"*Nett* yet." Faith stood at the same time as Gideon and both of them motioned to their chairs.

Gideon offered first. "This seat is open."

"It's okay, Gideon, stay seated," Faith said. "I need to look for a drinking fountain." She left the waiting room to search for something to soothe her dry mouth. Wandering down the hallway, she came to an intersection and wall with signs showing arrows to the X-ray and lab departments and to the left, the cafeteria. Having left the house without money, she wouldn't be able to purchase a drink, but maybe one of the workers would give her a cup and direct her to a water fountain.

Footsteps sounded behind her. "Wait up." Gideon strode toward her, his face contorted. "The *doktah* just came into the waiting room with an update on your parents."

Chapter 9

Bloomfield Hills, Michigan
Fifteen years ago

"We've located the car," Agent Sanderson announced.

Roslyn gripped the edge of the desk for support. Consumed in a fog of numbness, she swayed in place as Agent Sanderson dismissed two of his agents from the room with a head nod. She sucked in a breath and let it out slowly.

"And Adriana?" Roslyn searched the agent's eyes. His indiscernible expression masked what he knew, but she suspected he wouldn't have called them into the room without additional information. She gripped the desk tighter, her knuckles turning white with effort. The wait was too much. "Do you have news about my daughter or not?"

"Not yet," Sanderson replied. "Our K9 units have been dispatched. If the child was in the vehicle they took after abandoning the Jaguar, we'll know shortly. The dogs will pick up your daughter's scent in the Buick Skyhawk."

Brandon stepped forward. "Where did they find the car?"

Roslyn studied Sanderson's expression. FBI agents were trained not to reveal every detail. Tell as little as possible, it's how they catch criminals who slip up, know too much. She couldn't help but wonder if she and Brandon were under suspicion.

"Cheboygan," he said. "Forensics matched your nanny's prints taken from Adriana's bedroom with those in the recovered Jaguar, and soon we'll have confirmation on the prints in the Buick as well."

"What other leads are you following?" Brandon asked.

"At this point, state police are investigating a Yugo reported stolen from the same vicinity where the Buick was discovered. I'm not able to go into all the specifics," Sanderson added. "We also believe multiple people are involved. Your nanny didn't act alone."

Roslyn looked at her husband, whose jaw twitched. Last month he'd asked for a divorce, for no particular reason this time. His announcement hadn't shocked her. She blamed it on the scotch—his liquid courage. The next morning, hungover and mousy, he apologized profusely. He snuck out of the house only to return a few hours later with a gold bracelet. The dangling charm read: "Love Without End." But the damage had been done. He couldn't threaten to take their daughter away from her one minute, then try to make things right with a piece of jewelry.

"Don't look at me like that, Roz," he growled.

"I don't know any more than you. She told me she was going to school for architectural design and she wanted to work for the company after graduation."

Roslyn stared at him, uncertain whether to believe him or not. Outside of the agency's impeccable references, she knew nothing of the girl. Prior to employing Brittany, Roslyn had insisted on a drug test and background check. Her spotless record hadn't produced any red flags. Brandon planted his hand on Roslyn's lower back and she tensed. His supportive gesture wouldn't work to calm her down.

If the agent suspected tension between Roslyn and Brandon, he didn't show it. He simply continued asking questions. "Did she ever talk about friends or relatives?"

Roslyn shook her head. As the questions continued, realization dawned. She knew little about the person she'd hired—the person she had put in charge of her daughter. What was Brittany capable of? Roslyn's throat constricted. *If there's a God of mercy* . . .

"Agent Sanderson." The field agent seated with a laptop stood and pointed at the screen. "We've got an update."

Thank God. Roslyn's heart drummed as Sanderson viewed the monitor.

"Find out what roads are laying new asphalt," Sanderson instructed one of his men. He glanced up at Brandon. "The K9 unit confirmed your daughter was in the Buick."

"So what's this about asphalt?" Brandon's brow furrowed.

"Forensics found both horse manure and traces of asphalt on the tires."

Roslyn covered her mouth with a trembling hand. Last month she had read a magazine article about a kidnapped child. At the time, the factual statistics listed that only a small percentage of children returned home unharmed. Reading how most were never found hadn't made an impression at the time, but now she lacked the courage to ask what the odds of recovery were this late after an abduction.

"What does asphalt and horse manure have to do with Adriana?" Brandon pressed.

"Right now I don't know." The agent didn't, or wouldn't, make eye contact.

Numbness deadened Roslyn's senses. As Agent Sanderson said something about investigating all leads, his words muddled together. Roslyn's vision blurred with fuzzy white dots, and the high-pitched squeal in her ears distorted any comprehension. She leaned against Brandon's sturdy form as her knees buckled. Slumped over in his arms, she felt her weight lifted.

"Don't take me away." Her whimper was practically drowned out by the squawk of the radio static.

Brandon ignored her plea and crossed the room with Roslyn draped in his arms. On the opposite side of the office, he lowered her onto the cold leather couch. She attempted to sit up, but he gently placed his hand on her shoulder and eased her back down.

The scent of rubbing alcohol followed by a dab of cool wetness over her uncovered arm jolted her senses. Her eyes shot open. "I don't—"

The needle penetrated her skin prior to Leon's "little sting" comment. He Band-Aided the injection site, then stepped aside.

Brandon sat next to her. He stroked her hair, then kissed her forehead. For a moment, she drifted somewhere else, to a better time.

"The FBI is doing everything they can." Brandon's words jerked her back to reality.

She wanted to ask how much "everything" was, but overcome with both emotional and physical heaviness, her muscles relaxed. Her heart slowed its pace to a steady thump. Her eyelids closed as if paralyzed. In her dreamlike state, she heard Leon explain to Brandon how the sedative would help her sleep several hours. For Roslyn, the chemically induced sleep—a warped sense of abandonment of the body—felt like she'd been buried alive. An image of steam rising off asphalt flashed over her mind as her eyelids fluttered closed.

The phone rang . . . then rang again . . . and again.

She was dreaming, wasn't she?

"Hello . . . Yes, it is," Brandon said, his voice tense. "Where's Adriana?" His words partially registered with Roslyn in a slur of sounds barely distinguishable. "How do you expect me to raise that much so quickly?" Silence. "Yes, I understand. Unmarked. Small bills." The tunnel sound of his voice grew faint.

"Not enough time to trace," a male announced.

"Will you be able to secure that much money?" Sanderson asked.

"My banker will have to pull strings at the corporate level. He didn't give us much time."

Her husband's voice faded again as Roslyn fought succumbing to sleep. Her eyelids closed and refused to open. That must mean an exchange. Adriana for the money . . .

❧

Roslyn opened her eyes to a squawk of unfamiliar voices. She eased into a seated position on the leather sofa, waves of dizziness preventing her from standing. She licked her dry lips and blinked a few times to adjust her focus. Blinding light bled through the opened window next to her as Brandon peered between the wooden slats. She craned into a better position in order to glimpse around her husband's torso. Her gaze met a barrage of flashing strobes. More news vans. Reporters had gathered in a semicircle, microphones raised in the air. She squinted. A uniformed man stood at a podium.

Feeling weak, Roslyn fell back against the pillow. She should force herself to get up, to do something, but sinking into the couch, her muscles turned to mush. *Just a few minutes more . . .* Closing her eyes, she saw a familiar-looking man with red hair hold up the front page of the newspaper. The headline read: "Long Wait Over: Colepepper's Abducted Daughter Home Safe." Roslyn smiled. All was well.

"The Coast Guard is in position," a voice said over the radio static.

Roslyn pushed upright and stood, pausing long enough to adjust her balance. She located Brandon seated in the armchair in front of the desk. His elbows steadied on his knees and his face was buried in his hands. He didn't look up until she placed her hand on his shoulder.

Based on his downturned lips and fatigued expression, their daughter hadn't been found.

Brandon stood. "You should lie down." He turned her gently toward the door.

"What's happening?" The way everyone in the room hovered near the desk in silence, she suspected he was keeping pertinent information from her. "I heard you talking to the kidnappers."

His face paled. "That was five hours ago."

"When are they going to give us Adriana?"

He looked down at the floor. It was so unlike him not to have a solution to a problem.

A wave of nausea caused the room to spin. Roslyn covered her mouth as bile rose to the back of her throat. *Five hours. Something went wrong. Did he not get the money?* "Brandon," her voice squeaked.

He looked up, but his glossy eyes couldn't maintain contact with hers. He gathered her into his arms, his grip emptying her lungs of air. Something was terribly wrong. "Tell me what's happening. I heard something about the Coast Guard."

When he pulled back to arm's length, his face was wet with tears.

Roslyn's throat tightened.

"They shut down Mackinac Bridge." He closed his eyes and massaged his temples. "The helicopters were—"

"What?"

He waved at Leon seated near the bookcase-lined wall.

"Brandon, tell me." She glanced at Agent Sanderson perched next to the computer with the phone to his ear. Roslyn glared at her brother who was readying another syringe. "I'm not taking that," she said through gritted teeth.

"I want you to go upstairs and lie down," Brandon said, his voice strengthening. "When I hear something official—"

"No!" She jerked away from her husband and approached the agents. "I want to know about my daughter," she demanded.

Sanderson brought the phone down from his ear. "I'm on hold with the Coast Guard. The search-and-rescue dive team is still underwater."

Dive team? She shook her head. "No!" Her husband's image distorted as her vision clouded with images of her precious daughter underwater. Roslyn's entire body trembled uncontrollably. "Tell me what happened."

"The car went over the bridge," Brandon said slowly.

Chapter 10

Faith dodged two hospital workers pushing a man on a gurney as she sped down the hall to reach Olivia and the man dressed in a white coat and green scrubs. Gideon kept pace, muttering something under his breath that sounded like a short prayer.

As Faith neared the two, the doctor turned and disappeared behind a door, leaving Olivia standing in the hallway alone. *Lord . . . Your will be done, Father.* She braced for the news. "What did the *doktah* say?"

Olivia dried her wet cheeks with the back of her hands. "*Daed* is going into surgery. His leg is broken in multiple places. The *doktah* said something about him needing a pin or rod or something."

"And *Mamm*?"

"She's badly bruised, internally too. The *doktah* wants to admit her for observation and keep an eye on her organs." Olivia covered her face with her hands and cried.

A lump pressed against Faith's voice box and prevented her from speaking above a whisper. "Is the *doktah* aware of *Mamm's* kidney disease?"

Olivia nodded.

Faith glanced at Gideon, his expression pinched.

With a silence looming between them, Beverly came out of the restroom from across the hall, her gaze floating between Olivia, Faith, and Gideon. "What have you heard?"

Olivia updated their *Englisch* friend.

"Did the *doktah* say when we can see *Mamm*?" Faith asked.

"*Nett* until . . ." Olivia touched her hand to her forehead and closed her eyes a half second. "*Nett* until she's out of X-ray."

"How long will your *daed* be in surgery?" Gideon asked.

Olivia shrugged. "The ER *doktah* wasn't sure."

Faith looked up at the ceiling tiles, blinking tears off her lashes as quickly as they formed.

Gideon nudged her shoulder. "Should we go back to the lobby and wait?"

"Gideon is probably right," Beverly said. "I'm sure the hospital staff doesn't want us crowding the hallway."

Faith nodded, but as she turned toward the lobby, a woman behind them called Olivia's name.

"Admitting has just informed me that your mother's room number is 2218. Once she's finished in radiology, a patient transporter will take her directly to the second floor. If you would prefer to wait upstairs, you can. Otherwise, I'll ask Monica, the floor nurse, to call down when your mother is in her room."

"We'll be upstairs," Faith said, not waiting for anyone else to decide. She wanted to see her mother as quickly as possible.

"Very well." The nurse smiled and pointed to the right. "The visitor elevator is located in the main lobby."

Beverly led them down the hall, turning in the opposite direction as the cafeteria, according to the sign, and ending up in the main lobby where she stopped at the bank of elevators and pressed the Up button.

Faith scanned the seating area. People occupied several groupings of couches and chairs while two workers, a man wearing a security uniform and a woman dressed in a beige jacket, sat behind a round desk marked Information Center.

The elevator door opened and people exited. Gideon held the door from closing as Faith and Beverly stepped inside.

"Olivia?" Faith said when her sister hesitated.

"I, ah . . . I'll meet you there." Olivia waved them off.

Faith expected Gideon to stay with Olivia, but he released the door instead.

"What do you think she's doing?" Faith spoke softly in Pennsylvania *Deitsch*.

"I noticed her eyeing the courtesy phone," he said.

"Who would she be calling *nau*?" Faith clamped her mouth, noticing his doleful expression. She hadn't meant to salt his unhealed wound. "I suppose it's . . . important." She tried to sound positive, even though it was obvious. If Olivia had stayed behind to make a phone call, she was calling an *Englischer*.

Gideon lifted his shoulder in a half shrug. "Doesn't matter."

Faith understood. He might say it didn't matter, but it did. He was speaking from a place of pain.

A short time later, Faith sat in *Mamm's* hospital room as a nurse attached wires to small round patches on *Mamm's* skin, which were supposed to record her heart rhythm, then the nurse touched a button on the machine and it printed a long paper strip.

"If your mother wakes up and needs something, you can contact me by pressing the Call button on the remote," the nurse said. "Are you familiar with how to use the remote?"

Faith nodded. "Another nurse showed me earlier." She settled back in the chair beside her mother's bed. *Mamm's* bruised body looked as though someone had pulverized her with a meat mallet. Shades of plum and blue covered her swollen face, shoulders, and arms, and the way she held her stomach, her abdomen was probably just as colorful. No wonder her liver, kidneys, and spleen were involved.

Minutes after the nurse left the room, *Mamm* moaned.

Faith leaped up from the chair. "*Mamm*, it's Faith. How are you feeling?"

"Thirsty," *Mamm* rasped.

Faith filled a small Styrofoam cup with ice water from the bedside pitcher, then positioned the straw next to *Mamm's* mouth and held it as she took a sip. "Better?"

Mamm nodded, but winced. She touched the side of her head, palpating an egg-sized knot just above her right eye. Closing her eyes, tears slid down her face.

"You're in pain, aren't you?" Faith grabbed the remote attached to the bed rail and, not waiting for her mother to respond, pressed the nurse Call button. Her mother wasn't one to complain. The time *Mamm* had accidentally sliced the tip of her finger off, she wrapped her bleeding hand in a dishrag and matter-of-factly told *Daed*, who was reading the newspaper in the sitting room at the time, that she needed him to drive her into town.

A voice came over the speaker system. "May I help you?"

"*Jah*." Faith leaned closer and spoke into the remote. "*Mei* mother is in a lot of pain. Can someone bring her some medicine, please?"

"I'll send her nurse in," the woman responded.

A short time later, the nurse entered the room. "I

hear you're not feeling too good, Mrs. Pinkham? Can you tell me where it hurts?"

"All over," *Mamm* said weakly.

"On a scale of one to ten, with one being mild and ten being the worst pain possible, what number would you say your pain is?"

"Eight." She answered immediately, which meant her eight would equate to another person's fifteen.

"I'm sorry to hear that you're feeling so badly, Mrs. Pinkham. Your doctor ordered morphine for pain control, so if you'll give me a minute to get your dose ready, you should be feeling better soon."

The nurse left the room and returned a few minutes later with a syringe. After verifying *Mamm's* name, birth date, and scanning a barcode on her hospital bracelet, the nurse injected the medicine into the IV tubing. "You should start feeling better shortly. Can I get you anything else while I'm here?"

Mamm shook her head.

"Okay, I'll be back in a little while to check on you."

The medication made *Mamm's* eyelids droopy within minutes. Shortly after *Mamm* dozed off, the door eased open and Olivia entered. She took one look at *Mamm* and gasped. "How is she?"

Faith wanted to ask Olivia where she had been, but held her tongue. "I think she's doing better *nau*. The nurse was in a few minutes ago and gave her something for pain."

Mamm's eyes fluttered open. "Your father . . . how . . . ?"

"He's in surgery," Faith said, then turned to Olivia. "Are Gideon and Beverly still in the surgical waiting room?"

Olivia shrugged. "I wasn't with them so I wouldn't know."

Faith reached for *Mamm's* hand. "Try to rest. We'll let you know as soon as—" Her mother's eyes closed. Faith settled back into the chair at the bedside while Olivia stood teary-eyed at the foot of the bed.

"She looks like someone whose been dragged behind a plow team." Olivia moved toward the head of the bed and examined the IV bag hanging on the pole. "They're giving her dextrose and potassium," she said, reading the bag of fluids. Without missing a beat, she explained, "Dextrose is for low sugar and potassium replacement is important for your heart to function correctly."

Faith crinkled her brows. "How do you know all that?"

"I read a lot."

Faith didn't have much time to read anything but the Bible in preparation for joining the church. Even then, she was usually so tired she would fall asleep in the process. "Do you think she has something wrong with her heart?

The nurse hooked her up to that monitor on the wall."

"Maybe. Did the *doktah* say anything?"

"Nothing about her heart, but she was dehydrated, and they're watching her kidney function closely through blood work."

"That's interesting," Olivia mumbled, her attention on checking out the different pieces of equipment.

"What are you doing?"

"Just looking. Aren't you curious what any of this does?"

"*Nett* really." To Faith, the gauges, nozzles, and hoses embedded into the wall seemed complex.

The door opened and the nurse poked her head inside. "Are either of you Faith?"

"*Jah*, I am."

"There's a young man in the hall who is asking to speak with you."

Faith caught a glimpse of Gideon and bounded up from the chair. He wouldn't have left the surgical waiting room unless he had news. She rushed out of the room.

"I'm sorry to disturb you." He scratched the back of his neck. "How's your mother doing?"

"She's sleeping. The nurse gave her pain medicine."

"That's *gut*."

She eyed him shuffling his feet. "What did you hear?"

A hospital worker pushing a supply cart maneuvered around an empty bed parked against the wall. Faith waited for the man to pass, then grabbed Gideon's shirt sleeve. "Let's talk down the hall where it isn't so crowded."

She led him down the corridor and stopped near the elevators, though the area was just as congested with people coming and going. "Did you hear something about *mei* father?"

"Take a breath, Faith." Until Gideon placed his hand over hers, she hadn't realized she'd been squeezing his arm.

"I'm sorry." She slowed her thoughts and with it her racing pulse. "Is he out of surgery?"

He shook his head. "An OR nurse came into the waiting room and asked for the family of Mordecai Pinkham. When I stood up, she told me your father's surgery was taking longer than they had originally anticipated."

"What does that mean?" A whoosh of light-headedness caught her off guard and she staggered a step.

Gideon brought his arm around her waist. His gaze grew intense. "Are you okay?"

She waited for the dizziness to pass, but then realizing how close he was standing, holding her tight, concern filling his dark-blue eyes, another wave of sensations washed over her. "I, ah . . ." She shook free from under his arm. "I will be once you tell me what the nurse said."

"Nothing really. The surgery is taking longer than expected, and the nurse didn't want the family worried." He took a step back, increasing the distance between them. "I shouldn't have interrupted you. I'm sorry."

"*Nay*, don't be. Please."

An awkward second passed between them, Faith wishing she hadn't been so obvious about not wanting his arm around her. His gesture was a simple act of kindness. Of comfort. It was she who let her mind go in the wrong direction.

"Are you hungry?" he stammered. "Could I get you something from the cafeteria? Or maybe a coffee?"

She motioned to the drinking fountain on the wall next to the elevator. "Water will do, *danki*."

They strolled over to the fountain where she bent and took a long drink. The cool water was not only refreshing but it helped to relieve her dry throat. She stepped aside and he took her place at the fountain.

He finished drinking and wiped his mouth with his sleeve. "How's Olivia handling all that's happened?"

Faith's stomach hurt like it'd been kicked, but she faked a smile anyway. "I'll send her out when I get back to the room so you can ask her yourself."

She headed down the hallway, made a detour into the women's restroom, then returned to her mother's room. Faith shoved the hospital door open, surprised to find her mother now had a roommate. The patient, an elderly woman, must be hard of hearing because the TV was blaring.

"For more on the story of the kidnapped child, we will go to Sam Koen, who's in Cheboygan. Sam, what are the latest developments?"

Chapter 11

After surgery, *Daed* rested comfortably, or so the nurse who introduced herself as Mallory had said when Faith inquired. According to the nurse, the pain medication made him sleepy and not able to hold his eyes open more than a few seconds. Even then, his expressionless gaze alarmed Faith. She wasn't even sure her father recognized her or Olivia.

Daed's face twitched as the blood pressure cuff around his arm inflated. Seconds later, Mallory released the valve, deflating the cuff.

"How is it?" Olivia was quick to ask.

"Low, but that isn't uncommon for someone who nicked his femoral artery and had multiple compound fractures."

According to the doctor, the surgery had gone well. The surgeon described the process of using a metal rod and screws to put *Daed's* leg back together. Faith focused on the recovery process. Four to six weeks of physical therapy just to get back on his feet and most likely a limp and arthritis issues the rest of his life. *Daed* would not be pleased to hear that news. But more pressing were the barn chores, which hadn't been done today. Bishop Zook would make arrangements for someone to do them in the days ahead, but Faith or Olivia needed to go home and milk the cows and tend the livestock tonight.

"We were told he was given blood during surgery. Do you think he will need more?"

Olivia pushed up her dress sleeve and extended her bare arm to the nurse. "You can take mine."

Faith had never donated blood before, but if it would help her father, she would gladly offer hers as well. "Mine too. I'll donate."

The nurse removed the blood pressure cuff from *Daed's* arm. "That's very kind of you to consider donating. I know the blood bank is always looking for more donors. Do you know what blood types you are?"

Faith shook her head. "Is that a problem?"

"No, not at all. The blood bank will determine if you're a match." The nurse made a notation on a clipboard, then left the room.

Faith approached the bed. "How many blood types do you suppose there are?"

"Several," Olivia replied. "A, B, AB, O, and then there are the positive or negative Rh factors too."

"How do you—I know, you read a lot." Olivia was like a walking encyclopedia. "What kind of books are you reading, Liv?"

"Anything I can get *mei* hands on."

Daed flapped his arm against the mattress. Without opening his eyes, he called, "Irma?"

Faith reached for his hand and his arm relaxed. "*Daed*, it's Faith. Are you in pain?"

No response.

Olivia clasped the bed rail. "Do you think he was dreaming?"

"Probably." Faith held his hand a little longer before releasing it. He needed sleep, and one of them should head home and tend the livestock. Looking at Olivia, Faith motioned with a head nod at the door.

"What?" Olivia said, trailing her into the hallway.

"I don't think we should both stay when there are barn chores at home to be done. Snowflake hasn't been milked, and the calves and hogs still need feeding. Do you want to stay or go back to the *haus*?"

Olivia's mouth pursed for a second. "Since I'm the only one of legal age listed on the hospital paperwork, I should be here in case I have to make any medical decisions."

Faith hadn't thought about someone having to make medical decisions, but her sister was right. When the paperwork had been signed, the hospital worker made a point in asking if either of them were eighteen or older. Not yet seventeen, Faith reluctantly saw Olivia's point. "I agree. You should stay."

Moaning filtered into the hall from *Daed's* room. They went back inside as he called for *Mamm* once again.

Olivia placed her hand on his shoulder. "Try and relax."

"The truck's too close . . . Irma!" He grasped the bed rail and rolled slightly, apparently unaware of his limited mobility with his leg suspended.

"You're in the hospital," Olivia said calmly. "*Mamm* isn't here right *nau*—but she's okay."

Daed tried to push himself up and Olivia's eyes widened. "Faith, let the nurse know he's awake and restless."

Faith nodded but her feet didn't move. She had never seen her father combative in any way, yet nothing Olivia said or did could stop him from flailing his arms at her as he wrestled in an attempt to get out of bed.

"Faith, *geh nau*! I can't hold him down long."

As reality set in that he was close to falling out of bed, Faith rushed from the room. She found Mallory sitting at the nurses' desk in front of a computer. "Please, help, *mei* father is trying to climb out of bed!"

The nurse pushed off the chair and rounded the desk. She rushed into the room, relieved Olivia, and pinned *Daed's* shoulders down. "Mr. Pinkham, I'd like you to calm down. Your leg is in traction and you can't get out of bed." Her voice was steady and reassuring, but *Daed* didn't follow her orders. He continued to call for *Mamm*, telling her to hold on in Pennsylvania *Deitsch* as if reliving the accident. The nurse

123

pressed the Call button on the remote. "Code Yellow 3110," she said, repeating it three times.

A red-haired man rushed into the room and helped restrain *Daed*.

"You got him?" Mallory asked. "I need to get a dose of Ativan."

"Yep, go," the man replied.

As Mallory left the room, the man explained to her father that he'd been in an accident. Everything he'd already been told, but maybe this time it would register. "Mordecai," he said soothingly. "Let your mind relax and listen to my voice. Your help comes from the Lord, the Maker of heaven and earth."

The hairs on Faith's arms stood on end as the man spoke in Pennsylvania *Deitsch*.

Daed mumbled something in return, but his words were scrambled. His agitation simmered and within a short time disappeared altogether. He unclenched the bed rail and sank back against the mattress. Without uttering another sound, his eyes closed, a peacefulness taking root.

Two more nurses filed into the room along with Mallory, who stood beside the red-haired man and readied a syringe.

"He is resting in the hands of the Lord. He doesn't need the medication," the male nurse said.

Mallory studied *Daed*, then signaled the nurse on the opposite side of the bed, who began to buckle a strap around *Daed's* wrist, then fasten

124

it to the bed. "These restraints will help if he becomes combative again," Mallory explained, fastening the one on her side.

"He's *nett* a violent man," Faith said, feeling compelled to explain her father's unusual behavior.

His nurse smiled apologetically. "The restraints are precautionary. We don't want him pulling out his IV lines or trying to get out of bed. It isn't unusual for patients coming out of anesthesia to be disoriented or hallucinate. Sometimes they will say things that don't make sense. It's something we're aware of and will continue to monitor."

Faith hoped he remained sedated. It would be better for him to stay asleep than be awake and aware he was tethered to the bed rail like an animal. She scanned the room for the red-haired man to thank him, but he was already gone.

The nurse took *Daed's* blood pressure, made a few notations on a clipboard, then she and the other helpers left the room.

"You might as well go home," Olivia said matter-of-factly. She settled into the chair next to the bed. "Don't worry. I'll be here if he wakes up."

Faith eyed her sister. For some reason Olivia needed to stress the fact she wasn't going to leave his side, as if she was the loyal daughter. Jealousy flared, but Faith refused to give it fuel.

"I know he's in *gut* hands with you." She motioned to the door. "Beverly is sitting with

Mamm. I'll ask her to drive me home. Do you want me to see if she will bring me back into town after I'm finished with chores so I can relieve you?"

"*Nay*, I'll spend the *nacht*. But you'll need to find someone to work for me tomorrow."

"Okay." Faith had already planned to stop by her cousin's house on the way home and let her know about the accident. Once word spread through the district, it wouldn't be hard to find volunteers to help with barn chores and work at the restaurant. "When *Daed* wakes up, please tell him I'm praying for him and love him."

"*Jah*, I will."

Someone tapped lightly on the door, then opened it. A man entered wearing a pressed white button-down shirt, a navy tie, and a State of Michigan Police Officer badge clipped to his shirt pocket.

"I'm Officer Halbert," he said. "I'm here to speak with Mordecai Pinkham."

Faith blurted the first words that popped into her mind. "Why? Is he in trouble?"

"I'd just like to ask him a few questions about the accident."

"Oh." She gulped.

"The desk clerk said his visitation wasn't restricted, but if this isn't a good time, I can get the information for my report later."

"*Mei* father just had surgery and he's asleep." Faith stepped closer and lowered her voice. "May we talk in the hall so we don't disturb him?"

"Yes, absolutely."

Olivia joined Faith and the officer. "Is there something we can help you with?"

He consulted his notepad. "Were either of you passengers in the buggy?"

"*Nay*, but our mother was with him," Olivia volunteered. "She's also a patient, but her room is on another floor."

"Yes, I've already obtained Mrs. Pinkham's statement." He peered over Faith's shoulder into the room, then reached into his shirt pocket and removed a card. "This is a number where I can be reached." He handed the card to Olivia. "The investigation will remain open until I have the chance to talk with him, so it's important that I obtain his statement as soon as possible."

"I'll be sure he contacts you." Olivia looked at the information. "Officer Halbert."

Faith waited for the officer to walk away, then nudged Olivia. "Do you think we should have told him what *Daed* said about the truck being too close?"

Olivia shrugged. "We weren't eyewitnesses. Plus, you heard the nurse. *Daed* might have been delusional."

Daed wasn't delusional about his concern for *Mamm*. Her well-being was on the forefront of his mind. Faith sighed. Even somewhat sedated from surgery, her father demonstrated the type of man she hoped one day to marry. She glanced into the room at her father sleeping peacefully.

"Before you go," Olivia said, stiffening her back, "it takes some people longer to make a commitment to the church—and to marriage."

"I know."

"Gideon and I talked in the barn, and after I explained how confused I've been lately, he understands."

Of course he does. Faith forced a smile. "I'll see you tomorrow." She turned and rushed toward the elevators, her thoughts swirling. *Forgive me, Father. I should rejoice. I've been praying for Olivia and it seems You've answered* mei *prayers. She's no longer confused.*

She pressed the elevator button, silently confessing her guilty conscience to God. The door opened, and she nearly bumped into Gideon, who was holding a Styrofoam cup in each hand.

"*Hiya*," he said, smiling wide and extending one of the cups toward her. "*Kaffi?*"

Faith peered into the elevator—empty except for Gideon. "*Danki*, but drinking caffeine this late might prevent me from falling asleep tonight." She bit back sharing that sleep would be iffy at best, since she'd never been alone overnight before, not to mention thoughts of him and Olivia being back together would keep her awake.

"I wanted to see how your *Daed* is doing." The door started to close, but he stopped it with his knee. "Are you going up to see your *mamm*?"

"*Jah*." She stepped aside, clearing the way for Gideon to exit, but instead he gestured with a nod that she join him. "I thought you were getting off on this floor to see *mei* father."

"I'll ride up with you. If you don't mind *mei* company." He winked.

"That's fine." Faith stepped inside and averted her gaze to the tile floor. She knew enough not to take his flirting seriously. After all, they'd been good friends for a long time and he could be quite the tease. She pushed the playfulness aside. "I'm afraid I won't be the best company."

"So you say." He held up the drink again. "You sure I can't talk you into a cup of *kaffi*? I think you could use a pick-me-up."

She hesitated a minute, then accepted the drink. "*Danki. Nau* if I'm up all *nacht*, I'm going to blame it on you." She took a sip. Cream and sugar, just the way she liked it. Faith hoped the smile on her lips hadn't revealed how much she enjoyed the coffee, nor how impressed she was that he knew exactly how she took it.

He wiggled his eyebrows and grinned, which caused her to wonder if he'd somehow managed to read her thoughts.

Her cheeks were flaming, and while he pretended not to notice how her face lit up, his grin conveyed he was enjoying the time together.

"The *kaffi* is *gut*," she admitted with a surprisingly even voice.

"*Jah*, I know." His grin deepened but quickly faded. Instead of carrying the teasing any further, his expression sobered. "How is your *daed*?"

"His leg is suspended by a pulley system, much like the contraption used in the barn for lifting hay up to the loft."

He cringed. "That must be painful."

"I'm sure it is. He's been given pain medicine, which has helped him sleep. He only woke up once while I was there, or maybe he was having a nightmare. He kept calling out for *mei mamm*. I don't think he knew Olivia and I were in the room."

"I'm sorry." The concern on his face was mirrored in his eyes, which tugged on her heart all the more.

Recalling the officer's remark about having already spoken with her mother, Faith could hardly wait for the elevator to reach her floor to find out what questions the officer had asked and, more importantly, what her mother remembered.

"The accident must have been bad," Gideon said. "Have you heard what happened yet?"

"*Nay*, but while *Daed* was sleeping, a police officer came to talk with him." Faith replayed her father's words about the truck. Her spine chilled. No one mentioned Buttercup.

"What's wrong?"

Faith pushed the lump down her throat with a

hard swallow. "What do you think happened to Buttercup?"

He shook his head. "I don't know."

"Do you think she's still lying in the ditch? The officer would have said something, right?" Why hadn't she thought to ask the officer?

"Don't worry, Faith. Focus on your parents and leave Buttercup to me. I'll find out about her."

"And the buggy. *Daed* will need his buggy." Her stomach roiled at the thought of poor Buttercup. The moment the elevator door opened, she raced toward the first trash can she spotted. Pitching the Styrofoam cup into the receptacle, she gripped the sides of the waist-high trash can, hung her head, and vomited for several seconds.

Gideon handed her a hankie. "*Kaffi* too hard on your stomach?"

"*Jah*, I think so." She dabbed her mouth with the cloth, then gently cleared her scratchy, raw throat.

"There's a drinking fountain near the waiting room." He motioned to the right.

"I'm sorry," Faith said after taking a long drink. The cold water didn't completely take away the bitterness in her mouth, but it did soothe her throat.

"No apology needed. Are you feeling better?"

"*Jah*, I am. It's sweet of you not to mention how unladylike . . ." *Did I really just say sweet?* The same grin that appeared on Gideon's face moments ago resurfaced, and though he clearly had no way of reading her mind, once again it was as if he had intercepted her unspoken thoughts.

"Were you going to drink more?" He motioned to the fountain, his grin intact.

"*Nay*, I ah . . ." *I'm suddenly a blubbering fool around him.* She pretended to contemplate which direction to go, fully knowing *Mamm's* room was just around the corner.

He nudged her arm. "You sure you're feeling all right?"

She nodded, but the movement made her queasy again.

"This way." Gideon guided her to her mother's room, then he stopped short of the door. "I'll wait for you out here."

She gave a slight smile at his show of respect for *Mamm's* privacy. "Olivia is sitting with *Daed.* You might want to drop by and check how she's doing."

"Maybe later." Gideon usually went out of his way to spend time with Olivia. Why was he avoiding her now after their talk in the barn?

Faith opened her mother's door and smiled. *Mamm* was awake, and Beverly was keeping her company, sitting in the chair beside her. "How are you feeling, *Mamm*?"

"Sore. How is your father? I've asked to go to his room, but the *doktah* said I need to rest."

"He's sleeping."

"And his leg? How bad is it?"

"He came through the surgery all right. The *doktah* said it would take four to six weeks to heal."

"I'm thankful God spared us and we're still alive." Tears formed in *Mamm's* eyes that she wiped away with a tissue. "It could have been so much worse."

"I thank God too." Faith's throat swelled. She couldn't imagine what life would be like without her parents.

Before Faith could ask her *Mamm* about the conversation she'd had with the officer, her mother's eyes closed.

"We should probably let her rest," Beverly said.

"I think you're right." Faith leaned over the bed and gently kissed *Mamm's* forehead. She hated to leave her mother alone. But not only did the animals need tending, she had to open the restaurant in the morning. Her family relied on the busy season, and Fourth of July was only a few days away.

The door opened and a nurse stepped into the room.

Faith motioned to her mother. "She just fell asleep."

"I was actually looking for you. Your father's nurse called and there's a chance he'll need to go back into surgery. They said you volunteered to donate blood."

Chapter 12

Gideon debated whether to tell Faith the news about Buttercup now or wait until they were back at her place. Standing outside the hospital waiting for Beverly to pull the car around, he glanced up at the evening sky. No stars tonight. He wouldn't be surprised if it rained again.

Faith hadn't said much since she'd found out her A Positive blood type wasn't a match for her father's O Negative. Thankfully her father's second surgery to repair a tear in his colon went better than expected, and he didn't require additional blood.

"Tired?" *Stupid question.* Weariness and exhaustion were evident in her dull eyes.

"A little." She hugged herself. "It's been a long day. I went into the restaurant early to bake bread."

He'd forgotten that her day started a few hours before The Amish Table even opened for business. No wonder her shoulders sagged and her face looked drawn. "Maybe you should close the restaurant tomorrow. You could post a sign saying it's due to an accident."

"*Nay*, I have to be there."

"You're wearing yourself thin."

"*Mei* parents are counting on me. This is our busiest season."

Beverly pulled up to the curb and stopped the car. Gideon opened the front passenger door for Faith, then crawled into the backseat. The small talk was sporadic between Faith and the *Englischer* as the radio played softly in the background. Gideon leaned his head back and closed his eyes, grateful the women hadn't attempted to include him in the conversation. On Faith's request, Beverly stopped at Catherine's house so Faith could share the news and line up help for the restaurant. Gideon stayed in the car.

"Will you be needing a ride home, too, Gideon?"

"No, thank you. *Mei* horse is at Faith's *haus*." He hoped Bay's leg would be able to handle the three-mile trip now that he'd had a few hours to rest. Otherwise it would be a long walk home in the dark.

After a few minutes, Faith climbed back into the car. "I hope I wasn't in there too long," she said.

"Not at all." Beverly shifted the car into reverse. "Do you need to stop anywhere else?"

"*Nay*, *mei* cousin said she would tell the others."

Gideon picked up on the relief in Faith's tone. Hearing her sigh was like listening to the wheat field sway to a summer breeze.

Faith's sullenness continued even after she'd stepped out of the car and waved good-bye to the

Englischer, who pulled away slowly, then headed out of the driveway.

The last thing Gideon wanted to do was dampen Faith's mood, but he had to tell her what he'd been keeping to himself. He cleared his throat. "I have some bad news. Buttercup had to be put down."

As he studied her face and the news registered, Gideon regretted being so direct. Her lips started to quiver, and he reached for her hand. "I'm sorry."

The crease in Faith's brow deepened. "When did you find out?"

"While you were visiting your *mamm*, I called the police department, who referred me to the Posen Animal Clinic. Buttercup's injuries were too severe. The veterinarian couldn't do anything for her."

Faith touched her fingers to her gaping mouth. She stared at the barn, her expression bleak. He should have waited. She didn't need this news tonight.

"I need to milk the cows." She shuffled toward the barn.

"Why don't you go inside the *haus* and let me take care of the chores?"

Either dazed or ignoring him, she continued on course. Milking was often a time for him to mull over important matters. Maybe she felt the same. Over the years, he'd reasoned his way through a slew of problems while shoveling manure. Although his ideas didn't always match God's well-laid ones, he did feel better after hard work. Barn chores may be exactly what Faith needed. Only he wasn't about to leave her alone. He would find a place to ponder his own problems. Like on his walk home if Bay was still limping.

Faith removed a bucket from the shelf in the milking parlor. "I really don't need your help tonight," she said, adding soap.

"I want to help." Gideon reached for the bucket handle. "Let me take it out to the pump and fill it."

Her gaze darted around the room, obviously avoiding his, but why, he hadn't a clue.

"Okay, I'll ah—" Faith wrung her hands as she always did when she was nervous. "Why are you looking at me like that?"

He cocked his head, but that seemed to make her more uptight. *Women. Why did they have to be so difficult to figure out?*

Motioning to the door, she ordered, "*Geh*. Fill the bucket."

He marched out of the milking parlor and made his way to the pump. After a few hard thrusts on the iron handle, water gushed out of the spigot and into the pail.

Faith was busy pouring oats into the feed buckets when he returned to the barn. "You should probably check on Bay and see if he's able to make it home," she said.

Her father raised Jerseys the same as his family. Jerseys were known for a high quantity of butterfat in their milk, as well as for their gentleness. But as it was with any cow that went too long between milkings, the Jerseys tended to become temperamental. Not only did the pressure build up in the udders, making it painful, but the cow was at an increased risk of infection. "Don't you hear the herd bawling at the pasture door? We can't keep them waiting any longer."

"*Jah*, I hear them," Faith said.

Gideon unlatched the door leading to the pasture and pushed it open for the cows to come inside. He counted only three. "Where are the others?"

"We have several in the back pasture with their unweaned calves. We won't be milking them." She fastened the stanchions as the cows took their place.

Gideon placed the stool and suds bucket next to the first cow as Faith dumped oats into their feed trough. "This shouldn't take long," he said.

"Exactly why I said I could handle the chores." She tossed an extra rag into the sudsy water. She waited for him to finish cleaning the udders on the cow he was about to milk, then picked up the bucket and moved it to the next cow.

"You're beginning to make me feel unwelcome,"

he teased. "Aren't we friends?" He paused, waiting for her reply, but none came. "Faith?"

"*Jah*, Gideon," she said, wringing excess water from the rag. "We'll always be friends." Her tone didn't hold the same promise as her words.

He stood up and peered over the cow, but her back was to him and he couldn't see her expression. "Are you okay?"

"*Jah*," she replied without looking at him. "Why?"

"You seem . . . different." *Distant.* Conversation between them had never been a problem. They talked about everything. He plopped back down on the stool and resumed milking. After a moment of silence, he groaned under his breath. She was making it difficult to keep a conversation going. "You're usually more talkative."

"I suppose I am."

"I know you're upset about your parents, but is something else wrong?" Gideon milked faster. Normally if he pried too much, she would at least become frustrated and make some restrained squeal, which sounded more like a barn animal, before finally telling him to hush. If he could provoke a squeal, it would be better than silence. "What have I done to upset you?"

He crouched low to see between the cow's legs. Faith was hunched over, head against the animal's flank, and milking at a good, consistent pace. Even if she were crying, he wouldn't be able to tell over the noise of the livestock.

"One cow done." Gideon collected the bucket of milk along with the wooden stool he'd been sitting on, then moved to the last Jersey. As he passed Faith's milking stanchion, she didn't look up. Her lack of response brought back painful memories of when his older brothers ignored him. He moved his head from side to side, lengthening the muscles knotting his neck. Faith wasn't mean-spirited like his brothers had been growing up. She'd had a rough day, a lot on her mind. Still, he didn't want to be excluded. He wanted to be her sounding board as was the case when she vented about work.

"*Gut* girl, Snowflake." Faith released the cow back into the pasture.

Gideon tried not to notice when Faith walked up beside him.

"Are you almost done?" Her tone sounded more exhausted than curt.

"Yep." He kept milking.

"If you need more horse liniment for Bay's leg, it's on the shelf in the equipment room."

He glanced up, opened his mouth to say something about her red-rimmed eyes, but decided it was best not to mention it. "Are you heading back to the *haus* with the milk?"

"*Nett* yet. I still need to feed and water the hogs and chickens. I just wanted to let you know you're *welkum* to use the liniment."

140

"*Danki*." He studied her downturned head, gaze locked on the concrete or maybe her shoes. Her courteous yet impersonal demeanor wasn't the Faith he'd come to love—*like*—he *liked* hanging out with her. But until he could talk face-to-face without a cow in between them, he would keep things simple. "Do you need help tending the other animals?"

"*Nay*, I can handle it."

A calico barn cat curled its body around Faith's legs, meowing. Soon two more cats joined the chorus of meows, their tails twitching as they tried to get Faith's attention. She poured some milk into a shallow tin and watched them devour the treat.

Watching her gentleness with the cats, heat infused Gideon's veins. An uneasy feeling, something he hadn't experienced in a long time, coursed through him, making his hands clammy and his stomach queasy.

~※~

Hooking the lantern handle over the fence post, Faith tossed the sow feed over the wooden slats of their pen. "A slim supper tonight, but I'll make sure you eat better tomorrow." The hogs were used to having their feed supplemented by a variety of table scraps from the restaurant. They especially liked potato peelings and vegetables that had gone limp or were about to go bad.

141

As the sows wrangled for the best placement at the trough, Faith looked for the two runts that the others sometimes pushed aside. She removed the lantern from the post and waved it over the herd of eight. There, at the end, the smaller ones struggled to get their portion. The little one with a freckled snout looked up from the trough and snorted.

"*Nay* attitude please, Freckles," Faith said, leaning over the fence. "I've had a rough day."

"I know this has been a rough day," Gideon said, coming up beside her. "But why won't you tell me what's bothering you?"

She lowered the lantern to evade his stare. "You know, *mei* parents were in an accident," she chided. Wasn't that reason enough to feel sad, overwhelmed . . . useless? "I couldn't donate blood to help *mei daed*, and I couldn't stay to keep them company through the *nacht*. I'm feeling useless at the moment."

"Anyone can sit next to a hospital bed and watch someone sleep. But *nett* everyone can keep the farm and restaurant afloat. Trust me, Faith, you're *nett* useless."

She swallowed hard. He had a way of making her feel special.

"You'll feel better after you get some sleep," he said.

"I'm sure you're right." Faith yawned.

He placed his hand on her shoulder and pivoted

her toward the house. "Go inside. I'll finish feeding the animals."

She hesitated, then sighed and ambled to the house. Once inside, darkness surrounded her. Realizing this was the first time she'd been alone at night, she hurried to find a box of wooden matches in the drawer and light the lamp wick. A warm yellow glow bounced off the kitchen walls, contrasting the darkness with flickers of dancing light.

A heavy rap on the door broke the silence. "There's no reason to be jumpy." She drew a deep breath to settle her nerves, then opened the door.

Gideon lifted the milk canister. "I figured you would want me to bring this inside."

"*Jah, danki.*" She stepped aside, allowing him to enter.

He set the five-gallon stainless-steel container on the counter, then faced her. "Are you going to be all right here alone?"

She was bound to have a restless night having never been alone. But even if she stayed with her cousin, thoughts of Gideon in the loft with Olivia would keep her up. "I'll be fine. *Danki* for coming to the hospital with us. I'm sure Olivia appreciates—"

"Can we *nett* talk about Olivia right *nau*?"

Faith flinched at his sharp tone.

"I'm sorry." He lowered his head.

143

"This is the first time you haven't wanted to talk about Olivia," she said. "I'm guessing it has something to do with the barn loft."

"Faith, it's *nett* what you think."

"Really? That's what you told Olivia when she walked in the barn."

He sighed. "Okay, fine. I didn't want to bring it up because I know you're tired and you've been through a lot, and frankly, I'm exhausted. Olivia is . . . she isn't—"

An urgent knocking on the door startled Faith and she jumped.

Chapter 13

Standing in the Pinkham's kitchen, Gideon hemmed and hawed over telling Faith about Olivia. Faith most likely wasn't aware of the rumors about her sister, and after everything she'd gone through, tonight wasn't the night to bring it up.

Someone knocked and Faith scooted to the back door, leaving him alone with his thoughts. The bishop's voice spurred Gideon to action. He rounded the corner of the kitchen as the bishop's wife, Alice, pulled Faith into a hug.

"We heard the news about your parents and thought we would take the chance that your light was on." Bishop Zook looked Gideon's direction and narrowed his bushy white brows at him. "I didn't know you were here, Gideon."

"I, ah . . ." The censure in the older man's tone made Gideon temporarily tongue-tied. Then he spied the milk canisters out of the corner of his eye. "I *kumm* by to help with the barn chores."

The bishop's slight nod acknowledged his comment, but Gideon couldn't tell if he approved of his initiative. Usually as needs arose in their settlement, the bishop organized how the additional workload would be divided.

Gideon tugged on his collarless shirt, pulling it

away from his neck. Under the watchful eye of the bishop, sweat pebbled his forehead. Of course the closed windows made the July heat stifling. Now that the rain had stopped, someone should open the windows. The stale air was suffocating.

Alice Zook scanned the room. "Where's Olivia?"

"She didn't want to leave *Mamm* and *Daed* alone, so she stayed at the hospital."

"You're alone?" the bishop's wife pressed.

Faith gave Gideon a wary glance that begged for rescue. Earlier she'd been worried about someone spotting them at the river and spreading tittle-tattle through the district of them swimming together, which was a bit paranoid even for Faith. But he could see her point. She didn't want anything standing in the way of her joining the church.

"Either Olivia or I had to *kumm* home and see that the chores were done." Her simple explanation should have been enough, but she continued. "Gideon's horse injured his leg earlier today, so he needed to check on Bay."

Gideon's heart sank listening to Faith scramble with excuses, fearful of the repercussions due to their lack of a chaperone this late at night. As a baptized member of the church, Gideon expected the bishop would want to speak with him privately about the matter.

Bishop Zook stroked his beard, then turned to Gideon. "How is your horse?"

Gideon thought he heard doubt in the man's

question, but he straightened his shoulders. "Bay's still limping," he said, sounding more defensive than he wished.

Bishop Zook motioned to the door. "Why don't we go take a look at him?"

Gideon stole a glance at Faith as he headed to the door. She had no reason to be ashamed, and yet her downtrodden expression suggested remorse. Gideon groaned under his breath. *Don't let anyone heap guilt on you, Faith. We didn't do anything wrong.*

The breeze coming across the field felt good as he sloshed through shallow puddles that spanned part of the lawn and most of the driveway. Gideon's thoughts lingered on Faith—alone in that suffocating room with the bishop's wife.

"It sure rained hard today," the bishop said. "Most of the roads in the area are washed out." He crossed the driveway and stopped at his buggy to retrieve a lantern. He took time to light the wick. "Did your horse injure his leg in the storm?"

"*Jah*, Bay doesn't like thunder." He yanked the barn door open. "Mordecai's horse had to be put down. I haven't seen their buggy, but from what the officer told me over the phone, it's in bad shape. Faith's shook up."

"*Jah*, I noticed." He stepped into the barn. "I also noticed the two of you are spending more time together lately."

"We're friends."

147

Bishop Zook raised the lantern to shoulder height, throwing more light on Gideon.

"Bay's in the third stall." Gideon took the lead, not stopping until he was standing before the stall's half door. He unfastened the latch and slipped inside with the horse. "It's his front right leg."

Bishop Zook handed Gideon the lantern, then squatted next to Bay. When he ran his hand down the horse's leg, Bay flinched. "It's tender."

"I lathered him in liniment hoping it would reduce the swelling. I'm *nett* sure what else to do."

"It looks as though you've done everything you can do for *nau*." Bishop Zook stood, removed a hankie from his pocket, and used it to wipe the liniment off his hands. "The swelling isn't too bad, but he's definitely favoring it. I wouldn't suggest you drive him anywhere tonight. *Mei fraa* and I will give you a ride home."

"*Danki* for taking a look at him."

"If the swelling isn't down by tomorrow, you'll probably need to call a vet. He might have a stress fracture."

Gideon didn't want to think about the possibility of an injury that severe. A big vet bill would deplete the money he'd been saving to buy a farm. Not that he was in a rush to make that type of purchase. "I'll be praying that isn't the case." He'd put his heart into training the three-year-old and could kick himself for not getting him home before the storm. He should have seen the weather changing and left the river sooner.

"It's getting late," the bishop said. "Your parents are probably worried about you."

"*Jah*, I'm sure you're right." Gideon looked down at his muddy boots. *Mamm* did have a tendency to worry too much. It wouldn't be the first time she stayed up late, knitting into the night until all of her sons were home. Her hair didn't turn gray until his older brothers went on their *rumspringa*. Although Gideon had vowed not to put her through the same stress, he'd failed tonight.

He latched the stall door. "I'll plan on doing Mordecai's barn chores while he's in the hospital." He glimpsed Bishop Zook studying him and gulped. "Unless you have someone else in mind to assign the work."

"I know you're capable of handling the extra chores, but are you able to avoid temptation?"

Gideon coughed into his fist. He hadn't known the bishop to be so blunt before. But now that he was a baptized member, things were different. He was expected to follow the rules of the *Ordnung*.

"You're a member of the church," Bishop Zook said sternly. "Spending too much time with the young Pinkham *maeds* would not be wise."

"I haven't forgotten our talk about being unequally yoked, and Olivia and I haven't courted since she changed her mind about joining the church." He pushed a piece of straw with the toe of his boot. He'd recited the passage in Second Corinthians about not being yoked together with unbelievers until it became permanently etched in his mind—on his heart.

"Olivia isn't the only *maedel* I was talking about," Bishop Zook said.

Sure, he and Faith had been spending more time together, but she was in the process of becoming baptized, making the same lifelong commitment to the church. It wasn't like he was developing feelings for someone who had no intention of joining the faith.

"Faith's a *gut* person, and becoming a member of the district is very important to her. She's forgone *rumspringa* in order to surrender her life to God," Gideon said.

"Then I suggest you heed *mei* warning about temptation."

❧

Faith shuddered beneath the quilt each time the wind picked up and the old oak tree's long branches scratched against the glass. She flipped over, closed her eyes, and buried her face in the depths of the feather-stuffed pillow. Olivia's snoring usually drowned out sounds that were now noticeable in her absence. Faith had shared a bedroom with her sister her entire life, and while she had sometimes wondered what it would be like to have a room of her own, tonight she wished Olivia was home, filling the silence with her nasal-clogged breaths.

Faith tried to block out the moonlight projections of fingerlike shadows crawling over the chest of drawers and along the wall. Her mind was playing tricks on her. The shadows weren't moving closer, were they?

"Think about other things," Faith told herself, then pressed the sides of the pillow against her ears. She squeezed her eyes tighter, but just as disturbing was the conjured image of Gideon that her subconscious created. She'd never experienced the warmth of his gaze or seen his dark-blue eyes twinkle so intensely as in the barn seconds prior to Olivia arriving. *It's* nett *what you think.*

Faith flopped over on her back, the bed springs squeaking. She would never get to sleep if she couldn't stop him from invading her mind. Gideon was off-limits.

※

At home, Gideon removed his boots in the mudroom and placed them next to his father's by the back door. His mother was a stickler for not tracking in dirt and had trained him well. He tiptoed into the kitchen, his mouth watering as he inhaled the lingering aroma of fried chicken and biscuits.

Moonlight filtered through the kitchen windows, lighting the way around the oversized butcher-block island in the center of the room. He stopped at the stove, lifted the lid on the warmer compartment, and smiled at his discovery. Wrapped neatly in tinfoil was the supper plate his mother had saved for him. Heat radiated from the stove, which meant his mother must have recently banked it.

Gideon removed the plate from the warmer using a quilted potholder, then carefully carried the meal to the table. Leaving the plate covered to conserve heat, he went to the cabinet for a glass. Normally he liked coffee with his meal, but water would have to do. He didn't need caffeine this late. In order to do his chores plus the Pinkhams', he'd have to get up before the birds sang. As he filled a water glass at the sink, a petite figure appeared in the doorway.

"Why are you rummaging around in the dark?" *Mamm* whispered.

"I didn't want to wake anyone." Gideon kept his voice low. He fished a fork, knife, and spoon from the drawer.

Mamm shuffled into the room barefooted, her thinning gray hair down past her shoulders. She rotated the lazy Susan in the center of the table until she located the box of wooden matches. She ignited the lamp wick, and a soft yellow glow filled the table area.

"Did you get caught somewhere in the storm?"

No hint of sleepiness in her voice. Gideon recognized this was her roundabout way of prying. He pulled a chair out from under the table and sat. "I was at the hospital most of the *nacht*. The Pinkhams were in an accident."

"*Ach*! Are they all right?"

"Mordecai broke his leg in several places. Apparently a severe enough break that his bone nicked an artery, and he lost a lot of blood."

"And Irma?"

"The *doktah* admitted her for observation, although something was said about her organs being bruised."

Mamm covered her mouth. His mother tended to be one of the organizers when a family was in crisis. In the silence, she was probably already planning the meal deliveries.

Gideon peeled the tinfoil away from the plate, then breathed in his favorite meal before he bowed his head. *Heavenly Father, bless this food. Watch over Faith tonight, and please heal her mother and father. Amen.* His prayer was short and to the point, but God was certainly aware his stomach had been growling for hours.

Mamm removed the butter dish from the lazy Susan and slid it across the table for him to lather his biscuits.

"*Danki*." He bit into the crispy chicken thigh.

Mamm pushed away from the table. A drawer

squeaked open, then closed. She draped a dish towel over his shoulder and returned to her seat. "Did you hear how long Mordecai and Irma will be in the hospital?"

He wiped his face with the soft cloth. "Nothing definite. But Mordecai's leg will take anywhere from four to six weeks to heal. And that's if all goes well." He tossed the picked-clean bones on the plate and selected the fluffier of the two biscuits.

Mamm leaned forward. "How's Olivia?"

"Shook up, I guess." He concentrated on slathering the biscuit with butter. When he thought it was safe to look up, he lifted his gaze, but dropped it immediately when her brows crinkled and the lines across her forehead became more pronounced. Give her a minute or two and she would figure another way to slip Olivia into the conversation. *Mamm* always did. Even when he'd purposely kept her, as well as the rest of his family, in the dark about who he was courting. *"Mothers know these things,"* he remembered her saying. *"I'm praying for your future fraa."* Sparing her the details, he used to simply thank her. She did, after all, only want the very best for him.

He pretended not to notice that his mother had sunk back against the chair and crossed her arms. Gideon took a bite of the biscuit and savored the flavor as the butter melted in his mouth.

"I'll arrange meals and help around the house. Do you know if Olivia and Faith will need assistance at the restaurant?"

"Faith stopped at Catherine Glick's *haus* on the way home from the hospital and talked with her about working more hours." Perhaps the inflection in his voice when he mentioned Faith gave him away, but his mother's jaw went slack for half a second.

His mouth dried, the biscuit clogged his throat. Gideon gulped the entire glassful of water in one long drink.

"You gave Faith a ride home from the hospital?"

"Actually, Beverly Dembrowski was kind enough to give us both a ride to Alpena and back to Faith's *haus*." Realizing he'd said too much, he changed the subject. "Did I tell you Bay injured his leg? He became spooked by the thunder and lightning and ended up stumbling. I *doktahed* it with Mordecai's horse liniment, but Bay was still favoring it too much to chance hitching him to the buggy. Bishop Zook and Alice gave me a ride home."

Gideon pushed up from the table. "I think I'll turn in. I promised to help with the barn chores tomorrow at the Pinkhams'." He set his dishes in the sink, then escaped the kitchen before his mother found her voice.

Chapter 14

Bloomfield Hills, Michigan
Present day

"Adriana!" Roslyn shot up in bed, clutching her chest, breathing hard, and scanning the dark room. The way her nightgown stuck to her clammy skin, it'd be easy to assume the air conditioner had stopped working sometime during the night and the July heat had soaked through the satin material. But that wasn't the case. The overhead air vent blew cold air, raising the hairs on her arms and making her shiver.

Brandon's arm came around her. "It's okay. You had another bad dream."

"This was different," she whispered.

Her husband rolled to the edge of their king-sized bed and flipped on the lamp. "I'll get you something to drink." He tossed the covers back and climbed off the mattress. "Do you want water or something stronger?"

"Water, please." Roslyn didn't want anything to interfere with her ability to recall every second of the dream. Holding her forehead, she collapsed against the pillows and closed her eyes. Why the same redheaded man? Did she know him?

Brandon returned to the bedroom with a glass

of water. He sat down on the edge of the mattress on her side of the bed and handed her the glass. "I also brought you this." He handed her a blue oval-shaped tablet.

"I don't need Xanax."

"It'll relax you."

"It'll make me forget."

"Roz." He groaned. "You're exhausted. You're scheduled for multiple speaking engagements for the foundation and talking on camera always makes you nervous. You never sleep well between tapings."

"This isn't the time to remind me, Brandon. I'm flying to New York later today to do another segment on DiAnna's show." She glanced at the clock on the nightstand and tossed the covers back. "I have to go."

Brandon followed her into the bathroom. He leaned against the granite counter and crossed his arms as she turned on the shower. He was wearing only his pajama bottoms, and she could see his thick shoulders and strong chest, exposing his love of sports and the sculpted results of extensive daily workouts.

She slipped into the walk-in closet, selected a silk blouse and linen suit, then debated which pair of shoes would best fit the occasion. Flats or heels? Nude or white? Open- or closed-toe?

"You never said what your dream was about," he said, poking his head around the closet entrance.

"A redheaded man was holding a newspaper and on the front page it read: 'Long Wait Over, Colepepper's Abducted Daughter Home Safe.'" She withheld the fact that she'd had the same dream before, even the day Adriana went missing. "What do you think it means?"

Brandon grimaced.

She should have known better and not asked. Roslyn tilted her chin and marched past him, stopping to hang her clothes on the hook outside the shower.

"Roz." He turned her shoulders so she was facing him. "I think it's clear how busy you've been."

"This was real," she rasped. "I saw her."

***

Roslyn climbed into the backseat of the Lincoln Town Car and glanced at her watch. Hopefully Chrisla wasn't running late. "Have you checked the traffic?" she asked the driver.

"Clear all the way to the airport, ma'am."

"That's a relief." Roslyn opened her compact and studied her reflection in the mirror. Makeup had disguised the dark shadows under her eyes, lifted her cheekbones, and brightened her otherwise dull complexion with a soft peachy glow. Not too bad for no sleep. Her cell phone buzzed. *Chrisla, if you're running late . . .* But a quick check of the caller ID told her it wasn't her sister.

Unless she was calling from an unrecognizable number.

Roslyn pressed the answer button. "Hello."

"Mrs. Colepepper, this is Wayne Grant from the *Detroit News*. I'm calling to see if you would be interested in doing a feature story with us." He went on to explain how he'd been assigned to her daughter's disappearance and how he was aware this Labor Day weekend marked fifteen years since her abduction.

She pretended to remember him when he mentioned how he had covered the events from the news van outside her house, but numerous reporters, from all the media venues, had covered the story. At that time, she'd been too shaken up to talk with any of them. Brandon had given the statements.

"Mr. Grant," Roslyn said, interrupting his spiel about being with the paper twenty-five years. "Assuming you'd like to do a story on the Adriana Hope Foundation, let me direct you to my secretary. She will be happy to send you press release information and provide you with everything you need."

"Mrs. Colepepper, I'm aware of your foundation and the great strides you've made helping to recover missing children, but I want to do a story on Adriana. I believe I can help prove your daughter wasn't in the car at the time it went off the bridge."

Roslyn clutched her chest and pressed the phone closer to her ear as the reporter went on to explain various forensic advancements over the last fifteen years and how 3-D computerized models have proven beneficial. ". . . and more importantly, Mrs. Colepepper, I believe if your daughter is alive, my article will help bring her home."

Chapter 15

Posen, Michigan
Present day

The morning after her parents' accident, the rooster crowed twice before Faith summoned enough energy to finally open her eyes. She lay still, blinking. Her eyes—dry, scratchy, and weighted as if with sand—were hard to focus. After a moment, she pushed back the quilt and swung her legs off to one side of the bed, but didn't immediately bounce to her feet to start the day. Her shoulders dropped. This was the time of the morning when she'd hear *Daed's* footsteps clambering down the stairs. The screen door would creak open and snap closed, and he would be on his way to the barn to start the morning chores. *Mamm* would already be up, stoking the wood stove to cook breakfast. The synchronized rhythm of their family routine triggered a smile. She glanced at Olivia's empty bed adjacent to hers, then sprang to her feet.

Churning through a long to-do list in her mind, she slipped into her beige dress, brushed her waist-long hair, then pinned the thick fluffy strands into a bun at the back of her neck. Most days she spent more time making herself presentable, but Catherine would be here shortly to pick her up for work and Faith didn't want to keep her waiting.

Downstairs in the vacant kitchen, she longed for a hot cup of coffee to jump-start her morning, but decided against taking time to prepare a pot. Besides, she couldn't possibly drink all of it.

She donned boots and lumbered to the barn. Finding the door unlatched, she hesitated a moment. The only buggy in the drive was Gideon's, which had sat there all night. She yanked open the door and went inside. The milking parlor was empty. She continued into the main section, stopping short when she came upon Gideon bent over the grain barrel, scooping feed into a tin can.

She cleared her throat, and he shot upright, dropping the grain can back into the barrel. Faith stifled a giggle. "Sorry, I didn't mean to startle you." She'd never seen him this surprised. He was certainly handsome, even temporarily frozen in fear.

"I didn't hear you *kumm* in." He furrowed his brows. "I'm glad I was able to start your day off with a *gut* laugh." He leaned into the barrel mumbling something unrecognizable.

She cleared her throat in an attempt to gain control. "Should we start over?" Not wanting to come across as mocking him, she added, "*Guder mariye*, Gideon."

"*Mariye*," he grumbled, dipping his body halfway into the barrel.

She leaned closer to the barrel but drew back as he resurfaced with the can of feed. He must not have slept well. "What time did you get up?"

Gideon shrugged. "Before the rooster crowed."

"*Danki* for coming so early to help; I appreciate it." She went to the storage shelves mounted on the back wall where the feed buckets and milking pails were stored.

He came up behind her. "I've already milked the cows and fed the hogs."

She smiled. "You were up early to get all that done."

"I wasn't sure what time you needed to go into work," he replied. "Bay's leg is better. I'll be able to drive you to work."

"*Danki*, but it isn't necessary. Last *nacht* I made arrangements with Catherine to pick me up. I thought I mentioned it to you."

His smile faded. "You might have."

She appreciated his thoughtfulness, but increasing the distance between them was best.

"Can I drive you home?" His smile returned.

"I, ah—It probably wouldn't be wise to push Bay too hard. You know, the distance to town and back, the extra weight in the buggy." *Stop babbling. Either ask him about Olivia or leave.* Faith pivoted and snatched a tin can from the lower shelf. "I should probably feed the chickens

163

and collect the eggs. Catherine will be here soon." She scooped some chicken feed out of the barrel and left the barn, her heart beating faster than the time the bull chased her in the back pasture.

⁂

Gideon peered out the barn window and tracked Faith's steps as she crossed the lawn and opened the wire door of the chicken pen. Shaking the can of corn, she teased the hens into leaving their nesting boxes. Clucking, adjusting their feathers, the chickens were fully awake with piqued interest in whatever tidbit of food Faith had to offer them.

Gideon stretched as the first light of dawn peaked the horizon. A golden glow illuminated the thin layer of fog, and beads of dew hanging from blades of grass gleamed with morning light, calling for a new day. He didn't always take time away from chores to admire God's canvas. His masterpiece. Today was different. Gideon was drawn to the beauty—drawn to the sun's warm radiance surrounding Faith. He sighed and leaned back against the barn wall as she disappeared inside the coop. Faith was off-limits. The bishop had said so when he lectured about avoiding temptation and being unequally yoked. He wouldn't go down the road of courting before she committed to the church. Not again. Faith's baptism wasn't for several weeks. He could wait, couldn't he? The rough lumber against his back suddenly pierced his cotton shirt and caused him to adjust his position. More comfortable, his eyelids fluttered. The summer heat would soon absorb the kiss of dew on nature, evaporate the morning haze, and awaken the land. He yawned. Perhaps a mug of strong coffee would wake him up, relieve him of his stupor. Maybe he'd ask Faith to make a pot of coffee and they could share it. That was innocent enough.

Gideon left the barn and strode across the yard to the chicken coop. "Faith, I wanted to tell you about something I heard . . . about Olivia."

She continued collecting eggs. "What is it?"

"I heard she's . . ." Suddenly he wished he hadn't started the conversation. The rumors about Olivia stealing money from the restaurant till would break Faith's heart. A low groan wedged in his throat.

"Gideon," she said. "You're the one who brought this up."

"And I'm thinking *nau* it was a bad idea."

She huffed—and with reason. They'd shared secrets before. He'd told Faith things he hadn't told anyone.

He massaged the knotted cords in the back of his neck. He didn't like to keep Faith in the dark, and true, he'd brought it up. "I heard a rumor. Someone—and I'm *nett* telling you who—said

Olivia was taking money from the cash register," he blurted.

She blinked rapidly several times. "Who said that?"

"Faith." He cocked his head.

Her peeved expression morphed into sadness as her eyes hooded. "That's a big accusation. I'm surprised you listen to rumors, Gideon Rohrer."

He lowered his head. It wasn't just a rumor. He'd seen Olivia counting the hidden money in the barn loft.

Faith gathered the remaining dozen or more eggs, then darted out of the coop at the same time as Catherine's buggy pulled into the yard.

Faith climbed into her cousin's buggy with the basket of eggs. "*Guder mariye.*"

"*Mariye.*" Catherine motioned to the basket. "You taking those into work?"

"I might as well. I'd hate for them to go to waste." She'd collected several dozen and could never eat them all.

"How did you sleep? I thought about you all *nacht.*" Catherine's brows creased with worry. "Perhaps you should *kumm* to *mei haus* and stay with me until your parents are out of the hospital."

Three months from turning seventeen, Faith was more than capable of staying on her own. Catherine mothered her like a much older sibling, and normally Faith didn't mind. After all, Catherine was one of the kindest, gentlest women Faith had ever known. Still, she didn't want to be shuttled to a relative's. Not when she was expected to keep up with the household chores, the garden, and the animals.

"We can talk about it later." Catherine tapped the reins and her horse lunged forward.

Faith turned her gaze out the window as Gideon was leading Bay out of the barn. The horse showed no signs of favoring his leg, which was good news. Faith slumped against the buggy seat. She had liked the idea of Bay staying in one of their stalls, knowing it'd mean seeing Gideon more regularly.

"Something wrong?"

Faith sat up straighter. "I haven't had any *kaffi*."

Her cousin chuckled. "I'll be sure to get a pot brewing as soon as we arrive at the restaurant." Catherine carried most of the conversation on their way into town, talking about the warmer weather and how well she expected her tomato plants to do this year.

Faith's thoughts were on her parents. Was *Daed* still in a lot of pain? And *Mamm*, was she doing all right? The doctor admitted her for observation, but she longed to know if anything had changed during the night.

Catherine pulled into The Amish Table's parking lot and drove around back. She stopped the horse at the hitching post, directly under the maple tree's canopy of leaves, and set the brake.

Faith climbed out. Balancing the basket of eggs in one hand, she unlocked the kitchen door. The familiar scent of day-old cooking grease mixed with a hint of bleach traveled from the kitchen as she entered the building. She made a mental note to change the grease tonight, but in the meantime, she'd remedy the issue with the aroma of freshly baked bread.

Catherine started the coffeepot while Faith set the oven to preheat, then gathered the ingredients: flour, sugar, salt, oil, and active dry yeast. She knew her mother's recipe by heart. She measured enough to make eight loaves. Bread never went to waste. Today's loaves she'd use for French toast, breakfast toast, and sandwiches. She'd lather yesterday's leftover bread with garlic butter and serve it with pork pie and chicken parmesan orders, and bread older than yesterday she would douse with herbs and olive oil and turn into croutons.

Catherine returned with a mug of coffee in each hand. "The dining room is ready. All we have to do is turn the sign at seven." She handed Faith a steaming mug.

"*Danki.*" Faith took a sip of the dark roast, bitterness disrupting her stomach, then set the mug on the counter. Eager to get the work done, she mixed the ingredients and began kneading the dough. A few minutes later, she lightly touched two fingers to the smooth dough as her mother had taught, and it sprang back. Pleased with the degree of elasticity, she divided the mound of dough into eight loaves and placed them in the pans next to the oven to rise.

"I spoke with Lois last *nacht*," Catherine said between sips of coffee. "She mentioned coming in to help out a few hours if her mother-in-law will watch the *kinner*." Catherine wet a rag at the sink. "I don't know how she does it with triplets."

Faith couldn't help but detect regret in Catherine's tone. Zachary and her cousin had courted for several years, and at twenty-eight, she must be thinking he might never propose. Especially since the women in their district married as early as eighteen and often had several children by the time they reached their late twenties. Faith shifted the conversation to another topic. "Which would you rather do today? Cook or wait tables?"

"It doesn't matter," Catherine replied.

"You're the better cook," Faith freely admitted. "I'll take the dining room, and we'll put Lois on pitting the cherries if she comes in. I seem to recall she had an easy way of removing the pits using a paper clip."

Catherine chuckled. "I made the mistake of challenging her to a race one time and I ended up doing dishes for a week."

Faith started the next batch of bread dough with Catherine's help, then placed the raised loaves in the oven to bake. At seven o'clock she turned the sign in the window, and soon, a stream of customers began to file in.

Hours later, Faith was clipping orders on the wire for two different tables when a knock sounded at the back door. "It's probably the order," she told Catherine, heading to the back. But instead of finding a delivery man outside her door, she discovered a hunched over red-haired man wearing a grungy torn shirt and paint-splattered pants. He leaned against a shopping cart filled with what looked like the entirety of his worldly possessions, which amounted to a wool coat, an umbrella, a stack of newspapers, a few empty soda cans, and a garbage bag containing things she wouldn't venture to identify.

"Can I help you?"

He flipped the cardboard sign he was holding: "Will Work for Food. God Bless You."

She didn't have a job for him, but noticing how he sniffed the air, she couldn't let him go away hungry either.

"I like the smell of baked bread," he said. "Is it still warm?"

"I'll check." Faith left him standing at the door. She wrapped a loaf of warm bread in paper towels, poured some honey into a to-go cup, then took it to the man. She handed him the loaf. "If you *kumm* back after lunchtime, I'll make you a hamburger."

A childlike twinkle lit his eyes. "Cast thy bread upon the waters: for thou shalt find it after many days." He tore the bread in half and took a bite, his eyes closing as if savoring the flavor.

Cast thy bread upon the waters . . .

As if the man could read her mind, he said, "Your kind deed has not gone unnoticed."

"But I didn't give it to you for recognition." The *ding* of the cook's bell broke Faith's attention. "Excuse me, but I have to get back to work."

"Faith," he said, gaining her full attention. "Call your mother, child. She would like to hear how you're doing."

Chapter 16

Roslyn aimed her friendliest smile at the camera and maintained it until Walter, the network director, waved his hand and called, "Cut." She held the unwavering smile a second longer, then exhaled through pursed lips as tension seeped from her muscles. Even after fifteen years of hosting foundation-sponsored functions, she had trouble talking on camera, while her friend and longtime host of the syndicated talk show, DiAnna Rogers, coolly transitioned from camera to camera. The heat projected from the floodlights raised the surface of Roslyn's skin to broiling temperatures. Following the flashing red indicator light, meant to direct her to one of the three cameras currently filming, her eyes darted around the studio until they felt crossed. But the interview was done. She'd gotten through another taping without chewing her nails to the nub. Hopefully the information she shared would increase child abduction awareness.

Roslyn glanced over her shoulder at her sister standing a few feet away from the floodlights and photo umbrellas. Chrisla smiled wide and made a thumbs-up gesture. Roslyn touched her moist forehead, sure her makeup had run down the side of her face.

DiAnna tapped Roslyn's arm. "You did great."

"Could you tell I was nervous?"

"Not at all." Her college friend flashed a camera-ready smile that Roslyn had come to know as sincere.

"You probably have to say that," Roslyn half-heartedly teased.

A female stagehand approached wearing a black shirt, black jeans, and baseball cap with the show's logo. "I'm sure our viewers were choked up like me and reaching for their Kleenex. It must be difficult to keep reliving what you've gone through."

"Thank you," Roslyn's voice squeaked. Although she'd trained herself to relive her daughter's kidnapping to a point of numbness on the air, talking about Adriana's disappearance always triggered emotional upheaval. But, for the most part, she was able to conceal the debilitating truth.

Roslyn shifted on the cushioned chair and stretched her neck so the woman could unclip the microphone from her suit lapel. An egg-sized lump remained in her throat as thoughts of her precious daughter continued to overwhelm her mind.

"You're all set," the stagehand said, making a loop of the loose cords.

DiAnna placed her hand on Roslyn's shoulder. "I know these interviews are difficult so close to Labor Day."

Unable to speak for fear she would completely fall apart, Roslyn helped herself to a tissue from the box on the table, blotted her eyes, then leaned into her friend's embrace. DiAnna's support meant a lot over the years. When the authorities closed Adriana's case, despite Roslyn's adamant refusal to accept that her child was dead, DiAnna continued to help arrange national coverage to keep the tragedy in the public eye. But all news eventually becomes old, and Adriana's body never washed ashore. People lost interest.

Roslyn blotted away more tears as her sister climbed the stage steps.

"You didn't look nervous to me, sis," Chrisla said, shielding her eyes from the glare reflecting off the floodlights.

Roslyn reached for the glass of water sitting on the table next to her and took a sip. The lukewarm water didn't do much to quench her thirst, but it did wet her dry throat, making it easier to speak. "Thanks." She took another drink, placed the glass back on the coaster, then turned to her friend. "Ahem."

"Busted." DiAnna grinned as she snapped her compact closed. "Okay, so I'm a little vain."

"A little?" Roslyn's sullen mood lifted at the sight of her friend's smile.

DiAnna erupted in laughter. "I do love having you here in New York. When are you going to sell your place in Michigan and move here?"

"I'd never be able to convince Brandon to move the Colepepper headquarters." Besides, she refused to live in a high-rise. In fact, she didn't even enjoy staying in one of their hotels for any length of time, and there she had room service.

"You're probably right," DiAnna said. "So, I take it Brandon is still keeping himself . . . busy?"

"That's an understatement," Roslyn said, attempting to soften her sarcasm with a chuckle. Brandon had immersed himself in work once the authorities closed Adriana's case, and she'd begrudged his schedule for years. Granted, he tried encouraging her to accompany him on trips, but she refused to leave the house most days, let alone Bloomfield Hills. Then, teetering on the brink of insanity, she suffered a nervous breakdown, and Brandon assigned travel duties to the company's vice president. Ten years of therapy later, when she was finally doing better—or at least, when she had learned how to fool people better—her husband had resumed business as usual. "Brandon does ask me to go along with him on trips," she felt compelled to explain.

DiAnna lifted her brows. "So why don't you go? I'm sure a long vacation would do you good."

"You should have him take you to the beach," her sister added. "You could use a little sun."

"I have the foundation to run," Roslyn said.

Chrisla cleared her throat. "That isn't the only reason."

"I also work closely with the Missing Children's Network." Chrisla and DiAnna were well aware of her extensive organizational involvement. It was common knowledge among close friends and business associates that Roslyn also arranged meetings with legislatures to lobby for nationwide traffic cam installations. Had traffic cameras been available at the time of Adriana's kidnapping, the police could have tracked the car's whereabouts instead of having to rely on bystander information coupled with random parking-lot footage from banks and other businesses. But as Roslyn had learned all those years ago, private businesses were hit or miss when it came to quality recordings.

Suddenly aware of Chrisla's and DiAnna's stares, Roslyn blew out a long breath. Her best friend and sister were not easily fooled. "Okay," she finally said, knowing she had to spill the truth. "The *Detroit News* approached me on running a story about Adriana." Seeing their confused expressions, she continued. "Apparently the reporter is retiring after twenty-five years and is doing some sort of then-and-now on twenty-five of the most important stories of his career."

"Oh, I see. He's going to feature the foundation, that's great," DiAnna said.

Roslyn rubbed her trembling hands along her linen trousers. "He told me about new technology that's been developed since Adriana's abduction. Law enforcement have specialized computer programs to recreate crime scenes. Did you know President Kennedy's assassination was reenacted? A few years back, the Discovery Channel created a 3-D crime-scene simulation where they were able to analyze blood splatters with the bullet's trajectory to determine the shooter's location. Forensic investigators were able to calculate the angles and distances and wind pattern—"

DiAnna and Chrisla exchanged worried glances.

"Adriana's body was never found—and I'm not going insane—my daughter wasn't in that car."

Chrisla reached for her hand. "No one is saying you're going insane."

"Of course we're not, sweetie," DiAnna echoed. "But what does Kennedy's assassination have to do with Adriana?"

"The computer simulation would prove she wasn't in the car." Roslyn studied their faces. She wouldn't convince anyone if she couldn't stop her hands from shaking. "I was there when they pulled that dingy, red car out of Lake Huron." She squeezed her eyes shut, but wasn't able to block the image of the compact car being lifted out of the Mackinac Straights as water gushed out from every crack and crevice and cascaded back into Lake Huron. Watching from the shoreline, Roslyn nearly fainted as the crane hoisted the 1987 Yugo to the surface.

Think on other things. You've trained your mind.

Roslyn opened her eyes and, blotting tears with the wadded tissue, she directed her attention to the stage crew moving various pieces of equipment around the studio. They were easier to focus on than Chrisla and DiAnna's pitying expressions.

Roslyn's thoughts drifted back to Lake Huron. At first the authorities believed the passenger window was lowered in an attempt to escape, but later they ruled the window was already open—most likely a means to exhaust cigarette smoke, which was why Roslyn maintained Adriana wasn't in the car. She was alive . . . somewhere. Still, every investigator Roslyn had hired believed Adriana would not have escaped through the opening. Certainly not once the car submerged underwater, and not without eyewitnesses seeing a baby ejected as the car was falling. A computer simulation would prove everything.

"If the newspaper is willing to do a feature," Chrisla said, breaking the silence, "maybe we can convince the authorities to reopen the case."

"You know I'll help any way I can," DiAnna said.

Convincing her sister and best friend that it was a good idea to have the case reopened wasn't the same as convincing Brandon. Their marriage might crumble if she showed signs of madness. He might even have her committed again. Roslyn recalled the cold words she'd forced herself to say during one counseling session. *"I've accepted reality—my child is dead."*

Chrisla cleared her throat. "What does Brandon think about the *Detroit News* reporter wanting to do a story?"

Roslyn cringed. "He doesn't know."

Chapter 17

At seven p.m. Faith still hadn't called the hospital to check on her parents, and the homeless man's words hammered her conscience. She glanced at the wall clock and wrung her hands, antsy for the last customers to leave so she could turn the sign and make the phone call.

The little bell over the door jingled as Gideon entered the building.

Faith stepped out from behind the waitress station and greeted him with a smile. "Hello, Gideon."

"Looks like you've been busy."

"*Jah*, all day. News of the buggy accident spread through town and people wanted to get an update straight from the horse's mouth." A few *Englischers* had found the play on words cute, but Faith's tongue was raw from biting it all day.

Gideon grinned. "You don't look like a horse to me."

"*Danki*. I normally avoid talking about personal stuff around the customers, but the accident brought in a flock of curious folks, and, well, we need the business." She glanced at the tables she had yet to clean off and grimaced. More dishes to add to those already piled high in the sink. "I'm afraid if you've *kumm* to drive me home, I won't be ready to leave for a while."

"I thought you might need some help." He rolled up his sleeves. "I am a pretty *gut* dishwasher."

"You forgot to say you work for hamburgers."

"That too." He winked, and she noticed his long lashes.

Heat surfaced to her cheeks. She clasped her hands behind her back and looked down at the plank floor to regroup. Gideon had a way of sending shudders down her spine when he teased her like that.

He cleared his throat and when she lifted her gaze, he motioned to the customer at the register.

Relieved to have something else to focus on, she rang up the customer, then returned to the waitress station where Gideon was pouring a mug of coffee.

"Hope you don't mind that I helped myself."

"Of course *nett*, silly." Faith picked up her mug, took a sip, then wrinkled her nose. "I don't know why *Englischers* fuss over iced coffee. This isn't *gut*." She dumped the coffee down the sink and settled for a glass of lemonade to quench her thirst. She didn't need more caffeine this late anyway. It shouldn't be too much longer before the last guests finished their meals and left. Faith leaned against the counter and sighed.

"Tired?" Gideon sipped his coffee.

She nodded. "I've been worried about *mei* parents too."

"Do you want to go see them? I'm *nett* sure what time visiting hours end, but you could probably call and make special arrangements."

"*Jah*, I should try to go." All day Faith hadn't been able to shake the feeling that something was wrong, but she wasn't ready to tell Gideon about the homeless man. It wasn't as much what the man had said as the eeriness in the way he looked at her, like he could see through her.

"Call Beverly. I'm sure if she's free, she would drive you to Alpena. I'll go with you . . . if you want me to."

Faith smiled. "I would like that." *Wrong thing to say. You can't keep relying on him.*

"*Gut*, then I'll start the dishes." He disappeared into the kitchen. His and Catherine's voices drifted into the dining room as they greeted one another.

As Faith collected dirty dishes from an empty table, the last customers pushed their chairs back and stood. She set the stack back down, then retrieved their bill, which she hadn't totaled yet, and met the man and woman at the register. After quickly adding the meals and drinks together, she presented the man with the ticket.

"I heard there was a buggy accident last night," the woman said. "Was it someone you know?"

"*Mei* parents' buggy was hit."

The woman placed her hand on her chest. "Oh, my goodness. That's awful. Are they all right?"

"They're in the hospital." She took the money the man offered and completed the transaction. "Have a nice day."

"I heard the horse had to be put down and the buggy was destroyed. That's so sad. Did they catch the person who caused the accident?"

Faith shook her head.

"I hope they find the person responsible," the woman said.

"Thank you." Faith turned the sign in the window after the woman left, glad the day was over. She gathered a load of dirty dishes and took them into the kitchen.

Catherine covered the container of sliced onions with cellophane. "Did you turn the sign?"

"*Jah*." Faith set the plates on the dirty side of the sink, giving Gideon an apologetic smile. She went to the utility closet, grabbed the mop, bucket, and broom, then filled the pail with water.

"Did you remember to lock the front door?" Catherine asked.

"I'll do that *nau*." Faith retreated into the dining room with the cleaning supplies, locked the door, then swept and mopped the floors. Before leaving the dining room, she gathered the ketchup containers from the tables. She had already filled the salt, pepper, and sugar containers and restocked the napkin holders.

Catherine was busy cleaning the prep area while Gideon was elbow-deep in the soapy water. Faith put the ketchup bottles in the refrigerator, then sidled up beside him at the sink.

He lowered a stack of plates into the wash basin. "Weren't you going to call Beverly?"

"I thought we could get the dishes done first." Faith pushed her dress sleeves up past her elbows.

"*Nett* that I don't like standing shoulder to shoulder with you," he said, bumping his arm into hers. "But I want you to call."

She did want to ask about a ride. If not for tonight, then maybe after work tomorrow. "I'll make it quick."

Years ago, Bishop Zook had approved the use of phones in businesses, stipulating it be sparing. Faith only used it for ordering supplies or when customers called in take-out orders. Olivia, on the other hand, called *Englisch* friends and chatted freely when *Mamm* wasn't around. As Faith scanned the list of phone numbers on a piece of paper hanging on the wall, the phone rang.

"The Amish Table," she said, prepared to tell the caller they were closed.

"Faith, it's *Mamm*. I thought I would give you a call before you left work. Is everything going all right?" *Mamm's* voice sounded much stronger than it had last night.

"*Jah*, everything is fine. How are you?" Faith glanced over at Gideon, who had stopped washing dishes, and pointed to the phone and mouthed, "*Mei mamm.*" Now Catherine had stopped cleaning to bend her ear Faith's way.

"I'll probably be discharged in the morning," *Mamm* said.

"That's *wunderbaar* news." Faith covered the receiver with her hand. "*Mamm's* coming home tomorrow."

"That's *gut* news," Catherine said, and Gideon echoed.

Faith pressed the phone closer to her ear. "Do you want me to call Beverly to arrange a ride home for you?"

"Beverly is already here visiting me. She's going to take Olivia home. If I am discharged tomorrow, I plan to stay with your father. I don't want to leave him alone."

"How is *Daed* doing?"

"He had a rough day. Please keep him in your prayers."

"*Jah*, of course." Faith wished she was at the hospital with them now. It was difficult to interpret her mother's tone without seeing her expression. "We've had a busy day. Catherine cooked today and I waited tables. Lois helped for a few hours, and Gideon is here *nau* washing dishes."

"Sounds like you have everything under control."

"I think so."

"I knew I could count on you," *Mamm* said.

Her mother's melancholy tone alarmed Faith. Had *Mamm* told her everything?

Mamm coughed.

"Are you all right?"

"*Jah*, it's just a cough. I won't keep you on the phone. Be sure to lock up and don't forget to take the register drawer home. Did everything *kumm* in the delivery today?"

"*Jah*, why?"

"I'm *nett* sure how busy Fourth of July will be. You might have to pick up extra things at the market if you run low." She went on to mention several items they had run out of last year, then said, "Faith, I'm very proud of how well you're handling everything. Please tell Catherine and Gideon *danki* too."

"*Jah*, I will." Noting the tiredness in her mother's voice, she wrapped up the call. "Tell *Daed* we are all praying for him and you." Faith hung up the phone and leaned her head against the wall. *Watch over* mei *parents, Lord. Heal them please so they can* kumm *home.*

"Is everything all right?" Gideon studied her.

"I just needed to hear *Mamm's* voice." Faith had fretted all day when she should have left her worries in God's hands. But the homeless man had been right in that Faith wouldn't feel relief until she spoke with her *Mamm*.

186

Chapter 18

Driving Faith home from the restaurant after cleaning and locking up, Gideon was tempted to ask her if she was also awestruck by the shades of red, orange, and yellow that painted the sky. He gripped the reins, then stole a sideways glance at her. Seated on the edge of the bench, her back arched and neck stretched, she reminded him of a blue heron eyeing a rainbow trout. Faith was eyeing something, but it wasn't the sunset. "What are you so interested in?"

"Bay doesn't seem to be favoring his leg anymore."

"*Jah*, his strides are even." Gideon worked the reins. "I've had to hold him back. He keeps stretching his neck to gain more reins."

She sank against the bench, her shoulder brushing against his. "I was a little worried when you offered to bring me to town this morning that he wasn't ready, but the liniment must have worked."

"Must have." Gideon smiled. He had other thoughts running through his mind. Thoughts he'd have to suppress for another twelve weeks. Faith's baptism classes went through September, and she wouldn't be eligible to join the church until the first weekend in October when the next baptism service was held. *Twelve weeks.* Now he wished he hadn't made that vow to wait to court her.

Bay lurched his neck and the reins slipped in Gideon's hands as the gelding's pace increased. The rhythmic *clip-clopping* of the horse's hooves against the pavement indicated his legs were stronger. Still, Gideon couldn't risk another injury. He tightened his grip on the reins, applying steady pressure to slow Bay to an easy trot.

As the sun dipped lower on the horizon, the temperature was still unbearable. A hot summer evening like tonight would be a perfect time to sit on the porch and listen to the crickets sing. Gideon was about to make the suggestion when Faith yawned.

"You tired?" he asked.

"A little." She yawned again. "What about you?"

"*Nett* yet." He could stay up all night if they were sitting on the porch together, but he would wait for another day. He slowed Bay down even more, then turned into her driveway. He shifted positions on the bench to face her. "The barn chores are already done for tonight . . ." He left enough of a pause for her to offer him a cup of coffee, but she didn't. "I'll be over first thing in the morning to do the milking."

"Gideon, you've been such a blessing to *mei* family. *Danki.*"

Sincere, but distant. Because she was tired?

She opened the passenger door.

"I'd like to give you a ride to work tomorrow," he blurted.

"Okay." She slid off the bench and before closing the door, added, "I'll let Olivia know."

Sure, her sister would need a ride too. It only made sense for him to take them both. He waited until Faith was safely inside and the lamplight shone through the window, then released the buggy brake. But something prevented him from signaling Bay to move. Unable to shake Faith's disconnected tone of voice, he set the brake once again and piled out of the buggy. He bounded up the porch steps, taking two at a time, then knocked on the door.

Answering immediately, Faith puckered her brows. "Is it morning already?" A smile tugged her lips.

Twelve weeks. What happened to waiting to tell her how he felt? Despite warning bells going off, he stepped forward. "May I *kumm* in?"

❧❦❧

Faith opened the door wider for Gideon to enter.

He wiped his boots on the braided rug longer than necessary.

"Is something wrong?" She'd never seen him this befuddled.

"Remember what I told you about Olivia?"

"Are you referring to that rumor? Gideon, I thought you were different. I thought—"

189

"It isn't a rumor," he said.

She eyed him closely. "What are you saying?"

"Will you go out to the barn with me? I'd like to show you something."

"It's getting late." Olivia was due home anytime.

"Please? It'll only take a few minutes."

Faith motioned to the door. "Okay."

They walked in silence to the barn. Gideon lit the lantern. "It's up here," he said, putting one foot on the ladder that led to the haymow.

She narrowed her eyes. "In the loft? Really?"

"Will you trust me, please?"

She did trust him. With her heart, and that was a mistake.

He didn't say anything more until they had climbed the wooden ladder and were standing in the hayloft. "It's over here." He trounced across loose hay and went to the far side of the loft where he handed her the lantern, then knelt down. After a moment of searching under the hay, he produced a jar.

"This isn't right," Faith protested. "You should put that—"

Gideon unscrewed the lid and shook the money out.

Curiosity won out despite Faith's efforts not to snoop. She knelt beside Gideon and peered at more money than she'd ever seen. "Olivia told me you two talked the other *nacht*. She said she'd been confused and you . . . understood. Did she tell you she stole this money?"

"*Nay*. I didn't talk to her—I mean, we talked down by the stalls. And yes, Olivia said she was confused. She thought something was going on between you and me and—"

"You made it perfectly clear what Olivia walked in on in the barn *wasn't* what she thought." Faith pushed off the floor. "Make sure you put everything back the way you found it." Wishing she'd never seen the money, Faith fled the loft. She ran out of the barn and back to the house.

At least he had the sense to leave. She waited until his buggy pulled out of the driveway before going into the kitchen to make a cup of tea. The kitchen counters looked like they did when there'd been a wake. Noodle casseroles, fresh-cut vegetables, a three-bean salad, pickled eggs, cucumber sandwiches, and a wide assortment of fruit, brownies, cookies, and cobblers. She only wanted a cup of herbal tea. So much food. The bowl of raspberries would certainly go to waste. Faith hadn't eaten the berry since the time her lips puffed up like a yeast muffin. The doctor said allergies could get worse over the years and next time the swelling could close her airway.

Faith filled the kettle with water, but decided against making tea. With the windows closed all day, the July heat turned the house into an oven and making a fire to boil water for tea would only add to the misery. She filled a glass with tap water, then took it and the lantern to the bedroom. Maybe she would read her Bible while she waited for Olivia to get home.

Faith opened all the bedroom windows hoping to get a cross breeze flowing, but the stagnant air didn't flutter the curtains even a little. She gazed out the window at the moon's reflection on the pasture. God's guiding light.

Lord, please protect Gideon on the road home. Keep him safe. Watch over mei *parents, and, Lord, I ask that You take care of Liv. I don't understand why she would steal or why she wants to leave the district, turning her back on our ways. I pray our parents' accident was a wake-up call and she had a change of heart. Speak to her, Lord. Amen.*

After changing into her nightclothes, Faith crawled under the bed sheets. She opened the Bible to Psalms and began reading from where she had left off last.

For thou hast possessed my reins: thou hast covered me in my mother's womb. I will praise thee; for I am fearfully and wonderfully made: marvellous are thy works; and that my soul knoweth right well. My substance was not hid from thee, when I was made in secret, and curiously wrought in the lowest parts of the earth.

Faith read a few more passages, then closed the Bible. But unable to sleep, she stared at the ceiling and listened for strange sounds. This

192

was crazy. She climbed out of bed and retrieved her sewing project, a quilted journal cover for Olivia's birthday, from under the bed. She'd only sewn a few squares when her eyelids grew heavy. Melting into the mattress, her thoughts drifted to Gideon. Her eyes shot open hearing something creak on the other side of the door. She shoved the quilting project under the covers as Olivia tiptoed into the room.

"Sorry if I woke you up."

Faith pushed up on her elbow. "I heard *Mamm* might be discharged tomorrow."

"*Nett* anymore. One of her kidneys is failing."

"Failing!"

"I wanted to stay with her but she insisted I *kumm* home. She didn't want you having to do everything by yourself." Olivia crossed to her side of the room, retrieved a nightdress from the bottom dresser drawer, then began removing the straight pins that held the front of her dress together.

"She didn't mention it when I spoke with her earlier."

"I overheard her and the *doktah* talking about possible surgery to remove it, but like I said, she didn't want me to stay."

Faith squinted at the lamp's flickering flame. The wick had burned down to almost nothing. "What time did visiting hours end?"

"I don't know." Her sister slipped off her *kapp*

and combed her fingers through her hair. "We left after the nurse brought the supper tray."

That was hours ago. Faith rested her back against the wooden headboard. "Did Beverly have car problems?"

"Nope. I was in town for a while." She walked between the two beds and plopped down on the bed, collapsing against the mattress in a moan.

"How long?"

"A few hours. Why does it matter? You weren't home when Beverly dropped me off, so I went into town."

"Catherine and I could have used your help." Faith paused, but Olivia offered no apology. "I know about your plans to jump the fence."

"Is this about Gideon? Because I told you at the hospital, I'm confused." She flipped over, the mattress springs jangling under her weight.

"It's about *Mamm* and *Daed*. They need our help at the restaurant and around the *haus*. I'm sure *Daed* won't be able to do the barn chores for a while. And if *Mamm* loses a kidney . . ."

Her sister was silent, but feigning sleep wouldn't prevent this long-overdue conversation from happening. Hard to believe she'd actually missed Olivia last night.

"I know about the money you've been hiding in the barn," Faith said.

Olivia flipped over. She glared at Faith with piercing eyes and furrowed brows, her face turning a deep red. "Keep your hands off it."

"Oh, relax. I'm *nett* going to take it." Faith leaned toward the nightstand in between the two beds and turned the lamp wick down. The escape into darkness held surprising relief. At least she'd broached the subject. Now it was up to God to work in Olivia's heart.

As promised, Gideon was milking the cow the following morning when Faith went into the barn for chicken feed. She poked her head around the wall divider where he was seated on the stool next to the cow. "*Guder mariye.*"

He glanced over his shoulder and smiled. "I'm almost done."

Her gaze fixed on the rhythmic movements of his shoulders. He had the thickest, strongest shoulders she'd ever seen. She rested her head against the wall and sighed.

After a few seconds, Gideon turned back and faced her. He cleared his throat and smiled.

Faith straightened. A flash of heat spread up her neck and settled in her cheeks. She was too old for such silliness. "I have to go collect the eggs," she stammered, then scurried over to the grain bin and scooped some corn into a can.

The chickens didn't need much. The lawn held plenty of bugs to feast on. With the flock distracted by the corn she'd scattered, she ducked into the coop. The strong stench of ammonia burned her eyes. Holding her breath, she gathered the eggs quickly. Changing the straw in the nesting boxes was another task to add to the list of chores. Other duties crowded her mind, and she mentally categorized their importance as she carefully stacked the eggs into the apron around her waist. Then, satisfied she'd collected them all, she escaped the coop. The door slammed and she leaned back against the shed wall, sucking in fresh air.

"Fumes bad?" Gideon chuckled a few feet away.

Faith nodded and wrinkled her nose as she pushed off the wall.

"When was the coop cleaned last?"

She shrugged. "Probably a month ago." *Daed* kept the hen house clean. He changed out the straw every other week and tried to wash down the concrete floors at least monthly. She didn't pay much attention until it got bad like today. Her eyes were watery and she might not ever clear the stench in her nostrils.

Gideon walked with her to the house, carrying the milk canister. Faith held the door open, then followed him into the kitchen. Olivia wasn't up, not surprising.

Gideon nodded his head at the counter. "I see a food drive was organized."

"It showed up yesterday," she said, clearing a spot for the milk canister. "Do you see anything you'd like to eat? It's going to go bad if I don't do something with it."

"*Danki*, but I've already eaten breakfast." He set the milk canister down, then inspected the different containers of food. "The brownies look *gut*."

"Help yourself. Olivia and I won't eat them all."

"Olivia's home?"

"She's sleeping in." Faith hoped the sarcasm wasn't evident. She lowered the eggs one by one into the basin.

Gideon sidled up beside her at the sink. "*Gut*."

"*Gut*?" She eyed him hard. He seemed happy, his smile almost gloating. *Focus your thoughts.* She scrubbed an egg.

"Need help?" He picked up a dish towel.

She rinsed the egg and handed it to him. Although they worked in silence, the noise going on in her head made it hard to focus. She finished washing the last egg and handed it to him to dry. "I told Olivia I knew about the money she stashed in the barn."

"What did she say?"

"That I should keep *mei* hands off it."

Gideon didn't look surprised. As if allowing her to draw her own conclusion, he set the egg in the basket with the others, then handed her the dish towel without saying anything.

"Go ahead—say it—I told you so." Faith

wiped her hands on the towel and tossed it on the counter.

Gideon picked up the basket. "Is this all you're taking into town?"

She glanced at the food. "Would you mind if we make an extra stop? I'd like to drop some of this food off at the homeless shelter."

"Sure."

Faith gathered several containers, including the raspberries. "Don't tell anyone I'm getting rid of the food."

Gideon frowned. "You mean don't tell *mei mamm* you're giving away the raspberries I picked for her?"

"*Ach*, I didn't know your mother arranged all of this."

"That's okay. She probably doesn't know you're allergic to raspberries."

"Would you like to take them back home?"

"*Nay.* We have plenty. I think what you're doing is kind."

"I'm casting *mei* bread into the water," she said.

His brows crinkled.

"It's a long story. I'll tell you on the way into town." She handed Gideon the basket of eggs, then picked up the dishes of food and headed to the door.

The ride into town went quickly. Gideon chatted about his plans to clear more land and increase his crop size. He also shared his ideas of turning his apple groves into a U-Pick farm in the future.

The volunteers at the homeless shelter were thrilled with the donation, and Faith was pleased the food wouldn't go to waste. Once they reached The Amish Table, she shifted on the bench to face Gideon. "Do you want to *kumm* in for *kaffi*?"

He shook his head. "I have fieldwork to do before it gets too hot. After that I'm going to try to work on a new watering system." He explained how laborious it was to haul water from the pump to his orchards and his idea of building some sort of holding tanks at various locations in the fields to catch rainwater.

"Your day sounds full."

"I might be tied up for a few days," he said, adding, "I'll still take care of your *Daed's* barn chores, but do you think Catherine can give you a ride to and from work?"

Her heart sank, but she forced a smile, hoping it hid her disappointment. "I'm sure she will."

He lowered his gaze and a smile upturned the corners of his mouth. After a second he looked up and locked eyes with her. "But who knows, things could change."

Chapter 19

Roslyn stared at the drawings, tears clouding her vision. Her sister had captured Adriana's image so perfectly. Every detail, from the tiny dark ringlets on her forehead to her button nose and big, expressive light-blue eyes. If Roslyn concentrated she might hear her child's sweet voice again.

"What do you think?" Chrisla asked, her voice soft.

A bubble formed in Roslyn's throat that she couldn't swallow. Her sister's heartfelt work was evident in her drawings. She glanced furtively at Chrisla, who hovered with arched brows as if seeking approval.

"I, ah . . . I see Adriana's inquisitive expression and . . ." Roslyn squeezed her eyes shut.

"What is it?"

"I see my baby sitting in that clickety cart, reaching for those raspberries." Tears trickled down her face, saltiness collecting in the corners of her mouth. She hated that her last memory was of her being short with Adriana. Frustrated with the sticky mess she'd made on her face, her hands, and her dress. None of it mattered now. Roslyn turned away from the drawings and buried her face in her hands.

"Sis." Chrisla placed her hand on Roslyn's shoulder. "I know it's hard."

How could her sister possibly understand? She didn't know what it was like to lose a child. Chrisla watched her boys grow up, watched them take their first steps, get their first haircuts. She drove them to school and went with them on field trips. Unlike Roslyn, Chrisla had the opportunity to record every inch as they grew. She didn't miss out on anything with Ryan and Hunter. Her sister *didn't* know how difficult it was . . . she couldn't.

"I have a few more sketches of Adriana I'd like to show you." Chrisla reached into her leather portfolio and removed the pages. Unrolling the next set of drawings, she arranged them in front of Roslyn. "I used old photographs of you and Brandon as teenagers to combine your features."

Roslyn stared at the age-advanced images, noticing the resemblances right away.

"In this picture, I used Brandon's strong jawline with your high cheekbones." Her sister went on to point out the combination of dominate features.

The uncanny resemblance pricked Roslyn's arms with tiny goose bumps.

Chrisla placed the next print beside the first one. "I gave Adriana your heart-shaped face and Brandon's eyes in this one."

Roslyn always knew her artsy sister was talented, but Chrisla mostly painted landscape murals. In these drawings she captured the likeness of both Brandon and her. "The pictures seem so lifelike."

"Because you see yourself."

Roslyn pointed at the teenager drawing. "Whose pouty lips did you give her?"

Chrisla smiled. "Those are definitely yours. At least I hope she doesn't have Brandon's thin lips."

Roslyn wouldn't care which features Adriana favored: full lips, big eyes, pointed chin, or slanted nose. None of it mattered.

"I also didn't give her Brandon's broad shoulders or his receding hairline." Chrisla chuckled, then, widening her eyes, she clasped her hand over her mouth. "His ears must've been burning," she said under her breath.

Roslyn glanced over her shoulder as Brandon entered the kitchen, his overnight bag and briefcase in hand, but his expression didn't indicate he'd heard Chrisla's comment. "What time is your flight?"

"Not for a couple of hours." He tossed his travel bags on the floor next to the wall, then went to the refrigerator and removed a bottle of water.

It always amazed Roslyn how little he packed for a trip. A few polo shirts, trousers, exercise clothes, gym sneakers, and shaving gear were all crammed into one bag, while any time Roslyn traveled, she packed a minimum of three suitcases—one with nothing but shoes.

Brandon uncapped the water and took a drink. "What are you two looking at?" He craned his head toward the artwork. "Nice work, Chrisla."

"Thank you. Does the girl in the picture look familiar?"

Roslyn sucked in a breath as Brandon walked over to the table, then rotated the paper to get a better view and examined it.

"Nope." He chugged more water.

Chrisla unrolled the other sketches for him to view.

Color drained from Brandon's face. He looked up at Roslyn. "What's this all about?"

"It was my idea," her sister volunteered. "In two months it will have been fifteen years since Adriana went missing. I thought maybe we could—"

Brandon glared at Chrisla with a look Roslyn hadn't seen in a long time. "What are you trying to do? Send your sister back to the—"

He cut himself off, but they all knew what he was about to say.

"The loony farm," Roslyn said. Although Mission Stone Manor wasn't a farm at all, Brandon called it that because she had spent the majority of her lengthy stay working in the greenhouse and garden. As it turned out, repotting herbs, watering plants, and pulling weeds had been more therapeutic than the group talks. Spending time alone helped her form the idea of developing a foundation in her daughter's name.

Brandon tapped Roslyn's arm. "Will you help me find my knee brace?"

He only wore his knee brace to play basketball and it wasn't often that he played the sport. "I'm sure it's in one of the cabinets in the laundry room."

He tilted his head, giving her the I-need-to-talk-with-you-alone look.

Roslyn stood. "I'll be right back, sis." She dreaded what Brandon would say about the sketches. After she returned from New York, she mentioned having the case reopened. Brandon's response had been to remind her how many kooks had called the hotline number during the original investigation. How emotionally draining each call and the hope it represented had been.

Inside the laundry room, she reached to open the cabinet where he stored his sports equipment, but he stopped her.

"I don't need my brace. I just wanted a few minutes to talk with you privately."

"Oh." Roslyn leaned against the counter and crossed her arms. *Stay calm.*

"Had you seen your sister's drawings of Adriana before?"

She shook her head. "Not until today."

"I don't understand. Why would she be *guessing* what Adriana looks like as a teenager?"

"Do you remember me telling you that a reporter from the *Detroit News* contacted me about doing a story?"

"Yes, I remember."

"They want to focus on how the foundation was started and how we've assisted recovery efforts for more than a hundred abducted children." She swallowed hard. "They also want to include an update on Adriana."

The creases along his forehead deepened. "And how do the drawings . . . ?" Inhaling a raspy breath, he averted his eyes. This was harder on him than she'd expected. Over the years, he'd always been strong, resilient, relying more on logistics than emotions.

"Chrisla thinks we might be able to get the case reopened, given the anniversary of Adriana's abduction is coming up." Roslyn hadn't fully wrapped her mind around what it would mean to have her daughter's case reopened, or even *if* she would be able to convince the authorities to reinvestigate. Since she and her sister had returned from New York, they hadn't had much time together to discuss more on the topic.

"Our daughter's case was closed more than a decade ago—for a reason," Brandon said, a noticeable quiver in his tone. "She's gone."

"Her body was never found." *Even after the long winter.*

"Yes, I'm well aware of that fact." He rubbed the back of his neck. "Roz, without having new information, I don't see them reopening a cold case. Does any of this have to do with the recent kidnapping in Cheboygan?"

"No, that turned out to be a custody squabble. The boy was taken from day care by the father without prior arrangements with the mother. He's back home now."

Brandon lifted his hand to her face, gently touching her cheek. "Adriana's been gone a long time. Her case is cold. I don't want you to get your hopes up."

Losing her child was like falling into a bottomless dark hole. The only good thing that had come out of losing Adriana was their restored marriage. Brandon had credited God for providing wisdom to become a better husband. Roslyn wished God's wisdom included pointing them to Adrianna.

"I can't . . . forget about her," she said.

"Adriana will always be remembered." He drew her into his arms. "That's why you started the foundation."

Roslyn had learned to suppress the pain, mastered fooling others into believing everything was fine, but creating the foundation in Adriana's name had only redirected her grief into assisting others. A chill made its way down her spine.

Somehow Brandon sensed it and pressed her tighter.

"You have to keep moving forward," he said barely above a whisper.

"I can't let my baby go," she sobbed, resting her head against his solid shoulders.

"I know." His voice was raspy with emotion. "It's hard for me too."

It was right to keep looking. Even if doing so meant having to weed out the kooks, as Brandon called them. Adriana was alive. Roslyn just had to find her and bring her home.

Brandon buried his face in her hair. "Should I postpone my trip?"

"No." Roslyn gently pushed back and dried her eyes. "You're needed for the merger to go through." And she needed to pursue reopening Adriana's case while he was out of town and unable to talk her out of it.

"I don't have to fly halfway around the world to sign a few legal documents. The lawyers will take care of it. Wilson will Express Mail me the forms I need to sign."

"And miss golfing on the Howth peninsula? You love Ireland. I wouldn't ask you to do that."

"It isn't too late for you to join me. You could shop in Dublin while I'm in meetings. We can extend the stay and make a real vacation out of it."

Roslyn shook her head. "I have things I need

to do here." Persuade the authorities to open Adriana's case, something she should have insisted on long ago.

Brandon's scrutinizing gaze mirrored the worried look he'd given her all those years ago.

"I'll be fine," she said, adding, "really" when his expression didn't change.

"Roslyn, I'm not going to lie. I'm worried about you. You haven't been the same since you came back from New York."

Knowing Brandon, he wouldn't leave the country without first touching base with Leon. Her brother had been on call since the day of Adriana's kidnapping. When counseling wasn't enough to snap her out of it—or to free her from what Leon had diagnosed as Prolonged Grief Disorder—her brother suggested a more intense approach and convinced Brandon she needed to be institutionalized for an extended stint. Drowning in despair, Roslyn hadn't protested. Besides, the accommodations were more spa-like than the clinical straitjacket surroundings she had envisioned, but even those doctors couldn't take the pain away. When she first arrived at Mission Stone Manor, the interpersonal psychotherapy, psychiatrist's mental probing, and the mandatory group chats almost pushed her beyond return. But she adapted.

"I'll cancel the trip. I don't want to leave you alone."

"I'm not going to fall apart again," she protested. "I'm much stronger now. I won't allow it."

He studied her a moment. Probably wondering if she'd stopped taking her medication, slipped back into depression. Far from it. Chrisla's drawings had given her weary soul a reason to hope.

Roslyn rose to her tiptoes and planted a soft kiss on his jaw. "You need to get going or you'll miss your flight." Before he objected, she gently tugged his arm and led him back into the kitchen.

Thankfully, Chrisla had had the forethought to put the drawings away.

"Are you going to be in town this week?" Brandon asked her sister.

"He's worried about me being alone," Roslyn explained.

"The boys have a swim meet on Saturday, but it's in town." Her sister wiggled her brows at Roslyn as if trying to prompt more information.

"Good. Do you mind watching over my wife? See that she eats."

Roslyn rolled her eyes. Brandon always compared her to a kite—paper thin and easily blown away in a stiff breeze.

Chrisla looped her arm with Roslyn's. "Would you like to come for pot roast tonight?"

"Sure. Thank you."

"And the boys would love you to come to their swim meet."

"Fine." Roslyn stooped and picked up her

husband's bags. "Now that that's settled, please don't worry about me, Brandon." A smile underscored her words. "Okay?"

He nodded and a faint smile appeared.

"C'mon," Roslyn said as she led the way to the door.

"I'll call you." He kissed her lightly on the lips, then headed out to the garage.

Roslyn closed the door and spun to face her sister. "Where did you put the drawings? I need to see them again."

Chrisla removed the artwork from her leather portfolio, spaced the drawings over the table, then stepped back. "So, I take it Brandon's supportive of having the case reopened."

"No, but we're going to get the ball rolling while he's out of town."

Roslyn studied the pictures. Which, if any, of Chrisla's renderings were accurate? Adriana's big blue eyes stared back at her. "My sweet girl, if you're out there . . . Mommy's going to find you and bring you home."

Chapter 20

Posen, Michigan
Present day

"The customers have all left," Faith said, entering the kitchen with an armload of dirty dishes.

Catherine looked up from scrubbing the grill. "Did you flip the sign?"

"I will after I get these soaking." Faith lowered the stack into the basin. It'd been a hard day, especially without Olivia. Her sister arrived late, waited tables during the lunch rush, then complained of a headache and went home. But even though they were busy, Faith and Catherine worked as a team and the day sped by.

Catherine brought the dirty frypan over to the sink. "You think Olivia will feel better by tomorrow?"

"Something tells me *nay*. I'm sure she'll want to do something with her *Englisch* friends since it's the Fourth of July."

"I have to say, Faith, I'm impressed how well you've handled the weight and responsibility of the restaurant with your parents in the hospital. At the same time, I'm disappointed in Olivia. She's older than you, and she should have taken the brunt of the load. Instead, she's more interested in her *rumspringa*."

Faith considered telling Catherine about the money stashed in the barn, but decided it was best to change the topic. "If today was any indication of how busy the holiday weekend is going to be, we're going to need more help. Maybe we can stop by—" Faith sucked in a sharp breath as the back door swung open, then closed.

"Just me," Gideon called from the back. His boots scuffed the floor as he strolled out from the shadows of the storage shelving and smiled at Faith. "*Hiya*."

"Did you fix your crop watering problem?"

He shook his head. "*Nett* totally."

Catherine stepped away from the stove. "Hello, Gideon. Did you *kumm* to help?"

"Absolutely." He sidled up beside Faith at the sink and began rolling up his sleeves. "Busy day today?"

"*Jah*, but we need more days like today." She'd rather go home exhausted from being on her feet all day than go home exhausted from watching the clock tick with no customers to serve. "I feel bad you're always put to work when you *kumm* here."

"I wouldn't turn down free labor if I were you."

She chuckled. "Oh, trust me. I'm *nett* a fool." Except she *was* a fool, falling in love with her sister's *bu*.

He motioned to the sink. "I'll take over here

if you want to help Catherine and Olivia."

"Olivia went home early with a headache, or so she said." Faith spun toward the double doors and spoke over her shoulder as she pushed them open. "But *nau* that you're here, I have things to finish in the dining room."

Noticing the sign hadn't been flipped, Faith went to the front window. As she reached for the sign, the bell over the door jingled. "I'm sorry, but we're—"

A gloved hand with a turpentine stench covered her mouth and something cold pressed against the side of her head.

"Open the register," the man growled under the bandana draping the lower part of his face. He shoved her forward, then slapped a canvas bag on the display case. "Fill it."

Her hands trembled, pressing the buttons on the register.

The kitchen door whooshed open. "Catherine thought she heard—" Gideon halted midstep as the masked man slammed Faith's back against his chest.

"Stay back!" He pressed the gun barrel harder against her head. "I'll put a bullet through her skull!"

Gideon lifted his hands, soap suds dripping down his arms. "Let her go."

The man's grip tightened over her mouth as he aimed the gun at Gideon.

"Don't hurt him." His soiled glove muffled her voice, her plea in vain. *Lord, help us!*

"Put the money in the bag," he shouted at Gideon.

Gideon's hands shook as he emptied the cash from the drawer.

Don't shoot. Oh, Lord, stop him, please.

The gunman snatched the bag, but instead of releasing her, he pushed her toward the door.

No! She wouldn't let him take her. Not outside. Not in his vehicle. If he was going to kill her, she wanted to die here. Faith jabbed her elbow into his ribs, which seemed to irritate him more. His hand clamped down hard over her nose and mouth, blocking her airway. Dots of bright lights muddied her vision. She wasn't aware of the door opening until a red-haired man appeared at the threshold.

The newcomer approached the gunman. "Release the woman," he said authoritatively. "You're not going to shoot. Hand me the weapon."

In a split second, the gunman turned the gun on the red-haired man. *Click. Click. Click.* The man looked at the gun, then tossed it and released Faith before fleeing the restaurant.

Between hiccupping gasps, her legs wobbled and the room spun.

Gideon's strong arms pressed her against his chest. "It's over. You're safe, Faith. You're safe," he repeated.

Burying her face in the crook of Gideon's neck, she closed her eyes and let his soothing words melt the tension from her muscles. She was safe. It was over. *Lord,* danki *for keeping us safe and for sending the red-haired man to help.* Faith leaned back to look Gideon in the eyes. "Where's the man?"

"He ran off with the money. I'm sorry, Faith."

Tears washed over her face as she scanned the room for the homeless man. "Where's the man with red hair?"

Catherine pushed through the double doors. Her brows creased and worry lines etched her forehead. "Are you two okay?"

Faith broke from Gideon's embrace and, though she turned her attention to her cousin, she could still feel Gideon's eyes on her. "We are *nau.*"

Catherine rushed over to Faith and enveloped her in a hug so tight the air left her lungs. "I called the police. They should be here any minute."

Faith made a sidelong glance at Gideon, who was taking a few deep breaths. He'd been shaken as well.

A short time later, Officer Porter arrived. He collected the gun, then took notes as Faith and Gideon gave a full account of the event.

"The man's gloves smelled like turpentine or maybe gasoline." Faith's stomach knotted.

"Forensics should be able to get a sample of residue off the gun." He picked up the evidence

215

bag containing the weapon. "I'll need an idea of how much money was stolen for the report."

"I hadn't tallied today's receipts yet. Should I do that *nau*?" Faith wiped her shaky hands on her dress. She wasn't sure she could concentrate on the sales figures at the moment. Perhaps Catherine or Gideon could do the calculations.

"I'd like to ask you about the red-haired man you mentioned." The officer glanced at his notepad. "Did he leave at the same time as the gunman?"

Faith nodded. He'd left before she could thank him. The bold man had placed himself in harm's way and demanded the robber put the gun down as if he had authority over him.

As the policemen dusted the doorknob, the doorframe, the glass display case the register sat on, and numerous other objects in the room, Faith added up the meal tickets. When she finished counting, she asked Catherine to do the same. Catherine's figure matched Faith's. Clearly it'd been one of their busiest days all year, and now the money was gone. What would her mother think of her now? Just yesterday *Mamm* had praised Faith on how well she'd been doing at work.

Fighting back the tears, Faith escaped into the kitchen.

Gideon wasn't many steps behind her. "Are you okay?"

She shook her head. "*Mei* parents needed that

money to pay bills. They trusted me to run things and I let them down."

He tipped her chin up with his thumb. "Don't blame yourself. This isn't your fault."

She blinked, releasing the tears that weighted down her lashes. "I'm glad you were here, Gideon."

He cupped her face and brushed his thumbs against her wet cheek. "I'm going to drive you to work each day and be here before closing to take you home."

"Gideon, you have water tanks to build. You don't have to—"

"Shh." His gaze deepened. "Nothing matters more to me than your safety. Nothing."

A slew of emotions bombarded her all at once and she broke down sobbing.

Gideon took her into his arms. "Everything's going to be okay," he said, soothing her sorrows away.

After a moment, she pushed back and wiped her tears. "*Danki*, Gideon."

He smiled. "It will get better."

She nodded, though she wasn't sure things could. *Dishes.* Faith pushed up her sleeves and went to the sink. If she hurried, she could get them done before the police finished dusting for fingerprints.

"I'll wash." Gideon joined her at the sink.

Chapter 21

The morning following the robbery, Faith's hands trembled as she worked the key to unlock the back door of the restaurant.

Concern etched Gideon's face. "Are you going to be okay?"

"*Jah*." She faked a smile.

"I'm staying." He rolled up his shirt sleeves.

"Gideon, *nay*." She had to press through the day despite her balled-up nerves. Things would return to normal, she hoped.

"It's Fourth of July," he reasoned. "You might get busy."

She might get used to him facing her fears for her too. She followed Gideon into the dining room, but froze when an image of the gunman's masked face invaded her mind.

"Show me how to work this contraption." Gideon pointed at the coffee machine.

"You can't hover over me all day every day."

"Let's just concern ourselves with today," he said matter-of-factly without looking up from inspecting the buttons on the coffee machine. He picked up the pot. "I fill this with water, right?"

She gave in and nodded. "I supposed I'd be a fool to turn down help."

"I'd say so."

Faith measured the coffee, started the brewing process, then retreated into the kitchen to help Catherine, who had already started mixing the bread dough.

The morning went by smoothly. They managed the breakfast crowd without Olivia's help. Her sister arrived around lunchtime, though she started the shift complaining about having a headache.

Once the lunch crowd thinned, Faith made Gideon a grilled Rueben sandwich and fries. But as he ate, she caught him eyeing the wall clock more than once. "Gideon, you don't have to stay. You can take the sandwich with you if there is something you need to do."

"It can wait." He took a bite of the sandwich.

"We can manage." This Fourth of July hadn't been as busy as other years. "I feel bad for taking up so much of your time."

"Don't." He kept eating, and when he finished, he washed the dish.

Faith strode across the kitchen and peered through the window. The room was empty except for Olivia, who was dusting the display case, and Catherine, who was visiting with Zach. Faith faced Gideon. "There isn't anyone here. I know you have things to do."

He glanced up at the clock. "It shouldn't take me long."

"Gideon, I can get a ride home from Catherine."

He headed toward the back door. "I'll be back."

Once Gideon left, Faith went into the dining room. Without customers to overhear her, she could tell Olivia about the robbery. But the moment she walked into the room, Olivia begged off the remainder of the day, claiming her headache had worsened. Faith had overheard her sister on the phone with her *Englisch* friends earlier, talking about a barbecue and going to Rogers City to watch the fireworks.

"Go," Faith said. "I hope you feel better." At least Olivia had worked a few hours today. Faith used the downtime to peel potatoes and chop vegetables for tomorrow's stew. Her thoughts bounced from the gunman to the red-haired man, who would have been shot had the gun not jammed, to the stolen money and what her parents would say about the matter. Fretting over things she had no control over had worn her out. By the time Gideon returned at the end of the day, she was emotionally exhausted.

Catherine seemed pleased when Gideon rolled up his sleeves to help. Faith suspected Catherine and Zach had plans after work, the way she was hurrying to *reddy-up* the kitchen. She didn't even leave the grill on long enough to see if Gideon was hungry.

"Would you like me to warm up some *yummasetti* or pork pie, Gideon?" Faith asked.

Gideon stopped whistling. "I'm *nett* hungry."

Catherine wasn't the only one in a hurry. Gideon scrubbed the pots and pans at record speed. He pulled the sink stopper. "Done."

"Me too," Catherine announced.

Faith put away the dishes. "Let me check the front door one more time." She'd already triple-checked the lock, but checking one more time wouldn't hurt. Dead bolt in place, she scanned the room. The floors were swept and mopped, fresh place mats and napkin-rolled utensils were in place, and the coffeemaker was unplugged. The pie carrier was unloaded, and she'd wrapped the remaining slices in cellophane earlier, then stored them in the refrigerator. Satisfied the restaurant was ready for tomorrow, she returned to the kitchen.

"Would you like a drink to go?" she asked Gideon.

"Lemonade, please."

Faith filled to-go cups with drinks. "How about a piece of cherry pie?"

"Sounds *gut*, but let's take it to go."

"Catherine, what about you?"

"None for me, *danki*." She removed her apron and hung it on the hook.

Faith placed the pie in a to-go container while Gideon grabbed plastic forks, napkins, and straws. At the door she looked around the kitchen, then pressed the code to set the alarm, flipped off the lights, and locked the door.

"See you tomorrow." Catherine hurried across the parking lot to her buggy.

"I think she has important plans," Faith whispered to Gideon.

"*Mei* reason for hurrying tonight too," he said.

Mosquitoes buzzed around Faith's ears as they crossed the parking lot. Dusk was always the worst time of the day for the pesky creatures. In her parents' buggy she used to stash a small container of cedar leaf oil, which, dabbed on behind the ears, neck, wrists, and ankles, served to repel mosquitoes.

He untied Bay from the post. "Are you in a hurry to get home?"

"Why?"

He tossed his head and chuckled. "Do you always have to ask why?"

Gideon had commented more than once that she did too much thinking, and while she'd be apt to agree with him, it wasn't easy to turn off her thoughts. "I suppose I do have a curious nature, but seriously, why do you ask?"

He released the brake and, without saying another word, tapped the reins.

The stores on Main Street were closed for the holiday with the exception of the small party store at the edge of town. Anyone who wanted to watch the fireworks drove to either Rogers City or Alpena. Posen never managed to raise enough funds, and money earmarked for the Potato

Festival in September was sacred in this town.

Within a few minutes, he turned onto Leer Road, but as they approached her farm, he didn't slow down. Faith nudged his arm. "So, why are you being secretive?"

"Curiosity getting the best of you, is it?"

"You just passed *mei haus*."

They came to US-23 and he turned to the left. A few miles later, before the Calcite limestone quarry and Rogers City, Gideon pulled into an unpopulated roadside park and set the brake. "I thought we could eat our pie at one of the picnic tables." He gazed up at the sky. "It's a clear *nacht*. Maybe we'll be able see some fireworks."

"That's a lovely idea." Now it made sense why he was in such a hurry to leave the restaurant.

Gideon got out and tied Bay to the sign stating the park hours. "There's a table closer to the water," he said before stopping momentarily at the back of the buggy. He circled around to the passenger side and offered to carry the pie container.

Faith carried the drinks as she walked alongside him on a sandy foot trail, the waves of Lake Huron growing louder. Mosquitoes buzzed around her head, but with her hands full it was impossible to swat them away. She rubbed her ear on her shoulder, which shooed them away briefly.

Gideon smiled. "I brought a citronella candle,"

he said, lifting a glass jar. "Once we get to the table, I'll light it."

The pesky mosquitoes shouldn't be out much longer now that it was dark, but it was nice he'd thought to bring the candle. A popping sound in the distance caught her attention. Blues and reds lit the sky.

"You're right about it being a clear *nacht*," she said. The view was even better closer to the water. They opted not to sit at the picnic table but sat on a large piece of driftwood on the sand instead.

Faith removed her shoes and wiggled her toes in the cool sand. "I haven't been to the lake in a long time." She lifted her face into the wind and breathed in the dank scent. "I love the sound of waves washing ashore, don't you?"

"*Jah*," he said, hovering over the candle while striking a match. "Other than it's too windy this close to the water to keep the candle lit."

"That's okay." The mosquitoes weren't too bad, and the moonlight reflecting off the water and the fireworks provided enough light. She handed him one of the drinks, then pointed to the sky as more fireworks went off. "Ooh, they're so pretty. That one too."

"Too bad we couldn't have gotten a little closer to where they're being set off."

"*Nay*, this is perfect." Nothing could top being on the shoreline of massive Lake Huron and digging her toes into the sand while sitting next to Gideon.

He gently tapped her forearm with a fork, then rested the pie container on his knees and opened it. "Did you talk with your parents today?"

"*Nay*. I can't talk with them without telling them about the burglary, and if I tell them about that, they would only worry."

"They'll hear about it from someone else. Don't you think it'd be better coming from you?" Gideon stabbed his fork into the pie and began to devour the treat.

She leaned closer and took a forkful of pie, getting mostly crust. "Can we talk about something else?"

He pointed to the pie with his fork. "This is really *gut*."

"*Danki*, I used your cherries." She watched another firestorm of color dance across the sky. "I'm worried *mei* parents will be disappointed in me," she said. "I should have locked the door before cleaning off the tables."

"It was a mistake." He jabbed at more pie. "You checked the door at least three times tonight."

"Four."

"See, you're already more conscientious."

"But the money is still gone and that's *mei* fault."

He motioned to the pie. "You stopped eating. Don't you want more?"

"I'm *nett* very hungry."

"Has it crossed your mind that maybe your . . . thoughts are too consumed with money?"

"I don't think I'm consumed," she said. He should know money is an important factor in business.

"Maybe that's the wrong word. Too focused. Too worried." He shrugged. "You do talk about finances a lot."

Faith looked up at the dark sky. "I think the fireworks show ended."

"Maybe." He tilted the take-out container her direction. "Last bite. You want it?"

"*Nay, danki.*" Her stomach had soured from all the talk about her obsessive thoughts.

He dove his fork into the remaining pie, chewed it slowly, then licked the fork clean. "*Danki*, your pie was delicious." He took a drink of his lemonade.

"I'm glad you enjoyed it." She picked up her shoes, the empty drink and pie containers, and stood. "We should probably go."

"*Nau?*" He scrambled to his feet and followed her to the trash can. "Faith, we haven't had much time alone." He reached for her hand and held it. "I want to spend time with you."

"You do?" Faith's eyes darted from his to the sky as she struggled to compose herself.

"You sound surprised."

A burst of popping noises echoed, followed by

a spray of cascading silver and gold sparkles lightening the dark sky. Faith smiled. "That one seemed on top of us."

Without looking up, he stepped forward, closing the distance between them. "I wasn't watching the fireworks."

He leaned in closer, his warm breath fanning her neck triggering a pleasant shudder. Something had gotten into him—into her as well. *Kiss me already.*

He touched her cheek lightly, tracing her jawline.

"Gideon," she rasped.

Twigs snapped behind them. A flashlight flared in their direction. "I'm sorry, folks. The park hours are dawn to dusk."

Faith recognized the police officer's voice as one of the regulars at The Amish Table. Officer Porter, the officer who had taken their statement last night after the robbery. He knew most of the Amish in their district, her mother, father, probably Gideon's mother, and the bishop.

Gideon moved in front of Faith. "I'm sorry, Officer. We lost track of the time."

"You two should head home before it gets much later. Fourth of July is notorious for drunk drivers."

"Yes, sir." Gideon placed his hand on Faith's lower back and guided her toward the trail.

The officer aimed the flashlight toward the

path. "How are your parents doing?" he asked Faith once they reached the parking area.

Better than she was doing at the moment. "*Mei* father is still in the hospital recovering from leg surgery." She fought to suppress the nervous quiver in her voice. "*Mei* mother has internal bruising and problems with one of her kidneys."

"I'm sorry to hear that."

Gideon opened the passenger door for Faith. "Have you found the driver who ran them off the road?"

"Not yet, but we have a few leads we're working on."

"What about the man who robbed The Amish Table last *nacht*?"

"That's still under investigation too."

Faith slid onto the bench and cowered in the shadow of the lamppost while Gideon talked more with Officer Porter about the accident. After a few moments, Gideon was in the buggy and they were headed down the road. "Sorry I didn't realize how late it'd gotten," he said sheepishly.

❧

Traffic on US-23 kept Gideon focused on the road. Faith hadn't so much as made a peep since they'd left the roadside park.

He glanced at Faith, arms hugging herself and slouched with her head against the door. "You *kalt*?"

"*Nay*, I'm fine."

She wasn't fine. "You upset?"

Faith adjusted her position and wrung her hands together. "I wish the officer hadn't shown up."

Me too.

"The officer knows *mei* parents," she continued.

Her melancholy tone pricked his conscience. "Are you worried about your baptism?"

She shrugged.

"We haven't done anything wrong." Gideon divided his attention between watching the road and trying to glimpse Faith. "Don't fret, okay?"

She sighed heavily. "Okay."

It probably wasn't the best time to ask about tomorrow, but he did anyway. "Do you want to go fishing after work?"

Faith shifted on the seat to face him. "Do you *nett* care at all what Olivia will think of us spending so much time together?"

"Nope." He kept his eyes on Bay as a car passed. "Does that bother you?"

"*Nay*—well, *jah*, a little." She huffed out another breath and turned to look out the passenger window. "Olivia more or less indicated she might be ready to join the church."

"When?" Gideon said.

"The other day. I told her we were only friends."

Even focused on the road, he sensed her gaze burrowing into him. Dare he admit to wanting more than friendship? Gideon held his words until he pulled into her driveway and stopped Bay. "Faith, I'm *nett* in love with Olivia. I'm happy if she chooses to join the church, but I couldn't love or marry someone who stole money, especially from her parents."

Faith lowered her head and hand-pressed the folds of her dress.

He reached for her hand. "So what do you say about going fishing with me?"

❧❦❧

"I had a nice time watching the fireworks with you tonight, Gideon," Faith said softly.

"I had a nice time too." He gently squeezed her hand. "What's wrong?"

Her heart thumped against her ribs. If only this moment could last forever. She slipped her hand out from his. "You're basing your decision about Olivia on rumors."

"Let's *nett* talk about Olivia. I want to spend time with you."

Faith glanced out the side window of the buggy at the house. Dark, no sign of activity. Just as she suspected, Olivia hadn't gone home from work with a headache. Her sister had lied. Was she also lying about reconsidering Gideon's proposal? Joining the church?

"I can't go fishing with you. *Nett* when . . . *Gut nacht*, Gideon." Faith climbed out of the buggy and hurried up the porch steps. If she sat with him any longer, she would change her mind. She grabbed the doorknob but stopped to draw a deep breath. After having a gun pointed at her yesterday, going inside a dark house rattled her nerves.

Gideon hiked up the steps behind Faith. "Let me go in first."

Relief washed over her as she stepped aside. Once inside, she lit the lantern, then went to the cabinet next to the sink and removed a water glass.

"Do you want me to stay until Olivia comes home?"

She shook her head.

"Your hand is trembling."

So were her insides. Faith filled the glass with water and took a drink. "I'm better *nau*. You can go home."

Gideon inched closer. "I thought you were brave yesterday."

She shook her head. "I was terrified."

"*Jah*, me too." He clasped her upper arms. "I felt helpless. He held a gun to your head and I didn't know what to do."

Her eyes burned as memories came to life again of the man's glove over her mouth and cold steel pressed against her temple.

Gideon ushered her into his arms. "Please, don't think about it."

If only letting go of the memory was that easy. She rested her head on his shoulder a few moments, then mustered enough courage to break away. "It's getting late. You should go."

"Are you sure you don't want me to stay until Olivia comes home?"

Faith nodded. "I'll see you tomorrow?"

"Bright and early." He made his way to the door. "I'm bringing *mei* fishing poles. You need a break from all the stress."

"We'll see." First she wanted to find out if Olivia was still in love with Gideon—if she planned to stay Amish. Faith wasn't about to be the reason her sister jumped the fence.

Hours later, Faith ambled up the stairs to bed, yawning. Waiting up for Olivia to come home from the fireworks had been a mistake. Faith could have been asleep hours ago, but she needed answers. She slipped into her nightdress and climbed under the covers. Halfway through her prayers, she nodded off.

Footsteps on the stairs awakened Faith. The door creaked open, and moonlight spilling in through the window highlighted her sister's figure.

Faith pushed up in bed. "Olivia, where have you been? You left work because you had a headache."

"I went to watch the fireworks with friends." She changed into her nightclothes, tossing her dress on the floor.

"The fireworks ended hours ago."

"Faith, let it be." Olivia's bedsprings squeaked as she plopped down.

Faith rubbed her eyes. "What time is it?"

"Three."

Faith growled under her breath. "I suppose you're *nett* going into work today."

"*Nett* if you keep talking to me."

"The restaurant was robbed," she blurted.

"What! When?"

"The *nacht* before last a man wearing a bandana over his face came in after we closed and held a gun to *mei* head. He took the money from the till."

Olivia was silent a long moment. When she spoke, her words sounded like they were caught in her throat. "Why didn't you tell me?"

Faith refused to make excuses. "You left work early with a headache, which I gather was a lie. I thought you were ready to give up your *rumspringa* and join the church."

Chapter 22

One week after the restaurant was robbed, Gideon flipped through the pages of the *Detroit News* as he waited for the coffee to brew at The Amish Table. With Catherine late and Olivia a no-show, he wasn't about to leave Faith alone. He skimmed over the Flint water contamination problems and stopped on a story featuring farmer's almanac historical weather predictions and today's report expecting partly cloudy, high of eighty-four. He needed to water his blueberry bushes.

The aroma of fresh coffee filled the dining room. Gideon poured two mugs, adding cream and sugar to Faith's. He headed into the kitchen where she was busy making bread dough.

"*Kaffi's* done." He set a mug on the counter next to where she was working.

"*Danki.*" She sifted flour over the counter, then dusted her hands.

Watching her work reminded him of his mother. A knot formed in his stomach. "Do you have a few minutes you can spare before Catherine arrives? I want to ask you something."

"I will as soon as I divide the dough." She plopped the dough onto the countertop and began kneading it. A few minutes later, several bread pans were positioned near the stove and left to rise. Faith washed and dried her hands, then picked up her mug and blew on the coffee. "What did you want to ask me?"

"Did you sleep okay last *nacht*?"

"Are the dark circles under *mei* eyes that bad?" She smiled sheepishly before taking a sip of coffee.

"*Nay*." He just couldn't think of how to bring up having supper with his family when she'd already turned down fishing with him after work.

Faith lowered the mug. "What did you want to talk about?"

"I sorta promised *mei mamm* we'd have supper with her." He cringed. "Tomorrow."

Faith crinkled her brows. "We—as in you and me?"

He nodded. Bringing a *maedel* home to have supper with the family was a first for him. In their district courting was usually more private. "*Mamm's* curious—about us," he confessed. "In case you haven't noticed, it's been over a week since I've been home for supper—*nett* that I'm complaining."

"Curious about *us*—what does she think is going on?"

He didn't quite understand if that quiver in her voice was panic, fear, or excitement. Perhaps this was a mistake. "I told *Mamm* it might *nett* be possible for you to get off work, and if you can't then—"

"I'll see if I can arrange someone to work for

me." She smiled. "It's nice that you asked."

He blew out a breath, then felt silly for not covering up his nervousness better. "Ever since I told *Mamm* about the robbery, she's been worried about you—and Olivia."

"Oh, I see." Faith's smile deflated. "You invited Olivia too?"

"I didn't, but I'm *nett* sure—"

A hard knock on the back door caused Faith to jump. Her eyes grew large and she swallowed hard.

"Stay here." Gideon went to the back door and called, "Who is it?"

"Catherine."

He unlocked the dead bolt and opened the door.

"I'm so glad you thought to lock the door." Catherine set a basket of vegetables on the counter. "I thought we could make vegetable soup and use the rest in a potpie."

Faith stepped forward, her eyes widening. "This is very generous."

"I made a few stops on *mei* way. The turnips are from Patty and the carrots, celery, and onions are from Noreen's garden. Every little bit helps." Catherine removed an apron from the wall hook.

"*Jah*, it sure does." Faith turned toward the dining room and spoke over her shoulder. "I'll turn the sign."

Gideon joined Faith in the dining room. "Would you like me to stay longer?"

"*Danki*, but Catherine and I will be okay." She

flipped the sign, then unlocked the front door, her hands shaking.

Gideon groaned under his breath. Two women shouldn't be running this place alone. Where were Olivia and the others? His mother made it her mission to organize extra helpers, but no one had arrived and he refused to leave Faith until someone else showed up. Suddenly, chatter filtered into the dining room from the kitchen. He exchanged a glance with Faith, then rushed through the swinging doors.

"*Hiya*, Faith," Lois said.

Alice donned an apron. "We *kumm* to lend a hand."

Catherine came around the refrigerator with a bowl of shredded potatoes. "We have extra help today. Isn't it *wunderbaar*?"

Faith smiled. "*Jah, danki*." The bell over the front door jingled, drawing her attention back to the dining room.

Following Faith, Gideon recognized the local coffee drinkers as the *Englischers* headed to the round table.

Faith started filling coffee mugs as more locals arrived. "Gideon, I'll be okay."

"I, ah . . ." The blueberry plants and apple orchard needed watering, yet he wanted her to give him a reason to stay.

She lifted her brow. "You don't have to hover over me."

"I'm hovering *nau*?" He leaned back as if offended and exaggerated a frown. Hearing her soft chuckle brought a smile to his face. "I'll see you tonight—that is, if you still want me to drive you home?"

Her cheeks turned rosy. "*Jah*, I'll see you later."

Midafternoon, Faith was refilling coffee mugs at the corner table when a man she'd never seen before entered the restaurant. He removed his Tigers baseball cap, exposing gray thinning hair, and took the table in the back of the room next to the window.

Faith returned the coffeepot to the warmer, then took the newcomer a menu. "Would you like something to drink?"

"Coffee please."

She went back to the waitress station, filled a mug with coffee, then brought it to the man. "Do you need a few more minutes?"

"I'm ready." He closed the menu. "I'll have two eggs over medium, bacon, and potato pancakes."

"The potato pancakes come with our special sour cream and cheese sauce, is that okay?"

"Can I have it on the side, please?"

"Of course." Faith noted the request, then collected his menu.

The doorbell jingled and more customers entered. "Sit anywhere you like. I'll be with you in just a minute." Faith went into the kitchen, tore off the carbon copy, and handed the yellow slip to Catherine. "Sauce on the side, please."

"Are you getting busy?" Alice asked.

"It's starting to pick up a little." Faith wished it was busier. The restaurant didn't generate much revenue on just coffee drinkers and, outside of the recent newcomers, it'd been slow. She returned to the dining room and waited on the new table of customers.

A short time later, Catherine dinged the cook's bell announcing the meal was ready for pickup. Faith gathered the dishes, then served the man gazing out the window. She placed the meal before him. "Is there anything else I can get for you?"

He eyed the food. "This looks great."

"I hope you enjoy."

More customers arrived. It didn't take long before the restaurant was crowded. Faith tended to the tables and then walked the coffeepot around the room and refilled people's mugs.

"These are the best eggs I've ever eaten," the gray-haired man seated at the window seat said when she returned to his table.

"Thank you. I gathered them this morning."

"Farm fresh, that's wonderful."

"I baked the bread today, and the potatoes are locally grown," she added.

He pushed the plate aside. "I'll take another order."

"Of eggs?"

"All of it." He took a sip of coffee, then extended the mug for her to refill.

She'd never had anyone reorder a complete breakfast. Catherine would be pleased the man liked his food enough to order seconds. She rushed his request into the kitchen, loaded a tray with meals that were ready, and served the other customers. Catherine took no time to prepare another plate for the hungry man.

"Ma'am," he said, fiddling with his phone, "would you mind if I take your picture with the food? I'm a reporter for the *Detroit News* doing a story on back-road getaways and local small-town restaurants. I would love to feature your farm-fresh eggs and potato pancakes in one of my articles."

"Sorry, but we don't believe in having our pictures taken." She omitted reciting the verse in Exodus about why her people didn't believe in graven images. Although she was ready to give an account for her beliefs if the question arose, as it often did.

"I understand," the man said with a heavy sigh. "Is it all right if I take pictures of the food? I'd still like to feature your restaurant."

"Be *mei* guest." Had she known the food would be in the newspaper, she would have put a sprig of parsley on the plate to give it some color, but at least the egg yolks were bright yellow. A sure sign the chickens had gotten into the marigolds again.

The man snapped several pictures, taking time to arrange the utensils and paper place mat. After several minutes fussing with the food and jotting notes on a small notepad, he put his pen down and started to eat.

"Is the reorder as *gut* as the first?" She filled his mug with more coffee.

He wiped his mouth with his napkin. "I'm impressed. I think my readers will be too."

"Thank you. I'll be sure to tell the cook."

"I eat a lot of meals out, and I haven't come across a place yet that serves farm-fresh eggs collected the same morning. You should consider adding that information to the menu." He handed her one of his business cards. "On the back you'll find the date the article should appear in the paper. You'll find it in the Life-Home section."

Faith glanced at the information. They would need to raise more chickens if they were to supply all the eggs needed for the restaurant. As it was, she'd only brought them in to use so they wouldn't go to waste at home. But he'd given her a lot to think about. If farm-fresh eggs brought more customers in, then perhaps her mother would consider it. Then again, she might be upset Faith allowed pictures to be taken at all.

❧

All five of Gideon's brothers and their wives and children came for supper at Gideon's mother's house. In addition to his family, Bishop Zook and Alice were there also. Faith sat between Claudia and Phoebe, two of his sisters-in-law, each of them balancing a baby on her lap. Faith glanced across the table at Gideon, who looked ill at ease with the situation. Head down, he quickly ate his roast beef and mashed potatoes.

His mother passed Faith the bowl of peas. "Are you working six days a week?"

"*Jah*, but I don't mind. This is our busy season." Faith placed a spoonful of peas on her plate, then passed the bowl to Claudia.

"How's your father doing?"

"He's making progress. The physical therapist has taught him exercises for his leg and once home health is set up, he's supposed to be released."

The questions continued, first about Faith's parents' health, how she and Olivia were coping, then his mother brought up the robbery.

"You must have been terrified having a gun to your head."

"*Mamm*, please," Gideon said.

Faith appreciated his effort to stifle the conversation, but it didn't help once his sisters-in-law chimed in.

"I don't know what I would have done," Claudia said.

"Me either," Phoebe added.

"I was scared." Faith took a drink of milk. With

tomorrow being Sunday, everyone would want to know the details. She might as well get used to answering questions.

"This was a delicious meal, Elma," Alice said.

"*Danki*." Gideon's mother slid her chair back. "I'll get the dessert."

Alice stood. "Let me help."

The brothers' topic shifted to crops and Claudia and Phoebe chatted about babies. Faith stole a glance across the table at Gideon, who was chasing peas around on his plate with his spoon. Listening to the multiple conversations going on at the same time, she couldn't help but wish her family was larger. Sometimes she and Olivia hardly spoke to one another at the table. Most of their family conversations were about the restaurant.

When supper ended, Faith helped gather the dishes with the other women.

"It's been *wunderbaar* getting to know you better," Claudia said.

"You too." Faith was easily ten years younger than Gideon's older brothers' wives, and even though they all belonged to the same church district, she didn't know much about them.

It didn't take long to *reddy-up* the kitchen. Bishop Zook and Alice were the first to leave since church services would be held at their place in the morning.

Gideon cleared his throat. "If you're ready to

go," he said to Faith, motioning to the door.

"*Jah*, sure." Faith folded the dish towel and set it on the counter, then turned to his mother. "*Danki* for inviting me to supper."

"I've enjoyed having you," Elma said. "I hope Gideon will bring you over again soon."

Faith smiled as Gideon's cheeks shaded a deeper red. He looked as if he'd been in the sun all day.

Gideon cleared his throat again. "Ready?"

She nodded, excused herself, and followed him out the door.

He strode to the barn and stopped at his buggy parked by the fence. "Would you like to take a walk?"

One minute he wanted to leave, the next he wanted to stay.

Gideon motioned toward the cornfield. "*Mei* apple orchard is just beyond the corn. Do you want to check out the fruit?"

"Okay." She followed him into the tall corn. "I thought you were in a hurry to leave."

He kicked at a clump of dirt. "*Jah*, to get out of the *haus*."

"Why?"

"There you go with your *why* questions again." Gideon took off running, leaving corn husks waving in his wake.

"Hey, wait up." She ran after him.

Once she caught up, he slowed his pace. "*Mei*

family is a little overwhelming at times, but I'm glad you came."

"A lively supper table is certainly better than awkward silence, which is often the case between Olivia and me. In fact, I want to have a large family one day." Faith wasn't sure what prompted her to share her dreams, but she was comfortable talking with Gideon about almost anything.

As the orchard came into view, her gaze caught on chicken wire. "Why are some of your trees fenced?"

"In the springtime I put chickens in the pen. They eat pests like codling moths and beetles that overwinter in the debris. A few weeks of scratching around and feasting on insects, the chickens save the fruit trees from damage. I'd keep them here all season to keep the bugs down if they didn't tend to overfertilize the trees. That and having chickens this far away from the *haus* tends to draw foxes out of the woods."

"I never thought about wild animals. I'm sure the wire fence keeps the deer from nibbling on the tree bark and branches."

He nodded. "Deer, yes, but not the elk."

She canvassed the area with her gaze. "Your orchard is larger than I thought."

"It's taken several years." Gideon inspected a branch of apples. "Ginger Golds have a mild tart flavor. I press these into apple cider."

"Can I try one?"

"Sure."

She plucked a light-green apple from the branch and rubbed it on her hip, then took a big bite. The tartness instantly wrinkled her nose and mouth.

"Makes your lips pucker, doesn't it." He chuckled.

Faith swallowed hard, the sourness watering her eyes. "You said it was *mildly* tart."

"It is." Gideon shrugged. "It won't be ripe for another month. The skin will turn yellowish when it's ready."

"And you couldn't warn me?" She blotted her mouth with her dress sleeve.

"I wanted to see your mouth pucker." A broad grin spread across his face. He moved over to the next row. "These are Honeycrisps. They're sweet, crisp, and great for pies, sauces, or snacking on. They don't ripen until September."

She studied the apples. "I thought waxiness was something growers did for shipping fruit to the market, but these look shiny on their own."

"They have a natural wax. God's way of protecting the apples' water content. If they didn't have that waxy layer, apples wouldn't be crisp or moist. They'd turn soft and be more prone to insects. But you are right that growers wash and remove field dirt and, in the process, remove the natural wax. Many of the large growers rewax them prior to going to market so they last longer."

"You know a lot about apples," she said.

"I've done *mei* research." He motioned to her partially eaten apple. "You can toss that."

She studied it a moment, then pitched it down the grove. "One day you'll have a Ginger Gold tree growing amongst the Honeycrisps."

"Maybe. The orchard off the old railroad trail you walk was thought to be started by loggers spitting seeds and discarding cores."

She nodded. "You told me that once before, Mr. Walking Encyclopedia."

"Is that a compliment or are you calling me a know-it-all?"

Faith hesitated, pretending to size him up with her eyes. "A compliment."

He playfully blew out a noisy breath. "You had me worried."

"Oh, stop." She nudged his arm with her shoulder. "You're *nett* concerned with *mei* thoughts."

He smiled. "More than you know."

Hearing a songbird, Faith scanned the area. A silvery gray titmouse flitted through the canopy of branches and rested on the end of a twig. Faith found the walk with Gideon through his orchard peaceful. "I love daylight savings time, don't you?"

"*Jah*, but we should head back. The mosquitoes will be out in droves any minute." He swatted at one on his arm.

"Race you to the buggy." Faith took off running, but he was quick to catch up. He paced her until they reached the edge of the yard, then he hung back, letting her reach the buggy first. "You let me win."

"You didn't tap the buggy yet," he said, jogging past her. He went into the barn and a few moments later came out with the harness draped over his shoulder and leading Bay by the halter.

Faith helped him put the equipment on, fastening the buckle around the girth and slipping the reins through the metal rings.

"All set?" He opened the buggy door.

She climbed in and scooted over, making room for him on the bench. On the drive home, brilliant red, yellow, and orange colors filled the sky. The end of a perfect day. It was dark by the time they rolled into her yard. Faith noticed lights on in the house about the same time Gideon was pointing it out.

"Someone's home." He set the brake.

"Might be Liv."

Gideon jumped out, then held his arm out so she stayed behind him. "Let me go first." He peeked in the window at the same time the door opened.

"*Mamm*!" Faith rushed to her mother and hugged her. She felt frail in Faith's arms. "I didn't know you were being released from the hospital."

"We wanted to surprise you, but as it turned

out, you surprised us when we didn't find you home."

Faith's stomach knotted. Once word spread about her parents being home, news about the robbery would reach *Mamm* and *Daed*. Faith glanced at Gideon, then at her mother. "I need to tell you about what happened at the restaurant."

Chapter 23

In the past three weeks since her parents returned home, they still appeared frail despite Faith's prayers for their ongoing recovery. *Mamm's* weight loss gave her a washed-out, gaunt appearance, and *Daed*, whose leg cast had confined him to the house, was in pain and often frustrated with his inability to move around freely. Being unable to care for his livestock had seemed to somehow age him. Most days he sat quietly in the sitting room, gazing out the window. Thankfully, Gideon had volunteered to continue doing the barn chores, and he gave *Daed* a regular update on what calves were ready to be weaned and other important farming matters.

Faith worked hard around the house and at the restaurant so her mother could relax. Then, that morning, as Faith was getting ready for work, *Mamm* asked her to stay home and watch over *Daed*. The restaurant bookkeeping was two months behind, and now that it was the beginning of August, *Mamm* insisted it couldn't be neglected any longer. Had Faith been trained to do the end-of-the-month spreadsheets and tallies, she would have tried to convince her mother to let her do it, but as it was, even if she studied the previous months' entries, catching up both June and July would be a daunting task.

Faith didn't mind staying home with her father for the day. Especially since Gideon was part of the work crew who had come early to put up her father's hay. Arriving shortly after breakfast, the men had gone directly to the field and worked steadily all morning.

Faith gazed out the kitchen window at the workers in the field and spotted Gideon stacking hay on the wagons. *Make hay while the sun shines* was something she'd grown up hearing. It was certainly sunny. The August sun loomed hot in the cloudless blue sky. The kitchen was hot, too, with her having baked cookies all morning. Normally, she baked sweets at the restaurant and brought them home, but the cookie jar was almost empty and she wanted to offer all the workers a treat after the noon meal.

The men trudged across the field toward the barn, heads down. Leaving the hay wagons where they had stopped working, they brought the five-mule team to the barn to water and tie in the shade. Gideon went to the water pump. Distracted by Gideon splashing well water on his face, she continued to gaze at him as he combed his fingers through his damp hair. Her mind drifted to the day they'd spent at the river.

Boots stomped outside the window as the men kicked off the dirt before entering the house. While the men greeted *Daed*, she raced around the kitchen, placing spoons next to the potato salad. She set a plate stacked with cheese sandwiches on one side of the table, and a plate with sliced bread on the opposite side for those who wanted a cucumber, onion, or tomato sandwich instead.

Gideon meandered into the kitchen. "*Hiya*, Faith." His gaze went to the cookies cooling on the rack. "Those look *gut*."

She pointed to the food on the table. "You best *nett* fill your belly with sweets until after you've had a sandwich or two."

He opened his mouth, but closed it when the other men filed into the room. He lined up with the men and began filling his plate.

Faith waited until everyone selected their food, then put a cheese sandwich and a scoop of potato salad on a plate for *Daed*. The bishop and several of the elders sat with her father in the sitting room. Their conversation abruptly stopped as she stepped closer. "I brought you a sandwich," she said, handing her father the plate, fork, and napkin. "Do you want more *kaffi*?"

"*Nay, danki*, daughter."

"Let me know if I can get you anything else." Faith left the room. She hoped having company, even if only for an hour or so before the men returned to the fields, would help lift *Daed's* spirit. Being confined to the house had made him antsy. He wouldn't be happy again until he was able to do his own chores.

Several of the men, including Gideon, took their meal and went outside to sit under the shade tree. Now she wished she hadn't fired up the stove to make cookies. Even with the windows open the kitchen blazed with heat, though she shouldn't complain. Summer went by too fast. Soon the wintery chill, and the challenge to keep the house warm, would make her wish for summer again.

Faith filled the sink with soapy water and lowered the dirty dishes into the basin. Once she cleaned the kitchen, she planned to do laundry, then pull weeds in the garden.

Gideon entered the kitchen with a stack of plates and set them on the counter beside her. "I thought I'd bring these in. *Danki* for lunch."

"You're *welkum*. Are you heading back to the field?"

"*Jah*, but I didn't want to forget *mei* cookie." He snatched one off the cooling rack and took a bite. "Tastes *gut*."

"Would you like another one?"

"I'll wait." He grinned. "It'll give me an excuse to see you again." He turned to leave, but paused at the entrance. "Would you be interested in going for a walk with me after the evening chores are done?"

"*Jah*, that would be nice."

"Okay." He left the kitchen.

Faith gazed out the window as she washed dishes, her focus on Gideon as he strode across the field to join the others. He picked up a pitchfork, his strong shoulders working the hay. She still had a hard time believing he wanted to spend time with her, the tallest, gawkiest girl in the district. But Gideon had never once teased her or questioned her, like others had done in the past, about why she was taller than her parents, taller than her sister. A strand of stray hair fell out from the *kapp*. Or why she had frizzy, coarse hair, when Olivia's hair was silky smooth. Faith tucked the strand back under the *kapp*, then focused on the dishes. Once she finished the kitchen, she gathered dirty clothes from the bedrooms.

"I'm going to do some laundry, unless you'd rather I stay and keep you company?"

Daed turned away from the window and faced her. "Don't worry about me. I'll be fine."

"Would you like me to get you anything before I go out to the *washhaus*?"

"I'm all set, *danki*."

Faith hesitated. She didn't like leaving him alone in the house. Knowing him, he might try to move around on his own. Then again, the clothes needed washing and it might rain tomorrow. She picked up the wicker basket of laundry and headed outside. Her gaze drifted over to the workers. The wagon was almost full. They'd be hauling it to the barn soon.

Inside the *washhaus* felt hot and stuffy. Faith set the basket down next to the wringer washer, then grabbed two buckets and went to the pump. Washing clothes went faster when she, Olivia, and *Mamm* were doing it together. After several trips to the pump, the laundry tub was full. Scrubbing ketchup and mustard stains out of her work dresses then wringing out excess water from the garments made her muscles throb, but she worked fast. She wanted everything done before *Mamm* came home.

As she hung the clothes on the line to dry, Beverly Drombrowski's car pulled into the driveway and *Mamm* got out, the restaurant ledger in her hand. Faith clipped a dress on the line, then waved at their *Englisch* friend who was turning the car around. She met her mother in the driveway. "Were you able to get the records caught up?"

Mamm nodded, then directed her attention to the field. "Looks like they're finishing up. It'll be a relief when the hay is in the barn," she said, her voice sounding strained.

"*Jah*, it will." Every year her father fretted over the weather. Cut hay needed time to dry, but leaving it too long carried the risk of it getting rained on. Since wet hay tended to mold, and moldy hay was dangerous for the horses, *Daed's* concerns were justified.

"I'm going inside to check on your father,"

Mamm said, lumbering up the porch steps.

Faith continued hanging the laundry, stealing glimpses of Gideon when she could. When she had finished hanging the clothes, she went inside.

Mamm halted her words midsentence and snapped the ledger book closed when Faith entered the living room.

Faith chewed her lip as she went into the kitchen. She'd overheard enough to know the restaurant books hadn't balanced.

Chapter 24

Faith inched toward the wall which separated the kitchen from the sitting room. She leaned forward and pressed her ear against the wall to listen to her parents' hushed conversation. Her mother's fragile tone raised alarms as to the seriousness of the issue.

"How are we going to pay the hospital and *doktah's* bills?"

"We'll figure it out, Irma," *Daed* said calmly.

"But the restaurant isn't doing as well as we thought. According to the record books, we've lost money. I haven't been a *gut* steward of what God has given us."

"*Nay*, please don't say that. It might be a simple bookkeeping mistake. Remember when your numbers were off a few years ago and it took us four days to figure out what was wrong?"

"I remember," *Mamm* muttered.

"Then think on those things. It'll work out for the *gut*. Watch and see."

Heaviness filled Faith's chest, a crushing weight of indecision. She should tell her parents about the money Olivia had stashed away in the barn. But if she did, her sister would probably never talk to her again. Olivia hardly talked to her now as it was. Still . . . *Lord, I need wisdom.*

"Besides," her father continued, "the *doktah* doesn't want you overdoing it."

Hadn't *Mamm* been discharged in good health?

A car door slammed. Faith slipped into the kitchen and peered out the window. She recognized the blue four-door truck as the one *Daed's* physical therapist drove. *Mamm* greeted the *Englischer* at the door, welcoming him inside.

Faith wet a dishrag and washed the already clean counter.

Mamm entered the kitchen a few minutes later, eyes hooded and shoulders slumped. She placed the ledger on the table, ran her finger over the frayed cloth cover, and frowned.

Lord, I need to know what to do, what to say. "*Mamm*, would you like me to make you a cup of tea?"

She shook her head. "It's already too hot. Making a fire to brew a cup of tea would only make it worse."

"True." Faith smiled. "I'll put a jar of sun tea on the porch." She removed a large pickle jar from the cabinet, filled it with water, then added several tea bags. She scooped up the jug. "I'll be right back." The tea wouldn't be ready for hours, but her mother looked as though she needed a few minutes alone.

Faith took the jar outside and set it on the bottom porch step where the sun would hit it, then meandered over to the clothesline. She touched each garment, making her way down the line while sneaking a peek at the work going on in the barn. Gideon was busy, his back to her. The dresses and towels were still wet. *Daed's* shirts felt dry, but she might as well wait until everything was ready and bring them all in together. She decided to spend a few minutes working in the garden.

She squatted between two rows of tomatoes and grabbed a fistful of weeds. Usually garden work allowed a means to release stress and think through her problems, but today she couldn't think of anything but the conversation she had overheard between her parents. *What was wrong with* Mamm's *health? Was "not overdoing it" something* doktahs *instructed everyone they sent home from the hospital?* She yanked more weeds and tossed them on the pile. Lost in concentration, she hadn't paid much attention to the men leaving the barn. Now she saw that buggies rolled down the driveway and turned onto Leer Road one by one. Except for Gideon's. His horse was still tied under the tall oak, swatting flies away with his tail.

Gideon waited for the others to leave before strolling across the lawn to where Faith was working in the garden. She lifted her head as he approached and smiled.

"We finished putting up the hay," he said.

"So I see. *Danki*." Faith's attention shifted to something behind him.

Gideon followed her gaze. Irma and the therapist stood on the porch, talking too low to overhear, but deep lines wrinkled her mother's forehead. "Do you think everything's okay?"

Faith seemed to be studying her mother.

"Faith?" He touched her arm and she jerked. "I'm sorry. I didn't mean to startle you."

She offered a faint smile, then swiped the tears away from the corners of her eyes, smearing dirt on her face.

He moved closer. "What is it? Why are you crying?"

The *Englischer's* car door closed and the engine roared to life.

"I can't talk about it," she said softly.

"Is it about your father?"

She shook her head and choked down emotion as the therapist drove away.

"About the *Englischer*?"

"*Nay*!"

He took a step back. "I shouldn't pry. I'm sorry."

"I'm sorry I snapped." Faith gathered ripe tomatoes in her turned-up apron, but soon she had more than she could carry.

"I'll get a bucket." Gideon jogged to the barn and when he returned, he helped her transfer the tomatoes.

She moved on to the pole beans. The long hours she had spent at the restaurant and her mother being away was evident in the overgrowth of weeds. Gideon squatted down and began pulling them up by the roots. He stopped, hearing Faith sniffling a few rows over. "Are you all right?"

"*Jah.*"

He pretended not to notice the tracks of tears coursing down her cheeks. He picked weeds in silence. *Lord, what can I do? I hate to see her sad—I hate even more that she doesn't feel comfortable talking about what's bothering her.*

"The Amish Table lost money the past couple months. More than what was stolen," Faith blurted. "I'm sure *mei* parents don't want me talking about it—they actually didn't even share that news with me—I overheard it." She blinked several times, releasing a string of tears. "I had to tell someone. Please don't repeat anything I've said."

"I won't." He decreased the distance between them.

"On top of the restaurant *nett* doing well, the hospital bill came in the mail today, and apparently—" She covered her hand over her mouth and shook her head as if to say what he already knew, that she couldn't continue talking about it.

"You don't have to say any more." He reached out and clasped her elbow. "Things will work out. You have to have faith—*Faith,*" he said with a smile.

She rubbed her red-rimmed eyes. "I feel helpless."

"Did you tell them about Olivia?"

"*Nay.*" Faith opened her mouth, but closed it tight enough for her jaw muscles to twitch.

"I know you don't want to get Olivia in trouble," he said, drawing a deep breath. "But you have to tell your parents. They deserve to know."

Faith nodded.

Gideon could see the turmoil in Faith's eyes; she wasn't able to rat out her sister. Perhaps pushing her to do so was wrong. The bishop could break the news; maybe he could persuade Olivia to do the right thing and give the money back to her parents.

Gideon dusted the dirt off his knees. "Can we take a walk another time? I have a few things I need to do before milking time."

⁂

Faith shuffled to the house carrying the vegetables she'd picked. Opening the door, she heard her mother's muffled sob.

Mamm looked up from where she sat next to *Daed*, her eyes red and puffy. She wiped them with a wadded tissue. "I didn't hear you *kumm* in, Faith."

"I picked the ripe tomatoes." She pretended

not to notice the grief-stricken expression on *Mamm's* face. "I thought we could put a batch up for winter?"

"That's a *gut* idea."

"I'll get them started." She took the bucket into the kitchen and emptied it into the sink. Turmoil riled her stomach. Gideon was right. Her parents deserved to know about Olivia's hidden money.

A few moments later, *Mamm* came into the kitchen. She removed the canning pots from the bottom cabinet, filled them with water, then sank the jars into the deeper pot and the lids into the smaller one.

As the water heated on the stove, Faith cleaned the tomatoes. Gideon's words replayed in her mind. *"They deserve to know the truth."*

"The restaurant should be doing better than it is," Faith said. "If we hadn't been robbed . . ." *Or Olivia hadn't taken money from the till.*

"Honey, the robbery wasn't your fault."

"I didn't lock the door immediately."

"The important thing is that you weren't hurt. I'm so grateful—so thankful."

"I was glad Gideon was there. After the robbery, he insisted on taking me home each *nacht*."

Mamm placed the clean tomatoes into the strainer. "You and Gideon seem to be spending a lot of time together. Of course, he's a fine man, and we've certainly appreciated how well he's kept up with your father's chores."

Faith heard the *but* coming and stiffened.

The lines across her mother's forehead deepened. "There was a time, *nett* all that long ago, when I thought Olivia and Gideon might get married."

The tomato squished in Faith's hand, spilling its juices into her palm.

"Handle them gently," *Mamm* instructed.

Faith nodded and washed more tomatoes in silence. She'd helped wash tomatoes ever since she was old enough to stand on a stool and reach the sink. She and her mother never worked in silence. Faith wanted to say more about Olivia, but decided it best to change the subject. "Did the physical therapist leave early today?"

"This was his last day."

Excitement bubbled up within Faith. "He's improved that much? That's *wunderbaar*!"

Mamm turned her attention to the boiling pot of water. "This is ready for the tomatoes *nau*."

Faith plopped tomatoes one at a time, taking care not to get burned by the boiling water when it shot over the sides and sizzled on the stove's cast-iron surface.

"*Daed's* leg still needs time to heal."

Blanching only required a minute or two and afterward, dipping the tomatoes into cold water helped the skins to come off easier. Faith watched the tomatoes roll over in the boiling water.

"I overheard you talking with *Daed* about the books being off at the restaurant," she admitted.

"You were listening!"

Faith glanced up momentarily but, seeing her mother's furrowed brows, received the message loud and clear not to meddle. *"I haven't been a gut steward of what God has given us,"* her mother's words replayed. Bringing up Olivia now would only add to *Mamm's* guilt.

"I wish there was something I could do," Faith said.

"Please, honey, don't concern yourself with those worries. The Lord will provide."

Faith set down the tomato. "I'll be right back." She clambered up the stairs to her bedroom. Inside the top dresser drawer, she removed the jar full of money she'd been saving, then returned to the kitchen. "It isn't much," she said, handing it to her mother.

"What is this?"

"Money I was saving to buy Christmas gifts."

Mamm stared at the cash, tears pooling in her eyes. "I don't know what to say."

Faith smiled. "Merry Christmas—in August."

"You are very kind, daughter. *Danki*, so much."

"I wish I had more to give." One hundred two dollars and forty-eight cents wouldn't pay the hospital bill, nor would it get the restaurant out of the red. If only she had more to give. *Olivia has more—a lot more.* But Faith refused to add to

Mamm's sorrow. She would have to come up with another way to raise money. Maybe sell pies or cookies. *Mamm* had people approach her before about catering weddings and special events in the area . . . Faith's thoughts jumbled as she made a mental list of possibilities. Then she recalled the *Englischer* who took pictures for his newspaper article.

"*Mamm*, while you and *Daed* were in the hospital, Olivia and I didn't cook at home. I took the eggs into work each morning so they wouldn't spoil. Well, one day a man asked about the food and he even took pictures for an article he was writing."

Mamm frowned at the mention of pictures, but Faith continued.

"He seemed impressed that I had collected the eggs that morning. Apparently very few restaurants serve anything that fresh. He said we could charge more for that."

Mamm's expression relaxed. "That's certainly something to think about."

"Maybe we could start by increasing the number of laying hens we have," Faith said.

"Tell me more about the pictures he took. You weren't in them, were you?"

"*Nay*. I told him we don't believe in having our photos taken. He only took pictures of the food, which he said was so good that he wanted seconds."

"Two meals?" *Mamm's* mouth dropped open.

"I was surprised too." Faith chuckled as she dipped the tomatoes into the cold water. "I have his business card at the restaurant. He jotted down on the back of the card a few possible dates the article might appear."

A flicker of hope returned in *Mamm's* eyes, which pleased Faith.

It was early evening by the time the tomatoes were canned and the laundry was dry. Faith stood over the basket and unclipped the clothes from the line, breathing in the fresh aroma. She appreciated the flowery scent on her dresses after hanging outside.

Buggy wheels crunched over the gravel driveway. Bishop Zook climbed out of one buggy and two of the elders piled out of another. The three men ambled up the porch steps. A visit this close to suppertime was odd. Perhaps the bishop wanted to give *Daed* a count of hay since the men had cleared the fields earlier that day.

She clambered up the porch steps. "*Gut* afternoon, Bishop."

"Hello, Faith. I hope your father is up to having visitors."

"I'm sure he is." She opened the door, then followed her mother into the kitchen.

Mamm removed four mugs from the cabinet. "Would you put some cookies on a plate while I pour the *kaffi*?"

"Sure." Faith set the laundry basket on the table, then selected the cookies that hadn't burned and placed them on a plate.

Daed was smiling when Faith and *Mamm* took the coffee and cookies into the sitting room. "Irma," *Daed* said, unable to contain his excitement. "We've been given a horse and buggy. Isn't that a nice surprise?"

"*Ach*! That's *wunderbaar*!" *Mamm* clasped her hand over her mouth as tears collected on her lashes.

"That's very nice," Faith said. Her family was blessed to be part of such a giving district. The outpouring of help with the meals, the crops, and now their finances brought tears to her eyes.

Bishop Zook tapped Faith's arm. "Perhaps you can take the mare to the barn."

"I'd be happy to. What's the horse's name?"

"I was told it's called Starlight," the bishop replied.

Faith slipped out the front door, silently praising God for His providence. She stole a peek at the new-to-them buggy, then untied the horse's reins from the post and walked Starlight to the barn.

Gideon's buggy pulled into the yard. He stopped at the fence. "Faith, is something wrong?"

"*Nay*, something *wunderbaar* happened!" She dried her face using her dress sleeve. "We've been given this lovely horse and buggy by the district."

"That's *gut* news." He helped unhitch the buggy, then opened the barn door for Faith to walk the horse inside.

Faith led the mare into an empty stall. "Isn't she a beauty?"

"She is," he said.

She nudged his shoulder with hers. "You're *nett* looking at the horse."

He grinned. "The mare looks okay too."

His adorable dimples had a way of releasing tingles throughout her body. She snatched the water bucket from the floor. "You're a flirt, Gideon."

"Only with you."

She went outside to the pump and put her nervous energy into a strong thrust of the handle. The bucket filled in seconds. She lugged the fresh water into the barn and lowered the bucket into the stall. As she filled a tin can with oats, Gideon tossed hay down from the loft.

He climbed down the ladder. "Olivia's money jar is gone."

"Gone?"

He nodded. "She probably heard the men were going to put up the hay today and moved it."

"Or she was worried I would take it." Her sister had made it clear she didn't trust Faith. "I almost told *Mamm* about Olivia, but I couldn't. *Mamm* already feels she hasn't been a *gut* steward, I couldn't have her thinking she hasn't raised us right." She sighed. "I hope Olivia comes to her senses. She won't find peace in the world."

"Some people have to discover that the hard way." He scooped an armful of hay and headed to the mare's stall.

Chapter 25

Bloomfield Hills, Michigan
Present day

Roslyn paused outside of the police station and drew a deep breath to calm her nerves. The temperature gauge displayed on the building read ninety-two degrees, yet she was shivering as though it was early March. She turned to Chrisla. "What if the detective refuses to reopen the case?"

"You could always whisper a prayer for wisdom."

"Don't start." Roslyn hadn't uttered a prayer in years. Divine guidance happened in Bible stories, not in her life.

Chrisla reached for the door handle, but stopped. "Everything's going to work out."

"I want to believe that, but I . . ." Roslyn chewed her bottom lip and the waxy lipstick caused her stomach to roil. When she'd called to set up an appointment, she hadn't recognized the detective's name. At one time she knew all their names, their badge numbers too. She'd threatened the entire department more than once with filing a formal complaint. But in the end, even if a case was deemed open, if it lacked productive leads, it might as well be closed—the trail was cold.

Chrisla nudged Roslyn's arm with her elbow, then opened the door. "C'mon."

The front lobby was small and uninviting with its cement floor and metal chairs on opposing walls. Roslyn gave her name to the woman behind the administration window. "I have an appointment with Detective Bailey."

The woman made a quick phone call, then buzzed them through. "Fourth door on the right," she said.

A familiar coldness clung to the gunmetal walls, while their heels clacking on the cement floor echoed down the narrow hallway. She'd been down this passage hundreds of times, walking into the office filled with hope only to leave weighted in hopelessness.

A tall man with a flattop haircut, dressed in a long sleeved white shirt, dark slacks, and a wide belt sporting a shiny badge clipped at his waist, met her outside the office. Following him was a shorter man whom, once he stepped into view, she recognized as Detective Henderson. The last fifteen years had leathered his face and deepened the lines across his forehead, as well as thinned his now silvery-white hair.

The younger man extended his hand. "Good afternoon, I'm Detective Bailey. I believe you already know Detective Henderson."

Roslyn shook the younger man's hand, then greeted Detective Henderson. Over the years, Henderson had listened to her sob and rant when nothing was getting done—all with the patience of a saint.

Chrisla cleared her throat. "I'm Roslyn's sister." She offered her hand first to Bailey, then Henderson.

"Shall we go sit down?" The younger man motioned to the office.

Roslyn and Chrisla sat next to each other at the conference table while the two detectives took chairs on the opposite side.

Detective Bailey opened the conversation. "First, I'd like to say that even though I wasn't working for Oakland County PD at the time of your daughter's kidnapping, I am familiar with the case. Also, Detective Henderson filled me in on a few of the missing details after you set up the appointment. I understand you have new information about your daughter's abduction."

Roslyn's throat went dry. Technically, Chrisla's drawings were not new information as it pertained to evidence, which she had led the detective to believe over the phone in order to secure an appointment. Now she had to come clean. "The *Detroit News* is interested in doing a story on Adriana, and I thought if you would reopen the case . . ."

Bailey's brows slanted. "I'm sorry. I don't

273

think I'm following you, Mrs. Colepepper. Has a reporter obtained new information?"

"The first weekend in September will mark fifteen years that my daughter's been missing." She turned her attention to Detective Henderson. "Adriana's alive." Roslyn nudged her sister. "Show them your drawings."

Chrisla unzipped her portfolio, removed the artwork, and arranged the images to face the men. Leaning forward, she pointed to the individual drawings and described how she depicted Adriana's age, then sat back so they could study them quietly themselves.

Bailey looked up, frowning sympathetically. "I know it's only natural for you to revisit the incidents leading up to the kidnapping as it gets closer to Labor Day weekend, but without new information, we just don't have the manpower to reinvestigate your daughter's case. I'm sorry."

Roslyn leaned forward. "The kidnappers changed cars multiple times and the FBI found no evidence that Adriana was even in the Yugo." She rested her hands on the table, clenched her fists, then relaxed them. "You're right, there's rarely a day that I don't mull over every step I took in the grocery store, crossing the parking lot, putting the groceries in my car. But I've also counted the hours over and over between the abduction and the car going off the bridge. I can still vividly see that Yugo resurfacing in Lake Huron, water draining from every crevice. But what I don't see, Detective Bailey"—she narrowed her eyes at the investigator—"is my daughter in that car."

The younger man's Adam's apple bobbed. "True," he finally uttered. "But any DNA would have been destroyed the moment it submerged in the water."

"Your records should show how far the car window was down, and now you have the ability to digitally reenact the car going off the bridge. Based on the angles you calculate, I believe you'll discover the new evidence you need to open the case. My daughter wasn't in the car when it came up from the water and her body never surfaced. She wasn't in that car when it went over the bridge. She couldn't have been."

Detective Henderson cleared his throat. "Mrs. Colepepper, you've brought up a good point. The case was closed a number of years ago and since then, technology has improved. I would like to oversee a new investigation—pending data analysis, of course."

Roslyn's heart quickened its pace, and she barely felt her sister take her hand and give it a light squeeze. This was the news she'd wanted so desperately to hear.

Bailey rubbed his jaw. "I can't promise you much unless evidence supports those findings. And as for the drawings," he said, redirecting his attention to Chrisla, "we have computers to generate age-advanced images, which are highly accurate."

"I understand," Chrisla said.

Antsy to call the reporter, Roslyn stood. "I'll post a big enough reward that every young woman with even a vague resemblance to my daughter will be turned in to the hotline."

Chapter 26

Posen, Michigan
Present day

Tension swarmed the kitchen as Faith and Olivia worked around each other preparing supper. As *Mamm* had requested, they moved the table and chairs into the sitting room so that *Daed* didn't have to move far.

"How was work?" Faith asked her sister.

Olivia stirred the green beans. "Busy. We could have used more help."

Now you know how I've felt. Faith removed the plates from the cabinet. She fought back the urge to remind Olivia of all the times she either didn't show up or left early, including the day the restaurant was robbed. *Let it go.*

Olivia poured the beans into a bowl. "Are you working tomorrow?"

"All day," Faith said through gritted teeth. She walked the dishes into the sitting room and placed them on the table.

"Do you girls need help?" *Mamm* started to rise from the chair.

"*Nay*, we have it under control," Faith insisted. Both of her parents appeared weary when, after receiving such a wonderful gift of a horse and buggy, they should be rejoicing over God's blessing. Faith had to say something to Olivia. No more secrets.

"Olivia, are you aware the restaurant books didn't balance? The restaurant is losing money. Do you have any thoughts on why that may be?"

Olivia removed the pot roast from the oven. "Why would—hey, wait a minute." She set down the pan and faced Faith. "Are you trying to say that I have something to do with it?"

"You have a lot of money stashed, more money than a waitress—"

Olivia's nostrils flared.

"I overhead *Mamm* and *Daed* talking about the hospital bill." Faith paused, but Olivia said nothing. "The family's in financial trouble . . . Liv, are you even listening?"

She tossed the potholders on the counter. "What do you want me to say?"

"That you'll give *Mamm* and *Daed* the money hidden in the barn. I gave them everything I had. The members of our district provided a horse and buggy . . ."

"You told them about the money?"

"*Nay*," Faith said, picking up the bowl of beans. "Olivia, do what's right. Please." She took the food into the other room and placed it on the table.

This time *Mamm* stood and followed her back into the kitchen.

Faith grabbed the salt and pepper shakers and the bread and butter dishes while Olivia carried the pot roast and *Mamm* the pitcher of milk.

Conversation at the table revolved around the garden and canning. The new horse and how much hay the men had cleared from the fields. Once they had eaten, Faith and Olivia moved the table back into the kitchen and cleaned up the dishes in silence.

Faith yawned. "I'm going to bed."

Olivia followed her out of the kitchen but turned toward the front door.

"Olivia," *Daed* said sternly, "your mother and I want to talk with you."

"*Gut nacht* everyone." Faith hurried up the stairs. The last time her father had used that tone, Olivia had been caught lying about something. Faith knelt next to the bed. *Lord, please open Olivia's eyes. Don't let her become ensnared by the world. I worry about her soul. I also pray for* Daed *and* Mamm. *Give them wisdom and the right words of correction. Please bless our family. Heal* mei daed's *leg. Amen.*

Faith changed into her nightclothes and crawled between the sheets. She closed her eyes, her body becoming part of the mattress.

Sometime later, the door opened and closed hard. "Thanks a lot," Olivia snipped.

Faith stayed facing the wall.

"I know you're *nett* sleeping. I should have

known you would tell them about the money. You sabotaged *mei* dreams—*mei* plans. You're *nett mei schweschaler*. Do you hear me?"

Faith clamped her lips tight. Even if she placed her hand on the Bible, Olivia wouldn't believe Faith had nothing to do with their parents finding out.

Olivia's accusations last night had prevented Faith from getting much sleep, but she slipped out of the house early to collect the eggs. Forcing herself to focus on something other than her sister, she created a mental list of things she could do to help promote farm-fresh products at the restaurant. Information cards at each table would save the cost involved in printing new menus. Perhaps she should research grass-fed beef. She placed the egg in the basket and moved to the next nesting box.

Gideon cleared his throat. "Am I still driving you to work?"

"I forgot we have a horse and buggy *nau*. I better find out what *mei* parents want me to do." She collected the last egg and placed it in the basket.

"Maybe I should drive you. After all, you don't know much about that horse yet."

Faith smiled. "You're right about the horse."

"And your parents might need to go some-where," he added.

280

Gideon didn't have to convince her. She'd rather ride into town with him. "Can you give me a few minutes? You can *kumm* inside and have *kaffi*."

He motioned to Bay. "I'll wait in the buggy."

Faith hurried back to the house, the rich aroma of coffee meeting her at the door. She rounded the wall to the kitchen and stopped. On the center of the table was Olivia's jar of money.

Mamm looked up from the stove. "I'm making pancakes. How many would you like?"

"None for me. Gideon is giving me a ride into work, and I don't want to keep him waiting." She lifted the basket. "Do you want me to take the eggs to work or do you need them?"

"Leave me a half dozen and take the rest." She flipped the pancake.

Olivia walked into the kitchen yawning.

Faith counted out six eggs, placed them in a bowl, then picked up the basket. "*Guder mariye*, Olivia."

Her sister glared.

Faith ignored Olivia's daggers and went to the door. "See you tonight." She left before *Mamm* suggested taking Olivia into town with them. Her sister could try out the new horse.

"Something wrong?" Gideon asked once they were on the main road.

"*Mamm* and *Daed* know about Olivia's money. Of course, *mei* sister blames me for spilling the beans."

"She'll *kumm* around."

"You didn't see the look Olivia gave me. She may never talk to me again."

"Olivia's just upset she got caught. Give her time to cool down. Your parents needed to know. It was for the best."

"I don't know if they found the money or if Olivia gave it back, but the jar was on the table this morning."

"*Gut*." Gideon smiled.

Faith gazed out the window at the stalks of flowering thimbleweed scattered over the hillside. Only God could create such a beautiful landscape with weeds. She loved this time of the day when the temperature was still cool and the sun wasn't much over the horizon.

In light traffic, the trip to town went fast. Gideon pulled into the parking spot next to Catherine's buggy. "Do you think you might have some free time later this afternoon to go fishing?"

She smiled. "Perhaps."

As Gideon walked her to the back door, a buggy pulled into the driveway and stopped. Lois climbed out, then waved good-bye to her husband. She waited at the door for Faith and Gideon. "*Guder mariye*."

"*Mariye*," Faith replied.

"I ran into your *Mamm* yesterday and she asked if I could help out today."

"What about the *kinner*?"

"*Mei* niece volunteered to watch them."

Faith turned the doorknob. Locked. She knocked. "I forgot to grab *mei* keys," she explained.

Catherine let them in. "You'll never guess what I found resting against the door this morning." She didn't wait for any of them to guess. "A package." She picked up a large envelope from off the counter and handed it to Faith.

"Look—look inside," she said, sounding giddy.

Faith peered into the envelope. "I don't understand."

Gideon stepped closer. "What is it?"

"Money," Faith replied.

"Five hundred eighty-three dollars and seventy-eight cents in bills and coins." Catherine motioned to the package. "There's a note too."

Faith emptied the contents on the counter. She picked up the piece of paper and unfolded it. "Cast thy bread upon the waters: for thou shalt find it after many days."

She swallowed hard. "This is the amount of money that was stolen."

Gideon cocked his head. "You're sure?"

"*Jah.*" Faith studied the note again, recalling how the homeless man had quoted the scripture. "*Danki*, Father, for placing it on someone's heart to return the money. *Danki* for watching over us."

"Amen," Gideon said.

Faith returned the money to the envelope. Her

parents would be thrilled with the news. Perhaps the restaurant wouldn't close after all.

Gideon read the note, then handed it back. "Do you have any idea what this is about? I mean, I know it's a Scripture verse, but it doesn't make sense why someone would leave that note."

"Remember the red-haired man who came inside and spoke to the gunman?"

"*Jah*. I wasn't paying much attention to his hair color, but I remember the homeless man. I also recall him disappearing as quickly as he appeared."

"I think the note has something to do with . . ."

"With what?"

"A few weeks ago, he showed up here with a Will Work for Food sign. He quoted that same verse when I offered him something to eat."

Catherine's mouth dropped open. "Do you think he retrieved the money from the gunman?"

"Maybe." *But why would he confront a dangerous man?* Her mouth dried. "I need to start making the bread or we won't have any for the customers."

The day went smoothly having extra help. Olivia came to work, although she didn't have anything to say to Faith. But nothing could dampen Faith's spirit now that the money had been returned.

Gideon arrived two hours before closing time ready to wash dishes so they could get out on time. But Faith had already made arrangements with Catherine to leave early. On the ride home, Gideon talked about fishing.

"I need to run the money inside and make sure it's okay with *Mamm* if we go," she said once he pulled into the yard.

"Take your time. I'm going to water Bay."

Faith skipped up the porch steps, excited to share the contents of the envelope with her parents. "You'll never guess what was leaning against the back door of the restaurant." She used Catherine's opening line to spark their interest.

She dumped the contents on the table.

"Where did you get that?" *Mamm* said.

"It's the money that was stolen. Someone left it outside the door." She moved the bills around. "It's over five hundred dollars."

Mamm clutched her chest.

"This will help keep The Amish Table open, right?"

Mamm nodded. "On top of this blessing, and the money you and Olivia contributed, I found the bookkeeping error! We are *nett* as strapped for money as I had thought. Of course we still have looming medical bills . . ."

Mamm's words garbled in the back of Faith's mind. *Bookkeeping error? Did that mean Olivia hadn't stolen money?*

". . . I don't know how I did it, but I omitted a few deposits." *Mamm* shook her head. "*Daed* is going to take over the record books. I'm just *nett gut* at bookkeeping."

Faith lowered her head. "I heard a rumor about Olivia taking money from the till and I . . ."

"The bishop heard the same rumor. When your father and I confronted Olivia, she adamantly denied the accusations. But that was what prompted me to search through the records again. And I'm so glad I did."

"So Olivia was telling the truth?"

Her mother nodded. "The money in the jar was tips she'd saved. Saved for quite some time too. Olivia surprised me."

"*Jah*, me too."

Chapter 27

Gideon hadn't realized he'd been nervous until his hands started to sweat. Standing on the Pinkhams' porch waiting for Faith, he rubbed his palms on the front of his shirt. *What's gotten into you?* Gideon paced to the end of the porch where a hanging basket of pink geraniums was in full bloom. He checked the soil. Dry. If one plant was dry, the flower beds along the porch probably all needed watering as well. He grabbed the empty watering can from next to the porch swing and strode to the pump to fill it. He watered the flowers next to the house first, then fed the drooping geraniums.

The screen door opened and Faith stepped outside. "We'll need bait," she said, holding up an empty container. "That is, if you still want to go?"

"*Jah.*" He set the watering can down, then dried his hands on his shirt. "How long do you have?"

She shrugged. "Olivia is bringing supper home after her shift, so I don't need to help prepare anything." She handed him a container for bait. "If you want to start looking for worms, I'll grab *Daed's* pole from the equipment shed."

Gideon trekked to the back of the barn where

he found a log to turn. Without much digging he collected several worms.

"Need help?" Faith approached, pole in hand.

"I got 'em." He stood, brushed the dirt off his knees, then showed her the wiggling critters. "You think this is enough?"

"That depends," she said with an adorable smirk. "You going to feed them to the fish again?"

"What's that supposed to mean?"

She walked alongside him to the buggy. "I seem to recall you had several fish that stole your bait the last time."

"And I seem to recall that I was the one who baited your hook the time you caught the bigmouth bass."

"*Jah*, it was a big bass, wasn't it?"

He reached for her pole and put it and the container of worms in the back of the buggy next to the tackle box and his pole.

Faith climbed on the bench as he untied Bay. He turned the horse and buggy around, then climbed in beside Faith. One light tap of the reins and Bay started to trot. Without much afternoon traffic, they reached the fishing hole in a short time. Gideon unloaded the poles first and handed them to Faith, then grabbed the tackle box and bait.

She glanced up at the sky. "It's nice to be outside."

"You don't get much free time, do you?" He admired how hard she worked. When she wasn't at The Amish Table, she was doing laundry, canning, cleaning. Had he not volunteered to do her father's barn chores, she might have taken on that responsibility, too, since this was hay season and the other men in the district were working in their own fields.

"I don't mind. Makes me appreciate the days I do have off more." She drew in a deep breath, letting it out in a satisfied sigh, then laughed nervously when she caught him staring at her.

No denying his feelings—Faith was special. The bishop had been right to lecture Gideon about temptation, because at this very moment, he couldn't think of anything else but holding Faith in his arms and kissing her.

Gideon cleared his throat. "I guess if we're going to catch anything we better get down to the river." He tromped through the tall meadow grass toward the sound of rushing water. As he reached the river embankment, a hawk swooped down, snatched a fish with its talons, then flew off into the distance. "Did you see that?" He spoke over his shoulder as he made his way closer to the water.

"Are you going to say that should have been your catch?"

"Exactly. He stole it."

She laughed. "It might have been *mei* fish he stole."

Gideon sat on the sandy shore. He didn't have his waders on or he would walk in the current.

Faith sat next to him and began untangling her line.

"Do you want me to bait your hook?" he asked.

"And take credit for the size fish I catch, *nay danki*."

He baited his hook and was the first to cast a line. He glanced over at Faith fumbling with the squirming worm. "You sure you don't want help?"

She poked her finger and yelped.

"Here, hold this." He exchanged poles and, in doing so, her worm wiggled free from the hook. He chuckled to himself, knowing she would have lost her bait on the first cast. He fastened a new worm on the hook.

A moment later she pulled back on the rod while at the same time reeling in the line.

"Hey, I have something."

Gideon grabbed the net and waited for her to bring it in closer so he could scoop it from the water.

Her trout was legal but nothing to brag about. Faith found something to say anyway. "Less than five minutes in the water and I caught one. The first one, I should add."

"With *mei* pole, *mei* bait, and *mei* cast."

"Oh, don't be a poor sport, Gideon. Your turn will *kumm*."

He handed her pole back to her, then proceeded to remove the fish and rebait his. He cast the line, sending it up stream. Before he felt even a nibble, she caught two more.

"Got another one." She worked the line, reeling in a slightly larger fish than the last one.

The trout flapped on the sandy shoreline. Gideon placed his foot on the fish to stop it from flapping back into the water.

"This is fun," she said, watching him unhook her fourth fish.

"Smell your hands," he said, smirking.

Her face crinkled. "Why?"

"Just do it." He watched as she lifted one hand at a time to her nose. "Smell like fish?"

"*Nett* really."

"Smell like bait?"

She dropped her hand from her face and frowned. "You're *nett* jealous, are you?"

"You find that funny?" He finished baiting the hook, then set the pole down and stood.

"It'd be understandable if—"

"If what?" He moved within inches from her and lifted his hand. "Do mine smell like fish or worm guts?"

"You are jealous."

"Of you having all the fun?" He cupped her face with his hands, then finding her mouth dropping open in a gasp, leaned down and kissed her softly. When he lifted his lips, her bewildered eyes searched his, speechless. He kissed her again, this time more controlled and determined to take his time. She placed her hands on his shoulders, his neck, then she weaved her fingers through his hair, sending tingling sensations over his scalp. She'd melted into his embrace and was giving herself to him. He pulled back. "*Nau* that, Faith Pinkham, was fun."

Her dreamy expression morphed into a narrow-eyed stare as his words registered. "Fun! You—you kissed me because it was fun?"

"Yep." He picked up the pole, cast the line, and forced himself not to glance her direction while his insides were flapping like an oxygen-starved fish. He'd only meant to give her an up-close whiff of fish guts, not kiss her. Ignoring her probably wasn't the answer either, but his heart had never galloped this hard. He wasn't about to risk her seeing the effect she had on him. But even focusing on the water rippling around his line, he could feel her eyes on him, demanding an explanation. He needed to say something, but what? *Coward.*

"So," he said after a few moments of silence. "You going to cast that line back out?"

She huffed.

He pivoted just enough to notice her crossed arms in his peripheral vision. He opened his mouth to tease her about being so stiff when he got a tug on the end of his line. He reeled in the catch, which unfortunately didn't measure the legal limit. He tossed the pike back into the water, having to listen to Faith's mocking chuckle. He laughed along. "Are we going to debate what's funny again?" he asked with a wink.

Her rosy cheeks turned the shade of a ripened Macintosh, but the blushing glow quickly faded. She glanced up at the sky, then stood. "We should probably go."

Were those tears forming in her eyes? He scrambled to his feet, tossed the remaining worms into the water, then collected the equipment. He lifted the string of fish she'd caught. "You're *nett* wanting to go home because you've caught the most trout, are you?"

She smiled. "We'd be here all *nacht* if we had to wait for you to catch something legal."

Gideon wasn't sure why she'd sobered, but he liked that she was teasing again. They plodded through the meadow to where he'd left Bay tied under a tree. He loaded the poles, tackle box, and fish into the back end as Faith climbed into the buggy. Gideon untied Bay, then climbed onto the bench. But instead of releasing the brake, he shifted to face Faith. "I wanted to wait until you were baptized to . . ." His lungs tightened.

"To kiss me?" She fiddled with a loose thread on her dress.

He hooked his thumb under her chin and tipped it up. "To court you."

She blinked and tears rolled off her lashes. "I can't court you, Gideon."

Chapter 28

Gideon wanted to court her—exactly what Faith had dreamed about—but she had to say no. All because of Olivia. Faith cringed.

"Are you interested in someone else?" Gideon asked.

Only you. Faith shook her head.

"But you're *nett* interested in courting me?"

She hesitated.

He raked his fingers through his hair. "Faith, you kissed me back."

Jah, she had. And his lingering kiss would be impossible to forget. Faith watched a hawk take flight from a stand of aspens, his wings spanning wide as he glided toward the water.

Gideon mumbled something under his breath about another Pinkham woman trampling his heart. He released the brake, then tapped the reins.

A strong scent of fish wafted from the back of the buggy, or maybe the odor was on her cheeks where he'd cupped her face with his hands. Her lips tingled from the memory alone. Faith stole a peek at Gideon, looking straight ahead. His silence stung.

A few minutes later, he pulled into the driveway. He shifted on the bench. "Are you upset that I kissed you?"

"*Nay.*" She looked down and studied the hand stitches on her apron.

"We should have already been courting before I kissed you, and I take full responsibility for *mei* actions. I wanted to wait until after you were baptized, but—"

"You were wrong about Olivia. She didn't steal the money. *Mamm* found a bookkeeping error." There, she said it. Olivia wasn't the lying, stealing woman he said he couldn't marry. Olivia wasn't totally coldhearted either; she did give *Mamm* and *Daed* the money she'd saved. Faith opened the buggy door and stepped outside. "Rumors are destructive."

"Faith, wait." Gideon jumped out of the driver's side and leaped toward the porch as her foot landed on the bottom step. "Please, don't go inside. Let's talk about this."

His buggy rolled forward. In Gideon's quick exit he must have forgotten to set the brake. Now Bay was heading toward the barn. The young gelding had spent enough time on their farm that he must have thought it was time to eat and bed down in the stall.

Jogging next to the horse, Gideon was able to grab the reins.

Faith went inside. She kicked off her mud boots at the door and plodded into the kitchen.

Mamm glanced up from rolling out biscuit dough. "Did you and Gideon have a nice time?"

Faith forced a smile and nodded.

A knock sounded on the door. Gideon was peering through the screen when Faith rounded the corner.

He lifted the string of fish. "You forgot your catch."

She opened the door. "I forgot the pole too."

Mamm stepped around the corner. "I thought I heard your voice, Gideon. Are you staying for supper?"

"I wasn't planning on . . ." He glanced at Faith, then turned back to *Mamm*. "Maybe another time?"

"I see the fish were biting," *Mamm* said, motioning to Gideon's hand. She turned to Faith. "Take them outside and clean them. The trout will be a nice addition to whatever Olivia brings home for supper."

"Okay. I'll get a knife." Faith disappeared into the kitchen and searched the utensil drawer for the fillet knife. Her father usually gutted and cleaned the fish with a special knife he kept in the barn or maybe the *icehaus*, but she wouldn't interrupt his nap to ask. Instead she grabbed the sharpest paring knife in the drawer and an old newspaper from the box next to the wood stove.

Gideon eyed the knife in her hand and frowned. Once outside he said, "It'd be easier with a fillet."

"Couldn't find it." She strode to the tree stump they used for butchering chickens and spread out the newspaper.

Gideon set the trout on the paper. "I'll check the buggy for a better knife."

Faith didn't wait. She jabbed the knife into the fish, slit it down the middle, then removed the entrails. The barn cats must have picked up on the scent because they came meowing.

Gideon returned with the knife. "Couldn't wait?"

"It's getting late."

Gideon cleaned the remaining fish before she finished one. He scooped the entrails and fish heads off the newspaper and tossed them to the waiting cats. "Do you want me to finish that one?"

"I'm almost done."

"Here, use this." He handed her his knife, but said nothing about how badly she had mangled her fish compared to his.

"*Danki.*" Making the first cut with the sharper knife, she gashed her fingers. Bright red blood gushed out. Faith dropped the knife on the newspaper and clutched her hand. She wasn't sure what hurt worse, the actual cut or the sting of the oily fish juices seeping into the wound.

"Put pressure on it," Gideon instructed.

Faith squeezed her finger, but the bleeding wasn't stopping.

"Let's go to the pump." He ran ahead and cranked the handle.

She held her finger under the icy water as it began to go numb.

Gideon inspected the cut. "You might need stitches."

She had other things to try first. "I'll put some flour on it and if that doesn't work, I'll try coffee grounds. Would you mind flaying the rest?"

"*Jah*, no problem." He removed a hankie from his back pocket and reached for her hand.

"I should have been more careful," she said, watching him gently wrap the hankie around her fingers.

"Accidents happen. Have you had a tetanus shot lately?"

"I think so." She held the hankie tight and returned to the house.

Mamm took one look at the bloody cloth and ushered her to the sink. "I'll get the flour."

Faith held her hand under the cold water until *Mamm* had the flour ready to pour over the cut. At first it didn't seem like the bleeding was going to stop, but it finally did. As she held her hand still for *Mamm* to bandage it with a clean cloth, Gideon entered the kitchen with the fish.

Gideon craned his neck to see around *Mamm*. "Did it stop bleeding?"

"I think so," Faith replied.

"Where would you like me to put the fish, Irma?"

Mamm rinsed her hands, then removed a plate from the cabinet. "Are you sure you don't want to stay for supper, Gideon?"

"*Mei mamm* is expecting me home, but *danki*." He placed the trout on the plate, then washed his hands at the sink.

Olivia walked into the kitchen complaining about how much her feet ached. She set the pan of baked ziti on the table, the cheesy aroma filling the room. Olivia glanced at Faith's hand, but wasn't inquisitive enough to ask what happened. When her gaze reached Faith's, her sister scowled.

Gideon backed toward the door. "I shouldn't keep *mei mamm* waiting with supper." He turned and left.

Faith sighed. Those few moments at the river had changed her and Gideon's longstanding friendship. Now their relationship might always feel strained.

An hour later, as *Mamm* covered the fish in flour and placed them into the frying pan, Olivia and Faith carried the table into the sitting room so their family could sit together for the meal.

While Olivia answered a dozen or more questions about the new horse she'd driven into work, Faith wondered if the Lord provided a horse and buggy so she had her own transportation and wouldn't have to rely on Gideon.

Chapter 29

"Order up," Catherine announced, ringing the bell once to summon Olivia. Had Catherine tapped the bell twice, Faith would have responded. As women from the district volunteered to help wash dishes and assist Catherine in the kitchen, Faith and Olivia waited tables.

Faith removed the carbon copy of an order and clipped it to the wire. She moved aside as Olivia came up to the island with her tray.

Patty rushed by her with a plastic crate of stacked cups. She'd been elbow-deep in dishwater the last two hours straight. Faith liked it better when Gideon was washing dishes, but he hadn't been around in the last three weeks. He'd been scarce around the house as well, doing the chores before she was off work.

Faith kept herself busy at work, hoping the distraction would rid thoughts of him. But she seldom stayed busy enough, and she looked for him each time the bell over the front door jingled. His absence had the opposite effect. Instead of letting go, she held on to every second leading up to his kiss.

Faith picked up the coffeepot and made a loop around the room refilling mugs. She stepped aside as Olivia approached carrying a food tray.

Her sister stopped at the table behind Faith, and without intentionally eavesdropping, Faith overheard a conversation between her sister and an older gentleman seated by himself.

"Delight thyself also in the Lord: and he shall give thee the desires of thine heart," the man said. Before Olivia formed a response, he added, "Child, if you would learn to trust in the Lord, you wouldn't need to strive for things unseen. You will find contentment in His grace."

Faith glanced over her shoulder to see Olivia's brows pucker in response to his words.

"How do you know anything about me?" Olivia's voice trembled.

Another customer at a nearby table cleared her throat. "Miss," she said, lifting her mug. Faith quickly refilled the woman's mug while straining to hear the conversation at Olivia's table. Although Faith couldn't hear the red-haired man's reply, when she glanced over at Olivia, she noticed her sister's face had turned ashen. Faith filled more cups, emptying the pot. Then she returned to the waitress station to brew more.

Olivia darted behind the counter and ducked. "The man at table five would like more *kaffi*."

"He's your customer."

"*Nay*, I don't want him." Olivia shook her head. "The man is *narrish*."

The bell rang twice. Faith smiled. "Catherine's calling me." She pushed the swinging doors open and breezed into the kitchen. "What do you have?"

"Table three is ready. Table two is up next." Catherine flipped the eggs in the frypan.

Faith delivered the food to the customers. As she passed the man with the red hair, she noticed his mug sitting on the edge, empty. "Sir, we're brewing more *kaffi nau*."

"Bless you, dear."

She rounded the workstation and glared at Olivia. "What's wrong with you?"

"I told you he's *narrish*. He called himself a messenger. I'm *nett* going back to that table."

"Fine, I'll do it." She groaned when the order bell dinged twice again. "You'll have to serve table two." Faith handed Olivia the tray, then picked up the coffeepot.

She filled the man's mug, leaving enough room for him to add cream. "How is everything?"

"Very good." He dabbed his mouth with his napkin. "Do you know that the Lord Himself goes before you? He will be with you; He will never leave nor forsake you."

She hesitated, struck by an odd familiarity she couldn't place. She studied his gaze. Vibrant. Engaging. He reminded her of the homeless man, perhaps because he talked so openly about God. But this man seated before her was well groomed, wearing clothes neatly pressed. Realizing she'd been staring, Faith cleared her throat. "You're referring to the verse in Deuteronomy, *jah*?"

The man's green eyes flickered as if pleased with her answer. "The Israelites' journey to the promise land required blind faith," he said. "God went with them, leading them, yet they cried out in fear, even begged to return to bondage."

Faith listened, finding the man's enthusiasm for the Scriptures refreshing.

"The One who knows you by name has called you. Do not be afraid. Do not be discouraged. Remember He is with you always."

"I believe that He is with me."

"Then you shall find comfort in His mercy."

He was talking as if he knew something Faith didn't. Perhaps the man was suffering from dementia. "Can I get you anything else?"

"I'm satisfied now," he said.

"Okay, then I'll bring you the check." She returned to the waitress station and placed the coffeepot back on the machine's hot plate.

Olivia sidled up beside her, leaned closer, and whispered, "I told you he's *narrish*."

"He's an old man quoting scriptures. There is nothing *narrish* about that. We should all give account of our faith more freely."

"He got to you too. I can tell. You're shaking."

Faith glanced at her hands. Her sister was right, but Faith refused to agree that the customer had anything to do with it. What he'd spoken was the truth. God went before her—true. He was with her always—absolutely. If anything, the man's words had given her something else to think about besides Gideon. His words were like a blessing themselves—a holy distraction.

⊰⊱

Gideon inspected the apple and frowned at the crescent-shaped hole in the fruit. Plum Curculio beetles had burrowed their way into several apples, and a few pest-ridden fruit had already fallen to the ground. Why hadn't he seen signs of the infestation the other day when he was carting barrels of water out to the trees? He moved down the rows, checking each tree thoroughly for the extent of damages. So far he'd been able to avoid spraying toxic chemicals on his trees by pruning infected fruit and by using chickens. He also made a point to rake all the fruit that had fallen when the trees naturally pruned themselves in June.

The trees too infected to save, he chopped down and hauled to a clearing to burn. He didn't like losing mature trees, but he had no choice. It took most of the day, and even then he wasn't sure if he'd rectified the situation completely. As a last-ditch effort, he relocated the chickens from the henhouse to the fences surrounding the trees. They would eat well for the next few days.

As he worked, his thoughts flitted to Faith. He'd broken his own vow—went straight to kissing her. She deserved to be courted properly.

Gideon replayed her expression when he'd brushed her face with his fishy hands. Standing so close, seeing her mouth drop open . . . He shook his head. If he continued reviewing his actions leading up to the kiss, he might never master self-control again. Faith deserved better. Gideon glanced up at the descending sun. He needed to finish raking the infected apples and get over to Faith's house to milk the cows.

A short time later, Gideon was perched on a chair next to Mordecai Pinkham, updating him on the livestock and the limited feed remaining in the grain barrels.

"I could pick up a sack or two of oats from the feedstore if you'd like," Gideon offered.

"That would be *gut*, *danki*."

Irma came into the sitting room carrying two mugs of coffee and handed one to Gideon. "You're *welkum* to stay for supper tonight, Gideon. I'm making meat loaf."

"I'd like that, *danki*." His mouth had been watering since he'd arrived, taking in the tantalizing aroma.

The front door opened and Faith stepped inside. She looked his way and offered a tight-lipped smile.

"Hello, Faith," he said.

"What are you doing here, Gideon?"

Mordecai cleared his throat. "Is that any way to treat our guest?"

"I'm sorry if I sounded rude." Her gaze danced around the room, landing anywhere but on Gideon.

"I wanted to let your *Daed* know the grain is low," he said.

"And I invited him to stay and have supper," Irma interjected.

Gideon smiled. "Your *mamm's* making meat loaf. How could I refuse?"

Irma motioned to the kitchen. "Could you both help move the table in here so we can all eat together?"

Gideon stood. He and Faith managed to move the table into the sitting room without talking. He'd clear the air between them once supper was over.

Small talk during dinner consisted of crops and livestock. Gideon was sure his belly had stretched eating so much food. Irma's meat loaf was the best he'd eaten, though he wouldn't admit that in front of his mother. Faith hardly looked up from her plate, and she remained close-mouthed throughout the meal. He hadn't seen her in three weeks and now that the meal had ended, he half expected her to find a reason to scurry off.

"*Danki* for inviting me to supper," he told Faith's parents.

"You're always *welkum*, Gideon." Irma sipped her coffee.

"I'd like to show *mei* appreciation by offering

306

to wash dishes." He pushed away from the table and grabbed his plate, water glass, and utensils.

Faith stood. "That isn't necessary."

"But it's a thoughtful gesture," Irma said. "And I accept, Gideon." She turned to Faith. "Before you and Gideon *reddy-up* the kitchen, would you mind pouring your father and me more *kaffi*?"

"*Jah*, sure." Faith picked up their mugs and retreated into the kitchen.

Gideon collected a handful of dishes. Once everything was cleared off the table, he and Faith would move it back to the kitchen. Gideon placed the plates in the sink. "It's nice to see you again."

"I was surprised to find you here tonight. You've made yourself scarce." She gingerly touched the kettle to see if it was still hot.

"I've been busy in the orchard." Busy trying to sift through his feelings.

She wrapped a potholder around the cast-iron kettle handle, removed it from the stove, then poured coffee into the two mugs. As she delivered the drinks, Gideon prayed.

Lord, I need help. I know I got myself into this mess, but will You please give me the right words?

Faith returned, her mouth twisted in the same grimace as when she'd left.

He rolled up his shirt sleeves. Maybe not talking just yet was best. He scrubbed the plates and passed them to her to rinse. The serving dishes and glasses were followed by the pots and pans. Still, she didn't offer a word.

"How do you like the new horse?" he asked.

"Her gait is smooth. Fast."

"She's a retired racetrack horse. The bishop took up a collection and he and a few others bought her at the auction."

"The mare is certainly a blessing." Faith dried the plate and put it away. "At least I don't have to ask anyone for a ride to work. Although Catherine is always more than willing to pick me up or drop me off."

He sighed. She was more upset with him than he originally thought.

"And you," she added with phony chirpiness. "You've been a *wunderbaar* help to *mei* family. You've taken it upon yourself to keep up with the barn chores and it really means a lot to . . . *mei* parents."

He fished the silverware from the bottom of the basin and washed each piece with the cloth. After a miserable moment of silence between them, he handed her a washed fork without letting go. "We're called to help one another in times of need."

"*Jah*—and pray for those in trouble."

He released the fork and shifted to face her. Leaning his hip against the sink and crossing his arms, he said, "Do you need me to pray about something—someone in particular?"

She closed her eyes and shook her head slowly. "I merely repeated what the last baptism class was about."

"I see. Because I figured it had something to do with you avoiding eye contact with me."

She opened her eyes, but her gaze flitted. "Nope, it doesn't."

"You still looked away."

Faith straightened her shoulders, held eye contact a half second, then looked away. "*Mamm's* going to wonder what's taking us so long to finish the dishes." She put away the utensils, then washed the countertop.

He stood frozen, watching her scurry around the kitchen. Watching his best friend turn into a stranger. "How can we move past this uneasiness between us?"

She snapped the dish towel, then spread it over the counter. "You're the one who didn't *kumm* around for weeks. I know, you said you were busy in the orchard."

"That's true. I found grubs tunneling into the fruit. I had to do what I could to get the beetles under control. On top of that, I had to water the trees because we haven't had enough rain."

"You've been dealing with all that plus keeping up with our milking . . ." Her expression softened, and the imaginary wall between them vanished as her eyes flooded with concern. "Oh, Gideon, you must be exhausted."

He smiled. His best friend was back. "I'm *nett* too tired to sit with you on the swing for a while. Would you like to go outside?"

Her downturned mouth and the dull cast in her eyes answered that question. "Gideon," she said softly. "It wouldn't be wise."

He pulled the drain plug. "We have some things to talk about."

Faith eyed him a moment, then led the way outside, but she didn't sit on the swing. Instead she clutched the porch banister and aimed her gaze toward the barn.

The evening song of crickets chirping would have made the perfect backdrop to share time together—if Faith wasn't upset with him. He cleared his throat. "Are things better between you and Olivia?"

Faith shook her head. "She still blames me."

"I'm sorry." He hadn't meant to cause problems for Faith when he went to the bishop about Olivia. Now he wished he hadn't listened to the rumors. "It's *gut* your mother found the bookkeeping error."

"*Jah*, but it doesn't change everything. The hospital bills are high and our busiest season is almost over. After Labor Day weekend and the Potato Festival, things will slow down at work. According to *Mamm*, we'll be fortunate to stay afloat this winter. But this isn't what you wanted to talk about, is it?"

"*Nay*," he replied. "I want to know why you won't court me. I thought our friendship had turned a new direction—that you had developed special feelings for me."

She faced him. "You told me the reason you couldn't marry Olivia was because she stole from *mei* parents." She shrugged. "That rumor turned out to be a lie."

Gideon swallowed hard. He could have stopped the gossip from reaching the bishop's ears.

"Olivia's confused. She may join the church after all, and if that's her decision, I don't want to stand in the way of you two getting married."

He shook his head. "Faith, even if Olivia chooses our way, I'm *nett* going to marry her." He reached for her hands. "I love you and nothing will *kumm* between us—unless, of course, you change your mind about baptism."

Faith smiled. "Nothing will change *mei* mind about baptism. I'm *nett* ever leaving our community."

Chapter 30

The following morning Faith and Catherine zipped around the restaurant getting things ready. "I doubt Olivia will *kumm* into work today. She was out late again. So it might be just you and me."

"We've done it before," Catherine said, pinching the edge of the piecrust.

Faith nodded. Truth was, the day would probably run smoother without Olivia. But she wasn't about to say that out loud. She peeked inside the oven at the bread. Golden crust. Perfect timing. She grabbed a potholder, then pulled the pans out and set them on the wire rack to cool.

Catherine handed Faith the first pie to place on the oven rack, then the second. "I think we make a *gut* team."

"Me too." Faith and her cousin worked more like sisters than Faith and Olivia ever had.

"Maybe Gideon will drop by and offer to wash dishes for us," Catherine said, removing onions, mushrooms, and green and red peppers from the refrigerator.

"Wouldn't count on it. He's battling beetles in his orchard." Faith sipped her coffee, her thoughts drifting to Gideon and how he'd stolen her breath when he told her he loved her. They had agreed not to court officially until after her baptism, and she now wished her baptism was this week instead of in October. But she could wait five more weeks.

"Faith?" Her cousin's voice rose above the sound of running tap water.

Faith looked up to find Catherine rinsing a green pepper at the sink and smirking. "Did you say something?"

"I asked what Gideon used on the grubs? *Daadi* sprayed our fruit trees with a mixture of blackstrap molasses, vinegar, Murphy Oil soap, and something else, maybe a dash of baking soda."

"I'm *nett* sure what all he's tried." Faith grabbed a chopping knife from the drawer and helped Catherine dice the vegetables for omelets.

At seven o'clock, Faith turned the sign and unlocked the front door. To her surprise, Olivia came into work shortly after the first customers arrived. Her sister poured a mug of coffee and took a drink. Before now, Faith hadn't noticed the dark circles under Olivia's eyes. Some of her natural beauty, the peachy glow of skin that Faith always wished she had, was dulled by the worldly lifestyle Olivia had been living the past few months.

Faith glanced up from the waitress station and smiled at Olivia. *"Guder—"*

"Don't," Olivia snipped. "I'd rather we *nett* talk."

"You shall find comfort in His mercy." The words of the customer she'd served the other day echoed from the recesses of her mind. Faith wasn't sure what prompted the sudden recall, but just as the red-haired man had brought peace to her spirit the other day, his words did so again now.

Faith retreated into the kitchen. She'd give Olivia space—the entire dining room if it'd lessen some of the tension.

"How is she?" Catherine asked.

Faith's throat tightened. Unable to speak, she shrugged.

"This is her problem to work through. You have to trust God to soften her heart somehow."

"I know," Faith squeaked. "I've always wanted the two of us to be close-knit. I feel closer to you than *mei* own *schweschaler* and it's sad."

"It's *nett* sad for me." Catherine smiled. "I've always thought of you—both you and Olivia—as *mei boppli schweschalers*."

Olivia barged through the swinging doors and produced an order ticket. Without talking to either of them, she went to the ice machine, filled two glasses, pressed the water dispenser, then went back into the dining room.

"I see where this day is heading." Catherine rolled her eyes. "Let me know if she gets out of hand and I'll have a talk with her."

Faith nodded, though she had no intention of adding gas to the fire. As long as Olivia was pleasant to the customers, Faith planned to keep her mouth shut.

The front doorbell jingled, then jingled again. Faith didn't think much of the activity, assuming the local coffee drinkers were early today, but then Olivia pushed the door open.

"I'm going to need help."

⁂

Gideon inspected every apple before placing it in the wooden crate. He didn't want his first apple delivery of the season to The Amish Table to be infested. Considering the hassle trying to eradicate the grubs, he was pleased with the size and taste of the Honeycrisps. Hopefully Faith would be pleased with them as well.

He loaded the crate of apples into the back of the buggy, then wiped the sweat off his forehead with a hankie. It sure didn't feel like the end of August. He hoped the heat was an indication of an Indian summer this fall. The nicer weather prolonged apple season, which meant he had a chance of making up his losses from the beetle infestation.

Gideon climbed on the buggy bench and clicked his tongue to signal Bay forward. He'd timed the trip into town so he'd arrive between the breakfast and lunch crowds, hoping Faith would have a

315

few minutes to visit. Although they had agreed to wait for her baptism before they made courting official, he still planned to spend as much time with her as possible. Provided the beetles didn't take up all of his time. Five weeks. She'd be baptized, days away from turning seventeen, and they could start secretly making wedding plans—once he properly proposed, that is. It'd take another year, maybe two, depending on the number of damaged trees and loss of revenue, before he'd have enough saved to build a house.

Gideon pulled into the restaurant, amazed by all the cars. Labor Day wasn't until next week. He parked in the back and unloaded the apple crate. He tried opening the back door, but it was locked. He knocked.

The door opened, and Catherine waved him inside. "Irma's home with Mordecai and Faith's waiting tables."

"The parking lot is full." He set the crate on the counter, then went to the swinging doors and peeked into the dining room. "You're packed."

"Been like this all morning."

He glanced at the dishes piled high on the counter next to the sink.

Faith pushed open the door, greeting him as she strode to hang an order on the wire. "What brings you to town?"

He motioned to the crate. "I brought you some apples."

"That's *wunderbaar, danki.*" Faith didn't stop moving. She filled the drink order next, then practically ran him over on the way to the dining room. "I'll be right back. Can you wait?"

"*Jah*, I can—" He motioned to the sink, but Faith was already gone.

"Don't mind her," Catherine said. "We've been burning both ends of the candle all morning. The newspaper article really gave business a boost."

"What article?"

Catherine glanced at the hamburger patties frying on the grill, then darted around the island and grabbed the newspaper from the far counter. "*Detroit News* did a story about The Amish Table." She handed him the paper, then went back to flip the burgers. "You'll find the article in the Home section."

He flipped through the different sections until he found the right one, then scanned the pages. He noticed the picture of the building, The Amish Table sign out front, and the plate of eggs, bacon, and potato pancakes. Reading the write-up, he smiled when he came to the part about the farm-fresh eggs and bread baked daily. Gideon had never known anything different. His mother baked all their bread and cooked eggs laid by hens they raised.

Faith came into the kitchen and plopped down on the stool at the island. "I wasn't ready for so many customers. They're lining up outside."

"I read the article. What a nice review."

"*Jah*, who would have thought it would bring so much business?"

Olivia flew through the door and in her rush bumped into Gideon, knocking the paper out of his hand.

"I'm sorry." Olivia squatted down at the same time he did to collect the scattered pages.

Gideon picked up a section of the paper. The headline read: "Still Missing—Have You Seen Her? $100,000 Reward for Information." But it wasn't the headline that caught his attention. He studied the photograph. "Wow . . . I can't get over how much this person looks like you, Faith." He turned the paper so she could get a better look.

"If I were an *Englischer* maybe." She pushed off the chair. "I better take the *kaffi* pot around and check how everyone is doing."

Gideon followed Faith with his eyes out the door. So much for spending time with her.

Olivia tugged on the page. "May I see the picture?"

"*Jah*, sure." He handed her the disorganized stack of papers, then went into the dining room to speak with Faith. He ducked behind the wall partition near the coffeepot. He'd never seen so many people waiting for tables. The line stretched from the door, along the length of the building, blocking the view of the parking lot and road from the windows. Multiple conversations bounced off the walls, filling the room with garbled chatter. He gazed at Faith refilling coffee mugs, smiling, talking with the customers, radiating with joy.

"Gideon," Faith said as she approached, "is something wrong?"

"*Nay*, why?"

"You looked like you were staring into space." She set the coffeepot on the warmer and faced him. "What's up?"

"This place makes you happy, doesn't it?"

Faith tilted her head. "What's gotten into you?"

"I . . . ah"—he aimed his thumb over his shoulder—"I could help with dishes, if you agree to help me in the orchard after work."

Faith smiled. "*Jah*, I will. Anything to get out of doing dishes." She winked.

Chapter 31

"I hope you'll *kumm* back and visit us again soon," Faith said to the last customers of the day as she handed back the change from their bill.

"I only have one suggestion," one woman said.

"What's that?"

"You should consider opening a bakery shop too."

Faith chuckled. "I don't have enough hours in *mei* day as it is." She walked the group of women to the door, held it open, and thanked them again as they left. The Amish Table had closed over an hour ago, but like her mother, Faith didn't want to rush anyone out the door, even though it meant not getting out on time.

Faith locked the door, then leaned against it and sighed. *What a day—a glorious day, Father.* Even with her feet throbbing and as tired as she was, she wouldn't complain about God's way of answering her prayers. Between take-out orders and the constant flow of customers, this had to have been their busiest day ever. And, on top of providing an increase in revenue, God also provided a compatible environment where Faith and Olivia were able to set aside their differences and work together in a peaceful way.

Faith had already cleared most of the dirty

dishes from the table of eight. She just needed to grab the coffee mugs, dessert plates, and forks.

The kitchen door swung open and Gideon appeared carrying the busboy tub. "Need help?"

Faith smiled. "Did you think this day would ever end?"

He transferred dirty dishes into the tub. "I'm all for eating on paper plates after this," he said with a chuckle.

"Me too." Faith rolled the used place mats and set the trash in one corner of the tub. She motioned to the tables they had earlier joined in order to accommodate the women's group. "Would you give me a hand putting these tables back?"

Gideon placed the tub of dishes on a chair, then grasped the end of the table.

"I really appreciate your help today," she said, lifting the other end. "I'd forgotten the date the newspaper man said the article would be in the paper. To be honest, I had no idea one person could make such a difference." They moved the next table against the wall.

"So you met the person who wrote the review?"

"*Jah*, I thought it was odd that he ordered a second breakfast and that he wanted to take pictures of the food. He mentioned that he wrote tourism stories about local restaurants hidden away on the back roads of Michigan."

"That's interesting. He just stumbled into Posen?"

She shrugged. "Or God sent him." God had certainly sent the customers today, and the majority of them had mentioned the article. She glanced at the clock hanging on the far wall and frowned.

"Something wrong?"

"I didn't realize how late it was getting. *Mamm* and *Daed* were expecting us to bring home supper, and *nau* I'm *nett* sure if we even have some of the special of the day left over."

"Olivia took food home," he said.

"She did? I mean, I assumed Olivia was helping Catherine *reddy-up* the kitchen."

"It was Catherine who suggested she *nett* keep your parents waiting." He grinned. "And I offered to bring you home." He picked up the container of dishes. "I'll do these while you finish whatever needs to be done out here."

Faith watched him as he walked away. This day would have been a disaster had he not stayed to help. *Oh no!* She'd promised to help him in the apple grove and now it was dark. Faith hurried and wiped the tablecloths with a bleach rag. As she repositioned the chairs around the table, a newspaper fell on the floor. Picking it up, she reread the food critic's headline: "The Amish Table—A Place Where Farm-Raised, Hand-Picked, Baked-from-Scratch Daily Beckons Simple Living."

Faith pressed the paper against her chest.

"*Danki*, Father, for the abundant blessings You bestowed upon *mei* family. Forgive me for fretting about the restaurant's future. All the while I was wallowing in fear about the restaurant possibly closing, You were taking care of all our needs. I want to learn to trust in Your ways better and *nett* fret so much." She straightened the tablecloth. "Gideon needs help keeping the beetles away from his trees. Please allow his orchard to flourish. He's such a kind and considerate—"

Glass shattered, startling Faith.

Gideon poked his head around the waitress station. "Just me. I was putting mugs on the rack and one fell."

"I'll get the broom." She headed into the kitchen, grabbed the broom and dustpan from the utility room, then waved at Catherine, who was busy chopping vegetables for the next day.

Gideon was grinning when she returned. "I'm sorry I interrupted you."

Faith swept the pieces into the pile. "How long were you in here?"

He squatted down with the dustpan. "I heard you praying for me. *Danki*."

"We're supposed to pray for one another." She focused on cleaning up the mess. Plain people didn't usually pray out loud, and she prayed silently, too, but even as a child she talked with God as if He were her only friend. And the way she and Olivia got along, she needed someone to talk to.

"Will you keep *mei* apples in your prayers?"

"Of course I will, silly." She swept under the table. "I'm going to mop in the morning so we can leave anytime."

Gideon emptied the dishpan and the trash container.

"I appreciate your help, Gideon."

"Anytime."

Faith flipped the light switch on the dining room wall, her eyes feeling heavier in the dark.

Catherine snapped the lid on the container of chopped onions and placed it in the refrigerator. "I have things pretty well set up for tomorrow, so we shouldn't have as much to prepare." She removed her apron, hung it on the hook. "But if tomorrow goes like today, we'll need more workers."

"I agree." The way her feet were aching, Faith wasn't sure if she could keep up the pace another day.

"I'll stop by Lois's *haus* on *mei* way home," Catherine said as they lumbered to the back door.

"See you in the morning." Faith locked up, then she and Gideon headed to his buggy. "I hope getting out late hasn't interfered with your work in the orchard."

"It'll wait for tomorrow." He untied Bay from the post.

"But what about the beetles?"

"You prayed about it, remember?"

"So I did." Faith climbed onto the bench and yawned. The cool night air was calming, and she closed her eyes and listened to the rhythmic sound of Bay's hooves *clip-clopping* over the pavement.

"Faith," Gideon said, nudging her shoulder. "You're home."

She blinked a few times and looked around. "I fell asleep?"

He chuckled. "Snoring like a bear in hibernation."

"Remind me to ask you tomorrow what that sounds like." She opened the door and slid groggily off the bench. She didn't make it more than a few steps when Gideon sidled up beside her.

"I think you're still sleeping," he said, placing his hand on her lower back.

"Maybe." She giggled. "Maybe you're just a dream."

Chapter 32

Bloomfield Hills, Michigan
Present day

Roslyn paced the kitchen. Brandon should have been back from his run by now. Ten, eight-minute miles. Eighty minutes. She checked her watch and growled under her breath. *Brandon, you left two hours ago. Where are you?* She wrapped herself in a hug. *Don't panic.* She circled the island, stopped at the mini fridge, and removed a bottled water. Uncapping the bottle top, her hands trembled. She took a long drink, the arctic water sending a shudder through her body. She glanced at her cell phone. No missed calls or voice messages. Was he always this late and she just hadn't noticed?

The French door opening downstairs off the pool courtyard triggered a security alert to chirp and her phone to vibrate. She pressed the remote video feed on her phone and blew out a breath when she spotted her husband on the monitor. He'd either taken a shower in the spa downstairs or gone up the private staircase to the master suite.

Roslyn removed from the refrigerator the ingredients to make a green smoothie. Brandon liked the combination of kale, spinach, blueberries, ginger, and a splash of almond milk while she preferred the taste of spinach, apple, avocado, and Greek yogurt in hers. She blended his first and had it ready to hand to him when he entered the kitchen.

"Thanks." Brandon took a drink. "It's good."

Roslyn decided she didn't want one and put the items back in the refrigerator.

He motioned to the wall. "What's with the suitcases?"

"I booked us a weekend getaway up north," she said, rinsing the blender. "A cabin on Lake Huron."

He cocked his head. "Why would you want to go to—this has something to do with the hotline number for the reward, doesn't it?"

"If you're referring to following up on new information about our daughter, the answer is yes, it does." So much for waiting to talk with him when his endorphins were high after his run.

He closed his eyes and pinched the bridge of his nose. "Roz."

"When I showed you the 3-D simulation of the car going off the bridge, you said you'd support me in this."

"You said you were going to hire a private investigator to screen the calls. Don't you understand how dangerous it is for you to chase down leads yourself? There're nuts that will think you're carrying a hundred thousand dollars in your purse. They'll kill you for it."

"That's a risk I'll have to take."

"No." His authoritative voice sharpened. "Wait and go after the investigator verifies the hotline tip is legit. If it's her—"

"If it's Adriana, I can't take the chance of . . ." Her voice cracked. It shouldn't be this hard to convince the father of a missing child. "Brandon," she said, moving to the side of the island and placing her hand on his arm. "Maybe this is another dead end. Maybe we'll get up north, eat dinner at the little Amish restaurant the reporter mentioned, then in the morning watch the sunrise over Lake Huron and head home. But what if we find her? What if we're finally able to bring Adriana home?"

❧

Posen, Michigan

Faith diced cucumbers and placed them on the bed of lettuce, then sliced long strips of turkey, ham, and roast beef and arranged the different cuts of meat on the salad. She sprinkled the mix with cherry tomatoes and green onions, then added hard-boiled eggs she'd shelled earlier. She doubled-checked the to-go order. No croutons. Balsamic vinaigrette dressing on the side. She closed the Styrofoam container. "Chef's salad is done," she announced to Catherine, who was adding condiments to a row of opened hamburger buns in assembly-line fashion, and Lois, who was eyeing the grease-bubbling fries cooking.

"These are done, I just need to bag them." Lois flipped the basket of hot fries on the pan, then added more potatoes to the wire basket.

Faith placed the containers of food into an oversized bag. She hadn't been keeping track of the time, but today the workflow between the three of them seemed to run more efficiently. With *Daed* still unsteady on his feet, *Mamm* hadn't wanted to leave his side. Faith had seen her father moving around the house in the wee hours of the morning on his crutches, and she suspected he was purposefully delaying his recovery so *Mamm* would stay home with him and not wear herself out at the restaurant. Her parents were turning more responsibility of the restaurant over to Faith and Olivia, which pleased Faith that their parents trusted them. Of course Catherine was a huge help, and a few teens from the district volunteered to help clear tables and do dishes. The young girls were happy not to have to dig potatoes in their father's field.

Since the newspaper article a week ago, people arrived in droves, often waiting over an hour to be seated. Faith marveled at the immense love and support shown from the women in her district. Even those who couldn't work a full day due to other family obligations worked a few hours, which made a huge difference in serving the customers better. But one drawback Faith discovered earlier in the week was that having plenty of helpers meant Gideon didn't have a reason to wash dishes. In fact, she hadn't seen much of him all week and she missed him. She looked forward to Sunday when she would see him at service and perhaps sit on the porch swing in the evening. As long as she didn't fall asleep on him. Lately, it seemed the moment her body stopped moving, she couldn't stay awake.

Olivia bolted through the door, flagging multiple slips in her hand.

"Are you getting backed up out there?" Faith asked.

Olivia clipped the orders to the wire. "I'll let you know if I can't handle it," she said without looking at Faith, then addressed Martha, one of the young workers unloading the tote of dirty dishes. "I need one root beer, one lemonade, and three iced teas, please. I'll be back to get them." She breezed out of the room.

Olivia still hadn't acknowledged Faith with anything but a scowl. Her sister's sour attitude made working together awkward. Clearly, Olivia's heart was hardening a little more each day.

"How did your *daed's doktah* appointment go

yesterday?" Catherine asked, drawing Faith's attention.

"*Gut*. The *doktah* wants him moving around even more." Faith recalled how the first time he'd been outside since his surgery she had stopped the buggy next to the porch so he could have an up-close look at his new horse. Now he chomped at the bit to take the mare for a drive. Soon, Gideon wouldn't have a reason to do barn chores.

"Irma mentioned returning to work next week," Catherine said.

"She knows how busy we've been." Faith stepped aside for Martha to pass carrying a tray of drinks. "And the Potato Festival is always one of the busiest weekends of the year."

A hard rap on the back door summoned Faith's attention. She smiled at Gideon holding a wooden crate of apples. She opened the door and stepped aside. "I was hoping you would bring more apples today. Sunday service is being held at our *haus* this week and I wanted to make extra pies, or maybe I'll make apple strudel. *Hmm*. Which do you prefer?"

"Either." He set the crate on the back table, then dabbed his forehead with his hankie. "I like them both equally." He glanced around the kitchen. "You busy?"

"*Jah*, this is our busiest Labor Day weekend ever. Isn't that great?"

He chuckled. "It's nice to see you so happy."

His gaze flitted around the room as if spying who was within earshot. He leaned closer. "Any chance you can leave early?"

She shook her head. "I don't think so."

"Have you made any plans for Sunday evening?"

Faith clasped her hands behind her back and shrugged. *"Nett* yet." *Ask me to sit on the porch swing, take a walk, a drive . . .*

He smiled. "Don't make any plans."

The clanging sound of a pot falling on the floor grabbed their attention. But the noise didn't come from the work area, it came from behind the storage shelves. Faith took a few steps and stopped.

Gideon stepped in front of Faith, blocking her view of the redheaded homeless man. "Sir," Gideon said, "the customer entrance is in the front of the building."

The man mumbled something undecipherable.

"It's okay, Gideon. This is the man who chased away the robber that night." Faith sidestepped Gideon and approached the man. "I haven't seen you to thank you for returning the money. I feel awful that you put yourself in so much danger to retrieve it."

The grungy-clothed man rocked back and forth muttering incoherently.

"Maybe we should call the police," Gideon whispered.

The man stiffened and directed his piercing gaze at Faith. "Be strong and of a good courage, fear not, nor be afraid of them." He reached for her hand, but before he took it, Gideon stepped in the way.

"Sir—"

Faith peered around Gideon and asked, "Are you hungry?"

"God will not fail thee, nor forsake thee," the man said, then began repeating the same scripture.

Gideon nudged her arm. "I'll watch him if you want to make him something to eat."

She nodded and scurried over to the prep area. She grabbed a soup bowl, ladled the button-sized *knepp* dumplings into the dish, then sliced a loaf of sourdough bread. She handed the man the food as Olivia called Faith's name.

"I need you to take a couple of tables," Olivia said.

Her sister never wanted her help. Faith nodded. "*Jah*, sure."

Every table was occupied, and people were lined up outside. Faith grabbed a stack of menus. "Which tables should I take?"

Olivia hesitated.

"Obviously the place is packed and you need *mei* help."

"Table four, but I already gave them menus. The woman ordered hot tea, the man *kaffi*."

"Okay. Do you want me to take other tables as well?" Surely her sister couldn't wait on them all.

"Table three is getting ready to leave, so you can have whoever sits down next."

Faith could handle more than two tables, but she wouldn't press Olivia. This was the first her sister had spoken to her in days. She wasn't going to rock the boat now.

The woman seated at table four wore a bright-pink shirt with cream-colored pants, which didn't cover her calves or ankles. Her bright-pink lipstick stood out on her suntanned face. Across from the brunette woman sat a broad-shouldered man whose back was to the kitchen. The woman made eye contact with Faith, which usually meant the customer needed something, was growing impatient, or was about to leave. Faith picked up a pen and pad from off the counter and approached the table.

Chapter 33

Brittany Cox tossed the stolen cell phone into a trash container at the roadside picnic area, then removed a pack of cigarettes from her jean-jacket pocket. Her hands shook as she held the lighter to the tobacco. It had taken Brandon Colepepper four rings, twenty long seconds, to answer the phone, which meant the Feds had the wires tapped already. Still, she had to know if homicide had been added to the list of felonies she and Carlos had committed. Once Brittany heard Mrs. Colepepper's voice, the predictable snip in her tone, she was satisfied. Roslyn didn't deserve Adriana, but the woman didn't deserve to die. The crack to her skull with a tire iron hadn't been part of the plan. Carlos had messed up. If they hadn't pulled off a similar kidnapping before, she would have ditched him.

The cigarette ash turned red as Brittany pulled in a lungful of nicotine. *Just relax.* They'd gotten rid of the Jaguar at Carlos's cousin's scrapyard in Detroit within the first hour. Soon it'd be condensed to a cube-shaped chunk of metal, never to be found. Unless his cousin stripped it for parts. Even if he did dismantle the car, he wouldn't get caught. Detroit had reduced its police department by more than fifty percent due to budget cuts, so locating a stolen car wouldn't take priority over a liquor store robbery at gunpoint. Too bad they couldn't keep the Jaguar. Brittany liked the way the old car maneuvered and the feel of the soft leather interior.

Footsteps sounded. Brittany turned to look behind her. A man approached, matted red hair, wearing a tattered flannel shirt and grimy jeans.

"Good afternoon," he said.

Hit the road, jerk. I got nothing for you. Even if she wanted to help the bum out, she didn't have any money. Pumping coins into the vending machine for smokes and sodas had emptied her pockets. Brittany pulled a lungful of nicotine off the cigarette and held it in her lungs. *Ignore the man and maybe he'll bother someone else.*

The man stopped beside her. "Whoever trusts in his own mind is a fool, but he who walks in wisdom will be delivered."

"Yeah, sure." She had read somewhere that a high percentage of homeless people suffered from schizophrenia. The bum had clearly lost his mind. She'd certainly met a few weirdos while living on the streets of Chicago. It was best to ignore them. She dropped her cigarette on the sidewalk and snubbed out the ash with the toe of her shoe, then meandered down the piney trail toward the Presque Isle Lighthouse where Carlos had taken Adriana for a walk. It was almost closing time, and most of the museum visitors had already left. She spotted Carlos and Adriana on the shore, tossing stones into Lake Huron, and joined them.

"Well?" Carlos picked up a piece of driftwood.

"I couldn't do it."

He pivoted to face her. "What do you mean? All you had to do was push Play on the tape recorder and let the message tell them the drop location."

"I counted four rings. The line's tapped."

"Which is why you're using the stolen phone. You didn't use the pay phone, did you?"

Brittany shook her head. "The plan is all wrong. Too many variables. The nanny agency has my photo on file—my driver's license. If word has already started to spread . . ."

"What did you do, go soft since you left Chicago?"

"No, I didn't go soft!"

He hurled the piece of driftwood at the waves. "It worked the last time."

"The last time you jumped the Donovans' nanny and me both. The plan worked brilliantly because we had another witness." With the other nanny out cold, Brittany was able to provide a phony description of their attacker, precisely what the nanny confirmed in a separate report.

The ransom note threatened to hurt the family's other three children, so the authorities were not involved. Then the money was routed throughout Chicago, distributed through numerous carrier services, and eventually laundered at local flea and farmer's markets, where any marked bills would have traded hands multiple times that day. Those funds gave them enough to go to Las Vegas. But a losing streak at a blackjack table gobbled up the cash, so Brittany concocted another plan. One with higher stakes. Why settle for fifty thousand when the Colepeppers were worth so much more? In the months leading up to the kidnapping, Brittany had gained Adriana's trust. Even taught the child to call her *mum,* and right under Roslyn's surgically perfected nose. Every time Roslyn snubbed Brittany's nanny status, Brittany smiled and imagined sipping champagne mimosas poolside at one of the Colepepper hotel resorts. She'd never be a subway rat again. No more sleeping on the streets in Chicago.

"Well?" Carlos broke into her thoughts.

"I'm thinking," Brittany snapped. She'd run a dozen scenarios through her mind, but they all involved risk. Could she trust Carlos not to mess things up—again? The wind off Lake Huron picked up; its white-capped waves, increasing in size, washed farther ashore. Brittany shook her foot, now doused with lake water. The numbing cold water soaked through her Nike runners and socks. She went to reach for Adriana's hand, but the child was gone. "Where is she?"

"She was just—"

Brittany followed Carlos's line of vision and her lungs seized. The bum who had stopped to talk with her was now knee-deep in the water, reaching down for something . . . Brittany gasped when the man lifted Adriana out of the water. The child's blue-tinged lips quivered as she stared at the stranger with a stunned expression.

"Adriana!" Brittany rushed into the water and grabbed the child from the man. *Don't panic. You'll frighten the girl.*

"The waves must have washed the sand out from under her," the man said, combing his fingers through red hair that had flopped over his forehead.

"Thank you." Brittany turned her back to the wind in an attempt to shield Adriana from the cold air off the water. "Give him some money, Carlos."

Carlos dug his hand into his jean pocket, produced a five-dollar bill, and handed it to Brittany. "Give this to him. I'm going to warm up the car. We have to go."

Brittany handed the man the money. "Thanks again." She offered the most sincere smile she could muster as Adriana tried to wiggle free. Brittany tightened her grip. "Mum has you." She kissed the girl's chubby cheek. "I'm going to get you out of these wet clothes in just a minute."

"The child is not yours," the man said.

"What?" Brittany tried to smile, feeling the blood drain from her face.

"Don't you know? There is nothing hidden that will not be disclosed, and nothing concealed that will not be known or brought out into the open. For as it is written, He will bring to light what is hidden in darkness and will expose the motives of the heart." Compassion etched the man's face. "The truth shall set you free, child."

The truth would sentence her to fifteen to twenty years in Jackson Prison. Brittany clutched Adriana tight in her arms and ran to the parking lot. She opened the passenger door and dropped into the seat. "Go."

"Aren't you going to put her in the car seat?"

"No, just go. Just go!"

Chapter 34

Posen, Michigan
Fifteen years ago

"Are you sure you're feeling up to this?"

"I'll be fine, Mordecai." Irma tied the apron strings into a bow at her waist. She appreciated her husband's thoughtfulness, but this was their daughter's sixth birthday and a little kidney pain wasn't going to stop her from making this day extra special. So much had to be done yet. She still had the cake to make, the doll dress to finish sewing and wrap, supper to prepare, and all before their friends and family arrived to share in the celebration. Irma removed a bowl from the cabinet and placed it on the counter next to the sink where her husband was filling a glass with water.

"The *doktah* said *nett* to overdo it," he said gently.

"*Jah*, and I'm taking it easy." She dashed across the room to the pantry and removed the flour tin from the top shelf, trying not think about what the doctor had said about the possibility of one day needing a kidney transplant.

He turned off the tap. "I'm sure Olivia wouldn't mind if we have cake another *nacht*. You really should be resting in bed."

She glanced over her shoulder at little Olivia, sitting at the table, holding the wooden spoon and anxious as always to mix the cake batter. "I'll rest tomorrow, I promise." She set the bag of flour on the counter, then removed the sugar container from the cabinet.

"*Hmm.* Somehow I doubt that."

Irma slapped her hand on her hip. "Mordecai, I told you I would rest and I will." She smiled. "Unless you say I can go into the restaurant tomorrow and maybe Labor Day too. It is a huge weekend for our business."

He grimaced. "And the weekend after this is the Potato Festival and I'm sure the restaurant will be busy then too."

She reached for the vanilla extract on the spice shelf. "Last year was like feeding a horde of men at a barn raising who all wanted something different to eat." She exaggerated a bit since a typical barn raising meant feeding a hundred or more men, in addition to a large number of women and children. But everyone ate the same prepared meal. It wasn't uncommon to roast a pig, sometimes chickens, too, and have a variety of side dishes to choose from since the womenfolk all brought covered dishes to share.

Mordecai's expression softened and he chuckled. "The restaurant's taken care of. Meredith said she would cook, Catherine will wait tables, and Lois will wash dishes."

Irma frowned. She had developed many of the desserts offered on the menu, and her sister, Meredith, wasn't one to follow recipes. With the growing success of the restaurant, Irma worried they might lose customers if she was away too long. Replacing her wasn't as easy as Mordecai thought. She would need to make of a list of the specials. Monday, fried chicken; Tuesday, *yummasetti*; Wednesday, liver and onions; Thursday, sausage and sauerkraut; and Friday, she would have to come up with an alternative. Meredith's pork pie was bland even when Irma tried to offer advice.

Mordecai drank the water, then set the glass in the sink. "Do you need help getting ready for the birthday celebration?"

She could work much faster if he went into the other room, or better yet, out to the workshop. "Olivia and I have things under control." She gazed at her husband. As irritated as he made her about prearranging her sister to work at the restaurant, one look from him could still melt her heart. "*Danki*, though."

Mordecai smiled. "I have some chores to do in the barn."

A knock sounded on the door, and Irma groaned. She wasn't ready for company.

"I'll get it." Mordecai left the room.

Irma gathered the remaining ingredients for the cake, then pushed a kitchen chair up to the counter and motioned for Olivia to take her spot. Her daughter loved to bake. Irma looked forward to them working together in the restaurant one day. She measured the sugar and dumped it into the bowl as little Olivia readied the wooden spoon. Irma expected to hear her mother-in-law at the door, but heard a young woman's voice instead.

"Is there a lady of the house?" The unfamiliar voice sounded frantic.

Irma set the measuring cup down. "Stay here, Olivia. I'll be right back." She stepped around the kitchen wall to find a young woman holding a small child. Her panic-stricken face alarmed Irma and she drew closer. "Do you need help?"

"Yes, I do." The *Englischer* pushed past Mordecai and thrust the toddler at Irma, who automatically reached for the little girl. "I'll come back for her. I promise."

"What?" Irma gasped.

The child held out her arms. "Mum."

Irma tried to hand the child back to her mother, but the stranger held up her hands in protest.

"I can't take her. Not now." Her voice trembled. "You're godly people, right? You'll take good care of her. I can trust you, right?" The twenty-something woman seemed indifferent that her little girl was crying. The *Englischer* lowered her head and, shifting her feet from side to side in a nervous rocking motion, repeated, "You're godly people. I can trust you."

Someone should take the child from this young mother who was so obviously distraught. "Don't you have family you could leave her with?"

"No!"

The child couldn't fend for herself. Unless the mother had a chance to clear her head, the little one wouldn't be safe. Irma bounced the red-faced toddler to calm her down. "What's her name?"

"I—I call her Doll." The young mother backed up until she bumped into the door. "You'll take good care of her, right? I mean . . . until I come back."

Without looking at Mordecai, Irma nodded while trying to comprehend all that was happening. She estimated the toddler's age based on her mouthful of teeth to be around two years old. Did postpartum depression last that long? Her younger sister, Mary, suffered a breakdown after giving birth and an imbalance of hormones had put her on edge, making her more irresponsible than ever. If this stranger was suffering a similar mental breakdown, she probably believed the child was in harm's way. It made perfect sense that she would need time away—even if it meant leaving her child with strangers. But why did this *Englischer* choose to leave her daughter with them? Maybe the mother knew them from the restaurant. Irma studied the woman's face, but couldn't place her as having ever eaten at the diner. Irma stepped forward. "Do I know you?"

"Mum." The child lunged toward her mother, her little hand clasping the woman's wrist.

The stranger dropped the diaper bag on the floor. "I'll be back for you, sweetie." She bolted out the door.

The toddler let out a curdling cry, arms flailing.

Mordecai's mouth hung open, his eyes wide. Then as if what had just happened registered for the first time, he sprung out the door.

Olivia poked her head around the kitchen wall. Her eyes big and darting around the room, her little mind working to take in the scene.

"Go back in the kitchen, Olivia, and sit down. I won't be long," Irma said, bouncing the unhappy toddler.

Olivia scurried out of sight as the door opened and Mordecai returned, shaking his head in either disgust or disbelief. "She's gone. She jumped into an automobile and sped off."

At the moment, Irma was more concerned about calming the crying toddler. Red blotches surrounded her tiny mouth, and her lips had a bluish cast to them. "She's shivering," Irma said. "Would you add another log to the wood stove?"

Irma grabbed the log cabin quilt from off the chair and bundled the fussy child. "Are you hungry, Doll?" The girl's face pinched and she cried harder. Irma rocked the frightened little one in her arms, but that didn't seem to help. She carried her into the kitchen, and the moment

Doll noticed Olivia seated at the table, she quieted down.

"*Schweschaler*," Olivia said, her eyes bright with wonder.

Irma wished she could give Olivia a sister, or even a brother to grow up with. "This is Doll. Can you say *hiya*?"

Olivia wiggled her fingers in a wave. "*Hiya, boppli*."

The child mimicked Olivia's wave.

Mordecai brought the diaper bag into the kitchen and placed it on the table. He ran his fingers through his hair and paced to the window. He looked outside a half second, then faced Irma. "We can't keep this child."

Irma eyed him sternly. "*Nett* in front of the *kinner*," she said, using her friendliest Pennsylvania *Deitsch* voice.

He tugged her dress sleeve and she followed him to the other side of the room. "She's *nett* our child. We have to take her to the authorities."

"*Nay*, please." Irma's voice strained. "Obviously, the mother is under some sort of stress. She probably hasn't slept in months. I'm sure once she's rested, she'll *kumm* back."

He grunted, which was his way of not agreeing, but not totally disagreeing either.

"We helped Mary in her distress."

Mordecai groaned, but held back from reprimanding Irma for mentioning her younger sister's name. Since Mary chose to leave the faith and live in the world, it was forbidden to speak her name.

Irma glanced at the sweet, innocent child in her arms. "By the grace of God she found us."

"Found you," he corrected.

Tears sprung out of nowhere. She couldn't explain this emotional connection she felt toward the rejected child—and for the young, overwhelmed mother she didn't even know. How lonely and unloved the child must feel. *God have mercy.*

Mordecai touched Irma's cheek. "Don't cry."

"That woman trusted us—*strangers*—with her precious child. It shows how desperate she is. If the authorities get involved, they might send the child to a foster home. The woman might *nett* ever see her *boppli* again. I couldn't live with that on *mei* conscious."

Mordecai let out a sigh under his breath that sounded more like a growl. The noise he usually made in surrender, when he was at a loss for words and couldn't say no. "I stoked the wood stove. It should get warmer in a few minutes."

Irma smiled. "*Danki.*"

"*Danki,*" the toddler repeated.

Irma gazed at the child in wonderment. "Did you hear what she said?"

Mordecai chuckled. "By the grace of God."

"*Mamm.*" Olivia climbed down from the chair

and crossed the room. "Can the *boppli* help us bake?"

"*Jah*. Just as soon as we get her out of these wet clothes and fix her something to eat," she said, using a singsong tone, which seemed to please the little one. Irma rotated the child over to her other hip, went to the table, and peeked into the diaper bag. One disposable diaper and a baggy full of wet wipes. She glanced over her shoulder at Mordecai, leaning against the doorframe. "Would you mind going to Thomas and Noreen's place and ask to borrow a few cloth diapers, *nacht* clothes, and a dress?" Their farm was less than a mile down Leer Road, and their daughter was close to the same age and size as Doll.

Mordecai's eyes widened and he pushed off the doorframe. "How long do you think we'll have her?"

Irma didn't want to raise more concerns by bringing up the vacant look in the woman's eyes when her daughter held up her arms, crying for her mother. The *Englischer* was certainly detached, perhaps even bordering on deranged. Then again, the young mother acted responsibly by finding someone to help when obviously she was in no condition to care for the child.

Lord, have mercy.

Irma wouldn't dare talk about the mother's unsettling nature anymore. Not after she detected another wave of nervousness building up in

349

Mordecai's voice. He would insist on going to the authorities if she didn't calm him. "Even if the little one is only with us a few hours, she'll still need to be changed. Her outfit is wet and she's *kalt*. I don't want her to get sick while she's in our care."

He scratched his beard. "I don't know, Irma. This doesn't feel right. We don't know anything about this child—or the mother."

Irma gazed lovingly at the girl. "God will see us through. All it takes is faith."

Following Irma's mouth with her gaze, the toddler touched Irma's lips, then smiled. "Faith," she echoed.

"Can we call her Faith?" Olivia waved at the child. "*Hiya, boppli* Faith."

"Faith," the toddler repeated with a giggle.

Mordecai grabbed his hat from the wall hook, took a few steps toward the door, and turned. "Don't go getting attached to her, Irma."

But how could she not?

❧

Brittany yanked the Buick Skyhawk's rusted door open, jumped into the passenger seat, and slammed the door. "Let's go."

Carlos jammed the loaner car from his cousin into reverse and spun gravel until the tires screeched off the pavement.

"What are you doing, trying to draw attention

to us? Slow down!" She waved exhaust away from her face and coughed. Years of harsh road salt had eroded a hole in the floorboard, making it difficult to escape the toxic fumes.

Carlos let up on the gas. "Are you sure they won't call the police?"

"Let's hope they don't." She tugged the seat belt over her shoulder and clicked it in place.

"You don't sound very confident."

"It isn't as if we had any choice. That lunatic at the lighthouse said some weird things. His eyes were freaky, too, the way he seemed to be able to look straight through me. He knows."

"There's probably an all-points bulletin out. You should have waited longer before you called them."

"Don't blame this on me. I wasn't the one who knocked her out and left her for dead in the parking lot."

"What was I supposed to do, kidnap her too? Throw her in the trunk?" He accelerated. "What about the farmers once they see the news?"

Brittany tapped out a cigarette from her pack. "They don't watch TV or read newspapers." Her hands shook as she flicked the lighter, the flame catching the tobacco. She took a quick puff and exhaled a cloud of smoke. "Didn't you see the buggy? They're Amish."

Her city boyfriend crinkled his brows.

She took another drag on her cigarette, then

rolled down the window and exhaled. "They live like it's the 1800s, no electricity, no phones, no modern comforts."

Carlos laughed, then reached over and ruffled her hair. "That's my smart girl."

"Yee haw," she howled, then took another drag on her cigarette. "We better remember what house we left that million-dollar baby at." She turned to look out the back window.

"One? Try two or three million." He punched the accelerator to pass a string of cars on US Highway 23 North. "Let's just see how greedy we feel once we're in Canada."

"I still don't know why we couldn't have taken the Detroit Windsor Tunnel. We would already be in Canada now."

"I told you, I have connections in Sault Ste. Marie, Ontario. Stop worrying."

That wasn't an option. As the child's nanny, there would be plenty of video footage detailing every move she'd ever made while employed for the Colepeppers. The lighthouse man's albino face and red hair flashed before her eyes, sending an eerie chill through her body. "You think we should dump this car?"

"I already planned for that." Carlos kept his eyes on the road. "There's a car waiting on the other side of Mackinac Bridge in Saint Ignace, or if something comes up, we'll ditch this car in Cheboygan and hot-wire something."

A burst of adrenaline coursed in her veins as thoughts of national news coverage whirled in her mind. She trusted that the Amish couple believed her to be a distraught young mother, but with the Colepeppers' connections in the overseas market, they would broadcast her image worldwide. Canada. Oh, what had she been thinking? They owned hotels in Canada.

He glanced at her. "You're acting strange. What's wrong?"

"Colepepper Hotels are throughout Canada." For the first time since abducting Adriana, her palms went clammy.

"You brought the new passports, right?"

She nodded. "Still, we've got to go through border control."

"Don't worry." He reached for her hand. "They're looking for that kid. Once we swap cars, they won't have any evidence. Even if they search with dogs." He lifted her hand to his lips and kissed it. "Jewel Monty, you'll hire your own nanny one day."

Brittany cracked a smile hearing the name she'd picked for the fake identity. *Jewel.* Sounded like a millionaire's name. Her thoughts drifted to all the luxury items she would soon be able to afford. And then a breaking news report interrupted the music.

"Daughter of hotel mogul Brandon and Roslyn Colepepper of Bloomfield Hills has been kidnapped. The eighteen-month-old child was abducted from the parking lot of Best Choice Market on Telegraph Road in Bloomfield Hills. Her abductors are thought to be driving a dark-blue 1985 Buick Skyhawk. Anyone with information, please contact your local authorities."

Chapter 35

Posen, Michigan
Present day

Roslyn could hardly believe her eyes. The young woman standing before her and Brandon looked identical to Chrisla's drawings of Adriana, and was an even closer match to the computer-generated images produced by the age-progression software that Detective Henderson had provided.

"Would you like me to tell you about the special?" the woman who had introduced herself as Faith asked.

"Yes, please." Roslyn wasn't interested in eating; she wanted to listen to Adriana's voice, watch her mouth move, articulating certain words. The girl looked almost seventeen. Wearing no makeup to enhance high cheekbones or to thin her rounded face, she glowed with raw beauty—pure innocence. Roslyn studied the girl's hair, parted down the middle and pinned under a cap. She couldn't get a full look to see if it was thick like Brandon's or fine like her own. Then again, Roslyn couldn't even remember what her own natural hair color was. She'd been coloring and highlighting it since high school.

". . . and for dessert, the special today is shoofly pie."

"Shoofly?" Brandon echoed. "What kind of pie is that?"

"It's made with molasses and tends to be gooey; it's very *gut*," Faith said.

"Sounds interesting." Brandon smiled politely. He would never trade a ten-mile run for a piece of pie, not one made with molasses.

Roslyn avoided carbs, too, treating simple sugar as if she'd have an anaphylactic reaction if it landed on her tongue. That was how she kept her size-six figure. But today she wanted to know everything and anything about the menu in hopes of keeping the girl at their table. She unfolded the newspaper article written about the restaurant, which happened to run in the same edition as the story of Adriana's abduction. "I understand from this article that you make your bread from scratch."

"Yes, ma'am. We make our own recipe of sour-dough and wheat. Rye is available, too, but we don't make it here."

Brandon tapped the menu. "I'll try the roast beef sandwich with sourdough bread."

The young woman smiled. "It comes with mashed potatoes and one more side. Would you like green beans, corn, peas, house salad, or coleslaw?"

"House salad with ranch." Brandon closed the

menu and handed it back without so much as blinking an eye. Could he not look beyond the Amish costume and see their daughter?

"Are you still serving breakfast?" Roslyn asked.

"*Nay*, I'm sorry. Breakfast ended at eleven."

"Then I'll just have to come back tomorrow so I can try the potato pancakes the reporter raved about."

"I try *nett* to make a practice of bragging," Faith said, leaning forward slightly as though wanting to share juicy gossip, "but our potato pancakes are worth coming back for. You won't go away hungry, that is for certain. People say they're the best."

"The reporter certainly thought so. Which says a lot, coming from him. He isn't known to always give rave reviews." Roslyn studied the girl's reaction. The sparkle in her eyes, the wide, infectious smile spreading over her face, triggered memories of Adriana as a toddler. Her gaze clouded. She'd missed so many years. *Let it go. Adriana was here. Alive. Dredging up lost years would only feed resentment.* Roslyn put the years of counseling to practice and tried not to think about what she'd missed with her daughter, but instead, thought about the things she and Adriana would do, the places they would go, how they would make up for lost time.

"You said your name was Faith?" Roslyn asked.

"Yes, ma'am."

"Do you like raspberries or strawberries, Faith? I mean, do you eat a lot of them when they're in season?"

"Roz, honey, she has other customers to wait on," Brandon said.

The young woman's smile faltered, and her gaze darted over her shoulder. "If you need more time to decide," she said, not giving them full attention. "I can *kumm* back."

"No, I'm ready," Roslyn said. "I'll have the chicken salad."

The girl's expression softened and her smile returned. "The sandwich or salad?"

"Salad, please."

"I'll put your order in right away," she said, collecting Roslyn's menu. "If you need anything else, a refill on your drinks, please let me know."

Roslyn studied her missing child as she walked away.

"What was all that about?" Brandon asked.

Tears gathered on her lashes. "That's our daughter. That's Adriana."

His face paled as he reached for the glass of water. He took a drink, set the glass on the table, and folded his hands. "This is the lead you're following up on? Why you wanted to eat here?"

"Yes, she's—" Roslyn quieted as Faith stopped at the table next to theirs. She leaned forward and lowered her voice. "Don't you see the resemblance?"

He studied her a moment. "No, not really." His brows drew together.

Roslyn held up her hand before he spoke. "Please," she said. "A mother knows her child." *She hoped.* Her shoulders dropped and she slumped back in the chair. This was more than wishful thinking. The waitress resembled both of them. Roslyn peered at the next table over, eyeing Faith. The longer she stared, the more convinced Roslyn became. Her child had been found. Her feet began to bounce, her hands started to tremble. Unable to sit in one place for long, she shifted in her seat. She reached for Brandon's arm and gave it a gentle squeeze. Maybe she should step outside, calm herself . . . call Chrisla. Her sister would be ecstatic.

Brandon broke her concentration. "The cabin we rented is nice, don't you think?"

"Yes, it's very comfortable."

"Maybe we should talk to a real estate agent about looking at vacation homes for sale in the area. I'd like something on the water and larger than the cabin."

Roslyn smiled. "I'd like that too." They had talked about buying a summer home when they first were married, but after Adriana's kidnapping, they didn't have much reason for a family getaway. When they vacationed, they stayed in one of the Colepepper Hotels and Brandon worked most of the time. Now they would have a reason to escape the city and relax.

Brandon rambled on about tax write-offs if the second home was large enough to host executive weekend retreats.

Roslyn watched as the beautiful young lady refilled coffee mugs and chatted with the customers. She hadn't meant to make the child think she was being summoned but was pleased when Faith stopped at their table with the pot.

"Would you care for more coffee, sir?"

"Yes, please." Brandon handed her his mug. His gaze lingered on the teenager a few seconds too long. Then, when the girl's hands trembled, he seemed to panic. "So, have you worked here long?"

"All *mei* life. Well, I, ah . . . I didn't exactly work here *all mei* life. The last four years." Her eyes darted from Brandon to the coffee mug, back to Brandon.

The poor child was breathing hard and stammering. Brandon was making her nervous. Roslyn kicked him under the table.

Faith overfilled the mug. "*Ach*! I'm so sorry. I hope I didn't burn your hand."

"No," Brandon said, rotating his hand. "See, I'm fine."

"But maybe you could bring him an empty mug." Roslyn picked up the tin container of milk.

"He likes cream in his coffee, and now it's too full to add it."

"I don't need—"

Roslyn kicked his shin again.

"I'll bring another mug right away." The young woman hurried away.

"You can't stare like that, you were making her nervous."

He furrowed his brows. "What's up with kicking me under the table?"

"Here she comes." Roslyn looked up and smiled as Faith approached.

Faith set down the mug. "Are you sure you're okay? I feel awful for spilling *kaffi* on you."

"Please don't worry about it," Brandon said, using a calm, reassuring tone.

Faith pointed her thumb over her shoulder. "I'm going to check on your order."

Roslyn waited until Faith went into the kitchen, then addressed her husband. "You were staring again."

Brandon groaned. "You told me to look for resemblances."

"And?"

He half shrugged, half nodded. "You'll need better proof."

"I'm working on it," she said, thankful he didn't bring up all the kooks who professed to be their daughter or who said they knew Adriana only to stake claim to the reward money. Roslyn used the napkin to pick up the empty coffee mug. She glanced around the room, then slipped it into her purse.

Brandon frowned.

"I'm going to gather as much evidence as possible." Roslyn had nicely tucked the mug away when the food arrived.

"Can I get you anything else?"

"If it isn't too much trouble, I'd like a glass of ice water, please," Roslyn said, starting to feel guilty about taking up so much of the young woman's time, while at the same time, pleased with how well Faith handled herself. Her daughter was bright, friendly, and someone to be admired for all she must have gone through. Roslyn enjoyed her chicken salad. She ate slowly—until she realized this was Friday afternoon. How long would it take to have DNA samples tested?

Chapter 36

On Sunday, Faith spied Gideon through the kitchen window arranging the meeting benches under the large maple tree, its crimson leaves waving in the autumn breeze. With *Daed's* limited physical activity, Gideon had cut the grass and worked in the yard so the church meeting could be held outside.

Mamm scraped crusted potatoes from the bottom of the frypan. "How are you coming along with Olivia's birthday gift? Will you have it ready for tomorrow?"

"I finished it last *nacht*." Faith had worked hard to complete the quilted journal cover, but even though Olivia was always reading and taking notes, Faith wasn't sure her gift would be accepted. Olivia's silence stung. She wouldn't even acknowledge Faith asking to borrow her brush this morning when she couldn't find hers.

Mamm lowered the pan into the sink. "I'm sure Gideon's thirsty. He's been working hard all morning."

"I'll take him a glass of water." Faith filled a glass and scooted outdoors.

Gideon smiled as she approached. *"Guder mariye."*

"Hello." She held up the drink. "I thought you might be thirsty."

He guzzled the water, then handed the glass back. "The benches are in position. How many tables does your *mamm* want set up for the food?"

"Probably two." The last time her family hosted Sunday service, it had been February. For the preaching, they'd met in the barn and eaten the meal in the house.

The screen door opened, and *Daed*, using a cane, ambled outside and sat on the swing.

Faith smiled. It was good to see her father moving around more and able to enjoy the fall weather.

"He seems to be doing better," Gideon said.

"*Jah.*" Her father had gone through so much to even be able to walk again.

Buggies pulled into the yard, one after the other, and parked next to the fence. Service would get underway soon. Faith strode across the yard to greet the women. "Can I help carry anything?" she asked the bishop's wife.

"*Danki*, sweetie." Alice motioned to a crock. "If you'll grab the baked beans, I'll bring in the basket of rolls." A gust of wind flapped her shawl and she shuddered. "Sure is a breezy day."

"*Jah.*" Faith scanned the cloudless sky. "At least the sun's out. We could have the benches moved in front of the Jack Pines, which might block the wind."

"Oh, *nay*." Alice glanced at Gideon positioning a table. "Gideon's worked hard to get everything in place." She retrieved the basket from the back of the buggy and closed the hatch. "He's been a big help to your father. Worried about him too. When Gideon came to speak with *mei* husband about Olivia's shenanigans, he expressed how stressed your father has been."

Faith suppressed her surprise and nodded soberly.

Noreen King and her sister-in-law, Patty, strolled up to them. "*Guder mariye*, Alice and Faith," Noreen said. "It's such a beautiful day to hold service outside. *Nett* too hot or *kalt*."

The women's conversation buzzed around Faith, but all she could think about was how Gideon had gone to the bishop about the rumors he'd heard—lies he acted on—lies Olivia assumed Faith had spread.

Catherine's buggy pulled into the yard, and Faith dropped back to wait for her cousin.

"*Hiya*, Faith. I haven't seen you in a few hours," Catherine teased, removing a plate of cheese sandwiches from the buggy bench.

"I found out who ratted out Olivia. It was Gideon." Faith's shoulders dropped and heaviness filled her chest. "He didn't even have the nerve to tell me."

Catherine's brows wrinkled. "Don't be too hard on him. He was looking out for your parents, and besides, as a member of the district, it's his duty to report something of that magnitude. But it's *gut* your mother found the record keeping error. Otherwise . . ."

"What?"

"The men would have met to discuss the best way to handle her actions. After all, Olivia is at the age of decision, and she shows no interest in becoming part of the church."

Had her mother not found the accounting mistake . . . Faith didn't want to think of how disastrous it would have been. She set the crock of beans on the table. She glimpsed Gideon standing with the other men, but turned the moment their gazes connected. She slipped away from the women and dashed toward the barn. All the members hadn't arrived, so she had a few minutes to be alone before service.

When she entered the barn, Starlight neighed. Faith went into the stall and patted the mare's neck. She hadn't been there long before light shined in from outside. "Faith?" Gideon's footsteps tromped behind her and stopped. "Service is about to start. What are you doing out here?"

She continued petting the horse.

"Faith?" He placed his hand on her shoulder and gently pivoted her around. "Talk to me, please."

Faith stiffened her back. "You talk to me. Why

didn't you tell me you went to the bishop about Olivia? You know she blames me."

"I'm sorry." He bowed his head.

"Why did you repeat those lies *without* proof?"

He sighed. "I know it's difficult for you to understand, but as a member of the church I have an obligation to inform the elders when I see someone going astray."

"Acting on mere gossip, you severed any relationship I had with *mei* sister. She won't forgive either of us."

"I'll talk to her. I'll tell her the truth."

"It's probably too late." Faith marched off.

The members were starting to find their places on the benches. Men on one side and women and children on the other. Faith joined the group of youth who were taking the baptism classes.

The elder's teachings dealt with separating oneself from the world. Faith hoped God was speaking to Olivia's heart. She pondered Gideon's reason for telling the bishop about Olivia and concluded that she, too, would fully support the rules of their *Ordnung*—even the part about turning in a fellow believer if she found them doing wrong. A short time later, the baptism class ended with a prayer, and their small group joined the others for the meal.

While the men filled their plates with ham and baked beans, Gideon peered over the dessert table. Faith pretended not to notice him selecting a piece of apple strudel. Once the men filled their plates, the women and children went next. Faith waited for the line to go down before picking up a plate and going to the table. She looked for a place to sit next to Catherine, but the seats were already taken. Olivia was sitting at one end of the table. Surely she would slide over a little to make room. But even if she did, the meal would be awkward. Faith opted to eat inside the house. Fewer flies, anyway. She'd be alone for a change. Normally she enjoyed mealtime with the church family. But today a little distance between Gideon and her would be wise. At the moment, she couldn't talk about later this evening when they planned to sit on the porch together.

Faith entered the house, expecting to be alone, but found three young mothers with fussy babies sitting in the living room. She motioned to the kitchen and whispered she needed to get something, then tiptoed past the group.

The kitchen table was gone, used outside for the guests. She set her plate on the counter and nibbled on a piece of ham. Once she finished her food, she went back outside, making her way to the dessert table. The younger children were playing tag on the lawn, so more places had opened up on the benches. She selected a slice of her own apple pie and sat next to Catherine.

One of the younger boys playing tag shouted,

"A horse is loose," while pointing somewhere behind the barn that Faith couldn't see from where she was sitting.

Gideon and a few of the older teens jogged toward the fence.

Faith took a bite of the pie and let the apples and cinnamon melt in her mouth. Hearing commotion near the barn, she turned to watch Gideon approach Starlight. Had she not latched the stall door? The mare spooked and darted away from the youth flagging their arms.

"They're having quite a time of it," Catherine said.

"Starlight is a retired racehorse. She's got spirit." Faith smiled, eyeing the chase. When the group moved out of sight, she returned to eating her pie. But then another commotion broke out, and not from Gideon's group. Several police cars pulled into the drive and fanned out. Faith searched the crowd for her parents. *Mamm* stood next to the food table, her mouth agape. *Daed*, along with the bishop and elders, ambled toward the officers.

Faith dropped her fork on the plate and bounded up from the bench. She rushed to *Mamm's* side. Perhaps the officers had located the hit-and-run driver and wanted to let her parents know. But that wouldn't take this many officers. She leaned closer to *Mamm.* "Do you think it's something to do with the restaurant?" *Lord, I pray it wasn't a fire or vandalism. If so, we'll lose all the new business brought in from the newspaper article.*

Two officers flanked *Daed*.

Mamm's face cringed. She must have noticed *Daed's* watery eyes too. "Stay here." She rushed toward *Daed*, only more officers surrounded her as well, keeping them separate.

Faith glanced over to where Olivia had been sitting, but her sister was gone. At the same time, Catherine sidled up beside Faith and looped her arm around Faith's. Signaled by one of the officers, Faith clutched Catherine's arm tighter. "*Kumm* with me, please."

Catherine steadied Faith. "Take a deep breath," her cousin whispered.

Faith moved forward cautiously—until she noticed the police officers escorting her parents to separate cars. She broke from Catherine and ran toward the cars, reaching the nearest one where her mother was sitting in the backseat, sobbing. Panic infused her veins when *Mamm* didn't open the door or roll down the window.

An *Englisch* man, whose only indication he was a policeman was the handgun protruding from the holster strapped around his shoulder, said, "Are you Faith Pinkham?"

"*Jah*, where are you taking *mei* parents?" She gasped quick breaths, making her feel light-headed and out of control.

"I'm Special Agent Sanderson of the FBI,"

the man said, flashing what must have been his badge. "I need you to come with me."

"Why?"

"Faith," the bishop said calmly. "It will be best if you go with them."

"I haven't done anything wrong. Why am I being arrested?" *Why are you taking* Mamm *and* Daed *away?*

"You're not under arrest, miss, but I do have a court order, so you need to come with me."

Dozens of questions popped in her mind all at once, but as she opened her mouth to speak, she glimpsed the bishop shaking his head, and clamped it closed.

Gideon jogged up to them. "Is something wrong, Faith?"

"I don't know," she screeched. Blinking several times, she released the flood of tears, which had clouded her vision.

"If you will kindly step toward the vehicle, we can get on our way," Agent Sanderson said.

Faith looked again at Bishop Zook for his direction. When he nodded, she followed the agent's instruction and went with him and three others to the dark, unmarked vehicle. She climbed into the backseat, sinking into soft leather. Agent Sanderson took the seat next to her. "You're safe now," he said. "I won't let anything happen to you."

Safe? She was safe at home.

Faith assumed they were going to the police station in town, but the driver turned the opposite way. "Wh—where are you taking me?" Panic swelled in her throat. The vehicle was moving fast. Faith placed her hand on the door handle. *Wait for the oncoming car to pass . . .*

"You can't jump, the door is locked," Agent Sanderson said. "Please don't force me to put you in handcuffs."

"You can't take me away without *mei* parents' permission."

The man stared straight ahead.

She gritted her teeth. "You said I wasn't arrested."

"You're not in trouble."

Bishop Zook had given the impression that Faith should stay quiet. Perhaps she should do as instructed. Traveling south on US-23, they passed Alpena, then an hour or so later, Tawas City.

Seated next to her, Sanderson shifted to face her. "Do you need to use the restroom?"

The driver peered at her through the rearview mirror.

Faith shook her head.

The driver continued, merging onto I-75 a few miles later. Once on the interstate, she recognized the same Missing Children's billboard spaced several miles apart. The sign looked familiar. Where had she seen those pictures before? The *Detroit News*. The article about the missing child was in the same paper as the article the reporter ran about The Amish Table.

"Are you doing all right?" the agent asked.

How could any of this be all right? "Where are we going?"

"Bloomfield Hills. Are you familiar with the area?"

"*Nay*." The farthest she'd traveled from home was Alpena, and they'd passed that town hours ago. "Why are you . . . ?" She wept.

The agent handed her a box of tissues. "You're safe," he said reassuringly. "We've called a special counselor to help you through this transition. I'm sure it'll be overwhelming at first."

"I don't know what you're talking about."

"You don't see your resemblance to the billboard photograph you've been studying each time it comes up?"

"It looked familiar, is all."

"That toddler went missing fifteen years ago," he said. "The mother was putting groceries in the trunk of her car when someone hit her on the head and rendered her unconscious."

"Why are you telling me all of this? I don't know anything about the people involved. Do you think I know something? Is that why you're taking me away?" She spoke faster, unable to calm the panic growing inside of her.

"No," he said. "I believe you're innocent on all accounts."

"Then why am I . . . ?" *Oh, Lord.* The air left her lungs in a whoosh. "You think that girl is me?"

"I know this is all overwhelming and it'll take time to adjust."

"I don't believe any of it. I might look like the girl on the sign, but I'm *nett*. I'm Amish. I've never lived anywhere but Posen. You have the wrong person."

The corners of the man's mouth turned down. "Once we're at the station in Bloomfield, we'll run more DNA tests. If the blood work shows you're not the girl on the billboard, I'll drive you back to Posen. Okay? Will you trust me to look into it?"

Faith nodded, having no choice but to agree.

Chapter 37

Bloomfield Hills, Michigan
Present day

The Lord Himself goes before you and will be with you; He will never leave you nor forsake you. Do not be afraid; do not be discouraged. Faith recited the scripture from Deuteronomy multiple times before it dawned on her that the homeless man had quoted the same verse. Had God used the red-haired man to deliver the message or were the homeless man's ramblings a coincidence? Pondering the possibilities sent an unexplainable warmth through her. As if God Himself had shrouded her in peace, her hands stopped trembling. Suddenly the police station wasn't so gloomy. God hadn't abandoned her. He was with her, here in the gray painted room, awaiting the DNA results. And God would oversee her safe return home once the agent was satisfied she wasn't the missing child.

A thirtysomething woman entered the room. "Hello, I'm Kendra Hammond, an FBI psychologist." She extended her hand, shook Faith's firmly, then sat opposite Faith at the metal table. "Agent Sanderson asked me to stop in, introduce myself, and see if there's anything

I can do for you. Would you like something to drink? Something to eat?"

"*Nay*, thank you." Faith hadn't eaten since noon, and she had no idea how late it was now. Without windows in the room, she had nothing to go by but her growling stomach. Still, she couldn't eat. She'd already been offered food, drinks, newspapers and magazines to read, along with multiple invitations to talk about the situation. But she had nothing to say. She wasn't the person they were looking for. This mix-up was wrong. They shouldn't be holding her in a windowless room—she should be home sharing the porch swing with Gideon.

"I'm sorry the accommodations here are not more suitable." Kendra scanned the room and grimaced.

"I don't mind." She wouldn't be here much longer. According to the promise Special Agent Sanderson had made, he'd expedite the results from the blood sample.

"So what are some of your hobbies?"

"I like to cook and quilt. I garden in the summer, and sometimes in the winter I put jigsaw puzzles together."

"I might be able to arrange for a puzzle to be brought in. Would you like to work on one while we talk?"

Faith shook her head. "May I have a glass of water, please?"

"Absolutely." The woman left the room.

A few minutes later, the woman returned with the drink, along with Agent Sanderson holding a piece of paper in his hand. They sat opposite Faith.

"The test results you requested are back," Agent Sanderson said, glancing briefly at the psychologist.

Faith wrung her hands under the table as the agent placed the papers in front of her.

"With user error factored in, the results indicate that there is a 99.98 percent chance that you are Adriana Colepepper," Agent Sanderson said. "These figures are within fractions of the ones reported from the fingerprints and hair samples."

So it was true. She wasn't Faith Pinkham—never had been. Her parents were imposters. Numbness traveled over her body, deadening her senses. The agent's next words garbled, his mouth moved in slow motion. It couldn't be true. Her parents wouldn't have lied to her all these years.

"Maybe you would feel better if you drank some water," the woman said, sliding the Styrofoam cup closer to Faith. "We can talk about it when you're ready."

How could she ever be able to talk about something as earth-shattering as her parents' betrayal? She couldn't understand it herself.

"Your birth parents have been waiting outside," Agent Sanderson said. "Would you like to meet them now?"

Faith stared at him without really seeing him, or anything around her, for that matter.

"They've waited fifteen years to reunite with you—their daughter," the woman said softly.

Faith shivered. The thought of meeting two strangers who claimed to be her parents was more than she could handle. "I think I'm going to be—" She pushed away from the table and went to the small trash can next to the door. Vomiting didn't help relieve the nausea.

The woman came up beside her and tapped her shoulder. "A drink of water should help," she said, handing Faith the cup.

Faith took a sip. It didn't help settle her stomach, but she drank more. "What happens *nau*?"

"You'll meet your parents . . . and begin your new life." The woman smiled kindly. "I've had the opportunity to talk with your parents. They're anxious to get to know you, and they understand there will be an adjustment period. It'll be normal to feel awkward. But I promise you it won't stay that way. The Colepeppers have gone through a lot. I hope you will give them a chance."

Faith studied the worn paint on the cement floor. *Where are You, God? I thought I would be going home. I thought this was all a huge misunderstanding.* Her stomach roiled. She lunged for the trash can again.

After a few minutes, Faith agreed to meet

her parents. She stood in the room, next to the psychologist, as a man and woman entered. Faith gulped. The couple claiming to be her parents were the customers she'd waited on Friday, then again on Saturday for both breakfast and lunch.

Mrs. Colepepper's makeup ran down her face, leaving heavy black smudges around her eyes. She held out her arms and pulled Faith into a hug. "I knew you were still alive. I never gave up looking for you."

Faith wasn't sure how to respond. She stood stiff in the woman's arms, feeling dull, lifeless. Even if she tried, she wouldn't be able to share the same elation. Not with two strangers.

Mrs. Colepepper pushed back, but didn't let go of Faith's arms. "Brandon, look at our daughter. Isn't she beautiful?"

"We've missed you," Mr. Colepepper said, tears pooling in his eyes. "May I hug you?"

Faith nodded out of politeness. He must have sensed her resistance because his hug lasted a fraction of a second compared to his wife's clingy embrace. Faith wiped her face with her dress sleeve, but more tears flowed freely.

The agent swiped the tissue box from the table and offered it to Faith.

Faith forced a smile but was too choked up to speak. *Why, God? I don't understand. Why is this happening? Didn't I read* mei *Bible? Didn't I seek You?*

Mrs. Colepepper drew her into another tight embrace, her lilac perfume engulfing Faith's senses. "Let's go home," she said, half crying, half giddy with laughter.

Faith looked at Agent Sanderson for help. Did she have to leave the station with these strangers?

The psychologist cleared her throat. "Would it be all right if I drop by and check on you?"

Faith nodded.

Mrs. Colepepper turned to Agent Sanderson. "Thank you for putting a rush on Adriana's recovery and for everything you've done over the years. I'll send you an invitation to the celebration."

"I know you've waited a long time for this day, and our team was happy to help."

Mr. Colepepper shook the agent's hand. "I, too, am grateful for your prompt response."

Faith stared at the floor. She knew so little about the Colepeppers, about what had happened. The agent had explained how Mrs. Colepepper had been putting groceries in the trunk when she was knocked unconscious. The car was stolen with her inside—her . . . Adriana.

<hr/>

In the backseat, Faith gazed out the window and watched the buildings go by in a blur. She'd never been to a big city nor had she seen so many tall buildings.

"Tell me about yourself," Mrs. Colepepper said.

"There isn't much to tell. I'm Amish. We believe in—" Her statement of faith, of beliefs and plain ways, were they hers? "I like animals. On our farm we have milk cows, horses, hogs, chickens . . ." She teared up.

"Do you ride? The equestrian club is part of the country club. We could sign you up for lessons."

"That would be nice." Faith smiled, unaware that people actually took horseback riding lessons. She'd jumped on Buttercup and ridden bareback when she was younger, but no one taught her to ride. Granted, riding did take practice since the buggy horse's gait wasn't the smoothest without a saddle. Faith turned her gaze out the window and spotted another one of those billboards with her picture on it. She recalled the reporter who came to the restaurant. He had a camera. He said the photos were for his article. The newspaper printed both pictures of the food and of the building. Had he taken other photographs without her knowing? He could have compared the photographs he'd taken at The Amish Table with the images on the reward sign. She couldn't get over how the two articles appeared in the same paper. How, in the blink of an eye, everything had changed.

Mrs. Colepepper tapped her hand. "So what's your favorite subject in school?"

"I don't go to *schul*."

"What!" The woman's eyes grew large. "Why not? It's the law."

"We go through the eighth grade. I finished *mei* schooling a few years ago."

"Oh, that's just not right. For heaven's sake, what will you do in life without an education?"

Had she been asked this morning, Faith's answer would have been simple. She'd become a wife, a mother, a part owner in the restaurant one day. "*Mei* learning's been on the job, so to speak. I learned how to cook and clean and sew at home, then how to wait on customers and cook at the restaurant. That's how we do things, it's the Amish way." *Her way.*

Mrs. Colepepper shook her head, making *tsk-tsk* noises with her tongue. Obviously she disagreed with the Amish way of doing things, which most *Englischers* did. She pursed her lips as if she was about to say more, then stopped.

Mr. Colepepper turned off the main road, then slowed the car as they approached a small stone building. Inside the building, a man wearing a white button-down uniform shirt waved him through.

"Hon, you'll have to inform the gatehouse tomorrow to expect a high volume of guests over the next few weeks. You know everyone will be anxious to meet Adriana."

"Yes, I'll provide them with a list so they don't have to phone the house each time."

Adriana. Faith rolled the new name over in her mind. A pretty name—for someone else. Her name was Faith.

The pavement turned into cobblestone as Mr. Colepepper turned onto a long driveway. By the time he stopped, Mrs. Colepepper had her cell phone out and was pressing buttons. Outdoor floodlights aimed at the house came on.

Faith gulped. "Is this a hotel?"

"Oh goodness, no. This is our home," Mrs. Colepepper said. She waited for her husband to pull around the circle drive, then park the car, before scooting out of the vehicle. She held the door open. "Welcome home, Adriana."

It hadn't crossed Faith's mind to ask about siblings, but seeing the size of the house, she must come from a large family. Her stomach fluttered. What if her new brothers and sisters treated her like Olivia had—like she didn't belong? Then again, they'd be right. She didn't.

Mrs. Colepepper placed her hand on Faith's back. "Is something wrong?"

Everything is wrong, she wanted to say, but shook her head instead.

Mr. Colepepper drove off, the car's headlights disappearing behind thick hedges. A moment later, headlights flashed in a different direction and then one of five doors automatically opened and he pulled the car into the stall.

Motioning to the house, Mrs. Colepepper led

her through the front doors. Faith stood still, her gaze traveling up the winding staircase.

"Don't be shy," Mrs. Colepepper said, nudging her more into the foyer. "The kitchen is this way. Let's see what we can find to eat."

Faith followed, stepping gingerly across the shiny marble floors. She scanned the area. It must take days to scrub this much space. Oak cabinets lined the kitchen, and the countertops shined with what looked like flecks of gold embedded in the granite. Multiple ovens were built into the wall, and the stove resembled the size of the one at the restaurant. Copper pots hung from the giant center island.

Mr. Colepepper entered the room from a different door. "You looking for something to make?" he asked his wife.

"We should have picked up something while we were out," she said, closing the refrigerator door. "Georgette cleaned it out while we were gone. How 'bout Chinese?"

They both looked at Faith as if waiting for her to answer.

"I'm *nett* sure I can eat anything." She studied the gray marble swirls in the white floor.

"You should try. I would feel horrible if you went to bed hungry your first night home." Mrs. Colepepper pressed a few buttons on her phone, then held it to her ear. "Are you still delivering?"

"While she's ordering takeout, why don't

I show you where you can put your—" Mr. Colepepper tightened his lips in what looked like an apologetic frown. "You didn't bring any of your belongings, did you?"

Faith shook her head. "I didn't know . . ." *I'd be leaving forever.*

"Don't worry. Anything you want, we'll get for you. Roslyn loves to shop, so I'm sure she's already planning a trip to the mall. By the end of the week, you'll have a completely new wardrobe."

Faith glanced at her dress, her Sunday best. She recalled purchasing the plum material with the tip money she'd saved and how she'd taken great care in cutting out the pattern.

"Food should arrive shortly," Mrs. Colepeppper said, joining them at the foot of the winding staircase. "Have you seen your room yet?"

"No, ma'am."

The woman frowned. "I know it'll take awhile for you to feel comfortable calling me Mom, but until then, please call me Roslyn."

"And I'm Brandon."

Roslyn's phone rang and she took a few steps away to answer. "We just arrived home a few minutes ago. Yes, we're showing her around the house now. Yes, I know. We're taking it slow." Roslyn pulled the phone away and mouthed something Faith couldn't decipher.

"It's her sister, Chrisla," Brandon said. "I'm

sure the phone will ring all night. Everyone is excited about meeting you."

Faith cleared her throat. "Do you have other children?"

He shook his head. "We had a tough time after we lost you. Roslyn blamed herself and . . . she suffered a nervous breakdown."

"I'm sorry." Faith wished she could be more sympathetic, noticing the man's eyes glistening with tears. *Lord, I don't understand this.*

Brandon drew a breath and released it. "It was difficult to watch her unravel. Things happen for a reason, I suppose."

Faith lowered her head. "Only God knows what's in store." *Good or bad.*

A few minutes passed before Roslyn came back into the room apologizing for not being able to get off the phone sooner. "Your aunt Chrisla is excited to meet you," she said. "I convinced her to wait until tomorrow. I'm sure you must be exhausted." She glanced at her husband. "How much of the house have you shown her?"

"We were waiting for you," he said.

Roslyn motioned to the room off to the left. "We'll start in Brandon's study." She walked Faith through the different rooms on the main floor before the doorbell chimed. "We'll finish this after we eat," she said, going to the door.

Faith was already confused. The rooms were

large, with furniture she'd only seen in the magazines she flipped through while waiting for her mother at the doctor's office. She still hadn't seen the upstairs or downstairs. It was hard to imagine two people living in such a large house without getting lost.

They ate at the kitchen island. The chicken had a tangy citrus flavor with a hint of ginger. Something she thought she could mimic if given time in a kitchen with the right spices. Conversation at the table was awkward, as much for the Colepeppers as for Faith. When she finished eating, she rinsed her plate in the sink. Not wanting to snoop, she pointed to the cabinet below the sink. "Is your dish soap in here?"

"Just leave the dishes in the sink. Georgette will take care of them in the morning."

"It's really *nett* a bother." Three plates and three forks were nothing compared to the dishes, let alone the pots and pans, she washed after every meal at home. An image of Gideon, standing at the sink with his shirt sleeves rolled up to his elbows, popped into her mind. Would she ever see him again?

"I know you're tired," Roslyn said. "Let me show you to your room. Tomorrow we'll spend the whole day together."

Faith's stomach twisted. There was only so much small talk one could make. She followed Roslyn up the open staircase. Her heels clacked against the hardwood floors. The wide hallway seemed to go on forever.

"I think you'll like this suite." Roslyn opened the door.

Faith noticed the white carpet and didn't want to step on it for fear she would track dirt.

"It's okay." Roslyn waved her inside. "If you don't like lavender we can change the color."

"It's beautiful." The light-purple and green bedspread and matching pillows were offset by deep lavender walls. A white dresser and mirror sat opposite the bed with plenty of space to walk between. Flanking the bed were lamp tables and on the far side of the room was an inviting bay window seat. Her favorite piece of furniture was the white desk and chair. She could picture herself writing letters long into the night.

"Your bathroom is over here." Roslyn opened the door to the bathroom, which held a double-sink vanity, an oversized tub, and a separate glass shower area. Dark-purple towels hung from the towel rack, bringing out the tiny violet flowers in the wallpaper.

"You have a walk-in closet to your right." Roslyn opened the door and flipped the light.

Faith didn't know what a walk-in closet meant until she stepped inside the shelf-lined space. She turned a circle, eyeing all the room. The closet alone was big enough to hold a bed and nightstand.

"There are more towels and washcloths in the linen cabinet. You'll find soap and shampoo under the vanity. I'm going to find you something to wear to bed; I'll be right back." Roslyn left the room.

Faith turned a few circles. This was what living in a castle was like. She flipped the different light switches on and off, then went into the bedroom and sat on the cushioned window seat.

Roslyn returned with a nightgown, robe, and slippers. "Is there anything else I can get you before I leave?"

Faith hesitated a moment. "Would it be possible to get a pen and paper? I'd like to write and let my family know I made it safely."

Roslyn's smile faded. "Yes, of course." She went to the desk, opened the top drawer, then removed writing supplies, including stamps and envelopes.

"Thank you . . . for everything."

"Let me know if there's anything else you need," Roslyn said. "I'll see you in the morning." She closed the door.

Faith took the nightclothes into the bathroom, washed up at the sink, and changed. The clothes were thin compared to the heavy cotton she slept in at home. Anxious to write a letter, she sat at the desk.

Dear *Mamm* and *Daed*,

She stared at the stationery, unable to find the words. It wasn't that she lacked questions; she had plenty. Like how did she end up Amish? How did she get the name Faith? Did they even know she'd been kidnapped or that her birth parents had been searching for her for fifteen years? And most importantly, why did they hide the truth?

The air-conditioning vent above her sent a chill to her bones. Faith wadded up the paper and tossed it in the trash can. She started a new page, this one to Gideon.

Dear Gideon,

I'm still confused with everything that's happened. One minute I'm eating apple strudel and watching you chase the mare, and the next I'm whisked away downstate. They took blood samples at the police station. I was sure they had the wrong person, but I was wrong. I really am that girl in the paper. The one you said looked like me.

Please pray for me. I'm having a hard time adapting to this new life.

Faith

Faith folded the paper and sealed the envelope. Tomorrow she would ask about mailing it. She slipped under the covers and closed her eyes. Visions of Gideon paraded in her head.

Chapter 38

Faith fluttered her eyes a few times as soft morning light filtered through the blinds. Her eyes shot open. She had overslept. She sprang out of bed, but it wasn't until her bare feet landed on the plush carpet that her mind registered she wasn't at home. She sat on the edge of the mattress, covered her face with her hands, and breathed in and out deeply. *Get a hold of yourself.* But despite her best efforts to steel her nerves, she failed. "Why, God?"

When they took her away yesterday, she didn't have time to collect her belongings—the most important, her Bible. She had to rely on the scriptures she'd memorized over the years, but her thoughts were scrambled and words wouldn't come. In frustration, she lifted her arms in the air. "I surrender. Everything. The anger I feel toward *Mamm* and *Daed*. The lack of love I feel for *mei* new parents. Gideon . . ." She forced his name out with a groan. "Even Gideon. All to You, God. I lay *mei* burdens at Your feet." She pushed off the bed. "This is a new day. I shall rejoice in You, Lord." Faith winced under her conviction. "Truth is, I don't know if I can be joyful. I'm supposed to accept Your will, but I need help accepting all that's happened. Lord, this isn't *mei* home. I feel bad for the Colepeppers . . . Please forgive me."

Faith went into the closet off the bathroom, removed her dress from the hanger, then washed up before putting it on. She found a hairbrush in the top vanity drawer and brushed her long hair. Once her prayer *kapp* was pinned in place, she padded down the stairs and followed the cheerful humming sounds coming from the kitchen.

"Good morning," Faith said.

The older woman let out a screech the same time she jumped. She exhausted the sharp intake of air with ramblings in a language Faith didn't understand.

"I'm sorry I startled you," Faith said.

The gray-haired woman fanned her face with her hand. "I didn't hear you come in," she said, speaking English. "You up early."

Actually this was late for Faith, but she nodded. "Can I help?"

"No—no—no, I got this." She narrowed her eyes and made a strong suggestion to leave by shooing Faith with her hand. "I got this."

Faith lowered her head and turned.

"You baby Adriana?"

Faith pivoted around. "Yes."

"Welcome home. I'm Georgette," she said, lifting the corners of her mouth into a brief smile. "You have important things to do. Not cooking, no. Lady of the house no cooking."

"I was a cook at our—*a* restaurant. I liked *mei*

job." *She liked her life.* "But I'll get out of your way." She hung her head and turned.

"Eggs need scrambling," Georgette said.

Faith spun around. "I can do that." She went to the sink and washed her hands, then proceeded to crack the eggs into a bowl. "What time do the Colepeppers usually have breakfast?"

"Mr. Colepepper sometimes I no see. He leave early and come home late. I make green shake and leave for him. Mrs. Colepepper eat breakfast at eight. She also like green shake, but I make at lunch. Unless she has company, then she let me know what I make."

Preparing individual orders at different times of the day was like working in a restaurant, but Faith held her observation to herself and whisked the eggs.

Georgette removed the milk jug from the refrigerator, splashed some in the egg mixture Faith was working on, then continued whatever she was doing at the blender. Just as Georgette had said, Brandon arrived first, dressed in a business suit. He set his briefcase on the stool before addressing or making eye contact with either of them. "Good morn—Adriana, I thought you would have wanted to sleep in today."

"I did." She shrugged. "I normally get up at four so I can be in the restaurant by five to make the bread."

"Someone has to make the donuts, right?"

He chuckled, but sobered quickly. "Oh, you've probably never seen the commercial for—never mind. How did you sleep?"

"Very well, thank you. May I pour you a mug of *kaffi*?"

Georgette leaned toward Faith and whispered, "Mr. Colepepper doesn't drink coffee in the morning."

"Yes," he said, moving his briefcase from the stool to the floor. "As long as you pour one for yourself and sit down."

Faith glanced at Georgette, who answered with her widened eyes as strongly as if she were shooing her away with her hands. "Okay." She found the cups in the cabinet above the coffeepot and poured two mugs.

"So what are your plans for today?" Brandon asked as she sat on the stool next to him.

This was the first time since she could remember that she had no plans—nothing to do. Usually if she had a day off from the restaurant, she cleaned the house, did the laundry, and worked in the garden. She always had something to do. "I don't know."

Roslyn entered the kitchen dressed in tan pants that only went to her shins, brown sandals, and a bright-yellow shirt that made her tanned skin tone darker. "Good morning, everyone." She sat next to Faith. "How did you sleep, Adriana?"

"Very comfortably, thank you." Faith sipped

her coffee, feeling awkward that Georgette was doing all the work.

"I told Chrisla we would meet her at Nordstrom at ten," Roslyn said, briefly pausing to thank Georgette for the coffee. "We'll have lunch with her, then I'm sure she'll want to go with us to our hair and nail appointments. Tonight we'll meet Brandon for dinner." She leaned forward to look in her husband's direction. "Seven work for you?"

"Any time," he said.

"So we'll say seven-ish at Kapprello's Steakhouse. You do like steak, don't you, Adriana?"

"Yes, ma'am. I mean, Roslyn."

"Great. I can't wait." She sipped her coffee.

Roslyn had spoken so fast, Faith couldn't comprehend most of it. Except the hair and nails appointment. She wasn't sure how to tell Roslyn, but she didn't want fancy nails or someone changing her hair.

Brandon left for work once Georgette blended his drink. Faith hadn't watched everything that went into the shake, but it was certainly a spring-green color. Georgette served Faith next with scrambled eggs, a slab of ham, toast, and a large glass of milk. Roslyn's plate of food was identical except Georgette forgot the toast.

"I'll share *mei* toast," Faith said.

Roslyn shook her head. "I don't eat bread. It goes to my waist."

Faith wanted to remind her how she'd eaten the

sourdough bread that she had made at the restaurant, but held her tongue. Her thoughts drifted to work. Catherine would have already baked the loaves for today. She took a drink of milk and cringed.

"Something wrong?" Georgette cocked her head. "Milk sour?"

"*Nay.*" Or at least Faith didn't think so. "I'm *nett* used to store-bought milk. We drink it unpasteurized where I'm from," she explained. The altered version coated her tongue with a bad taste. Maybe it had soured.

Two hours later at the mall, Faith was jerked into a tight hug by a woman who introduced herself as Aunt Chrisla. The woman pushed back, eyeing Faith hard. "Adriana's a younger version of you, Roz."

Roslyn smiled. "Much prettier version. She has Brandon's sparkling eyes."

"Yes, I can see that," Aunt Chrisla said.

Faith hadn't noticed the resemblances, but then again, she'd been in denial and hadn't looked for similarities. The height made sense. *Mamm*, *Daed*, even Olivia, were all shorter than her.

Faith blushed as the two women went over each aspect of her parents' features she had. A part of her wished, for Roslyn's sake, she could share in the excitement.

"I cannot get over how much she looks like the drawings," Chrisla said.

"Doesn't she, though?" Roslyn glowed with pride. Pride she'd been denied so many years.

Aunt Chrisla scanned the area. "Where shall we head first?"

"Nordstrom. Adriana will need everyday outfits and a nice dress for the celebration. I wish we had time to take her shopping in New York."

Aunt Chrisla turned to Faith. "Have you ever been to New York?"

"*Nay.*"

"You'll love it. The shops on Fifth Avenue are to die for."

Faith crinkled her nose.

"Not literally." Aunt Chrisla chuckled. "It's going to be nice having a girl in the family to spoil. I have two teenage boys myself, and neither of them cares if their socks match or if they wear the same gym clothes all week."

They reached Nordstrom, and Faith soon discovered why the women were so giddy. She had never seen so many clothing selections or had so many people offering choices to try on at once. After declining everything, she tried to explain. "If I had a few yards of material, I could make *mei* own dresses."

Roslyn and Chrisla exchanged glances, then shook their heads at the same time, their expressions aghast.

Faith peered at herself in the mirror. The floor-length sequined gown covered her legs, but the plunging neckline and strapless style made her feel naked and ashamed.

"That one is perfect," Roslyn said.

Chrisla agreed. "The shimmering brings out your blue eyes."

Faith turned side to side. It shimmered all right, but she worried people wouldn't be looking at her eyes. "It's too . . . worldly."

"You're up and coming in the world," Roslyn said, erecting her spine as though ramrodded into position. "You're the heir to the Colepepper Hotels. People will expect you to—"

Aunt Chrisla thrust another dress toward Faith. "Try this one on; it's your size. The neckline is higher. I think you'll feel more comfortable in it."

"Okay." Faith disappeared into the changing stall.

"Roz, you have to take things slow."

Faith leaned her ear against the small opening near the door hinges and listened as Aunt Chrisla scolded her older sister.

"Ever since you told me about her, I've been reading about the Amish."

"They're a cult, aren't they?"

Faith's throat tightened. The members of her Old Order settlement were devoted followers of the faith—faith in Jesus Christ. They believed in His teachings.

"By the way, what did you learn about the people who had her?" Chrisla asked.

"Nothing conclusive. The FBI is still investigating. They won't say when they will be finished with the investigation." Roslyn lowered her voice, but not low enough that Faith didn't hear. "They stole her."

"No, Brittany did."

"They kept her from me all those years. Years I lost."

"Let's focus on Adriana. You have your daughter back. Let's spoil her."

The FBI is investigating what? Faith's shoulders sank.

"How does it fit, Adriana?" Roslyn asked.

Faith didn't want to try anything else on, but she slipped into the dress and pretended not to have heard the sisters' conversation.

Roslyn eyed her in the mirror when she exited the fitting room. "Do you like it?"

Faith nodded. She couldn't let them think she'd been part of a cult. Who knew the depth of Aunt Chrisla's probing? Amish people were often misunderstood for their simple lifestyle.

Roslyn turned to the clerk. "We'll take this one. Now bring us a selection of your khakis, jeans, and shirts that teenage girls wear nowadays."

Faith tried on several outfits, saying yes to everything Roslyn said she liked. Even the jeans that hugged her waist and felt snug in the legs.

"Miss," Roslyn said to the sales clerk, "would you be a dear and cut the tags off the shirt and jeans? Adriana will want to wear them home."

"Yes, ma'am." The woman slipped between the racks of clothes and returned a few moments later with a pair of shears and a bag for Faith to take her plum dress home.

Faith clutched the bag, fearful Roslyn might discard her favorite dress if given a chance. One thing she did like about wearing jeans was the pockets. She no longer had to carry the letter she'd written to Gideon tucked up her dress sleeve. They continued through the different shops in the mall, and even with the new clothes on, people stared. Her head covering and black shoes stood out, but Roslyn remedied that, too, insisting Faith try on multiple pairs of shoes.

Faith spotted a shipping store near the exit and stopped to mail her letter. She was happier knowing Gideon would tell the others she was safe and be praying for her as well. Maybe she would write her parents a letter later today.

After lunch, they finished their outing at the nail and hair salon. As if Roslyn had spoken with Jay, the hair stylist, prior to their arrival, the first thing the man did was clip off her ponytail. Faith widened her eyes as Jay then separated her hair into thin sections using tinfoil, then painted it with blue-tinted chemicals that made her eyes water.

"Don't worry," Jay said. "Your hair won't be blue when I'm done."

Faith squeezed her eyes closed anyway. After processing under a drier, then washing, rinsing, more cutting, blow-drying, and styling, Faith opened her eyes. Her once below-the-waist locks now rested on her shoulders. The hairdresser was correct, her hair wasn't blue. The golden highlights looked like she'd spent long hours in the sun without her *kapp*, and for the first time ever, she had bangs flopping in her eyes. Roslyn, Aunt Chrisla, Jay, and his entire staff stood with their mouths agape. But when Faith looked at herself, she no longer knew the person in the mirror.

Faith managed to disguise her tears enough that everyone thought she was overjoyed with the results. She thanked the hairdresser—he'd done a beautiful job—and in the end, children with cancer would benefit from her donated hair, but she couldn't stop chiding herself. Made to look more pleasing to the eye, she blended in with the world she had tried so hard to avoid. And worst of all, she did it to please people.

Chapter 39

As Roslyn and Chrisla's team of florists, designers, caterers, waitresses, groundskeepers, and event planners all merged together for last-minute party instructions, Faith stepped out of the commotion of the room and into another whirlwind going on in the kitchen.

Faith dodged someone carrying a large glass bowl of fruit and almost ran into two men toting what looked like a giant birdbath, which by their strained expressions must be heavy. She sidled up to Georgette, who was busy directing the catering crew and slicing a block of cheese at the same time.

"Are those people supposed to be bringing a birdbath inside?" Faith asked.

Georgette glanced up and chuckled. "That's a water fountain, only tonight champagne will be flowing through it."

Faith looked at it again and crinkled her nose.

"Strong drink not for you," Georgette said as if reading her mind.

"I'll keep that in mind tonight." Faith snatched a piece of cheese off the tray and popped it in her mouth.

"I saw that." Georgette wagged the knife.

Faith pushed out her bottom lip, then reached

for another piece, but she pulled her hand back when Georgette looked up from slicing the block of cheddar.

"You eat whatever you want, darling," she said, adding in a firm tone, "but wash your hands first."

"Yes, ma'am." Faith went to the sink and scrubbed her hands. "Do you know if the mail came today?"

"You ask me this every day. Same question always."

Faith glanced over her shoulder. "Did it?"

"Nothing for you." Georgette returned to her duties.

A lump formed in Faith's throat. Since leaving Posen a few days shy of a month ago, she had written Gideon three times, but had yet to receive one reply. Had he forgotten today was her birthday? Perhaps he'd been busy. After all, October was one of his busiest months. Picking apples, making cider, taking the fruit to market, and all while preparing his other crops for winter. But if she'd been important to him, he would have found time to write even a short note. His silence had kept her awake nights, praying for him, her parents—both sets, and Olivia. Faith longed for news from home. She had to figure out a way to go back without disappointing Roslyn and Brandon.

"The guests will be arriving soon. You best go

get ready for your party," Georgette said.

Faith sniffled. "Do you need me for anything?"

"You go upstairs, take a hot bubble bath, and relax. Tonight is going to be very special."

Faith nodded, then shuffled out of the room. The flurry of activity outside of the kitchen was even more chaotic. Workers were placing flower arrangements, decorating indoor trees with white lights, and setting up tables. It was all too fancy, too much. She slipped up the stairs. Perhaps Georgette was right, a hot bath might help her relax. But it made her too relaxed. The only time she had ever napped during this time of the day was when she was down with the flu. But today when she crawled between the satin sheets, she fell asleep immediately. She might have slept all night had someone not knocked on her door.

"I'm Candice and I'm here to help you get ready for the party," the woman said, holding up what looked like a tackle box. "Hair and makeup."

Surely the woman with the two-toned, black with bleached tips crewcut wasn't going to change Faith's hair. "I've already had *mei* hair cut. This is as short as I want to go."

The woman chuckled. "I'm only styling your hair and doing your makeup."

Faith hesitated, but finally let her in.

Candice scanned the room much like Faith

did the first time. "If you want to change into the dress you'll be wearing, then we can get started."

"Okay." Faith went into the closet and carefully removed the royal-blue gown from the protective covering the store had sent it home in. She wiggled into the formfitting fabric, her stomach knotting with nerves. This party, the social event of the year, as Roslyn called it, was in Faith's honor—or rather Adriana's. Her *Englisch* mother's way of introducing her to the world. Faith wasn't sure what to expect, and as the time ticked closer, the more she wanted to stay hidden in her room.

"That's a beautiful dress," Candice said, displaying the makeup products on the bathroom counter.

"Thank you." Faith brushed her hands over the smooth fabric. "I've never worn anything like it."

Candice pulled the vanity chair out and motioned for Faith to sit in front of the mirror. She rolled Faith's hair with hot rollers, then as they were cooling, she started on the makeup.

"I'm using a medium foundation and a peachy blush."

Faith wasn't sure what any of it meant. She had seen Olivia wearing makeup before, but had pretended not to notice. Now she was doing the things she had condemned her sister for. She closed her eyes as Candice brushed makeup over her eyelids. Her thoughts drifted to her family. She had missed Olivia's birthday last month, and today was her own. Faith pushed those thoughts aside. "Can I open *mei* eyes?"

"Almost." Candice applied something waxy to Faith's lips.

"Okay, you can look."

Faith opened her eyes and stared in disbelief.

"Do you like it?"

"*Jah*, I do."

Candice unrolled her hair, and the ringlets bounced up at least an inch. Her hair no longer rested on her shoulders, but was the shortest it had ever been.

"Well, what do you think?"

Faith stared at the mirror. She touched the springy, soft curl and smiled. "I feel like a different person—a phony."

"Okay if I spray it down?"

"Whatever you think." Faith closed her eyes and held her breath as Candice sprayed her hair with hair spray. "I hope you have an enjoyable evening," she said, capping the can. She began packing up her equipment, then when she had everything put away, she handed Faith a business card.

"In case you have another event," she said. "Or if you want someone to teach you how to apply your own makeup."

"Thank you." Faith slipped the card into the

vanity drawer. "I don't usually wear makeup or do anything to my hair, but I'll let you know if an occasion comes up."

Candice nodded. "It's been a pleasure meeting you. I'll see myself out." She left the room.

Faith practiced walking in the shoes Roslyn had picked out. Her legs wobbled in the heels, but she liked being taller. She would even tower over Gideon at this height.

Sometime later, she heard a knock on the bedroom door. "The guests are arriving," Georgette said. "Are you almost ready?"

"*Jah*, almost." Faith opened the door.

"You look like a princess."

"I'm nervous." Faith chewed the corner of her nail, chipping the polish.

"You don't need to be. Think of them as your friends."

"You'll be there, right?"

"I no work tonight. Mrs. Colepepper no want me in caterer's way. You tell me about big party tomorrow, yes?"

Faith nodded.

"Now, shoulders straight and smile."

Faith sucked in a deep breath, turned side to side in the mirror one last time, then headed down the hall with Georgette. But once they reached the staircase, Georgette stayed behind, shooing her with her hand.

Chattering voices and clinking glasses mingled

with soft piano music, which reminded Faith of falling raindrops.

As she reached the landing, Roslyn and Brandon flanked her, Roslyn wearing a black sequined gown and Brandon wearing a black suit and tie. She hadn't even greeted her *Englisch* parents before people started snapping pictures, flashing strobes of light firing every second.

Faith turned her face and leaned into Brandon's shoulder. No one said anything about pictures.

"Please, everyone," Roslyn said, lifting her hand. "If you could refrain from taking pictures until introductions are made, I promise, we will pose for a family photo before the evening ends."

Faith cringed. *Tell them it's wrong. Tell them you don't believe in having photographs taken.*

"As most of you know, our daughter, Adriana, was stolen from us fifteen years ago. She's why I started the Adriana Hope Foundation. Why I believe strongly in providing financial resources, tools, and education for helping to recover missing children. Most of you have heard me say that roughly eight hundred thousand children go missing each year. That's two thousand children a day. Many of those cases are unsolved. Many of those parents will never hold their child in their arms again." Roslyn's voice cracked. She looked at Faith, then at her husband, tears gleaming in her eyes. "Brandon, will you—"

"What I think my wife is trying to say is that life is precious. It's not guaranteed. One moment you can be loading your groceries in the trunk of your car and then the next you're watching a stolen car being lifted from Lake Huron, hoping and praying your child isn't in the vehicle. Roslyn has dedicated—made her life's mission finding missing children. And in her steadfast diligence, she's helped recover hundreds . . . and most importantly to me, she found our daughter." He glanced at Faith. "Everyone, Roslyn and I would like to introduce you to our daughter, Adriana Colepepper!"

Clapping hands echoed across the room as the audience welcomed her home. Faith brushed the tears from her face, her makeup coming off on her hand. Roslyn and Brandon had shared the story with her before about the nanny stealing the car and later it going over the bridge. How years later, computer reenactment helped determine Faith wasn't in the car. And how Roslyn spared no expense in plastering billboards along the interstate.

"Roslyn, can we get a picture for the *Detroit News*," a reporter called.

Roslyn laughed. "For you, my friend, we'll stand here posing until tomorrow."

Strobes fired, temporarily blinding Faith with rings of bright lights. More people called out to look to the right, to the left. It was all too much.

You shall not make for yourself any graven image . . . Instructions she had heard and obeyed since childhood bombarded her thoughts.

Faith leaned toward Roslyn. "Would it be okay if I use the restroom?"

"Of course it is, darling."

Faith fled through the crowd before it crossed her mind she should have gone upstairs. The landing was full of people, all wanting to know more about how Roslyn and Brandon found their missing daughter. She crossed the room, passed by an ice sculpture she recognized as her infant picture on the billboard, and ran into Agent Sanderson.

"I'm sorry," she said.

"The party is a bit overwhelming, isn't it?"

Faith nodded, then asked, "How are *mei* parents?"

The agent's gaze flitted to Roslyn and Brandon.

"*Nay, mei* Amish parents. I heard you were investigating them."

"I'm not at liberty to discuss the case," he said.

"Why? It's about me."

The crowd spread as Roslyn crossed the room to join them. "Agent Sanderson, I'm glad you were able to join us."

"It's always a blessing when a cold case is closed for good."

"I couldn't agree more." She motioned to the fountain of bubbling champagne. "Would you care for a glass of champagne or a drink from the bar?"

"No, thank you. I just stopped for a few minutes." He turned to Faith. "If I don't see you again, good luck with everything."

"Thank you." Faith darted away. She found solitude in Brandon's office. It didn't matter how hard she cried, the crowd's laughter would drown out her voice. It felt good to sit in the dark, to be alone. But it wasn't too long before the door opened and a tall figure entered the room and flipped on the light.

"Adriana? What are you doing sitting in the dark?" Uncle Leon motioned to the sofa. "May I sit with you?"

Faith nodded. She'd been introduced to Roslyn's older brother at a family dinner the first week after she arrived.

"Do you want to talk about why you're crying?"

She shrugged. Hunter, Chrisla's son, had said Uncle Leon played with people's heads. She wasn't interested in playing mind games. Faith had learned over the past month that when Kendra Hammond, the police psychologist, called to check on her progress to say what people wanted to hear—Yes, she was adjusting. The Colepeppers were treating her fine, and yes, she had everything she needed—because no one really wanted to know her concerns. Every time she asked about her parents, the subject was changed.

"Why don't you start by telling me about being Amish," he said. "I've done some reading about the Amish since I met you, and I'd like to learn more."

"What do you want know?"

"Tell me about your typical day and what you did for fun."

"*Mei Daed* and I were the first ones up in the morning. He milked the cows and I collected the eggs. Then I went into town. *Mei* par—"

"It's okay," he said calmly. "They were your parents for fifteen years, and from what I've seen, they did a fine job raising you."

Faith's eyes clouded with tears. "I think so too." She sucked in a breath and released it slowly. "*Mei* parents own a restaurant, and I bake the bread every morning, or I did. After work, we ate supper together and had Bible devotions."

"And for fun?"

"There's plenty to do that's fun. We have regular sewing bees, and gardening—lots to do in the garden. I went fishing sometimes. Even caught the largest a few times."

"That all sounds like fun."

Faith nodded, unable to push down the lump in her throat.

"Why are you in here alone?"

She shrugged. "This isn't *mei* kind of gathering.

I'm used to barn raisings and getting together for meals after Sunday services. Not anything fancy like tonight." She didn't know why she was telling him all of this, but Georgette wasn't around to talk to. "And today's *mei* birthday. I was sort of expecting a card or letter from back home."

The door opened and Roslyn poked her head inside. "There you are. I've been looking all over for you, Adriana. There're some people I want to introduce you to."

Uncle Leon cleared his throat. "Will you give us another minute or two?"

"Okay, but please don't stay in here long. This is her welcoming home party." Roslyn closed the door.

"Did you tell Brandon and Roslyn that you celebrate your birthday on this day?"

"*Nay*, why?"

"Because this isn't your birthday. You were born in March."

She lowered her head. Another lie.

"I would like to talk with you again. Would you like that too?"

At least he seemed more open and eager to listen to her talk about growing up Amish. "I suppose so."

"Great. I'm going to recommend to your mother that we start counseling. You need to be able to express your feelings and talk about your

Amish upbringing. I understand how difficult it must be to walk away from that lifestyle."

"Roslyn thinks I was in a cult. Do you?"

❧

The following month Faith nervously sat in the chair across from Uncle Leon's desk as Roslyn waited in the lobby.

A red-haired man wearing a wool coat and carrying an umbrella entered the room. "Your uncle was called away unexpectedly," he said, removing the overcoat. "I've been assigned to talk with you in his absence." He sat behind the desk. "I understand you were raised Amish."

Faith wrung her hands. At the welcome home party she thought she'd made a connection with her uncle, but that had been a month ago. Now she wasn't sure this was a good idea. Without saying why, Roslyn had been leery of her attending counseling sessions. Perhaps it had something to do with what Brandon had told her about Roslyn's nervous breakdown. This morning she looked forward to talking with her uncle more, but talking to a stranger . . . ? That wouldn't be easy. "Should I *kumm* back at a better time? I don't mind changing *mei* appointment."

Kindness shone in his emerald-green eyes. "That's *nett* necessary. I'm familiar with your raising up."

"*Ach*! How *wunderbaar* you speak Pennsylvania *Deitsch*."

"*Jah*. How are you?"

"I'm *gut*, *danki*." Thrilled to finally find someone who would truly understand her struggle, Faith sat on the edge of her seat, eager to talk.

"Tell me what's troubling you, child."

Faith exhaled. Where should she start? "I feel like a sheep that's lost *mei* way." She motioned to her jeans. "I wear these *Englisch* clothes, cut *mei* hair—*nett* for *mei* vanity, *nay*. I did it to appease *mei* birth *mamm*." She lowered her head. "*Lecherich, jah*?"

"No, it's not ridiculous. God sees your heart. I know what you've been taught. Modern conveniences, fancy clothing, all inspire worldliness and, while it's true it might inflate one's mind with pridefulness and keep you from being with God, God also sees your brokenness. He sees your difficulty. He's pleased with you, Faith. Don't let your mind tell you otherwise."

Faith sank into the cushioned sofa, her muscles relaxing. "I don't even have *mei* Bible with me to read. How can He be pleased with me?"

"Oh, child. You placed His words upon your heart long ago and committed them to memory. You are *nett* without His promises. He is with you always. His Spirit will lead you with instruction. Lift your hope higher in the One who has called you by name. For it is written: 'Before they call I will answer; while they are still speaking I will hear.' " He paused. "So you see, child, God's mercy is abiding. His love is everlasting."

Faith sniffled.

" 'The Lord Himself goes before you; He will never leave nor forsake you. Do not be afraid; do not be discouraged.' Will you take these words to heart?"

Faith nodded.

He folded his hands on the desk, giving her time to dry her tears. "*Nau*, what else do you wish to talk about?"

As Faith unloaded her burdens about how she had planned to get baptized and join the church, how she'd fallen in love with a good Amish man that one day she wished to marry, and how she always planned to work at the restaurant, somehow her soul felt restored. They talked longer than her scheduled time, and speaking in Pennsylvania *Deitsch*, she didn't have to guard her words knowing Roslyn was waiting in the lobby outside the door.

"Will I see you again?" she asked when it was time to go.

"I'm sure you will."

Faith smiled. Her uncle being called away was divine intervention—or so she liked to believe.

Roslyn wasn't in the lobby when Faith left the office. She noticed the women's restroom and pushed open the door. But the conversation she overheard stopped her in her tracks. Roslyn was on the phone with someone.

"I want to know if the nanny had an Amish background. She had to know them somehow. Yes, I know. But I think it's time to press charges. They stole my child. I want them punished."

Chapter 40

The next day Faith managed to sneak into Brandon's office and call Beverly Dembrowski. She had too many unanswered questions and needed help sorting things out. Although reluctant at first, Faith managed to talk her *Englisch* neighbor into coming to get her and driving her to Posen.

The northern November wind off Lake Huron sent chills down her spine. Thankfully, she'd remembered to bring the winter coat Roslyn had bought her. Faith gazed at the familiar scenery. The maples and oaks had shed most of their beautiful crimson and gold leaves, and the overcast sky suggested snow flurries. As they passed the roadside park where Gideon had taken her to watch fireworks, stirred-up memories brought tears to her eyes. July seemed so long ago.

Beverly cleared her throat as they neared the city limits. "Where do you want to go first?"

"*Mamm* is probably at the restaurant," Faith said. "Can we stop there first?"

"No problem." Beverly pulled around back and stopped the car.

Faith noticed the police car in the parking lot and cringed. "If I don't *kumm* out . . ." *Lord, have mercy.* "Maybe you should drive around or something."

"I'll wait for you here." Her *Englisch* friend held her voice steady, playing like she wasn't nervous, but Faith knew different. After Faith shared Roslyn's plans, Beverly developed a twitch in her cheek. No doubt nervous that she would also be accused of kidnapping.

"I'll be quick." Faith pushed the door open. She entered the building at the rear entrance and stepped cautiously toward the grill.

Catherine gasped. "Faith! You're back."

"Shh." She placed her finger over her lips. "I *kumm* to talk with *Mamm*."

"Irma isn't here today. She wasn't feeling well yesterday so she went home early. How are you doing? You've been on *mei* mind and I've been praying for you."

"*Danki*." Faith hesitated. With a police car in the parking lot, this wasn't the place to go into a long discussion, but she had to ask. "Did you know about me?"

Catherine sighed. "I knew you weren't *Aenti* Irma's *boppli*. She was very hush-hush about you."

"You didn't ask? Your *mamm* didn't question her sister?"

Catherine gulped. "Have you heard whispers of *Aenti* M?"

"M? *Nay*."

"Our mothers haven't spoken their sister's name since her shunning. I've only heard them address her by her initial."

"What about her?"

Catherine shrugged. "*Mei* mother and the rest of the district all assumed you were *Aenti* M's *boppli*. That she had gotten herself in a fix and had left you for *Aenti* Irma to raise."

Faith's shoulders slumped.

"We all love you and miss you—especially Irma. Please go see her."

Faith nodded.

Catherine pulled her into a tight hug. "I'm praying things work out."

"*Danki*." Faith couldn't help but feel betrayed. All the years she and Catherine had been close and she hadn't mentioned the dark secret. She said good-bye not knowing when or even if she would see her cousin again.

"That was short. Are you okay?" Beverly started the engine once Faith put on her seat belt.

"*Mamm* wasn't there." She swallowed, settling the quiver in the back of her throat. She went in the restaurant to get answers and came out with even more questions. "Can we stop by the *haus*?"

"Of course." Without needling Faith for tidbits of information, Beverly put the car into drive and headed out of town.

Faith hand-pressed the wrinkles in her dress. She recalled having her eye on the plum material for weeks before saving enough money to purchase the yardage needed for the dress, an apron, and matching thread. Then the long hours she spent cutting out the pattern, hand sewing the dress and apron. So different from walking into a store and purchasing a dress with a plastic card.

"Don't be nervous," Beverly said, stopping the car next to the house. "And take as long as you want."

"Thanks." Faith blew out a breath, then climbed out. "Lord, give me the right words," she whispered, lumbering up the steps.

Mamm opened the door. "Faith!" She drew her into a suffocating hug. "It's so *gut* to see you." Ushering her inside, *Mamm* held her gaze for a long moment.

Faith nervously touched her bun. If *Mamm* noticed her shorter, highlighted hair, she didn't mention it.

Faith removed her coat and hung it on the wall peg, then sat across the table from her mother. She wasn't sure where to begin. "Why didn't you write?"

Her mother's smile faded. "The police said I'm not allowed to have any contact with you." Her lips tightened and eyes glazed. "But I think about you all the time. I wonder how you are getting along, if they are treating you *gut*." She wiped her eyes and drew a ragged breath. Then pushing her chair back, she stood. "I have your birthday present in the sitting room," she said, weeping as she left the room.

Faith stared at the grooves in the wooden table, remembering her father working on it in the barn to surprise her mother for Christmas.

"It isn't much," *Mamm* said, handing her the brown paper-wrapped package.

Faith swallowed the egg-sized lump in her throat. "You didn't miss *mei* birthday. I wasn't born in October."

Rounding her shoulders, lowering her head, her mother seemed to shrink in the chair.

"Why didn't you tell me I wasn't your daughter? I don't understand. How could you let me believe something that wasn't true?" She closed her eyes briefly to pray for guidance. "You kept me hidden all those years. Why?"

Her mother looked up. "Faith, I didn't know anyone was searching for you. A young woman came to the door with you in her arms. She looked frightened and distraught—desperate for help. She begged me to take you and promised to *kumm* back. I didn't know what to do. I couldn't say *nay* when I held you in *mei* arms. For a long time I believed she would come back." *Mamm's* voice faded. "After a while, I didn't want her to."

"Who was she?"

Mamm shook her head. "The woman never gave me her name. She called you Doll."

"Then how did I get the name Faith?"

"Olivia named you, and it stuck. You were a bright child. You picked up on Pennsylvania *Deitsch* immediately."

"What did you tell the members of the church about me?"

"I told them we had a *boppli* dropped off . . . and I let them assume you were *mei schweschaler's* child."

Faith kept the information Catherine had told her to herself. "Why would they make that assumption?"

"*Mei* younger sister, Mary, left the faith to go her own way. She had a child, a daughter, but soon after, she fell into a deep depression. Mary's mental anguish was too great. She asked me to take her *boppli* and raise her as *mei* own."

"What are you saying?"

"Olivia is *mei schweschaler's* child. I raised her from an infant. Only a few weeks old. So when you arrived, it was easy for the others to believe you were also Mary's daughter. Since it's forbidden to mention her name, no one asked questions." She lowered her head. "It was wrong of me, but I didn't correct their assumptions."

"Does Olivia know the truth?"

"She does *nau*." *Mamm's* hands shook as she reached for the box of tissues on the table. She blew her nose. "Olivia found out her blood wasn't a match when she wanted to donate for your father's surgery. She started asking the nurses questions. Even checked a book out from the library. That's when I told her about her mother."

Faith sank back in the chair. Olivia's change of attitude was starting to make sense. "Where's Olivia *nau*?"

"She's gone."

Faith reached across the table for her mother's hand and gave it a gentle squeeze. "*Mei* heart breaks for you. I wish none of this was happening."

"Me too."

"But I have to tell you something. Roslyn wants to press charges. She thinks you were in cahoots with the nanny who kidnapped me. She wants you and *Daed* to be punished."

"I heard. Officer Porter told me yesterday at the restaurant there was more to *kumm* from all of this and it might *nett* be *gut* news. He told me I should hire a lawyer." She shrugged. "There is little I can do. The Lord will be with me. When the time comes He will provide the words."

Her mother forced a smile and pushed the birthday gift closer to Faith. "Will you open your package, please?"

"*Mamm*, please. They're going to interrogate you."

Her mother eyed the package.

Faith unwrapped the gift. "It's beautiful." She removed the knitted scarf from the box and wrapped it around her neck. "*Mei* favorite color."

"I know. It matches your dress."

"*Danki.*" She started to cry. "This isn't how I wanted things to go." She reached for her mother's hand. "This is *mei* home." *Where I belong.*

"You're *nett* supposed to be here," *Mamm* said, her voice straining.

Faith winced at her words. Although she understood that she'd been there too long. Her mother could be in even more trouble if they were discovered together. "Someone had to warn you."

Her mother looked as if she'd withered under her shawl as she pulled it tighter.

The back door opened and *Daed* entered along with a gusty wind. He limped a few steps, then stopped, eyeing Faith. "When did you get here?"

"Just a few minutes ago. I had to warn you and *Mamm* about the kidnapping charges." Tears washed over her face. "I'm *nett* supposed to be here. I don't want you to get into more trouble." She removed her coat from the wall hook and slipped it on.

"You were our daughter for fifteen years and we'll never forget you," *Daed* said. "Please don't forget how you were raised. Keep God close to your heart."

She pushed a short strand of hair under her *kapp*. He must think she'd already turned away from her upbringing to have changed her hair so drastically. "I won't ever forget. But, *Daed*, they think we're a cult." She rushed into her father's strong arms.

"Put your trust in God, child."

❧

Gideon picked a handful of apples and lowered them into the basket. With the weather changing and frost expected, the season was over. He needed to gather what apples remained and store them in the cellar.

Twigs crunched behind him. He stood still. This time of the year deer were often spotted at the edge of the orchard, nibbling on apples that had fallen. He'd seen black bears eating what they could in preparation for their long winter sleep.

The steps grew closer, louder. Wildlife usually wasn't so brazen. He turned.

"Hello, Gideon," Faith said.

His jaw dropped. She was the last person he'd expected.

"Don't you have anything to say?"

He could think of plenty to say. None of it in her chipper, nothing's happened tone. *Guard yourself.* Faith had closed the gap between them. "What brings you back?" he said, hoping to sound indifferent.

"I wanted to see you. I thought I might find you here. It looks as though it might snow. First for the year if it does." Her expression sobered.

426

"Why didn't you write back? I sent you multiple letters. Didn't you get them?"

"*Jah*, I received them." He studied the apple in his hand instead of watching the tears roll down her face. He had to distance himself for his own soul's sake. Otherwise he might succumb to worldly temptations and take her in his arms.

"I—I thought . . ." Her shoulders began to shake as she wept softly.

"In your letter, you asked me to pray because you were having difficulty adapting. *Adapting,*" he repeated louder. "I didn't want you adapting to the world. How could I pray for that? I was praying for you to *kumm* back home." *Back to me.*

Faith was silent.

"But you adapted just fine without *mei* prayers."

Her tear-stained face pinched.

"I saw the pictures in the paper, Faith. You, wearing a fancy dress, your face painted with makeup, and your hair not even shoulder-length. Did you think the gossip wouldn't reach *mei* ears?"

"I was in a difficult situation," she rasped. "That woman posing for the photograph isn't me— *nett* the real me. Had you looked beyond *mei* appearance, you would have seen vacancy in *mei* eyes. Do you really think I want that lifestyle?"

He squeezed the apple he'd been holding, hoping to diffuse some of the pain pressing on his heart.

"I have to go *nau*." Faith turned away.

Gideon threw the apple with all the force he could muster. "Faith!" He crossed the rows of trees and caught her arm before she reached the edge of the field of drying corn stalks. "I need to tell you something before you go."

"What?" She kept her head down.

"Have you talked with your mother?"

Faith flinched. With a roll of her shoulder, she looked up at him. "I went to see *Mamm* first."

"So she told you about The Amish Table? That it's closing next month?"

"*Nay*," she rasped. "Isn't business still booming?"

"The media camped out several weeks, hounding your parents about their part in the kidnapping. But I think the main reason they're closing is because of Irma's health. Something to do with her kidneys *nett* functioning like they should. She's unable to work long hours and without you and Olivia . . . Well, they feel it's for the best." At least the district had agreed to help pay the medical bills and they wouldn't have that burden to bear alone.

"I wish there was something I could do."

"They've been told *nett* to contact you. If you want to help—stay away." He motioned to the house. "I'll walk you—" He stopped midstep. A police vehicle with flashing lights pulled into the driveway.

Chapter 41

Bloomfield Hills, Michigan
Present day

Roslyn studied the security footage on her laptop where it showed Adriana leaving the house before sunrise. Her child was missing—again.

The doorbell rang.

Roslyn and Chrisla jumped up to answer it at the same time.

"I came as soon as I heard," Leon said, unbuttoning his overcoat in the foyer.

Roslyn narrowed her eyes on her brother. "What did you and Adriana talk about yesterday?"

"I thought my secretary made you aware of my schedule change. The deposition ran late. I was out of the office for the better part of the day."

"That's impossible." Roslyn's knees wobbled, and Leon and Chrisla helped her to a chair. "I don't understand," Roslyn said. "I heard you and Adriana talking in your office."

Leon glanced at Chrisla, skepticism arching his brows. "Roslyn, you couldn't have heard me talking. Like I said, I was tied up downtown."

The front door opened and Roslyn shot up from the chair.

Brandon entered the house, set his briefcase

on the stand in the foyer, and went straight to Roslyn. "Honey" was all he said before crushing her in his arms. After a few seconds, he pulled back. "Have you heard anything yet?"

She shook her head. "I had to threaten the police department with withdrawing our pledge to the beneficiary fund if they didn't open a missing child case. They tried to tell me I had to wait twenty-four hours before filing a report. I have the security footage on my laptop if you want to see it."

Brandon watched the film silently. "She wasn't abducted, and it doesn't appear she was lured away by anyone. She's wearing her Amish dress."

"I noticed that too."

"She didn't take a suitcase, so I doubt she's planning to be gone long."

"If Adriana went back up north she wouldn't need anything."

Sadness hooded Brandon's eyes as he placed his arms around her waist. "Adriana's going to be all right. We're not going to lose her again." He pulled her into another hug.

"You don't know that," she whimpered. "They could hide her or shuttle her to another settlement."

He gave her a gentle squeeze, then pulled back to look her in the eyes. "I know we'll make it through whatever happens, just like we did before."

Roslyn closed her eyes as he leaned closer and kissed her forehead. Fifteen years ago, she and Brandon were on the brink of divorce, but in the disaster, they found one another again. When most of the marriages of The Adriana Hope Foundation families she had helped over the years had dissolved, she and Brandon had beaten the odds. And they had only God to thank for not giving up on them.

Roslyn's cell rang. She reached into her trouser pocket and read the caller ID. "It's the police department." She pressed the Answer button. "This is Roslyn Colepepper." Hearing her daughter was safe, she released a pent-up breath. She glanced at Brandon. "They have her."

Chrisla cheered.

"Yes, thank you." Roslyn disconnected the call. "Adriana will be home shortly."

"Where did they find her?" Brandon asked.

"Up north." Roslyn was unsure what to think about Adriana running away to the Amish community. She had to find a way to make her daughter happy. "How about we all go out for dinner once Adriana gets back? I'm sure she'll be hungry, and I haven't eaten anything all day."

"What are we going to do, pretend nothing happened?" Brandon asked, then turned to Leon. "How should we handle this?"

"It's a delicate matter. The type of abrupt transition she's been forced to—"

"Forced!" Roslyn huffed. "She was stolen from *me*—her mother."

Leon nodded. "I'm only trying to share a different perspective. Through Adriana's eyes, she was forced from the family and life she had. She's going to have difficulty adjusting. Not only to the truth about who she is, but also the lifestyle. She was clearly uncomfortable having her picture taken at the party. When I found her sitting in the dark in Brandon's office, she was hiding from the large crowd, the photographers, the loud music, the drinking."

Roslyn sighed. In her excitement to introduce her daughter to the world, to celebrate her return, she hadn't considered how uncomfortable it would be for Adriana. Her daughter had so graciously gone along with the planning . . . hadn't she?

"You might consider canceling the interview with DiAnna," Chrisla said. "I know how much you wanted to take her shopping and show her New York when it's decorated for Christmas, but it might be too much."

Brandon rested his hand on Roslyn's shoulder. "Things will work out, you'll see."

When the doorbell rang, Roslyn sprang from the chair. Opening the door and seeing Adriana wearing her Amish clothes, hanging her head like a beaten dog, Roslyn's heart went out to her daughter.

"I'm sorry for worrying you," Adriana said.

Roslyn drew her into a hug. "You're not familiar with the city. I thought you were lost."

Adriana stepped back. "I went home to warn *mei*—" She clamped her mouth in obvious distress.

"Why don't we sit down and talk," Brandon suggested.

They joined Chrisla and Leon in the formal living room, Adriana taking the chair next to Leon.

Roslyn started the conversation again. "You went home to see your family."

"Yes," Adriana said. "I overheard you talking on the phone. You said the police should press charges. But they didn't have anything to do with my kidnapping. I asked them what happened. *Mei mamm* told me about the young girl."

"The nanny," Roslyn said. "Brittany Cox."

"They didn't know her—had never seen her before that day. When she dropped me off, she said *mei* name was Doll."

Roslyn batted tears off her lashes.

"They saved *mei* life," Adriana said. "They took me in, raised me up. If they hadn't done that for me—a stranger—I would have gone over the bridge with the kidnappers."

"But they should have taken you to the police," Roslyn said.

"And what would have become of me? Would you have known to look for me under that name—Doll? Would I have been shuffled around the foster system, unclaimed?" Her gaze darted from Roslyn to Brandon, then settled on Roslyn. "You gave birth to me—gave me life, but the Pinkhams raised me to know and love God, my Father, who gives everlasting life. I know you believe they should be punished, but I'm grateful for *mei* upbringing. I shudder to think how different *mei* life would have been growing up not having a relationship with God." She lowered her head. "It took me a little while, but I've forgiven them for withholding the truth. I ask that you forgive them too."

Roslyn was silent.

"You turned out to be a fine young lady," Brandon said. "I think your Amish parents raised a well-adjusted child. We're proud of you."

"Thank you," Adriana said.

Roslyn stood. "Let's go out to eat. I'm starved. You must be hungry, too, Adriana, after all the traveling you've done today."

The doorbell rang. Odd that the gatehouse hadn't called about a visitor. Perhaps Adriana forgot something in the police car. Roslyn stood, but Brandon made it to the door first.

"Is Faith here?"

❧

Faith dashed to the door upon hearing her name. Her eyes widened at the sight of her sister, dressed in a thick sweater, tight-fitting jeans, and pointed-toe boots. "Olivia, it's so *gut* to see you." Faith hugged her sister. She had so many questions, but first she needed to introduce her to Roslyn and Brandon. "*Kumm* with me. I want you to meet . . . *mei* family." She choked out the words. Ever since she'd prayed on the trip from Posen to Bloomfield Hills for God to give her strength, her heart had been heavy with conviction. Roslyn and Brandon were her family now. She needed to obey the teachings in the Bible and honor her father and mother.

Noticing Olivia hesitating, Faith reached for her hand and gave it a tug. "It's okay, *kumm*." She led the way to the living room. "Everyone, this is *mei* sister, Olivia. Olivia, this is my mother, Roslyn. My father, Brandon." She pointed to Chrisla, who was busy eyeing Roslyn from across the room. "My aunt Chrisla, and lastly, Uncle Leon." Faith turned to Roslyn, who within seconds of the introduction had turned ashen. "Is Georgette in the kitchen? I'd like Olivia to meet her too."

"She's out for the evening," Roslyn said hoarsely.

Brandon stood. "I'll get you a glass of water, honey." He smiled at Olivia and said, "It's nice to meet you," then left the room.

Olivia scanned the towering ceiling, then shifted her gaze to the large windows overlooking the lake.

Faith leaned closer and whispered, "It's over-whelming, isn't it?"

"Very much so," Olivia said, her gaze still roaming.

"So how did you find me?"

Olivia shrugged. "It wasn't all that hard." She glanced over her shoulder, then lowered her voice. "Can we go somewhere to talk?"

Faith faced Roslyn and the others. "Would it be okay if I show Olivia my room?"

"Try not to be too long. Your mother wants to go eat," Brandon said. "But, Olivia, you're welcome to join us."

"Thank you," Olivia said.

Faith led her up the stairs, and when they reached her bedroom, she watched as her sister's mouth dropped open. Faith showed her the bathroom, the separate shower and tub, the big walk-in closet, then finally dropped onto the bed. "You can spend the *nacht* if you want. Listening to you snore would be like old times." She propped up one elbow. "What is it?" Her sister looked like the time she'd swallowed a horsefly. "Are you going to be sick?"

Olivia shook her head. "Do you like it here?"

"The room is—well, it's bigger than ours."

"No, here. Living with the Colepeppers?"

"They're nice people." Faith exhaled noisily and fell against the mattress. "I want to go home," she admitted. "I want my life back to normal."

Olivia's face pinched. "It's all my fault."

"What are you saying, Olivia?"

"Why you're here. It was me—I called the hotline number. The Colepeppers wanted proof, so I gave them your brush the day they came to the restaurant. They were going to use a sample of hair to test your DNA. I'm sorry."

Faith needed a moment to absorb the news, to settle her stomach, which was threatening to pitch what little food was in it.

"Remember the newspaper article? How Gideon teased that the person looked like you?"

Faith nodded.

"I not only agreed with Gideon, but I recognized the *boppli* in the picture. I remembered the day you arrived. The dates matched. The *boppli* was kidnapped on the same day the woman left you with us: *mei* birthday. *Mamm* and I were making a cake when she came to the door."

"So you knew all along we weren't *schweschalers*?"

"I didn't remember everything. Not until I saw the newspaper, then it all came back to me. I'm sorry, Faith. I didn't mean to—that isn't true—I was angry that you told *Mamm* and *Daed* about the money. I had been saving *mei* tips so I could go to school to become a nurse, maybe a *doktah*."

"I told you the truth. I wasn't the one who told them." Faith sighed. "Gideon told the bishop, who told *Mamm* and *Daed*." She felt tears welling. All along she thought the reporter had recognized her and turned her in. It hadn't occurred to her it might have been her sister.

"Gideon?"

Faith nodded. "He'd heard a rumor. I have no idea who started it."

"Probably his sister, Claudia. She came into the restaurant to buy a pie when I was in the middle of counting the till. I put the uncounted money in *mei* pocket long enough to get her order." Olivia closed her eyes as if finally taking in the truth. "I'm sorry I blamed you." Tears spilled down her cheeks, tracking her makeup. "I hope you'll forgive me, Faith. I tried to give the reward money back to Mrs. Colepepper, but she refused to take it. I feel like Judas when he betrayed Jesus."

Faith placed her hand on her sister's arm. "I forgive you, Livie. I'll always think of you as *mei* big *schweschaler*."

Olivia cried harder. "I destroyed your life."

"*Nay*, you didn't. It's *nett* like the Colepeppers are bad people. They treat me very well."

"But you don't want to be *Englisch*, do you?"

"*Nay*, but one of the police officers said something interesting. When I turn eighteen I'll be free to live anywhere I want. So I'll wait out *mei* time. Sixteen months isn't long." *Unless Gideon doesn't wait.*

"You don't hate me?"

"*Nett* even a little." She hugged her sister, and for the first time in years, she felt her sister hug her back. "But I do want to know what your plans are."

"I never wanted to work at The Amish Table forever. I even paid someone I met at the library for tutoring so I could earn *mei* GED. I want to go to *schul* to become a nurse or maybe a *doktah*."

Faith recalled how interested Olivia was in the instruments at the hospital. "If you want to work in medicine, then you should talk with Sadie about becoming a *boppli* catcher. The district is growing. She could use an assistant."

Olivia shook her head. "Without joining the church no one would have me. *Nett* Sadie, *nett* any of the expecting mothers."

"Sounds like you've made up your mind."

Olivia nodded.

"God has placed a calling on your heart. I believe if you're willing and trust God, He will direct your steps. But please, promise me you'll never forget about God or your upbringing."

Chapter 42

Posen, Michigan
Present day

Two days before Christmas, Irma pushed through the double doors separating the kitchen from the dining room at The Amish Table. It had been a long day, and her feet were feeling it. She lumbered to the window, and as she flipped the Closed sign, she spotted a new customer in her peripheral vision. The elderly man must have slipped in without the bell over the door jingling to alert her. "I'm sorry," she said, going to the menu holder behind the workstation and removing a menu. "I didn't hear you come in."

"You're closed," he said, pushing up from the chair. "I should go."

"*Nay*, please stay." She hadn't turned a single customer away in the twenty years she'd been open, and on the last official day The Amish Table was open, she couldn't send someone out into the snowy night without serving him first.

The man removed his hat, exposing a mat of red hair, and placed it on the chair next to him where he'd draped his raggedy wool coat and placed his umbrella. Waiting for him to remove his worn gloves, she couldn't help but wonder how he kept his hands warm. The tips of his fingers poked through the holes. Once he was situated, she extended the menu. But the man lifted his hand. "I already know what I'd like."

"Okay." She readied the pen and pad. "What can I get you?"

"I'd like a cup of hot water and a piece of your homemade bread."

"That's all?" She couldn't help but wonder if the man's order had something to do with lack of money to pay for an actual meal. He certainly looked cold. The tip of his nose and his cheeks looked raw from being outside too long.

"Bread and water is all I need. All any of us need."

"Very well." Irma hurried into the kitchen. "Catherine, don't shut down the grill. We have a latecomer."

Catherine chuckled. "*Nau* why doesn't it surprise me that on the last *nacht* we're open to the public, you take in a stray at the last minute."

Irma smiled. "God blessed this business for many years. The least I can do is bless the hungry stranger. Grill him a steak, please." She placed a thick slice of sourdough bread on a plate, then ladled vegetable soup into a bowl. To go with his hot water, she selected a berry blend tea bag.

"This should get you started," she said. "Your steak should be out shortly."

The man smiled. "But I only ordered—"

"There's no charge. So eat your belly full."

"You extend your hand to the poor and reach out to the needy," he said. "A virtuous woman indeed."

"I hope you enjoy the meal." She stopped from mentioning the restaurant was closing. She planned to serve food for Second Christmas tomorrow and give the meats from the freezer to Catherine and the others.

"You shall rejoice in time to come. Your children shall rise up and call you blessed."

Her *kinner* were gone. How could she believe the ramblings of an old man? "I should check on your steak." She returned to the kitchen, and a few minutes later, Catherine had it ready to serve the customer.

"God has heard your petitions in secret," the man said upon her return. "Do not be dismayed. For God is with you. He will uphold you with His righteous right hand."

"I, ah . . ." Her tongue tied.

"Do you believe what I'm telling you?"

"I believe God is with me." She motioned to the kitchen. "I'm going to see if we have any pie left."

Catherine glanced up from organizing the refrigerator. "I have everything ready for Second Christmas."

"*Danki.*" Irma placed a piece of apple pie on a

plate and went back into the dining room, but the man was gone.

⚜

Roslyn shot up in bed, clutching her chest and panting for air.

Brandon rolled over. "What's wrong?"

"I keep seeing Adriana, wearing her Amish dress and kneeling beside the bed praying."

"And that frightens you?" He propped up on his elbow.

"She's praying for our eyes to be opened. For us to come to the saving knowledge of Jesus Christ."

"What's wrong with that?"

She pushed her bangs away from her face. "I haven't had a full night's sleep since being plagued with these dreams. Tonight she prayed about forgiveness. She asked God to forgive her for not wanting to be here."

Brandon pulled her into a hug. "Maybe God is trying to tell you something," he said, patting her back.

"I've already dropped the charges against the Amish couple. What more can I give—my daughter?" Her husband's silence stirred fire in her belly. She pushed off his chest and flipped the light on. "You're quiet. What are you thinking?"

"I think there's a reason you only see her in the Amish dress." He pushed a strand of hair behind her ear. "Why don't you ask God to show you what to do?"

"And you're okay with—with whatever that is?"

He nodded. "Adriana's heart is heavily burdened. I want what's best for her."

Roslyn fell against his chest and sobbed. If she asked God, she already knew what the answer to her prayer would mean.

❧

The following morning Roslyn was the first to rise despite the sleepless night she'd had. The floors were chilly on her bare feet as she padded into the bathroom. A quick shower and she was wide-awake. She glanced outside at the snow-covered lawn. Not much snow here in Bloomfield Hills, but northern Michigan weather was much different. As the coffee brewed, she gazed outside at the cardinal pecking seed from the bird feeder.

"Good morning," Adriana said, coming into the kitchen.

"Happy Christmas Eve." Roslyn poured a mug of coffee and handed it to her daughter. "I have a surprise," she said.

Brandon wandered into the kitchen, his hair askew after a restless night. "Did you pour me a cup?"

Roslyn removed another mug from the cabinet.

"I was just telling Adriana that we have a surprise."

He lifted his brows. "An early Christmas present?"

"I suppose it is." She faced her husband with tears pooling in her eyes. "We're going to spend Christmas at the cabin," she said, struggling to keep her tone even. "I've already called the real estate agent who sold us the place, and she's sending someone to plow the driveway and leave a load of wood by the back door. All we have to do is . . ." She reached for a paper towel and blotted her eyes.

"I'm all for the new journey," Brandon said. "I hope you'll be able to show us how to use a wood stove, Adriana."

"*Jah*, I can do that." She sipped her coffee.

"We'll need to pack some winter clothes," Roslyn said. "And food. I'm sure all of the grocery stores will be closed in the area, and of course, we need to bring the presents." Roslyn lifted her mug, eyeing her husband over the rim. His reassuring nod helped calm her nerves. "We shouldn't waste too much time before we get on the road. The weather is supposed to get bad later on." And given any reason to postpone, she probably would change her mind. Roslyn glimpsed Adriana at the sink. "Please, go pack."

Adriana set her cup in the sink, then left the kitchen.

Roslyn unleashed her tears.

Brandon came up behind her and wrapped his arms around her waist. "We're doing the right thing," he said, kissing her neck.

"I hope so."

⁂

Faith recognized the wooded area a few miles south of Posen even in the dark. Being so close to home was bittersweet. Growing up, Christmas Eve was a time when her family gathered in the living room with mugs of hot cocoa and floating marshmallows, and *Daed* read the story of Jesus' birth from the book of Luke. Afterward, Faith and Olivia would stay up late playing the guessing game—if their gift was knitted, quilted, or sewn, and the color.

This Christmas season she and Roslyn spent endless hours shopping in crowded stores and humming catchy Christmas tunes. Faith enjoyed the frenzy, enjoyed spending time with Roslyn, then later, when guilt tugged at her heart, she repented. Christmas was supposed to be simple, and she had easily made it materialistic.

Brandon stopped the car in front of the cabin tucked under giant snow-covered pines. "I'll leave the lights on while you unlock the door, Roz."

Faith climbed out of the warm backseat and into the cold. She inhaled the frosty air and took in the scent of pine. Once inside, the cabin seemed larger than it appeared from the outside. Two leather couches flanked the two-story stoned fireplace, and off to the left was a dining room table and chairs. The kitchen had plenty of room for multiple people to work in it at the same time, and its eat-at countertop sat eight.

"It's a bit nippy in here. I can see my breath," Roslyn said, blowing into her hands.

"I'll get a fire started." Faith went outside and picked a few smaller pieces of wood; later she would bring in the larger logs to burn throughout the night. She looked forward to sitting by the fire and listening to the crackling sounds. At least tonight, she could go to sleep under cold sheets and dream about being home.

Brandon brought the suitcases inside, then went back to the car several times for the food, supplies, and presents.

"Who wants hot cocoa?" Roslyn asked.

Faith and Brandon both replied "me" at the same time, then laughed. Faith found spending the evening together delightful. She almost didn't want to go to bed.

On Christmas morning, Faith rose early and made breakfast. The fully equipped kitchen had all the pots and pans needed to make eggs, bacon, fried potatoes, and toast.

"I thought I was dreaming of bacon," Brandon teased, sniffing the air. He poured himself a mug of coffee and sat at the table. "You like to cook, don't you?"

"It's one of my favorite things to do," Faith said. "I would have baked bread this morning, but we didn't bring any flour." She shrugged. "So we eat store-bought toast this year."

Roslyn plodded out to the kitchen in a bathrobe and furry slippers. "You're so sweet to make breakfast," she said, going to the coffeepot first.

"It was *mei* pleasure." Faith loaded the plates and set them on the table. The conversation felt awkward. Roslyn hadn't said much, as though she was on the verge of tears. Brandon went overboard to keep the conversation going. He talked about putting an addition on the cabin in the future, hunting on the eighty acres, and buying a boat in the spring to go fishing.

"Gideon and I fished a lot together," Faith said.

"Gideon sounds like a special man." Roslyn pushed her potatoes around on her plate.

"He is." Faith wished she could introduce them to him, but what would be the point? Their worlds were separate now. Gideon had made that clear.

Roslyn sighed, then pushed away from the table. "I have something for you." She disappeared into the bedroom, then came back a few minutes later with an envelope. "This arrived last month. Not long after you went up north."

Faith ran her hand over Gideon's handwriting.

"I hope you'll forgive me. I was afraid you might run away again." Roslyn sniffled. "I wanted you to be happy living with us, being part of our family, but when I hear you talk about your past, your face lights up . . . I know you'll never be happy living outside your Amish district. I'd like to think Gideon has a lot to do with why you want to go back to Posen . . . and it's not that you don't like us."

Faith set the letter on the table and hugged Roslyn. "It isn't you," she said, crying. "You'll always have a special place in *mei* heart."

"Even if you move back to Posen?"

Faith nodded. She wanted to start preparing them for when she turned eighteen and was free to live where she wanted.

Brandon stood and encased them both in a big hug. "I think it's time to open gifts."

They sat down in the living room and exchanged presents. Faith had picked out things when she was shopping for them, but had also knitted them each a wool scarf.

"I hope you like this," Roslyn said, handing Faith a large package tied with a bright-red bow.

Opening the box, Faith's eyes watered. She reached in and removed the blue Amish dress. "It's beautiful."

"I had a seamstress copy your dress to make a pattern." Roslyn motioned to the box. "There's more."

Faith counted a different colored dress for each day of the week. "Thank you. I love the dresses." She especially loved that Roslyn had accepted her wearing the Amish clothing.

"I'm glad you like them. Maybe you can pick out your favorite to wear tomorrow."

"I already know *mei* favorite. The blue one," she said. The three of them talked most of the evening, and it was late when Faith was alone to read her letter from Gideon, which was a wonderful Christmas present by itself.

Dear Faith,

You might not have known that before you left I had been counting down the days to your baptism. I not only wanted to court you, as we spoke about, but I also wanted to ask you to be my wife once we were both committed to God and to the church.

I guess what I wanted to say in this letter is, I haven't stopped counting the days. Nor will I stop. I hope you understand why I refused to pray for you to adapt to your new life. I'm praying for you to come home—where you belong.

Love,
Gideon

Chapter 43

Posen, Michigan
Present day

Gideon wasn't sure why he agreed to go to Second Christmas. Sure, there was plenty of food, but he'd done his best to avoid the restaurant since Faith had left town, and being here now only served to remind him of how much he missed her. He moved down the serving line and placed a spoonful of macaroni and cheese on his plate.

Irma set another large bowl of broccoli salad on the table. "I'm going to tell the new owners about your seasonal fruits. Hopefully they will continue to buy your produce."

"*Danki*," Gideon said. Irma was kind to think of him when her mind must be overloaded with so many other things. "Is the new owner taking over at the beginning of the year?"

Irma shook her head. "I'll turn the keys over tonight once the celebration has ended and everything is cleaned up." Her voice frayed. "I see empty dishes." She snatched a vegetable tray from the table and rushed it into the kitchen.

The bell jingled above the door and the crowd parted like a polecat had been let inside. Gideon glanced toward the door at the person who had stirred the whispers. "Faith." The word caught in his throat.

Mordecai limped toward the door, the bishop with him.

Gideon pressed forward. Perhaps if her father or the bishop couldn't talk sense into her, he could. She would only bring more condemnation on the district showing up like this.

Faith spoke first. "Merry Christmas, *Daed*. Bishop Zook." As she scanned the room, her gaze landed briefly on him and she smiled. "Hello, Gideon."

"Merry Christmas, Faith," he said.

She continued to scan the crowd. "Where's *Mamm*?"

Irma bolted through the swinging doors. "Faith!" The two hugged for a long moment.

"I am home, *Mamm*," Faith muttered, buried in the embrace.

Mordecai and the bishop shared the same sullen expression.

Gideon hoped to have a few minutes with Faith, too, but he wouldn't interrupt the attention she was getting from her parents.

Several of the members gathered their children and put their coats and capes on as they headed to the door. The room thinned quickly, leaving Faith, her parents, the bishop, his wife, and Gideon.

A gust of wind swept through the door, and as

Gideon turned to make sure the door was closed completely, an *Englisch* man stepped into view.

"Good evening," the man said, removing his hat and shaking the snow off the brim. He stomped snow from his rubber boots, then shuddered, jowls flapping and red hair dropping over his eyes. "The temperature is dropping fast out there," he said, combing his fingers through his damp hair.

Gideon eyed the man. "By the looks of your wool overcoat, it must be snowing hard."

"It is indeed." The man carefully removed his coat and draped it over his shoulder, then moved past Gideon and took a seat at one of the tables.

Perhaps the man thought the restaurant was open. "Excuse me, sir, the restaurant is closed." Gideon motioned to the long table of food. "If you're hungry, please, help yourself."

The *Englischer* removed a thick envelope from an inside coat pocket. "I have business to discuss with the owner."

"I'll let them know you're here." Gideon hoped the man's presence wouldn't dampen the joyful mood. He approached Mordecai. "Excuse me. There's someone here who asked to speak with you and Irma."

Irma glanced over her shoulder. "Faith, why don't you share the news with Gideon while your father and I see what this is about." Her mother drew a raspy breath, then tightened her hand around the dangling set of keys Gideon recognized as belonging to the restaurant.

Gideon elbowed Faith's arm. "Could we step outside?"

"*Jah.*" She glanced over her shoulder briefly toward her parents, then went with him out the front door.

"You didn't write back," Gideon said the moment they were outside.

"I was just given your letter yesterday." She hugged herself, her lips quivering in the icy weather.

"I wrote you the day you found me in the orchard."

"You saw the pictures of me in that *Englisch* dress and wearing makeup . . . I thought you'd given up on me."

He looked down at the snowy sidewalk. "I thought finding out you were *nett* Amish had changed you and I assumed—"

"You assumed wrong." Faith sniffled. "These last few months have been hard. *Mei* whole life was turned upside down, but that didn't change *mei* beliefs. I wasn't born Amish, but I believe in the Amish way. I still want to be baptized and join the church."

His shoulders dropped under the weight of knowing it'd go against the *Ordnung* to be Amish living a worldly lifestyle. "Perhaps when you're legally old enough to choose . . ."

"You said in your letter you would wait for me. Is it still true?"

"*Jah*, I'm still waiting. What about you?"

"*Nay, nett* anymore."

He groaned under his breath and waited for the white fog around his mouth to clear. "You don't have to sound so giddy." *She no longer wants to wait for me and now she's smirking.* "Look, I'm sorry I misjudged you."

"You misjudged Olivia too. She was so upset over being accused of stealing from the till that she called the tip hotline number. That's how the Colepeppers found me."

It made sense now why Faith didn't want to wait for him. "I'm sorry, Faith. I hope you'll find it in your heart to forgive me. I didn't mean any harm to *kumm*, and I understand if that's why you don't want to wait for me."

"Gideon, I have already forgiven you."

"*Danki*." He lowered his head. He'd made a mess of everything and now he'd lost the woman he loved.

Faith reached for his hand. "I don't want to wait any longer, because Bishop Zook has already agreed to baptize me as soon as I finish the remaining classes. I don't have to wait for the next baptism in spring."

"I don't understand. You live in Bloomfield Hills *nau*."

"*Mei Englisch* parents live there. But I'm

455

moving back home—here—where I belong. The Colepeppers are letting me choose where I want to live. I choose *mei* Plain life—I choose you, Gideon. If you'll still have me."

"You don't have to ask." He brought her into his arms and kissed her slowly, savoring everything about the moment. "I love you, Faith."

"I love you too."

Warmth spread to his core despite the wintery weather. He'd never experienced this much joy and he wanted to hold on to these feelings forever. "Faith," he said, leaning back to look her in the eye, "we've been good friends for a long time. I already know I want to marry you."

She smiled. "Don't you think we should court first?"

He kissed her forehead. "I'm just telling you *mei* intentions are to never let you go."

"I like the sound of that."

"We'll probably have to wait until you're eighteen, but that should give me time to build our *haus*. I hope you don't mind the view of apple trees."

"Sounds perfect." Her smile morphed into a frown. "But there's something I have to tell you."

He cringed. "What's that?"

"*Mei* birthday is in March, *nett* October."

Gideon smiled. "That's *gut*. It gives me time to make you something different for your birthday."

"Something different?"

"I made shelves for the restaurant. Only . . ." He glanced over his shoulder at the window. The Pinkhams were still busy talking with the man.

Faith tapped his shoulder. "What's wrong?"

"Your parents are selling the restaurant. The man sitting with them has *kumm* with the documents." He brushed the back of his hand over her moist cheeks. "I wish it wasn't happening tonight."

"Me too." Tears pooled in her eyes.

Gideon reached for her hand. "We better get back inside. Icicles are going to form on your lashes."

She wiped her face and smiled. "It's going to be strange *nett* baking bread every morning."

"Things will work out," he said. "They did for you coming home."

She nodded. Once inside, she kicked the snow off her boots at the door. She looked at the floor and sighed. "I better get a mop and clean up this puddle so someone doesn't fall."

The redheaded man approached. "I understand you are Adriana Colepepper?"

Faith shot a look at Gideon that sent a shiver down his spine.

"*Jah*, I am she."

"I was instructed to give this to you." He handed her a card with her name scrawled on it and the set of keys Irma had been holding.

Faith opened the card. Tears flowed freely by

the time she finished reading it and handed it to Gideon.

Dear Adriana,

Your father and I were thrilled when we finally found you after so many years. There hadn't been a day that I didn't think of you or remember holding you in my arms. But you are no longer a baby, you're a lovely young woman whom we are proud to call our daughter. I thank God that you were taken care of so well. As much as it pains me to say good-bye, I know your leaving is for the best. The restaurant is our gift to you. I look forward to eating potato pancakes and sampling your homemade bread when we come up to the cabin for visits.

Please don't stop praying for us.

Love,

Mom and Dad

P.S. Don't worry about your sister. I insisted Olivia keep the reward money, and I'll see that she has everything she needs to go back to school.

Gideon glanced up from the letter, but Faith was gone.

"Is everything okay?" Irma asked.

"I'll find out," he muttered. Gideon went into the kitchen and found Faith removing the mop from the utility closet. "Are you all right?"

She sniffled.

"Faith." He stepped closer. "That was a *wunderbaar* thing your *Englisch* parents did for you."

She nodded.

He swallowed hard. "Does it make you want to go back?"

"*Nay*," she replied. "*Mei* place is here—with you."

"*Gut*." He rolled up his shirt sleeves. "I suppose you're going to need a dishwasher, *jah*?"

Faith chuckled. "You know I won't turn down help."

Acknowledgments

So many people have helped me, but I want to thank God first. To God be the glory, for He's given me the words and storyline for another book! I pray that God speaks through the words in this book and that everyone who reads *Abiding Mercy* will feel God's presence.

Thank you to my husband, Dan. I REALLY appreciate everything you've given up to help me achieve this dream of writing. Thank you for understanding when the characters in my head steal my time. I love you.

Thank you to Lexie, Danny, and Sarah for your love and support. I love you!

I wish to thank some Facebook friends who helped name some of the characters seen in *Abiding Mercy*: Kay Bossard, Amy Champion, Emilie Clawson Hinton, Alicia Isreal, Shawna Jackson, Rhonda Moulton, Judy Rickman, Merry Sunshine, Mallory Fry Tompsett, and Jessie Powers Young. I wish I could personally thank each one of you for reading my books and showing support through kind words of encouragement and FB interactions.

A special thank you to Adriana Miller who inspired the *Englisch* name. You're beautiful, sweetie.

Thank you to my editors: Becky Monds, Natalie Hanemann, Jodi Hughes, and Becky Philpott who believed in the story when I pitched it. I am so honored to have all of you in my life! Thank you, Kristen Golden! You have helped me out so much with marketing, and you do it so well! Thank you, Daisy Hutton, for allowing me to be part of the HarperCollins Christian Publishing family!

I would also like to thank my agent, Natasha Kern. You are a godsend. Thank you for your valuable input on this book and for your ongoing career guidance. I am so blessed to have you as my agent!

Thanks also to my scribes critique partners: Sarah Hamaker, Ginny Hamlin, Michele Morris, Colleen Scott, and Jennifer Uhlarik. I love our group and how it's more than just critiquing each other's work. Your prayers and support have seen me through—chapter by chapter.

Discussion Questions

1. Have you ever taken your child from the shopping cart and put him or her in the car before loading the groceries? Do you think after reading this book you'll change your routine?

2. After Adriana is abducted, Brandon and Leon work together to medicate Roslyn against her wishes. What was your reaction to this? Did they have her best interests at heart or was something else going on?

3. Ecclesiastes 11:1 reads, "Cast thy bread upon the waters: for thou shalt find it after many days." Can you think of a time when a generous act you showed one person was repaid to you through another?

4. Was Roslyn a character you had a hard time relating to? How did you react when she brought Adriana/Faith "home," took her shopping for new clothes, and had her hair and nails done? If you'd been in Roslyn's shoes, would you have transitioned your daughter so quickly? At this point in the story, was Roslyn thinking more about herself or of Faith/Adriana? Were there elements of Roslyn's situation that you empathized with?

5. Gideon had his heart broken by Olivia when

she decided to jump the fence. When he begins to have feelings for Faith, he asks her to confirm that she plans to commit to the Amish way of life. Imagine how Gideon felt when he saw Faith's photo in the newspaper, wearing a fancy dress, her hair and face made up. His best laid plans didn't account for the mystery that unravels about Faith. Think of a time in your life when you took out all possible obstacles and your plan was still thwarted. What did you learn about your own plans compared to the plans God has for you?

6. How did you feel when Faith begins to settle in to life with the Colepeppers? Did you feel like it was a betrayal to her friends and family in Posen? Her Amish way of life? Can you recall times in your life when you accepted God's will for you even when it went against everything you preferred?

7. Roslyn makes the difficult decision to let Faith go after finally getting her back. In what ways does Roslyn's character grow over the course of the story? Is the person she becomes someone you'd want to befriend?

8. The man with red hair shows up in several scenes of the book. Who does this man represent to you? In what ways did he affect the outcome of the story? Could this story have had the same ending if this character hadn't been present?

Center Point Large Print
600 Brooks Road / PO Box 1
Thorndike, ME 04986-0001 USA

(207) 568-3717

US & Canada:
1 800 929-9108
www.centerpointlargeprint.com